THANK YOU!

Dear Reader,

Thank you for reading DIABLO SPRINGS. I hope you enjoyed this journey into my imagination. For the history buffs, Diablo Springs is loosely based on Agua Caliente, a real life ghost town which became popular around the turn of the century. Socialites flocked there for the healing waters… until in the late 1890s an enterprising engineer decided to make them bigger and better, resulting in the springs draining into underground caverns and disappearing altogether. The writer in me thought, *what better place for a ghost story than a town where even the water is a ghost*…. All other similarities between Diablo Springs and Agua Caliente ended there, but it was the seed I needed to sprout my story.

If you have a minute, please consider leaving a short review for Diablo Springs and the other great reads in this set. Authors and readers alike love reviews!

To receive an email when my next book comes out, please enter my monthly contest at:

http://erinquinnbooks.com/Contest.htm

I'm always giving something. My newsletter only goes to those who sign up and is never sent unsolicited. Expect to receive it no more than a few times a year. (I will never spam you with constant updates—life's too short *smile*).

If you like time travel, please check out my award winning *Mists of Ireland* series which Diana Gabaldon calls "complex, mysterious and very satisfying." If a fast-paced, dark paranormal is more to your taste, try my award winning *Beyond* series which was a RT Book Reviews Top Pick, "Fascinating... powerful... beautifully wrought"

As always, thank you for reading my books!

Erin Quinn
www.ErinQuinnBooks.com

PRAISE FOR THE NOVELS BY ERIN QUINN

"A richly developed time-swept paranormal series that should be on every romance lover's shelf."
USA Today Books

"Beautifully written. One of the pure joys of reading a Quinn novel is the incredible visual nature of her writing." *RT Book Reviews*

"I simply adore this series. The world is lush, layered, and wonderfully complicated. Emotionally charged with love, betrayal, forgiveness, and sacrifice."
Smexy Books

"Complex, multi-faceted foundation of myth and magic, intense emotional drama, and hopeful redemption."
Romance Junkies

"Erin Quinn is one of the most powerful writers I have ever read."
The Book Reading Gals

"Ms. Quinn weaves an unforgettable tale that will leave you yearning for more. An absolute must-read!"
Two Lips Reviews

DIABLO SPRINGS

ERIN QUINN

CHAPTER ONE

B rendan thought lying to Analise's mom would be the trickiest part, but Analise said she was spending the night at a friend's house and she was such a good kid that her mother never even questioned it. No, the biggest challenge had been keeping their destination a secret from Analise. He'd never considered how hard that would be. But that was the way he was. He didn't see the big picture, didn't realize he wasn't seeing it until it was too late.

He'd been obsessed with the town they were headed to for weeks now, ever since he'd taken the detour and seen it for himself. Now returning to Diablo Springs was all he could think about. That and bringing Analise with him. It felt urgent, the need to bring her there.

Tomorrow they'd be breaking the news to Analise's mother that her sixteen-year-old daughter was pregnant, but that didn't seem as important as what they'd be doing tonight.

Tonight, they'd be sleeping under the stars in the back of his pickup. In Diablo Springs.

"We're almost there," he said, glancing at Analise as she shifted restlessly beside him.

"I wish you'd tell me where *there* is."

"Just a little farther. It'll be worth the wait. I promise."

Analise's mom had grown up in Diablo Springs and her great-grandmother still lived there, but Analise had never even visited. Every time she'd asked about it, her mother got cagey and shut her down. Not a big deal, except Analise suspected her father lived in Diablo Springs, too, and that her mom had been lying about not knowing how to find him.

He shifted, eyeing the sky. Lightning exploded across the surface and blackened clouds dipped low, scraping the mountains and teasing the parched and cracked desert floor with promises of rain it didn't deliver. The air felt electric.

Rain would mess up all his plans.

At last the exit sign appeared, Diablo Springs Next Exit. Analise leaned forward, her lips moving silently over the name as she read it.

Her eyes widened and she shot him a stunned glance.

"I saw the exit when I was driving home from my sister's house a couple weeks ago. There was construction and I had to take a detour." He shrugged, grinning.

"And you didn't say anything?"

He should've expected that, should've had a ready answer. "I . . . I wasn't sure it was the right place. I didn't want to say until I was."

"Did you go there? Did you stop and see it?" Analise asked.

He could feel her gaze on him, but he didn't want her to see his eyes. Just in case.

"I didn't have time to stop. It was late and I had to work the next day."

More lies. He'd swerved to take the exit, answering a call that had felt like a tug at his gut, a lure in his brain. He had stopped. More than that. He'd stayed so long that he never made it to work the next morning. Or the one after.

He couldn't tell Analise that, though. She'd want to know what he'd been doing.

"I found something on the Web, too," he said brightly. Another lie, but he couldn't tell her the truth. "The town's got a lot of history."

Her jaw dropped. "You researched its history?"

Brendan flushed. "I didn't *research* it. I just saw some stuff."

"Like?"

He'd been hoping she'd ask. "Apaches used to live there before someone found silver in the mountains and chased them off. After that, it was all gunslingers and wild west. Like in the movies."

His voice had grown wistful and a strange yearning formed in his chest. He could almost taste the air, as it must have been over a hundred years ago. He could almost see himself with a pistol strapped to his leg and a rifle to his saddle.

"The Apaches used the hot springs for sacred ceremonies. That kind of thing. The water's gone now, though."

"What do you mean it's gone?"

He shrugged again. "I don't know. Gone. There's just a big dry hole there now."

"How come?"

"I just said I don't know."

"Okay. Just asking." Her eyes narrowed.

"Are you giving me shit because I didn't read that far?" he countered, his voice sharp.

It stopped him for a moment. He never spoke to Analise that way.

"What's wrong with you?" she asked. "You're acting weird."

He swallowed, suddenly uneasy. "I just thought you'd be excited, is all."

Analise reached over and squeezed hand. "You're freaked out about the baby, aren't you? It's okay. Me, too. I'm scared to tell my mom. She's going to have a meltdown . . ."

She kept talking but her voice faded as his thoughts returned to Diablo Springs. He could smell the dark lore, the sulfurous history, the hot violence. It'd been the kind of place where you'd either get screwed or killed, sometimes both. It fired his blood, imagining it.

"Did you hear me?"

Analise's hurt tone snapped him out of his reverie.

"Everything's going to be okay, babe," he rushed to reassure her.

Apparently it was the right thing to say. She gave him her sweet smile and went back to looking out the window as they zigzagged into the mountains. Finally, they peaked and started down the other side into the basin where Diablo Springs squatted like a dirty smear on a pretty painting.

"It feels like we're in the middle of nowhere," Analise murmured, frowning.

Brendan shifted uncomfortably as doubt nudged through his anticipation. He'd been so excited to bring her here, but as they crossed the town's border, a feeling of dread began to curdle in his stomach. He didn't understand it.

He turned onto Main Street where one traffic light blinked yellow in all directions. The building fronts looked like they must have a century ago only now most of them had boarded up windows or FOR SALE signs on their doors. It looked desolate and ugly. It looked like the last place on earth he should have brought Analise Beck.

"Everything's closed up," Analise said, looking out the window. "It's creepy."

"I thought you were curious about where your mom came from," he said defensively.

"Curious, yeah, but . . . I didn't know you were going to bring me here. I thought we were going someplace nice, you know, like a hotel."

Brendan swallowed hard. Of course she'd thought that. Only an idiot would think a surprise trip to a ghost town would make a sixteen-year-old happy. The big picture had eluded him again. Scowling, he clenched his hands around the steering wheel and kept driving.

* * *

Less than a quarter mile of open scrub and cactus stretched between the road and the place where the old springs had once flowed. A bridge and walkway used to lead from the Diablo Springs Hotel to the hot pools, and guests would make the short journey by foot. Brendan knew that decking had once surrounded the springs where bathers could sit and dangle their feet in the water.

Now the splintered railings poked up from the remnants like broken bones. It was all overrun, devoured by the hot sun and burning grit of the desert. As he pulled closer, he could see what was left of it, ruins around a black chasm.

Following the road to the huge hollow, he watched the horizon devour the last glow of sunlight. In the fresh dusk, he stopped and hopped out of the truck. Before he went around to Analise's side, he took a deep breath of the seared air. Even the heat felt good.

Analise opened her door and Brendan hurried over to help her down. She was so small and fine boned; he couldn't touch her without wanting to protect her. And now, with the baby coming, he had that much more to worry about.

He knew her mom thought he was too old for her. Too old with no future. He couldn't blame her. He worked for a landscaper, which was a fancy way of saying he mowed other people's lawns for a living. What mother wanted her superstar daughter attached to a man with dirt under his fingernails and grass stains on his clothes? Once they told

Ms. Beck about the baby, she'd hate him. Actually, she'd just hate him more.

The air was thick and close, still a hundred degrees even at sunset. The low scrub crept down the surrounding mountains and right up to the sides of the dirt road. Beyond, a wild assortment of spiky and thorny desert plants sprawled out on the abandoned grounds, some blooming with wild pinks and corals. Not a blade of grass was in sight. The land was tough, barbed, dead inside. Abandoned and hard to love. He'd felt an instant bond with the place.

Analise looked around with something akin to horror. What had she expected? Picket fences and petunias?

He pointed to the black ravine sloping down just ahead. It had shocked him the first time he'd seen it. It opened so suddenly, like a hole straight to hell. As dry now as the crackling air. Hard to imagine it had ever held healing waters.

Analise turned away from the dirt fissure and stared out at the silhouetted town. A few lights twinkled in windows as night worked its way into homes. Her expression, her reaction to his surprise, wasn't at all what he'd imagined. Anger stirred beneath his breastbone.

He reached in the back seat and pulled out a blanket, which he spread over an unlikely patch of even ground. As he smoothed it down, he discovered a miniscule sprouting of what looked like grass. Grass, even here. Feeling somehow betrayed by it, he twisted it until its grasping roots snapped and hurled it away.

"Sit down, babe. I brought us a little picnic."

Analise gave the blanket a nervous look. She held her self stiff as a doll, seemingly undecided about which way to face. The town and the ravine were like warring poles and she the metal pin in between. Brendan frowned.

"I don't like it here, Brendan. Let's go."

How like his little princess to find this place that welcomed him like family distasteful. It was nothing but dirt. Just like him.

"Go where?" he said bitterly. "Maybe to the Ritz? You think I got that kind of money?"

Analise looked instantly contrite, which only made him feel like a bigger shit.

"Brendan, I'm sorry. This was a great surprise. I do want to see it all, but it's getting really dark."

"So?"

"It's . . . I mean . . . Don't tell me you don't feel it."

In fact, as she spoke, pointing out the clustering darkness, he did feel it. A disturbance, rippling through the air like the hot and gritty breeze. It held a tension, a feeling of violation, a sense of aggression. And he liked it. Brendan shook his head.

"You afraid of the dark now, babe?"

Her smile was small and forced.

He got up and went to the truck where he rummaged for his flashlight, hoping its batteries were still good. He turned it on and a pale, buttery beam chased back the shadows. It waned after the initial burst, but held.

"Better?" he asked.

Analise nodded without much conviction. "I guess. It's just really creepy here."

It didn't matter that she was right, it made him mad. "Do you know how hard it was to get off work so I could bring you here?"

Tears made her eyes shiny and luminous. "I know, I'm sorry. It's just . . . I'm scared, Brendan."

"You're scared of everything. You—" He stopped abruptly and scanned the area around them. He'd heard something.

"What?" Analise said.

"Shh." He stood, searching the darkness. The feeble glow of the flashlight reached only a foot or two in front of him. Past that it was all huddled shadows and looming shapes. He strained with the effort to hear. The quiet folded in and stretched out in a hiss. Then a slight, slithering sound reached his ears. Like dirt spilling into an empty hole.

In unison, he and Analise looked to the ravine. He took a step closer.

"No. Brendan, no. Let's just get out of here."

He waved her off and took another step. Frozen, Analise watched. The sound came again. Loose soil and rock sliding down the side. As if something were climbing up.

"What do you see?" she whispered.

Brendan shook his head and moved closer to the edge of the chasm. A rock joined the slight avalanche of dirt. It clicked and thumped down and down and down. Analise made a whimpering sound and for a moment, his foggy mind cleared with a suddenness that made him stagger. He shook his head, stunned by the sudden clarity. What the hell were they doing here?

Analise was right. This place . . . It wasn't natural. It felt wrong. Something rank hovered in the air like a layer of dust.

More rocks, the earth slide increased. As if something had lost its foothold and slipped back a few feet, causing the rocks to cave in around it.

Brendan was almost to the edge. His flashlight crawled over the terrain and then inched up to the piled dirt circling the chasm. The blackness around him seemed more complete because of the tiny rent he and his light put in it. He acknowledged the fear that threatened to buckle his knees even as he refused to give into it.

He stopped a few steps from the plunging brink.

"Brendan," Analise said, her voice a shaky whisper in the disturbing dark.

He leaned forward, trying to peer into the pit without actually going to the rim. He couldn't see a damn thing, but more dirt shifted and skipped into the depths. Dirt he'd dislodged? Or—

"Brendan, please come back. Please?"

A deep and dank odor wafted up toward him. Like something dead and long ago rotted had escaped its sealed chamber. What the hell was it? Another step and then a rush of air blasted out in a gust that lifted his hair and scared a *"What the fuck!"* right out of him. The scrabbling sound raced up the ravine wall and Brendan stumbled back, shouting again as he tried to catch his balance. Behind him, Analise began to scream.

"Run!" he hollered, racing past her to the truck.

She didn't even know from what, but she didn't stop to ask. She scrambled through the door he held open, over the seat to her side as he jumped in behind the wheel and threw the gear into reverse. The truck fish tailed before spinning around and out the way they'd come. Shaking and crying Analise turned in her seat and looked back.

"What do you see?" he demanded.

She was sobbing, too hysterical to even answer. He tore his gaze from the road and looked in the rearview mirror. A pale light seemed to hover over the pit. What was it? A face? But it glowed, not like skin but— Without warning, it shifted and it felt . . . it felt like it looked at him. Analise screamed.

"What is it?" Brendan shouted. "Is it following us?"

"I don't know," Analise sobbed.

Brendan had the pedal to the floor and the truck felt like it had wings as it flew across the desert, barely staying on the excuse for a road. It hadn't taken them this long to get there, had it? Shit, was he lost? Had he gotten turned around? Where was the moon? Where was the fucking *town*?

"Why did you bring me here?" Analise was crying over and over. "Why, why?"

He turned in his seat and looked back. Nothing following, and yet . . . a glimmer. The town. How had the town ended up on his right? Didn't matter, as long as he got there. He cranked the wheel, his instincts telling him he was backtracking while his eyes told him he was headed the right way.

"No," Analise shouted. "You're going back."

He opened his mouth to tell her she was wrong, but now he was completely disoriented and his headlights picked out the gaping ravine ahead. At seventy miles an hour, they were going in.

He turned hard left, taking the truck into a crazy spin at the edge of the abyss. He felt the wheels lose traction. Felt the pull of gravity trying to suck them down. The back end hovered for an instant over the great nothingness of it, and then slowly, the truck began to slide down.

CHAPTER TWO

S ome say destiny is unavoidable. Some say a person's whole life is determined before he or she is even born. Reilly Alexander didn't buy into that, which wasn't the same as saying he didn't believe it. When he looked back on his life, it seemed fate had done more than drive him around; it had plotted out a specific course that brought him here, now, to a bookstore in Los Angeles where he would meet his destiny.

"We've put your table right up front," the Barnes & Noble manager told him.

"Thank you."

"I think you'll have a good turnout. Your book has been selling quite well for us."

This was his fourth book, and he still couldn't get used to hearing that it wasn't complete crap. Maybe he'd never get used to hearing it. A part of him still believed that it was his nefarious and disastrous venture into the music business that brought the readers to his books, not the writing. Not *his* stories, but *the* story of a failed rocker turned literary genius. He smirked to himself at that. Yeah, that.

But fans did come. The women, as often as not, looking for something better than a book to take to bed. The young musicians came because they thought some of his luck would rub off on them. It didn't matter that his luck in the music business had run out fast. The others . . . He still hadn't figured out what drew the others. All in all, though, he ate well, traveled in fair style, and lived a life of quasi-fame. In honesty, more than he'd ever expected of himself.

He ran a hand over his nearly shaved head, still expecting the shoulder-length shag he'd worn until a few months ago when he'd decided it was time to cut even that from his life. The impeccably dressed manager he followed to the table hadn't said a word about Reilly's appearance, but it was there in the look that skimmed his Flogging Molly T-shirt and faded blue jeans. In the beginning, when the first book had come out, he'd tried the dressing up and felt like an even bigger idiot and imposter. The slacks and button-down had fit his image like panty hose and a sunbonnet.

"Just let me know if you need anything," the manager said before going about his business. A cold beer would be nice, but Reilly refrained from asking and simply thanked the man. All he could hope was that the next two hours went fast.

During his college years Reilly had made his living as a lead singer and songwriter of a band called Badlands. When the group broke up after three years and one hit single, Reilly had been left with a bit of fame and little fortune. Individually, each of the band members had branched out and failed to produce anything worth listening to. Reilly had resorted to writing songs for others until he'd finally settled down and pounded out the novel he'd been thinking of for years.

Four books later, he'd gained enough traction to warrant a fifth. Riding the infamy tide with Badlands had taught him not to believe his own press, though. They loved his books today, but only if he had something better to provide tomorrow. His problem of the hour was that he didn't. The channel of ideas he'd been surfing had disappeared and left him lost and in a panic over what came next. Was it time for yet another career change?

The signing started like clockwork with a steady trickle of readers who had fished his other titles off the shelves and now wanted his signature on the new one. It never felt real to scrawl his name on the title page, but he tried not to let it show. A few strays showed up, too, most of them looking for the bathroom, a couple in search of Cinnabon and its seductive aroma.

When a young man in board shorts and an old Badlands concert T-shirt came up to the table, Reilly immediately took note. He hadn't seen one of those shirts in years. It made him feel nostalgic for a minute.

The kid told him, "I'm writing a report for my music history class about one-hit wonders. You know, where are they now?"

"They're all in hiding," Reilly said. He knew for a fact that one or two of his own one-hit disaster group would probably shoot the pimply kid if he tried to out them. Oblivious, the kid sat on the edge of Reilly's table and picked up a copy of his latest book, *Broken*.

"So is this based on your life?" he asked.

Reilly gave him a steady look. "It's about a maniac who stalks groupies and murders them."

The kid nodded, still wearing the idiot smile.

"So, no," Reilly said patiently, "it's not about my life."

The kid let go a snort of laughter. "Good thing, huh?"

And so it went, until finally, the lull gave him a chance to sit back and drink the water so thoughtfully provided by one of the cute sales clerks.

"Excuse me?"

Reilly looked up to find an older woman standing in front of him. Fine-boned and birdlike, she had paper-thin skin the color of toffee—not black, brown, or white, but a mixture that defied racial claims. Deep lines fanned from the corners of eyes that sparkled like black diamonds. She wore pink lipstick—a young girl's color, but she managed to carry it off. Perhaps it was the white-toothed smile. A turban in bright African colors wrapped around her hair and a long flowing tunic matched it. Black pants with precise creases covered her legs and black sneakers completed the outfit. Reilly stared at the athletic shoes with a bemused smile. The words *super granny* came to mind.

Behind her stood a hodgepodge of humanity that Reilly couldn't have dreamed up and fictionalized if he'd tried. Like some kind of comic book depiction of a crowd, they clustered together, some extremely tall and others excessively short, some unnaturally thin and others uncommonly fat. Their clothes crossed the spectrum from white gauze to fuchsia, tie-dye to black satin. One man wore white gloves and a priest's vestments. Either this was the weirdest book club on the planet or they'd been beamed down from a circling vessel. The group watched the old woman with avid interest.

"You are Nathan Reilly Alexander?" she said, her voice strong and clear.

No one called him Nathan. If it wouldn't have been such a pointless pain in the ass to do it, he'd have had the name removed from record. "It's Reilly. Reilly Alexander."

He reached for the book she held out and opened it to the title page.

"You can make it out to Chloe Lamont," she said. "Your guide to your destiny."

He paused, pen poised over the page. "Come again?"

"You've been waiting for me, haven't you?"

Reilly gave her a slanted look and a head shake. "Can't say that I have."

"You haven't been thinking of fate, of your destiny? Of where you go from here?"

He wanted to scoff, but of course he'd been doing more than thinking about it. He'd been dwelling on it. He wrote, *To Chloe, enjoy the book*, signed it, and handed it back to her. She took it with a strange smile.

"Don't you wonder why I'm here?"

"It's a book signing. People are supposed come to them."

"There's a town called Diablo Springs," she said, ignoring his sarcasm. She had a rich and melodic voice with a trace of an unidentifiable accent that teased the ends of her words. "It was a notorious place once. Do you know how it got its name?"

Reilly shrugged. He knew, but obviously she had her own theory and was dying to tell him.

"It's not named for the hot springs, as many mistakenly believe," she said. "It's called Diablo because it's haunted by the devil himself."

"Interesting," he answered, wishing she'd move along.

She stared at a point over his shoulder and her body became unnaturally still. For reasons he couldn't explain, every hair on Reilly's body stood on end. He thought of pushing away from the table and bolting, but the idea of it was ridiculous enough to keep him rooted.

As if hearing his thoughts, she snapped her attention back to him. "Diablo Springs is home to spirits that will never find peace. You're familiar with this place, of course."

"Obviously. You know the answer to that."

She nodded. "I've been called there."

"Then you should go."

"I've been called to bring you. I'm leaving tonight."

"Listen, Ms. Lamont—"

"You may call me Chloe."

He'd pass on that offer. "I don't know what you've heard about Diablo Springs, Ms. Lamont, but I can pretty much guarantee that it isn't true. It's just a dried-up old town."

"A ghost town, but only the ghosts know it."

"If you say so."

"Aren't you curious about who is calling me?"

"No."

"Not even if it's Carolina Beck?"

Had she said *Carolina Beck*? That got Reilly's full attention. He hadn't thought of Carolina Beck since the last time she'd slammed the door in his face. Her granddaughter, Gracie, was another story altogether. He was pretty sure he'd never stopped thinking about Gracie. Once upon a time, sparkles and unicorns had filled Gracie's eyes and Reilly Alexander, her heart.

But that was a long, long time ago.

"You're friends with Carolina Beck?" he asked skeptically.

"Her spirit."

Her spirit? "She's dead?"

Chloe didn't answer.

Reilly leaned forward, intrigued now. "How is she calling you?"

Chloe leaned in, "How did I know you'd care?"

A pale man appeared at Chloe's side, younger than she by about twenty years, but still graying at the temples. Tall and skeletal, he struck Reilly as a hybrid of a vampire and Abraham Lincoln. Where Chloe was color, he was transparent. He put a protective hand on Chloe's waist and a watchful eye on Reilly.

"You're looking for your next story," Chloe went on. "You're worried because you can't find one. It's a question of destiny, but you can't see what's right under your nose."

"And you can?" Reilly said.

"You're part of this story, Nathan Reilly Alexander."

"And just what kind of story would that be?"

"A ghost story, of course."

CHAPTER THREE

Gracie Beck leaned back from her computer and stared at the brochure she'd created for a distance education program. The banner read, "See the world from the other side of the textbook." It was the kind of program she'd longed to go on when she was in college. But by then she'd had a baby, a job, and more life experience than she cared to remember.

She saved the file and leaned back in her chair. This evening, the house seemed cavernous, though in reality it was just a tiny one-story bungalow built in the giddy days following World War II. San Diego was filled with houses like this one. Apart from the two bedrooms—hers and her daughter, Analise's—there was a nook that doubled as an office, a living room/family room, and a kitchen with enough space for a dinette. The yard was small, but Lake Murray, where she could walk her pair of horse-sized dogs, Tinkerbelle and Juliet, wasn't far off.

Her third dog, a petite Yorkie named Romeo, sat on her lap while she worked. Gracie absently scratched behind his ears.

She supposed she should get used to the silence in the house. Analise was sixteen and soon she'd be off to college. She was an honor student with gifts that ranged from math to music. First-chair orchestra, accelerated calculus; she'd have her pick of universities. Gracie would miss her, but she was so proud.

Analise was at a sleepover tonight at her girlfriend's. Nothing uncommon and yet the twilight hours had been filled with a bad feeling that wouldn't go away. Her daughter had texted an hour or so ago—the kind of sweet check-in she always did—but still . . . something felt off. Gracie had tried to talk herself out of worrying but finally she'd called Analise and gotten her voice mail.

Again, nothing to worry about. So why was she so anxious?

Standing, Gracie stretched, wincing as her joints creaked and muscles groaned. She'd just celebrated her thirty-third birthday, but she felt ancient. All three dogs stood when she did, but Juliet gave a sudden, low growl that lifted the fine hairs at Gracie's nape. Tinkerbelle raised her head, ears pricked.

Probably nothing more than the wind in the trees, but Gracie scooped up Romeo and let the big dogs escort her to the hall. She paused at Analise's door and listened, though she didn't expect to hear anything. Analise was gone. Quietly, she turned the knob and pushed the door open.

The darkness and shadows seemed to fold over one another as she stepped inside her daughter's bedroom and stared with a mixture of worry and confusion. On any given day, a chaos of jeans, peeled off and left where they dropped, shirts discarded with sleeves half in, half out, shoes strewn in between with stray socks and hair things—all would have littered the floor. But tonight it was spotless.

The whole week Gracie had noticed little things that seemed out of character for Analise. Her hair styled out of her face, her makeup less severe, a grouchy mumble in the morning instead of a smile. But none of it sent up the kind of red flag the clean room did.

A sound came from the front of the house and both Juliet and Tinkerbelle spun around with bared teeth and deep barks. Romeo joined in, late on the uptake but determined to be as fierce as his giant counterparts. He squirmed to get down and Gracie set him on the floor. Immediately he tore out of the room.

Gracie strained to hear beyond the yapping animals as she followed their furious barks. The hallway had never seemed so long, so dim, so cut off from the rest of the house. Gracie rounded the corner into the front room, filled with irrational fear. It was empty, of course. No intruder could make it past her dogs and the front door remained closed, the windows shut tight. Everything locked up. But Gracie couldn't shake the nagging apprehension.

Without warning, Juliet launched herself at the front door, barking like a rabid wolf. Tinkerbelle charged just a half step behind and Romeo hopped between them. Over their ruckus, Gracie heard a sound, a scratching from the other side. Slowly she approached as the dogs frothed in their excitement.

From outside Gracie heard a long, agonized shriek echo on the wind. High-pitched and loud, it raced through her blood like ice and brought the word *keening* into her head.

Anxious, Gracie stepped forward. Her palms were damp as she braced them on the door and stood on tiptoe so she could see out the peephole.

The porch was empty, lit by the bright light over the door. A strong wind blew the branches of the giant pepper tree in the front yard, making a rustling sound as it blustered through the dangling limbs. For a moment, it seemed that someone stood beneath it. A woman ... a small, bent woman. Familiar, yet too unlikely to be more than a trick of the eye.

Still, the woman looked like her Grandma Beck.

The telephone rang, startling a scream out of Gracie. She spun around and let out another scream when she saw the woman from outside sitting calmly at her dinette.

Gracie's eyes had not deceived her. The woman's face was deeply lined, aged since the last time Gracie had seen her, but unmistakable. She wore a house dress of pastel plaid, pearlescent snaps down the front with big square pockets. A lighter and box of Virginia Slims menthol cigarettes was in the right one. Numb, Gracie stared into her rheumy eyes and felt tears prick her own.

"Grandma Beck?" she whispered.

A sane part of her mind recognized that this could only be an illusion, but every beloved feature seemed so *real*. The gleam of pink scalp beneath the tufts of white hair, the downturn of her eyes at the corners, the deep groves around her lips from puckering as she drew on her cigarettes. Gracie smelled the smoke that clung to her and beneath it, the light scent of Skin So Soft bath oil, her grandmother's favorite.

The phone rang again, insistent. Gracie ignored it. No one called the house phone anymore except telemarketers and politicians.

Grandma Beck said nothing. She lifted a book she held in her lap as if to show it. Frowning, Gracie tipped her head and stared at the worn, brown cover, the word Ledger embossed in elaborate scroll at the center. Her grandma's hands shook as she held it out. Gracie reached for it as the phone rang again, a shrill demand. Annoyed, Gracie reached for it, intending to hang up on whoever called, but Grandma Beck began to fade.

"No," Gracie said, snatching her hand back. "No, don't go."

Silly, when she knew her grandma wasn't really there. A gentle smile curved the woman's thin lips and Grandma flickered, like a candle in a breeze, and vanished completely.

The third ring of the phone made her spin, snatch up receiver and jab the talk button. "What?" she demanded, still staring at the chair where her grandmother had sat, still smelling the faint scent of smoke and bath oil. Her heart hurt and those prickly tears began to spill. Some spiritual part of her recognized what had just happened, but she didn't want to acknowledge it.

"Gracie Beck?"

The man's voice on the other end stirred a memory, though she didn't place it until he told her his name.

"Eddie Rodriguez?" she repeated with both confusion and disbelief.

"Yeah. Remember me?"

They'd gone to grade school, junior high, and high school together. How could she forget?

"Listen, Gracie, I've got some bad news. I think you'd better come home."

"Home?" she said, reaching for the edge of the counter to brace herself. Diablo Springs was a lot of things to her. But it wasn't home.

The tears came faster, and she clenched her eyes, the memory of her grandma seated at her table so sharp and poignant that she had to bite her lip to hold back the sob.

"It's your grandma," Eddie said, like she'd known he would.

He paused and took a breath. Gracie did, too, steeling herself for his next words. "I'm sorry. There's no easy way to say it. Or explain it for that matter. Gracie, your grandma's dead."

The words rolled over her like a numbing tide.

"Are you there?"

"Yes. I'm here."

"Okay." He stopped again and this time it made Gracie's heart lodge somewhere in her throat. "There's more," he said finally.

She swallowed, feeling like she'd been sealed in an airtight silo that filtered every sound but her thumping heart.

"Is— Gracie, do you have a daughter?"

CHAPTER FOUR

Reilly had always thought Diablo Springs looked like a Hollywood rendition of the town that time forgot. With the lightning storm giving it a strobe effect, it seemed to loom up like a spooky relic in a bad horror flick. Ironically, when he'd lived here, he'd thought the world ended at the town's borders. He was right, he realized now, just not in the way he'd thought back then.

He glanced in his rearview mirror where Chloe, the Abraham Lincoln-vampire look-alike, and the priest with the gloves followed in a minivan. He wondered if they were as freaked out by the weather as Reilly was by the turn of events that had unfolded in just one short night.

The clouds had gathered during the drive from Los Angeles, and each mile east had brought them deeper into brooding skies and quaking thunder. Now the storm seemed to hover just over Reilly's SUV like a twelve gauge with a tight trigger. According to the weather report, this was just the precursor to a tropical storm blowing up from Mexico. He planned to be back home long before that one hit.

He still couldn't believe he was on his way back to Diablo Springs. What had possessed him to go home? To pack his bags and hit the road with complete strangers? Chloe said he needed a story, and God knew it was true. But no story was compelling enough to drag him across the desert to his home town . . . except his own.

Sure, Chloe walking into the bookstore with her entourage of weirdos and her bizarre claims that she'd been called to Diablo Springs by ghosts had piqued his interest. He couldn't pretend that he wasn't intrigued by the fact that she'd shown up to take *him* with her, either. But, in truth, he'd come for only one reason: It was time to finally write the painful ending to his brother's chapter and reclaim the pieces of himself that had been torn out by Diablo Springs.

Honestly, he'd been brooding about it for weeks, months even. Since he'd learned that Matt had died. Since he'd acknowledged the relief he'd felt—the kind of relief that came from offloading the two-ton ball and chain he'd been dragging most of his life.

Matt's death, however, hadn't put an end to anything. In fact, it had opened flood gates inside Reilly and spewed a toxic mix of memories into his bloodstream. He'd sent instructions to Digger Young—Diablo Spring's undertaker—to have Matt cremated and shipped to him in Los Angeles. He'd locked the ashes up with his memories and gone on like neither existed. But each day since, getting out of bed had been a little harder. Going to the computer, a bit more difficult. Facing himself in the mirror, a lot more painful.

He'd lost weight, lost his drive. Last week he'd shaved his fucking head. Next week he might move onto something more permanent . . . like maybe shave a few years from his life. The fact of the matter was, he needed to bury his ghosts and Matt was only one of them. Diablo Springs and all the blood and pain of his history there— that one needed to be buried, too.

He'd made the decision to come in a split second, because he knew if he thought about it, he'd talk himself out of doing it. And every survival instinct he possessed was telling him now or never. Deal with the shit or let it suck him down so deep he'd never come out.

Chloe Lamont was merely the resounding clap that began the avalanche, the instigator of a collapse long in coming. Reilly either came home and faced his past or he would self-destruct. Simple as that.

But how had she known that Carolina Beck would be the bait that made him snap? What did she know about her or Gracie Beck, her granddaughter?

He turned after the Circle K—run-down but holding on even here—and made his way into downtown Diablo Springs. Feeling pensive, he passed Rough Street and glanced at the fourth house on the left where he'd been raised. Now, it was boarded up and overrun with scrub and, most likely, rodents and bugs. This was the desert and no place on earth was more hospitable to vermin. He'd written a number-one single and two bestsellers about the things that creeped and crawled across the hot sands of Arizona.

At last he parked at the curb in front of the Diablo Springs Hotel, where they'd be staying for the next few days if Chloe could be believed, and just sat there for a moment as memories flashed in his head like the storm in the sky.

Gracie Beck, the girl not quite next door but close enough to walk. She'd been sixteen to his eighteen and she'd lived here with her grandmother. Gracie Beck, so beautiful his heart had clenched whenever he looked at her. He'd known even then that he wasn't good enough for her, but in his youth he'd thought love was stronger than blood, even bad blood. The night before *The End*, he'd learned otherwise.

Chloe had told him that she'd spoken to Carolina Beck just yesterday and confirmed reservations for herself, her two companions, and one Nathan Reilly Alexander. He would've argued, but he sure as hell couldn't stay in his old house and the Diablo was the only place for a hundred miles in any direction.

The Diablo Springs Hotel might have been considered a hotel in the 1800s when it was built, but by today's standards it was just a big house with six bedrooms and saggy eaves. Carolina Beck had lived there for her entire life. From where he sat, it looked like a good wind could blow it over, but as a hard gust rocked the SUV, the hotel stood steady, letting him know it was sturdier than it looked.

Lightning sizzled and sparked overhead, turning the windows of the Diablo into jack-o'-lantern eyes. The howling wind pounded the giant mesquite and sucked the grit from the rock and cactus garden along the walkway. On cue, a tumbleweed bounced its way past them to lodge in the neighbor's fence.

Reilly glanced at his watch. It was nearly midnight, but lights blazed on the ground floor, sending a tickle of unease down Reilly's spine. Carolina Beck was the kind of woman who rose with the sun and worked like a farmer's wife until dusk. She'd never burned the midnight oil.

The brooding storm intensified the oppressive heat as he climbed out of the Jeep. It felt like he'd stepped into a damp electric blanket with a buzzing short deep within its circuitry. In the distance the ruins of the old hot springs stuck up like black bones against the lightning-struck sky. Reilly squinted as spinning flashes of blue and red whirled against the backdrop. Police cars? He frowned, wondering if the Dead Lights had lured another victim into the cavernous pit of the dried-up springs.

The minivan that had followed him out of Los Angeles pulled up behind his Jeep and the old woman and her two companions piled out. Between Count Lincoln, Father Ghoul, and Chloe the Gypsy Queen, he couldn't say which of the three was the strangest.

The air held a fetid smell that brought home a million memories. Hot summer nights swimming with his brother, Matt, in Danny Green's aboveground pool. They'd frozen water in milk jugs and floated them in a vain effort to cool it off. They'd slept on cots in the backyard, braving the bugs for the chance of a breeze. They'd learned the sun could be an enemy. And so could a lightning storm, like the electric light show going on now.

As Reilly grabbed his bag from the back of the SUV, the sharp scent of sulfur joined the loamy smells in the air. No rain yet, just a few sprinkles that seemed to evaporate before they reached earth, leaving a filmy steam that made his skin sticky and the air thick.

Chloe Lamont approached, followed closely by the Count, who Reilly guessed to be her bodyguard or an adopted son . . . or maybe her significant other. Hard to say. He easily topped Reilly's own six foot two and looked like he might never have seen the sun.

"Nathan," Chloe said in her soft, mysteriously accented voice. "Do you feel them?"

"No."

"Liar. I know you sense them. You've always sensed them."

"I sense we're going to get hit by lightning if we don't get inside."

Her grin was smug. He gritted his teeth.

"We're late," she said, unconcerned with his prediction. "Not too late, but late. Let's go in."

Reilly gave one more glance at the police lights out at the dried-up springs and then followed Chloe and the Count up the walkway. The priest fell in step behind him.

Chloe paused on the porch, looking at him expectantly as he joined her.

"No one home?" he asked.

She gave a shrug that conveyed absolutely nothing. "You go first," she said. "You'll have to face . . . Is it Faith?" She tilted her head to the side and narrowed her eyes. "No, it's Grace, isn't it?"

"Gracie?" Reilly glanced at the front door and then back to Chloe.

Chloe gave him an enigmatic smile. "Gracie, yes, of course. You didn't really think you were through with her, did you?"

"Gracie's *here*?" he repeated with a step back.

"Not yet."

It took a moment for common sense to overpower his knee-jerk reaction. He gave a low laugh. "You've got your wires crossed, Chloe. Gracie Beck hasn't been back to Diablo Springs since she took off. She's never coming back."

"That's what they say about you."

The door swung silently open as a huge bolt of lightning struck nearby with a crack and a hiss, releasing a smattering of raindrops that broke through the vapors. It seemed they should sizzle as they hit the ground below.

A diminutive gentleman in a gray sweater and black trousers stood on the threshold. He gave them a benevolent smile and stood aside for them to enter.

"I wondered if you'd beat the storm," he said.

Reilly didn't know who he was, but he seemed at home here.

They filed through the door in twos, like kids using the buddy system for their field trip. Reilly dropped his bags and closed the door behind them. Every light in the house seemed to be on, but there was no sign of life anywhere.

"I'm Jonathan Stevens. Welcome to the Diablo," he said, holding out a hand. Reilly shook and introduced himself. Then, because it seemed to be expected, he said, "This is Chloe Lamont and . . ."

Abe the Vampire held out his hand. "Bill Barnes." He flashed a frosty glance at Reilly. "It's easier to remember than Abraham."

Reilly's eyes widened. The guy could read minds?

"Michael," the priest mumbled, but he didn't offer to shake. Instead he clasped his gloved hands behind him defensively.

"I'm sorry Ms. Beck isn't here to greet you," Jonathan said.

"Where is she?" Reilly asked.

"It's not my place to say."

Reilly shot a sideways glance at Chloe. The old woman looked solemnly back.

"Your rooms are ready, however, and I'll take your bags right up. Feel free to make yourselves at home during your stay. I can make coffee if you'd care for it."

"No, thanks," Reilly said and the others declined as well.

They didn't have a lot of baggage—if you didn't count the figurative kind—but Reilly moved to help carry it upstairs. When he returned, the others had moved into the front room. Reilly followed, feeling like he was stepping back in time.

"It's changed, since the last time you were here, no?" Chloe's voice came deep and melodic and way too close. She was like a spider, creeping up on him.

"I only made it past the porch once," he muttered.

Although her granddaughter had loved Reilly, Carolina Beck had made no pretense of overlooking his inferiority. Matt and Reilly Alexander gave white trash new standards. The first time Gracie had brought him home had been the last. After that he and Gracie had met in secret.

From that one brief encounter, Reilly remembered the place as being bright and cheery, though. TV-mom clean and neat. In this room, there'd been a serviceable sofa of everyday blue and a matching chair in front of a console television set. Nondescript, outdoorsy paintings had adorned the walls and blue-checked curtains covered the windows. It had looked clean and happy. He'd felt like he sullied the place just be being there.

What he saw now was the opposite of that. A long, gleaming bar stretched the length of the western wall and hard wood tables with stiff, spindle-back chairs filled in the space where that sofa had been. The bar wasn't stocked—not even a glass waited to be filled behind it and the empty shelves had an eerie feel to them that was almost as disturbing as the strange change in décor.

"Maybe she was trying to bring in tourists with the rustic feel," he said, confused.

"Maybe," Chloe answered with a smile that mocked him.

Ornately framed pictures of people long dead perched on yellowed doilies atop the mantel or hung from big heavy frames on the walls. The subjects in the pictures seemed to look out, watching him back as he stared in disbelief. The room was still, the wood dark, the curtains heavy, and the cloying atmosphere smelled of old sex and booze.

Jonathan entered, looking like Mr. Rodgers mistakenly cast in an episode of *Gunsmoke*.

"Ms. Beck remodeled," Reilly said.

"A few years ago," Jonathan answered. "Right after I started working for her."

Carolina had a suspicious nature that didn't lend itself to live-in help. He was surprised she'd hired Jonathan at all.

"She wanted the Diablo restored to its original glory," he went on. "All of this came from the attic."

"Huh."

Reilly wandered to the fireplace where of a faded picture of four women in various stages of undress hung. The women sat at a table in front of a bar—the bar in this very room, from the looks of it—pinned in place like butterflies on a board by the sharp rays of sunlight cutting through cloudy windows. None of them looked old enough to be in the profession their attire suggested. Until you looked at their disillusioned eyes.

Beyond their circle of light, a scattering of dusty and disreputable men watched, as if picture taking was the most interesting thing to behold. A large black woman stood in the background, balefully eyeing the men watching the women.

Reilly used his sleeve to rub away a smudge on the glass, his gaze caught by one of the women sitting at the table. There was something hauntingly familiar about her clear, light eyes, but it took a full minute before he realized what it was. She looked like Gracie Beck. She looked a *lot* like Gracie Beck had the last time he'd seen her.

She stared back at him, her gaze filled with questions, accusations . . . hurt. He felt trapped by the weight of guilt that look dredged up. Which was stupid. It wasn't Gracie in the picture and even if it were, Gracie had moved on without a backwards glance. What did he have to feel guilty about?

"Think we could open some windows?" he asked, turning away. "It's hot in here."

And obviously, miserly Caroline hadn't ever put in air conditioning.

The storm had picked up momentum in the short time they'd been there, but it hadn't brought cooler temperatures. Still, it had to be better than the stale and stifling air inside.

"They don't open," Jonathan said calmly.

Doubtful, Reilly tried anyway, but none of them budged. Frustrated, he brushed the dust from his hands when a loud whirring came an instant before the feel of air blowing through a vent.

Air-conditioning. Miracles did happen. He found the thermostat by the swinging door. It seemed anachronistic in its surroundings, but Reilly was relieved it existed at all. He laughed when he saw the control fixed at ninety-five. Leave it to Carolina Beck to install air, but refuse to keep it turned low enough to cool.

"Do you mind?" he asked, not caring if Jonathan did. He moved the lever to sixty-five, knowing she'd go nuts when she found out, but too hot to care. *Sorry, Carolina, but this is hard enough without being steamed alive.*

He turned around just as the front door burst open and Gracie Beck, two dogs the size of ponies, and a third drenched ball of fur blew into the room. Reilly's heart stuttered to a stop as he stared at the woman he'd never been able to forget, no matter how hard he'd tried. And he had. Every damn day since.

She'd always been small—even before he'd filled out and shot up to his six-two height, the top of her head had barely reached his chin. She still was, but age had rounded the sharp angles of her shoulders, added fullness to her breasts, smoothed the slope to her waist. She wore khaki capris that followed the curve of her legs and a black T-shirt that had been dampened by the rain. He could just make out the faint outline of a lace bra. It drew his gaze and started a slow burn from a spark that had never really gone out.

Her soft brown hair was drawn back in a ponytail, but a few wisps escaped to frame her face. Her eyes were still storm-cloud gray, overflowing with the kind of secrets that drove a man insane with wanting to know. But gone was the cocky defiance that had marked Gracie Beck from the cradle. Gone was the devil-may-care smile that had teased him into wet dreams as a teen. In its place was a somberness that had no place on a mouth so soft.

A feeling welled up inside him, as powerful as the winds buffeting the house, as deep as the pitted crevices in the dried-up springs. A longing to touch her, to cup her face and taste her lips, to press his nose to her temple and breathe her in. It caught him unaware and put him on guard. Wary, he braced for her to notice him, too.

She scanned the room quickly, eyes widening as they moved from one stranger to another while he waited with tension knotting inside him.

"What . . ." she began, and then her gaze found him and her words faded away.

Their eyes locked and held. Confusion turned hers silver and made him want to charge across the room while at the same time urging him to run in the opposite direction. She took a hesitant step forward, as if she couldn't help herself. He did, too, pulled by the same insane compulsion.

"What . . ." she said again, and then suddenly her eyes shuttered and she stiffened. "What are you doing here?"

Moment lost, Reilly allowed himself a breath of relief. Only relief was hell and gone from how he really felt. "Good to see you, too, Gracie."

CHAPTER FIVE

Gracie had driven across the desert at breakneck speeds, thinking of nothing but Analise. Now she was here, expecting to see Eddie Rodriguez waiting with her contrite daughter nearby. She'd never thought she'd find Reilly Alexander instead.

"What are you doing in my grandmother's house?" she demanded, staring at the man who'd destroyed her life with as much dignity as she could muster while wrestling two Great Danes on leashes and holding one wet Yorkie in her arms. "Where are Eddie and my daughter?"

"Eddie Rodriguez?" Reilly said, shock widening his pretty eyes, reminding her of the boy she'd fallen in love with so long ago. The boy who'd promised to sweep her away and care for her forever. The boy who'd knocked her up and then disappeared with her hopes and dreams.

He was a man now. Taller, broader through the shoulders and chest, bigger all around. She'd never forget those hazel eyes, though, or the face of the man who'd hurt her so badly she'd thought she'd never recover.

What was he doing here? And where was Eddie with her daughter?

She gave the dogs a sharp command to sit and put Romeo down next to them before pulling out her cell phone and hitting the last number dialed to reach Eddie. She'd talked to him a half hour ago and he'd said he'd be at the Diablo with Analise by the time she got here.

As the phone rang, she took in her surroundings. Nothing looked the same as it had when she'd lived there with her grandmother seventeen years ago. Not the furniture, the pictures, the curtains. Not the strangers crowded inside, either. She tried to sort through her confusion as she stared at the clustered group of people. A man who looked as if he'd neglected to remove his Dracula costume after Halloween; an older, dark-skinned woman wearing an African turban and tunic. Hanging back stood a priest wearing dingy white gloves and rounding out the group was an older man with silver at the temples, wearing a gray sweater with leather patches at the elbows. He must be Jonathan, the caretaker Eddie said her grandmother had finally hired. He'd described him as distinguished looking, in a seedy kind of way. The man seemed to fit the bill.

At their fringes stood Reilly Alexander. Her heart stuttered at the sight of him.

Eddie's phone kept ringing in her ear, but headlights shot through the windows and climbed the walls. Gracie hit the "end" button and hurried to the porch as Eddie Rodriguez got out of a police car and ran around to the other side. Sheltering his passenger from the rain, he hurried them both up to where Gracie waited. When he

43

lowered the umbrella, Analise stepped forward into her mother's waiting arms.

Gracie cried as she embraced her only child, mumbling words that didn't need to make sense as they held one another.

"She's fine, Gracie," Eddie said, patting her shoulder awkwardly. "Dr. Graebel checked her out. She has a bump on her head and she's shook up, but no permanent damage. He thinks the boy will be okay, too."

The boy?

"Brendan?" she asked, pulling back to see Analise's face. "Brendan brought you here? Why?"

"He thought I'd like it," Analise mumbled, wiping at her tears. She looked pale and Gracie suspected she was in shock.

"He's still at Dr. Graebel's?" Gracie asked Eddie.

"Yeah. He isn't conscious yet, so the doc wants to keep overnight, but he says he doesn't think it's serious. Thinks the boy will be coming around soon."

"Mom," Analise said, looking around. "Who are all these people?"

Analise brushed her hair back from her face and scanned the cluster of strangers, giving Reilly his first clear look at her face. Gracie froze with dread, wanting to shove Analise behind her and race for the door, but a train was already barreling through the tunnel and at any moment, it would jump the tracks. There was no way to stop it, just as there was no way in hell Reilly could look at his daughter and not recognize her for who she was.

The blood drained from his face and his mouth fell open. Uncomfortable with his fixed stare, Analise shifted and looked away. Fortunately, *she* hadn't made the connection yet, but Gracie wouldn't be able to keep it from her now. Scared, angry, and uncertain about what came next, Gracie lifted her chin and met the incredulous gaze that swung her way.

Eddie had been scribbling on a notebook he carried. Now he looked up just as the woman in the turban stepped forward.

"We have reservations," she said with a smile, oblivious to the turmoil churning among Gracie, Reilly, and their confused daughter. She looked anxious as she went on. "Mr. Stevens assured us our rooms are ready."

"Reservations?" Eddie repeated like it was a foreign concept. His gaze moved suspiciously through the room until it landed on Reilly. He gave a bark of laughter, finally wrenching Reilly's gaze away from Gracie.

Reilly and Eddie had known each other most of their lives, but it still bothered Gracie when Eddie pulled him into an embrace and patted him soundly on the back. "Son of a bitch. Never thought I'd seen you here. How the hell are you?"

Reilly made a sound that wasn't quite laughter and stepped back. "I could use a drink."

So could Gracie.

"What the hell are you— You with these guys?" Eddie asked.

The suspicion was back in his voice. Good.

"No," Reilly answered at the same time the woman said, "Yes."

She smiled again, her turbaned head bobbing. "Nathan is looking for his next story," she said. "He thinks he'll find it here."

Eddie's eyes narrowed at that. "What makes you think so, Reilly?"

With a sick feeling in her stomach, Gracie tucked Analise against her and waited for Reilly to answer. He'd come for a story? Had he heard about Grandma Beck's death and decided to sensationalize it? She wouldn't put it past him.

"Time out," Reilly said, making a *T* with his hands. "Rewind. They"—he jerked his thumb at the small group—"are the story. Seriously, look at them."

Only the priest appeared to be offended by the comment. Jonathan cleared his throat to draw attention and then greeted Eddie with a friendly smile. Eddie returned it with a curt nod.

"Ms. Lamont is correct. These people reserved their rooms a few days ago. Carolina took the reservation herself."

Gracie let out a deep breath. "I'm sorry for the inconvenience, Ms. Lamont, but you'll need to find other accommodations. My grandmother died tonight. The Diablo isn't available for guests anymore."

"Carolina's dead?" Reilly exclaimed in a deep voice. "Are you serious?"

"Your grandma died?" Analise cried. *"Tonight?"*

Cursing her own stupidity for blurting that out in front of Analise, Gracie pulled her closer.

Eddie nodded, confirming it. "We found her body out by the ruins."

"By the *ruins*?" Analise said. "But . . ."

Reilly looked like he was having as hard a time processing everything as Gracie and Analise. He gave Chloe Lamont a hard, accusing look and the old woman stared serenely back, but deep within the black wells of her eyes, Gracie could swear she saw satisfaction.

Disturbed, Gracie shifted her gaze to Reilly.

"I'm sorry about your grandmother, Gracie," he told her. "I didn't know."

"I did," Chloe said.

Gracie's jaw dropped. "What does that—"

"Ms. Lamont is a spiritual woman," the man who looked like Dracula said. "She communes with the dead."

"We've been studying Diablo Springs for some time now," Chloe offered, her voice clear and strong, tinged with a compassion that seemed misplaced, considering the fact that she was a complete stranger. "There's a psychic phenomenon here that's beyond anything I've ever experienced. It's incredible, really. Like a vibration. I'm surprised even you can't feel it."

The "even you" comment was the last straw. Gracie was too tired to even feign politeness. "For the love of God," she said in disgust. "I'm sorry, but you and your friends will have to leave."

Chloe's eyes widened. "Miss Beck, I understand you're upset, but you can't turn us away in the middle of the night. In a storm, no less."

"I'm afraid I can."

"We've already paid."

"I'll give you a refund."

"Gracie," Eddie said beneath his breath. "Take a look out the window. At least let them stay until morning. It's only a few hours."

Gracie narrowed her eyes at him before turning back to woman.

"Check the books," Chloe insisted. "I'm sure you'll find everything in order."

The leather-bound book Grandma Beck had always used to record the comings and goings of the Diablo's temporary residents was on the entry table, just like always. Gracie traced her fingers over the word Ledger on the bright blue cover, thinking of the aged brown ledger she'd seen in her grandma's hands just before Eddie called.

Swallowing the lump in her throat, Gracie opened it to the page marked with a strip of red ribbon.

The entry was dated and written in Grandma Beck's scrawl. *Bill Barnes, four rooms.* Beneath that, in small block letters: *Paid in advance. Check with bank. Wire transfer??? Full price.*

Damn it, they'd been telling the truth. Reluctantly, she faced the group watching her. "Who is Bill Barnes?"

Dracula stepped forward. Surely not?

"She wouldn't take a credit card, so I had Bill wire the payment to her bank account," Chloe said. "She was very suspicious about it."

"Why didn't you just pay her when you got here?"

"Because I knew you'd throw us out if all the accounts weren't settled."

The old woman's dark voice sent a chill through Gracie. She didn't like Chloe Lamont. Not at all.

"I still might."

"No, you won't. Not in good conscience and you are a person guided by your conscience."

Gracie wanted to spite this woman and damn the consequences, but Chloe cut her off.

"She called to us," Chloe said softly. Again, Gracie heard that ring of compassion. "All the way across the desert, we heard her. All of us."

"All of you?" Eddie repeated, staring from one face to another.

Reilly leaned against the wall, looking up as if wondering how he'd come to be here. Gracie wondered the same thing.

"What do you have to say about this?" she demanded.

The look Reilly gave her was hard and filled with accusation. As if he had the right to be angry with *her.* "Not a damned thing," he answered.

Bill Barnes touched Chloe lightly on the arm and murmured something in her ear. Chloe nodded. "You're right, Bill." She looked at Gracie. "We think it's best if we discuss this in the morning." She looked at Jonathan. "Would you be so kind as to tell us what rooms we're in?"

Gracie glared at her, wishing with all her might that she could tell them to take a hike, but thunder shook the house as the wind rattled the windows.

And damn it to hell, Chloe was right. Gracie's conscience guided her and she'd have to be heartless to send them out in this when she knew there wasn't another place to stay for at least a hundred miles in any direction. She was too exhausted to be heartless tonight. But that didn't mean she'd be nice.

With a tight-lipped smile, Jonathan led the *guests* upstairs, leaving Gracie, her daughter, Eddie, and Reilly alone on the first floor.

Feeling like the day had lasted forever, Gracie looked around. "Now, would someone please tell me what the hell happened here tonight?"

CHAPTER SIX

May 1896
Somewhere in Colorado

The first scream carried across the plains like the howl of an October wind. It brought my head up and around. I was on all fours, trying to pull some deadwood free from a tangle of roots. As the sound settled around me, I perched up on my knees like a prairie dog to see over the waving sea of grass, but that didn't help much. All I saw was more of the same.

I though it must have been a crow or a buzzard I heard. There'd been plenty of each on the way, and I hated them both. In fact, today I hated just about everything and everyone.

I'd been angry for days, ever since my daddy came home and said we were pulling up roots and running away. He hadn't said "running," but that's what it was all the same. I wasn't old enough to argue, but I was old enough to be mad about it. I hadn't even gotten to say good-bye to Charlotte or Willie Johnson, who'd been acting like he might want to be more than friendly with me. Seventeen was only old enough to do a woman's share of chores, not speak my mind.

The fact that we were running like cowards bothered me as much as anything. I'd begged my daddy not to testify in court about the holdup, but of course he didn't listen. Men. The bank sure didn't deserve his loyalty, but he'd given it all the same. And look how it had paid him back. Momma had tried to sway him, too, but then he'd become stubborn and decided that, as the man of the house, he'd say where and what and why things got done.

We were five days from Alamosa now, and I still hadn't forgiven him. I didn't like walking day in and day out. My momma looked like she was carrying a litter of babies, though we both prayed just one would come out. Even though her ribs must have felt like they were ready to burst, Momma still took in the scenery like she'd been blessed to even step foot on God's green earth. I couldn't see it that way. Not when I was sleeping on the hard ground with bugs sure to be creeping and crawling over me all night and my bed at home as empty and neat as could be.

I picked up another stick, shifting the bundle in my arms and giving myself a splinter in the process. That only spurred my anger.

And then I heard the next scream.

This time, there wasn't any doubt. That was no bird. I rocked back on my heels, looking over the swaying seedpods toward our camp on the other side of the hill. The sun arced low in the sky, dragging shadows out with the wind. A gun fired, and an instant later a gray puff of smoke wafted upward.

I scrambled to my feet, dropping the wood I'd been gathering as I raced without thought toward the sound. More gunshots cracked the dusky blue day, followed by a triumphant whoop of glee that made my blood run cold. Indians? Was it Indians?

I dropped to my knees at the top of the hill and scooted forward to look over. My skirts tangled about my legs and ripped when I didn't heed them. Belly flat to the earth, I peered down at our camp. Five men on horseback rode circles around it, firing pistols into the air just for the fun of it, I guessed. Not Indians. These were white men, men who looked like they'd not seen a bath for many years. They seemed to be playing a game of some sort, turning and riding and darting around. I couldn't see beyond the wagon, though, to what was at the center of their sport. I cupped my hands to my eyes to block the glare of the setting sun and searched for my momma and daddy, grandma and brother. Had they gone to gather wood or hunt? Were these bandits robbing us while they were gone? But even as I thought it, I recognized the flaw in my thinking. It was Momma I'd heard scream. I was sure of it.

The men down below laughed and shouted happily to one another as they raced around. I made my eyes squinty, trying to make out features through the dirt and dust that caked their faces. Who were they? Why were they here?

I scanned the far hillside, praying the rest of my family was there, on the other side, watching with the same horror I was. A pot of stew Momma had set to cook still hung over the fire and the fresh breeze brought the smell of it to me.

Momma, where are you?

Johnny's toys lay atop the quilt Momma and I had sewn when he was born and spread out for him to play on when we'd struck camp, but he wasn't anywhere around it. Beyond that . . .

A wave of sickness hit me. Beyond Johnny's blanket, Grandma's wheelchair lay on its side, wheels peeking out from behind the crates we'd unloaded when we set camp. I stared, one part of my mind jamming like gears in a windmill as another part spun out of control. Why was Grandma's wheelchair all tipped over? And where was Grandma?

A rider charged up the hill, and I ducked down.

He shouted out to the others. "Lonnie, Jake, come on. Let's git."

"Ain't done," one of them hollered back. "Not by far we ain't. And I'm hungry. I'm going to sit me down and have some of this fine stew Mrs. Beck done cooked up for us."

The rider muttered something and then reined his horse around.

Lonnie . . . Jake . . .

I flattened myself to the earth, inhaled the dark scents of dirt and worms, and tried to batten down my fear. Lonnie and Jake . . . The Smith brothers. I bit hard on my lip to keep from crying out. The brothers were identical twins, just a year older than my seventeen, and they were murderers. Cold-blooded murderers. Last month my father had stood as the only witness to their thievery and murderousness and convinced a jury to hang the two men.

A movement from the opposite hillside caught my eyes. Daddy and Johnny, running toward the wagon. My daddy held his rifle in one hand, Johnny clung to the other. They'd heard the gunshots, as I had, but from their angle, they couldn't see the men, now gathered at the fire. I wanted to stand up and shout, wave my arms and warn them, but if I did . . .

My daddy's footsteps slowed as he stared at something out of my sight. What? What did he see? He stilled, Johnny at his side, and stared. Just stared.

Then slowly he pushed Johnny back, pointed at a boulder. Johnny didn't want to do what Daddy ordered. I could see it in his posture. In the defiant tilt of his head. He was six, but tried to act sixteen. At last he crouched down where he'd been told. Daddy cocked his rifle and advanced on the camp.

"*No,*" I breathed. "*No, Daddy.*"

One of the men, maybe Lonnie, maybe Jake, sensed him coming and looked up. He reached for his gun. In my mind I could hear the metal clear the leather. Time seemed to slow down. I felt each beat of my heart, watched paralyzed as my daddy advanced on the gang. What could I do? If I stood, they'd kill me. I knew they would. But if I didn't, my daddy would certainly die. I tried to make my legs move. Tried to get to my feet. But I was frozen, flattened on the hillside like one of the stones beside me.

The man with the gun stood quiet as a shadow and sidled up to the wagon, peeking around. Daddy saw, took aim, and fired. The shot splintered into the bed and sent wood shards flying in all directions. It made a loud boom that echoed across the open plains and hills. A yelp broke from my lips, but I clapped a hand over my mouth to mute it. The man with the gun howled and grabbed at his eye.

Fast as lightning, the other men reached for their weapons and rounded the wagon. Daddy got off another shot, but that was all. The four men fired with abandon and my scream lodged in my throat as Daddy's body danced with the impact. They riddled him full of lead, moving forward as they fired like the mindless killers they were. The sloping foothills around me sucked up the sound and threw it back in resounding echoes that seemed to pierce me. I covered my ears and shut my eyes, but I couldn't block out the sound or the tears squeezing through my tightly closed lids. I couldn't erase the image of my father's body jumping in a death jig of gunfire. Suddenly the shots stopped. I opened my eyes. Daddy lay still and broken on the ground, arms and legs askew in angles no arms or legs were ever meant to be. One of the outlaws raised his pistol and put a final shot in his head.

I prayed as hard as I could that Johnny would remain behind his rock. But even as the sobbing plea lodged in my throat, I saw my baby brother emerge from his craggy hiding place, heard his scream, a tormented sound filled with more humiliation, anger, and agony than a child could ever endure.

He charged across the clearing. The sound he made matched the anguish trapped inside my breast, but they didn't stop what came next. The army of four turned like soldiers and opened fire.

"No," I cried. Yet the word came dry and silent, a fiery whisper that burned and crackled in my throat. "No," I tried again, but it was too late. Now both my daddy and brother lay flat on the ground in a twist of blood and gore. The same filthy killer who'd put his gun to Daddy's head now did the same to my brother. The vibration of the shot traveled through me like a quaking of the earth. Hot tears streamed down my face, but still, I couldn't move.

The man twirled his pistol like a gunslinger, grinned at his friends, and then joined them back at the fire. They ransacked the kitchen crates for plates and spoons, laughing as they scooped Momma's stew onto their dishes. They sat in a circle as they fed themselves, ignoring the crumpled, bloody bodies of my daddy and brother.

I scanned the craggy knolls around me, looking for Momma. Where was she? Hiding like me? Or didn't she know? Maybe she was close to the river? There, she might not have heard the shots. How would I face her when she came back to find her husband and son murdered while I'd done nothing to help?

And why was grandma's wheelchair turned over?

The horrible men glutted themselves on the stew for interminable minutes, and then one of them moved to the back of the wagon and urinated on Grandma's wheelchair. This . . . this horrible act of disrespect finally loosened my numbed limbs. I stood without thinking, but then another man's head whipped around, and I dropped to my belly with such force I knocked the breath from my lungs.

Excited voices came and then the sound of horses. They'd seen me.

On all fours I scrambled down the hill, trying at once to keep low and move fast. I looked behind and saw that the grass was flattened where I'd lain on it. In a full panic I stood straight, hiked up my skirts, and tore across the open land. Ahead were bushes and beyond a smattering of pine trees leading into the foothills. I made it to the first of them just as the men crested the hill behind me. My heart hammered against my ribs and my constricted lungs fought to bring in air. I crept back and back until I reached a tree with low branches. I crawled beneath the skirt of its boughs and then up two, three limbs. Overhead the branches grew tight as a cage. I could go no higher. I stayed as still as I could, making myself small as I peered through the pine needles. The wind teased around the trees, disguising my movements.

The riders came down the hill, following the tracks I'd left until they reached the place where I'd stood and run. From that point they worked their way back and forth, bickering as they rode, one calling the other stupid, the other retorting in kind.

They entered the trees and circled among the pines. I crouched still as time, waiting for them to see me. The man with the wagon splinters in his face stopped at the tree next to the one where I hid. The side of his cheek was puffy and bloody, the eyelid swollen nearly shut. Still, if he moved, if he looked straight on . . .

My heart thudded, and the terror I'd held down threatened to swoop up and out in a never-ending scream. My eyes streamed with the effort to be silent, to be still. The man coughed and spat, his face coming up and around to where I huddled. I closed my eyes and silently whispered a prayer.

"Jake!" one of the others shouted. "Anything?"

To my left, Jake answered, but I dared not turn my head to look. I dared not move. Someone else called something from beyond the trees.

"She's gone," the bloodied man beside me said. "I say let's git, too. Ain't nothing she can do out here but die."

The truth of that added another layer to my horror.

The four of them gathered together and I trembled with the effort to remain motionless. They conferred for a moment that lasted so long my hands ached and my legs felt weak. Finally they rode away, single file. As the last man spun away, I caught one clear look at him.

It was Lonnie Dean Smith all right. I bit hard on my lip, choking back the sob. The bastard.

I stayed where I was until they'd left the cove, until they'd ridden up and over the ridge. They passed my hiding place close enough that I could have reached out and touched them as they went by. The last man towed

Daddy's two horses behind him, the supplies they'd pilfered weighing heavy on their backs.

Unmoving, I stared at their tracks. Is that how they'd found my family? Followed our trail from our front door? But how were they free? I'd seen the brothers taken away in handcuffs to await their execution. How were they here when they should be in jail? Locked up. Ready to hang?

My daddy must have known they'd break free and come for him. That's why he'd wanted us to leave as we had, in the dead of the night with only a wagon full of possessions. Daddy had known the Smith brothers wouldn't hang. He'd known they'd hunt for him. He hadn't known how fast, though, or with what determination.

Branches pulled at my hair and snagged my clothes when I finally scurried down from the tree. My hands were sticky with sap, and my arms were scratched and bleeding. I hit the ground, wiggled out from under the boughs, and raced toward the camp, silent lest my voice carry and bring the outlaws back. Great billowing waves of black smoke rose up from the valley where we'd stopped. From the hilltop, I saw our wagon ablaze and all our things burning like bonfire. I half-ran, half-stumbled down the to the inferno.

"Momma!" I shouted. My daddy and brother still lay where they'd been gunned down. I ran to them, touching their bloodied and broken bodies with shaking hands. Most of Johnny's face had been blown away, half of Daddy's head. There would be no miracle survival for either.

I stood, my hands red with their blood. "Momma!" I cried again. "Grandma!"

No one answered. Holding my apron up to my face, I circled the hot flames to the place where I'd seen my grandmother's wheelchair. Now I saw what had been hidden before, my grandmother's wasted body, bloody with gunshots, sprawled on the ground. I dropped to my knees beside her, sobbing, my eyes streaming with tears from grief and pain and smoke. The ground near Grandma's gray hair was wet, and I realized with sickening rage that the man I'd seen had been urinating not on Grandma's chair, but on her body.

"No!" I screamed at the sky.

I still hadn't found my mother. I stood and hurried to the far end of the wagon, where the smoke was like a black wall holding me back. I saw a foot sticking out from beside the wheel. Dropping to my hands and knees I crawled under the smoke to where my mother was sprawled in the dirt. Her dress had been ripped down the front, her swollen, pregnant belly sticking up to the sky. Skirts bunched, privates exposed and legs splayed at an awful angle. I wasn't too young to know what they'd done to her. After they'd finished, they'd shot her in the head and stomach.

Sobbing, I smoothed my mother's clothes down and collapsed on the ground next to her, curling myself into a tight ball of misery. The wagon, weakened by fire, gave an ominous groan, lilted to the right, and then shuddered in warning. Before I understood what that meant, it collapsed on top of my mother's body. I scrambled back just in time to avoid being crushed by the burning bed.

They were all dead. Everyone but me, who'd been too cowardly to save them. I wanted to curl up and die beside them, let the fires burn away my anguish, but I was too yellow for even that.

I scooted back as the flames burned hotter and higher, watching with dumb fear as the wind shifted, and the flames moved to the long grasses on the outskirts. In a blink they caught like tinder and exploded into an inferno. In moments I'd be trapped.

Instinct kicked in when the urge to survive did not. Keeping my apron to my face, I moved to the railings at the back of the wagon where my daddy kept one shotgun hidden and loaded for me and my mother. She'd probably been going for it when Smith's riders attacked. I didn't have time to search for more bullets. From my father's dead body, I took his heavy hunting knife. And then my feet were moving away as my mind stayed with my family.

The fire chased me, happily making sport of this run for my life. With each pounding step, I thought of my mother, my brother, my father, my grandmother. Their names alternated in my mind, keeping time with my steps. I raced to the shallow river and splashed across, the wet cold bringing me from shock into the full realization that whether I lived or died depended on what I did next.

CHAPTER SEVEN

G randma Beck had done away with the sofa and loveseat that once dominated the front room and replaced them with tables, uncomfortable chairs and a bar. A *bar*. Grandma Beck, who didn't even drink wine on holidays. That the bar was dry made the situation no less bizarre, and in the grand scheme of the unending night, it fell low on the list of weird.

Arm around Analise's shoulders, Gracie moved to one of the tables and took a seat beside her daughter. Tinkerbelle and Juliet flopped on the floor behind them, where they could keep their eyes on everyone. Romeo jumped into Analise's lap and licked her hand. Smiling, Analise cuddled the little dog and took the comfort he offered.

Eddie pulled out the chair opposite them. Reilly stayed where he was against the wall, arms crossed over that broad chest, long legs braced, brooding tension bunching his shoulders.

The strangers he'd brought with him were upstairs finding their rooms, and their footsteps sounded like an elephant stampede from down below. It felt like an invasion on every level. Gracie hoped by some miracle they'd all disappear in the morning, but the storm outside sounded like it was gaining momentum instead of waning. A dreadful pessimistic voice in her head told her they wouldn't be departing anytime soon.

"Analise," Eddie said, leaning forward with his arms on the table. "Let's go over what happened tonight one more time."

Analise's lashes were wet and spiky, and her eyes were shiny from tears. She looked so young and vulnerable that Gracie thought her heart might break. She'd spent her life trying to shelter her daughter from pain and fear, yet here she was, captive to both anyway.

"I told you, I don't remember," Analise said in a thick voice.

"Why are you here, honey?" Gracie asked. "Start there."

Analise bit her lip and looked down. "Brendan brought me here as a surprise. For my birthday."

"When's your birthday?" Reilly asked, his deep voice abrupt in the surprised silence.

Analise frowned at him. "Next week," she said, "But I'm going to be in Orange County for the Newspaper Club convention. We get to go to Disneyland."

"How old are you?"

His sharp tone confused Analise, but Gracie knew exactly why the demand had such an aggressive edge.

"She's sixteen, Reilly," Gracie answered flatly. "Any other questions?"

"Give me a minute."

Stiffening, Gracie turned away and rubbed Analise's back. "So you lied to me about staying with Karen," she said.

Analise nodded. "I'm sorry."

"Why did Brendan think a trip to Diablo Springs would be a good birthday surprise?" Eddie asked.

"He knew I was curious about where my mom came from. Who my dad is." She glanced at Gracie and quickly away.

Gracie fought the urge to look at Reilly, but the pull was too strong. She didn't have a clue what he might be thinking. Hell, she didn't have a clue what *she* was thinking. Reilly snagged her gaze as soon as she lifted it but he didn't give anything away. His features might have been carved from stone, his eyes from ice.

Tears burned Gracie's eyes, but she didn't let them go. She'd known that Analise was curious about where her mother came from, who her absent father might be. Gracie had lied and said there'd been several boys and she'd never known which one was the father. The fabrication of her promiscuity had fit nicely with the truth of how Grandma Beck had shipped her pregnant granddaughter off to live with strangers until the baby was born and then never let her come back home.

All the other questions Analise asked, Gracie managed to answer with as much honesty as she could, sharing the bare minimum, glossing over the rest. She'd never guessed that Analise had kept digging, searching for more. In retrospect, that was a big fail on her part. She should've known an overachiever like Analise would never settle for half-truths and lies.

"Analise, I didn't realize how important it was to you."

"You didn't think knowing my dad was so important?" Analise shot back, astonished.

Yeah, Gracie deserved that. "So you came here thinking you'd miraculously find him?"

"I thought Grandma would tell me."

Grandma Beck wouldn't have given up that secret under torture. She'd have turned Analise around and sent her home so fast, the kid would have been dizzy.

As for Reilly, well he'd packed up and hit the road before she'd even known she was pregnant and by the time she'd learned his whereabouts . . . Well, she'd been too hurt and betrayed to hunt him down. He'd promised her a future and left her without a word, her life in ruins. At first, her pride wouldn't let her ask him for anything, not even help with his child. Later, when maturity and distance had given her perspective, there'd been other reasons not to tell him. That didn't make it right or fair, but few things in Gracie's life had ever been right or fair.

She glanced at him again. She couldn't help it. Even after all this time, having him in the same room was like sitting next to a power line. She felt him beneath the skin, a low frequency hum that made her hyperaware and jittery.

He wore a T-shirt that couldn't hide the thick, corded muscles of his arms and chest. His faded Levi's hung low on lean hips, drawing her eye down and stirring memories she didn't want to wake.

A black and white tattoo covered his right forearm, and a series of colorful ones wrapped his left bicep. His hair was just shy of shaved and a five-o'clock shadow darkened his jaw. At eighteen he'd been walking, talking sex appeal. At thirty-five, he was potent enough to make her swoon. He looked older, harder. A lot less boy, a lot more man. But it was working for him.

With a start, she realized he'd been watching her, watching him. A hot blush heated her face and she jerked her attention back to her daughter. Fortunately, Analise wasn't paying attention to anyone else.

"Did you see your grandmother tonight?" Eddie asked.

Technically, Grandma Beck was Analise's great-grandmother, but they'd never bothered with the formal title. Besides, Analise had never even met her.

"We didn't see anyone. It was just starting to get dark when we pulled into town and Brendan wanted to see the springs, so we went straight there. It got dark really fast, though, and I didn't like it out there, by the springs. It was creepy and I had a bad feeling, but Brendan kept talking about how it used to be. He said he'd read some Web page." She paused, sucked in a shaky breath. "Some stupid Web page he kept going on about. I said I wanted to go and he got mad. He'd been acting really weird for a few a days because of . . ."

She stopped and shook her head.

"I mean, I think he was stressed about work and that had him uptight."

"Laying sod stressed him out?"

"*Mom*," Analise said reproachfully. "Quit being so judgy."

Inside, Gracie cringed. They'd had this conversation before, but now, in front of Reilly, Gracie realized for the first time how much she sounded like Grandma Beck. She could feel Reilly's eyes burning into her, but she didn't look up.

"Go on, Analise," she said softly.

"We heard something," Analise said.

"What?" both Eddie and Gracie asked at the same time.

"I don't know. It sounded like . . . like . . . it was in the hole," she blurted on a shaky breath.

"The springs?" Eddie said sharply.

Analise swallowed and tears began to slide down her face again. Gracie could feel her daughter trembling and wrapped her arms around her.

"It's okay. You're safe, sweetheart."

"Why is it so hot in here?" Analise asked.

Reilly pushed away from the wall and moved to a thermostat by the old-fashioned swinging doors that led to the kitchen. Gracie hadn't noticed it before. Now she stared in surprise.

"Grandma Beck put in air-conditioning?" she exclaimed.

Reilly gave her a sardonic look over his shoulder. "Would it make you feel any better if you knew she set it at ninety-five?"

Gracie almost laughed.

"I turned it down earlier." Reilly paused and frowned at the control. "Who pushed it back up?"

"Sure as hell wasn't me," Eddie said, wiping the sweat off his face with a handkerchief.

Reilly adjusted the temperature and they all waited, faces tilted up, for the whoosh of air in the vents and the cool to come. At last it did, tepid but promising some relief. Reilly gave the thermostat a suspicious glance and moved back to where he'd stood against the wall.

"You heard something in the springs," Eddie prompted. "What did it sound like?"

"Like there was something down there," Analise said vehemently. "Something that wanted out. Brendan went to look. I told him not to. I was so scared. It was so . . . I told him to come back and then all of a sudden he shouted to run. We got in the truck and started to drive and we saw the lights. We thought it was the town, and we turned, but we couldn't find the way and . . . and . . ."

She glanced from one face to another, as if expecting someone to be able to fill in the blanks for her. Gracie knew they were all thinking the same thing. Dead Lights.

Technically, it was a nautical term that she'd looked up once in an attempt to understand the reference to the lights everyone in Diablo Springs had seen at one time or another. The closest she could come to an explanation was the floating quality the light behind a port window—shuttered or not—would have when viewed from the shore. Diablo Springs had never been large enough for a boat and there were no shores here—not anymore. The term, however, managed to perfectly represent the fear inspired by the lights that could be seen hovering over the deep dry spring where nothing should ever float again.

"You saw Dead Lights," Reilly said calmly.

Gracie shot him a disapproving look. Now Analise had a name for her overcharged imagination to build upon.

"Dead Lights are a phenomenon of the dried springs, honey," Gracie explained. "Probably something to do with the gases trapped under it and the heat."

Gracie saw relief in her daughter's eyes at an explanation that she could believe. "I don't remember anything after that."

"You never saw your grandma?" Eddie asked.

"No, we never made it here."

Gracie knew what Eddie would ask next and she stood quickly, hoping to stop him. He'd already told her over the phone where Grandma Beck's body had been found. Analise didn't need to hear that. Not now. Not yet.

"I'm going to take Analise upstairs and show her where she's sleeping. I think she's had enough for one night."

Eddie looked at Analise's drawn features and nodded. "After you're done, come down. I still need to talk to you."

Analise set Romeo down with Tinkerbelle and Juliet, and all three dogs followed diligently behind her. Gracie could feel Reilly's gaze tracking her as she led her daughter to the stairs but she didn't look back. Looking back never did anyone any good.

At the door to her old bedroom, Gracie hesitated, suddenly afraid of crossing the next threshold. Being back in this town, in the home where she'd grown up . . . seeing it so transformed while trying to cope with the reality that she'd never see her grandma again...it all felt like too much. She'd been gone for half of her life and she felt it down to the bone.

"I have no idea what's behind this door," she told Analise with a tight laugh. "She might have burned my bed."

Analise stared into her face, trying to see all that Gracie wanted to hide. "I don't get how she could do that to you. Throw you out when you were pregnant. How could she let me grow up and never try to know me?"

The pain in her daughter's voice tore through Gracie. She'd cried herself to sleep many nights with that question spinning in her head. "It was another time, honey. People were different back then."

Analise snorted. "It was 1998, Mom. Not that long ago."

"It's like dog years in Diablo Springs."

Analise gave a halfhearted smile. Tinkerbelle and Juliet waited patiently, following the conversation like a tennis match while Romeo pranced around them.

Gracie braced herself as she reached for the doorknob. She doubted her grandma would have turned it into a rented room as she'd done the others. Grandma Beck had strict, if often cryptic, rules about such things. No guests in family quarters was one of them. Most likely she'd stripped the room bare and left it as a stark reminder of all of Gracie's failings.

With a fake smile for Analise, she opened the door.

Surprise didn't describe what she felt when she saw inside. Shock was closer, but still not big enough. The room looked exactly as it had when she'd left. Not even dust had moved in to change it. Gracie gripped the door frame, staring at this metaphor for her relationship with Grandma Beck. She'd shut her out while keeping her memory in pristine suspension.

Analise brushed past her with a look of wonder, her fear forgotten for the moment as she stared back in time to her mother's life as a teenager. Posters of The Backstreet Boys, Hanson, and *Titanic* decorated the walls and a bed with a bright purple comforter butted up to a nightstand in the corner. A picture window overlooked a huge mesquite in the front yard and polka-dot curtains that Grandma Beck had sewn herself framed the glass. Once the sun came up, they would be able to see the ruins from here. Now it was just a dark void in the distance.

A hot pink beanbag chair sat next to a CD player with bright lights and fat knobs for volume and the radio. Gracie had saved her babysitting money for months to buy it. A cracked plastic CD case had been tossed on top. Spice Girls.

Yearbooks and photo albums lined her bookshelves, along with her favorite stories from kindergarten up. She'd always kept her books and she remembered how much she'd missed them after she'd gone. She'd only been able to take what she could fit in her second-hand Volkswagen when Grandma Beck had shown her the door. Everything else she'd left behind. Until she walked through the door at that moment, she hadn't realized how much of herself that included.

"I can't believe she kept all this stuff," Gracie murmured, entering her past with its bittersweet memories.

Analise gave her a troubled look so filled with questions that Gracie couldn't quite meet it. Before she could voice any of them, Gracie raised her hand and shook her head.

"I'm too tired to talk about any of this tonight, sweetie. Why don't you get ready bed and try to sleep. If I know Eddie, he'll be back with more questions tomorrow. We can talk then, too."

"We can go see Brendan in the morning, right?"

Gracie nodded. "Yeah."

"Okay." Analise gave her a good night hug. "I'm sorry I lied."

"We'll deal with that when we're back home."

"I know."

Tinkerbelle and Romeo stayed with Analise in the bedroom. Both dogs would take up their usual posts at the end of her bed. Tinkerbelle would wait until Analise went to sleep, though, before she made the jump from the floor to the mattress. She thought she was sneaky.

Ever faithful, Juliet followed Gracie back downstairs where Eddie and Reilly waited. The house still felt unbelievably hot down here—much warmer than upstairs, though it should have been the opposite. Or maybe it was her anxiety that made it feel so warm. Her grandma was dead. She didn't even know how she'd died yet.

And Reilly Alexander was back in Diablo Springs.

"Can we try to open some windows?" Gracie asked as she entered the front room.

Reilly had moved to the bar. He stood at the end, arms resting on the battered surface, head bent as he contemplated the wood grain. Gracie wished she could hear his thoughts. She wasn't looking forward to the confrontation that was certain to come.

"Reilly already tried to get them open," Eddie told her. "They're either painted or nailed shut."

"I think all the air is going to the rooms upstairs. It's cooler there."

A large, aged photograph hanging on the wall above the fireplace caught her attention. In a bright flash of lightning, it seemed that the eyes of the subjects had shifted. Gracie moved closer and stared at the women gathered at a table that looked just like the ones here now. She hadn't heard him move, but suddenly Reilly was behind her.

"That one looks like you," he said in her ear.

Startled, she stumbled back and into the solid wall of his chest. His hands came up to steady her, and the feel of him, the scent of him tumbled Gracie down a long tunnel of memory. He'd always felt so solid to her, someone certain and strong in her teenaged world of chaos. Grandma Beck had never seemed mentally sound. Even as a child, Gracie had understood that a few of her hinges had rusted over. By contrast, Reilly had been constant and reliable.

What a farce.

She turned quickly, stepping away when a traitorous part of her wanted to lean. Eddie was flipping through his notes.

"From what I got earlier," he said, "your daughter and this Brendan kid arrived just after seven. Mac Conner came out when he saw the sirens and told me he'd seen them drive through town."

Gracie and Reilly looked up in unison, both with the same bemused expression on their faces.

"I'd forgotten what it's like to live in a town so small a strange vehicle is noticed," Reilly said.

Eddie frowned. "We know our neighbors here."

"No offense intended."

"Mac said they were speeding," Eddie said. "That's why he noticed."

"I've talked to Brendan about driving fast," Gracie said. "He doesn't listen. He's eighteen and still missing the connection between his ears and his brain."

"You sound just like your grandmother," Reilly said.

Stung, she raised her chin. "I sound just like Analise's mother. That's how I'm supposed to sound."

His jaw hardened and he looked away.

"The sun set about six-thirty, seven," Eddie continued. "I was at the Buckboard having dinner when my radio went off. Monica over at the municipal office said Carolina Beck had called in, all upset and shouting. Said there was trouble out at the springs. Said to get my ass out there right now."

"She said that?" Gracie asked. "She said *ass*?"

"According to Monica she did."

"I never heard her use so much as a *darn*."

"Maybe Monica threw the *ass* in for effect. However it happened, I jumped in my car and went straight there. That was just about the time the storm blew in. It was lightning like there was a short in the sky. I haven't seen a storm like this in years. Hell, the rain alone is enough to dance about. We're going on a ten-year drought."

"Eddie . . . my daughter?" Gracie prompted before he could go on too long about the drought. She'd heard it enough times to know the subject of drought in a conversation could last almost as long as the drought itself.

He nodded. "When I got there I didn't see anything. Not a damn thing. Then as I was turning, I saw a pickup truck perched at the edge of the springs. Lights were out, and it was so dark, I almost missed it. So I backed up and aimed my headlights and that's when I saw your grandma."

Stomach churning over the thought of the balanced truck, her daughter possibly still inside, Gracie braced herself.

"Before I could get out of the car, I saw the truck start to rock. Still couldn't see anyone in it, but it looked like it was shaking." He lifted a hand and made a back-and-forth motion. "Then, Carolina, she shouts at it. I couldn't hear her over the wind and the thunder, but she was screaming like a banshee. She started running toward the truck. So did I, but she got there first. She was still screaming, though I couldn't make heads or tails out of what she said. Next thing I knew, she was falling and there wasn't a damn thing I could do to stop it."

"She slipped?" Reilly asked the question Gracie was afraid to.

Eddie released a deep breath through his nose and shook his head. "I guess. No one pushed her and I hope to God she didn't jump. I've told the city council a hundred times we need to fill those springs in. Never enough money. No one will work out there." He shook head some more. "By the time I reached the edge, I couldn't see her anymore, but I saw the kids in the front seat of the truck. They were scared shitless, practically catatonic. I tried to get to them, but it was like the wind was against me and lightning was striking all around. I thought I was going to be laid out next to your grandma in a minute. And then the truck went over." He whistled and made another gesture. "It all happened so fast."

"Oh my God," Gracie breathed. It was almost too horrible to believe. Her grandmother wasn't the first Beck woman to lose her life at the old springs. Gracie's mother had died there when Gracie was just an infant. And now it had nearly taken Analise.

"I jumped on the horn and called for help," Eddie was saying, "and then I got my winch and fed it out into the hole."

"You went down?" Reilly asked.

Gracie understood his shock. They'd all grown up with stories about what lurked in Diablo Springs. Demons, ghosts, three-headed monsters. Fear of the springs was part of the fabric of their childhood. Call it superstition, call it wise—even adults stayed away from the treacherous springs. The thought of going down inside it in the dark, during a storm, made Gracie's blood run cold. The idea of her daughter being trapped down there made her sway.

Reilly reached out to steady her again, his hand warm against her arm.

"What did you see down there?" Gracie asked, when she didn't really want to know.

"Not a lot. It was damn quiet, like being inside a vacuum. I couldn't hear the storm. Couldn't hear the kids. Couldn't hear nothing. Not ashamed to tell you I was spooked, because I sure as shit was."

"How did you get them out?" Reilly asked.

"The truck caught not far from the edge. Don't know how or on what yet, but it was just dangling. I was scared to death I was going to tap it and it would just go. I got to your daughter's side first, Gracie. The boy was unconscious, but Analise had enough wits left to help me get her out. About that time, backup came and we pulled Brendan up, too. After we got them off to Doc Graebel's, we found your grandma."

"Did the fall kill her?" Reilly asked in a strained voice.

"Won't know until Digger files his report."

The name startled Gracie out of the dread that had overcome her. Digger Young, the town's coroner and undertaker. His family had been handling the dead of Diablo Springs for over a hundred years. She didn't know if it made her feel better or worse to know her grandma was in his hands now.

"It was a crazy night," he said, "with your grandma out there struck dead and the kids screaming . . . I guess it kicked my imagination into overdrive. Because it didn't feel like any other accident I've been to, and I've been to a lot, small town or no."

The seriousness of his last words left both Gracie and Reilly silent. Eddie Rodriguez was not the kind of man who was easily shaken, yet even now they could see that he still wasn't completely recovered.

CHAPTER EIGHT

After Eddie left, Reilly stood beside Gracie in the entryway, listening to the storm outside, feeling a different kind of storm rage at the heart of him. The kid was his—no doubt about it. He could see his family's traits in the shape of her eyes, the line of her chin, the slant of her cheekbones. Straight on, she looked like Gracie. Beautiful, ethereal in some ways. But there was no escaping the Alexander blood that ran in her veins. Even her eyes were the same hazel, flecked with blue and green. They were his father's eyes, his brother's eyes and his eyes. Now, they were his daughter's.

Holy fuck.

Gracie had given birth to his child and he'd never even known. He shoved his hands in his pockets, trying to decide if he was more pissed off at her or himself. Gracie's horse-dog pricked its ears, watching him with a predatory look.

The animal stared at him with a look that teetered between expectation and dismissal. Evidently, he wasn't the only one who couldn't figure out what to feel.

"I'm too tired to think," Gracie said at last. "This has been the longest day in history."

He nodded. "You look tired. I mean, you look good. But tired."

"You had it right the first time."

"No, really. You look good."

Tired, stressed out, and road worn, she looked better than most women did fresh and ready to paint the town. Her eyes darkened, as if she'd read his mind, and something flashed in them that hit him down low and hard. But before he could put a name to what he'd seen, it vanished and in its place he saw cold anger. And just like that, his indecisive pissed-off made up its mind.

"That's what you want to say to me?" she said. "You just met your daughter for the first time, and *that's* the conversation you're going to strike?"

Okay, they could play it her way. "You look good. Why the fuck didn't you tell me I had a daughter?"

Her eyes widened and she actually sputtered for a moment. "How was I going to do that, Reilly? You left. Without a *word*. No forwarding address, no phone call. No *see ya later, Gracie. Changed my mind.*"

It was his turn to be speechless. That's how she remembered it?

"You're a little confused."

"I'm a lot confused. But for the record, I didn't tell you because I didn't know until after you'd left."

"You could have found me."

"I could have. But by then I realized you weren't worth the effort."

"So you told our kid she didn't have a father?"

Her cold laugh pricked at him, and for the first time in a long time, he began to wonder if he had his facts right. She was indignant, so certain that she'd played no role in what had happened between them.

"I told *Analise* that I didn't know who her father was. I told her the truth."

That cut through his sheltering anger and struck blood. Gracie had been the only person in his entire life who'd ever *really* known him. She wouldn't believe that, though, and he certainly didn't want to share the knowledge.

"She looks like you," he said softly.

Gracie said nothing.

"She's beautiful. Is she a good kid?"

Grudgingly, Gracie nodded. "When she's not running off with her no-good boyfriend." She shrugged. "She's smart. She likes music."

Her voice hitched over the last words and Reilly felt something pull tight inside him. He wanted to howl at the unfairness of this situation. He wanted someone to give him the playbook on how to fix it.

He needed to extricate himself from the conversation and fast.

Instead, he asked, "Why aren't you married?" Like the answer didn't matter to him.

"That's none of your business."

"You couldn't find a replacement?"

"I'm going to bed."

She turned away and began switching off lights. The heat downstairs made the air feel thick, heavy from the storm. The rain had eased up, but distant thunder still rumbled and the clouds created a lid over the basin. Her shirt clung to her shoulder blades. The fine hairs at her nape curled from the humidity. A million years ago, he used to love to kiss that vulnerable place on her body. It would make her go boneless and lean back against his chest like he was Hercules, holding up the world.

The guard dog trailed close behind as she moved around the room. Every so often it would curl its lip at him, just in case he had any ideas of getting close to her. After checking the door, Gracie started up the stairs.

"I'm sorry about your grandmother. She was a tough old bird, but she had her moments."

She shot him a dirty look over her shoulder. "I haven't seen her or heard from her since she sent me away. I hardly know what to feel now." She looked down at the staged saloon below. "Pity. I guess that's what it is."

Reilly heard how she ended the sentiment, but his thoughts had stuttered over the words that began it. *Carolina had sent Gracie away?* "I heard you left but I didn't—"

"You heard?" she said, her voice sharp and disillusioned. "You heard I *left* and that never struck you as odd? My leaving home at sixteen? You never looked back, never wondered what happened to me?"

"No," he said, and his voice gave him away. "I always wondered." And God knew he was still looking back. "I was dealing with a lot of shit from Matt."

"Good for you, Reilly. Glad you could be there for him."

She reached the landing and turned left. In a matter of steps she'd be at her door, through it. He'd be off the hook. In the morning, he'd get up, spread Matt's ashes out where their mom was buried, and hit the road. He could be back in Los Angeles by early afternoon.

"He's dead now," Reilly said.

Gracie turned, surprised. "Your brother's dead? When?" Her soft voice managed to sound injured and impregnable at once.

He hadn't meant to mention it—not any of it. His brother's death was far too personal to share with anyone.

"Shot himself out at the springs a few months ago."

The breath she let out was slow and full of a million things she didn't say. He could feel them, though, all her conflicted sentiments about his brother. Now was the time to tell her where he'd been during the handful of days when she'd decided to bail on him, yet the words felt like another kind of betrayal when his brother's ashes were still stashed in his bag.

"He'd only been back in town for a couple of weeks," Reilly heard himself say. "He spent most of the past sixteen years in jail. No surprise there."

"He always ran on self-destructive."

A family trait. As did an obsession with a certain girl next door.

Reilly rubbed the back of his neck, looking anywhere but at her face. An awkward pause filled in the shadowed spaces between them. He figured the best thing he could do was leave it at that. He caught his lower lip between his teeth and glanced up at her from beneath his lashes, unable to make his feet move away. There was so much he wanted—*needed*—to say, but there were no words that could make up for the disillusionment and pain that stood between them.

He followed her all the way to a door at the end of the hall where she stopped. The horse-dog waited at her feet, watching him with a steady, menacing look.

"Gracie." He reached out as he said her name, but the dog advanced with lightning speed and a low growl. Reilly took a hasty step back.

"Juliet," Gracie reprimanded in a harsh whisper. "No. Friend. Friend."

She stepped forward and wrapped her arms around Reilly's middle in a meaningless hug meant to convince the dog that the hostility it felt was false. The warmth of her body came through the light embrace and on their own, his arms went around her, pulling her closer. Her hair smelled of coconut, her skin of something sweet and seductive, the scent of Gracie. He'd chased that scent since the last time he'd held her.

The tension in her body seemed to travel like a current to his. He turned his face into the crook of her shoulder and held her tight for just a moment more, just as long as she would let him.

When she pulled back, a mixture of hurt, anger, and mystified hunger lurked in her pretty eyes. She stepped away and opened the door before he could see more. A blast of icy air rushed out at them. Not just cool, but subzero. It snapped him out of his daze.

"Jesus," he said. "You'll be frozen before the sun comes up. Maybe she had the air set so high downstairs because all the cold stops here."

"Maybe," she agreed, crossing into the room that must have been her grandmother's like a stranger who'd taken a wrong turn. Slowly, she turned in place, her gaze brushing over the surface of a heavy wood dresser that looked older than the Diablo itself. An antique grooming set was laid out on dainty doily. Pretty little boxes lined the edge by the mirror, oddly shaped and metal. Gracie met her own eyes in her reflection and the desolation he saw would've broken his heart if he still had one. Her relationship with her grandmother had always been troubled.

The horse-dog *grr*'d as Reilly crossed the threshold, but didn't try to eat him so he started looking along the floorboards for the vents—no easy feat when Gracie's grandmother had the room packed with heavy furniture.

"This bedroom set belonged to her great-grandmother, I think."

"It's probably yours now," he said softly.

Gracie swayed and reached for the bedpost. Slowly she sank to the edge of the bed, watching him as he continued his search for air vents. He could almost see his breath now.

"She never even met Analise," Gracie said. "I sent her an announcement when she was born. I sent her Christmas cards, every year with pictures. She never responded."

Crouched down by the roll top desk, Reilly paused and looked back. "Why?"

"Not a clue."

They stared at one another from across the room, and he was pretty sure they were both thinking of the mysterious twists and turns of life. From her expression, she didn't like thinking about it anymore than he did.

He couldn't see behind the desk, so he stood and pulled it out from the wall.

"I saw her tonight," Gracie said.

The tone of voice, the reluctance of her words made Reilly pause. He had no doubt who she meant. "At the springs?" he asked, thinking Gracie must have stopped there before coming to the house. Yet he remembered how she'd burst through the door, frantic to see her daughter. *Their* daughter.

"In my kitchen." A quiet laugh. "The dogs were all freaked out, barking, and the telephone rang—Eddie, calling to tell me what had happened. Before I answered, Grandma Beck was just *there,* sitting in the kitchen, holding an old ledger."

He turned and leaned against the desk. "Same thing happened with Matt. In my car," he said. "I looked over and Matt was riding shotgun."

He was breathing heavy, but the air felt thin, icy. Like they were atop a frozen mountain.

"How long was he there?" she asked.

"A couple seconds."

Her gaze traveled up to his shorn head and lingered. Like she knew that he'd gone home after that and stared into the mirror until his reflection blurred, wondering if he'd finally cracked. He'd started with scissors, whacking off his brown hair like it was somehow to blame. When that hadn't solved anything, he'd gone for the razor.

Feeling way too exposed, he turned and looked at the floor again.

"I don't see the vent," he said, his voice pitched low. Husky.

Despite the instinct urging him to walk away, he glanced up and met her eyes. Gracie lifted a shoulder, her gaze never leaving his.

"I can figure it out tomorrow."

I not *we*. Because Gracie had been figuring things out on her own for a long time.

He came to stand in front of her. She had to tilt her head back to see his face. The position was intimate in itself—Gracie sitting on the bed, him standing before her. The urge to cup her face, to hold it while he bent and kissed her . . . it was almost too much to resist.

"Why are you here, Reilly?" she asked. Now her voice was husky, too.

He hesitated, wanting to give her the answer she desired. He might have, too, if he'd been sure what that was.

"It was time," he said finally.

She frowned and he knew she was looking for the hidden meaning. Even *he* wasn't sure about that.

He couldn't help himself. He brushed the pad of his thumb over the puckered skin between her brows and then, because he couldn't help that, either, he smoothed a lock of hair behind her ear, his fingers softly skimming the silk of her cheek. Her eyes widened and for a moment, he was lost in the swirling grays and blues, knowing that if she looked hard enough, deep enough she'd see right to raw and wounded center of him. This was an impossible situation and if he didn't do something quick, he'd be in too deep to ever get out.

She shook her head and pulled back. Disappointment and relief waged a war inside of him. Reluctantly, he dropped his hand.

"You should leave," she said.

Reilly agreed one-hundred-and-one percent. Leave. Go. Get as far away as fast as he could.

"You sure?"

"You had your chance to be a stand-up guy with me, Reilly. You didn't take it. I've moved on. I've built a good life for me and my daughter. We don't need you."

"Your daughter dragged you all the way back here, looking for her daddy, Gracie. You haven't moved on quite far enough."

She stared at him, wounded. If she'd been cruel, he'd been pitiless. But he was right. The past was over, but tonight their daughter had decided to bring history into the present, whether they liked it or not.

He'd had every reason to walk away all those years ago. Reasons that had ripped out his heart and made him the man he was now. He'd betrayed his brother—the one person who'd always been there for him—so he could come back to her, only to find she hadn't waited.

He shouldn't be asking for a chance to make things right. Gracie should.

He laughed, low and without humor. She scowled at him.

"Good night, Gracie."

CHAPTER NINE

B etween the cold in her room, the turmoil of her thoughts and emotions, and the thunder outside, Gracie never really fell asleep. She kept going over everything that had happened. Eddie's call, Grandma Beck, Analise.

Reilly.

Reilly and the mystifying yearning that his touch had dredged from her soul. She'd loved him since she was a girl. She'd hated him with every fiber of her being as a woman. For years she'd told herself she was over him and in a matter of hours, he'd turned her inside out. It infuriated her that with everything she had to deal with— all the trauma of coming home to the death of her grandmother and the realization that her trustworthy daughter wasn't quite so trustworthy after all—Reilly seemed to have the front seat in her thoughts.

Silent and drawn, she dressed, uneasy in the freezing room. A dozen times she found herself spinning to look behind her, sensing something that was never there. She didn't believe in ghosts, but it was hard to remember that when Grandma Beck had paid her a visit from the beyond on the night of her horrible, tragic death.

She didn't become truly spooked, though, until Juliet lifted her head and growled at the corner where the desk was wedged against the wall. Slowly, Gracie let her gaze track the room as that fierce snarl revved. The watery daylight coming through the window did little more than cast shadows deep in the overstuffed room. Thunder still rumbled outside, but the lightning had eased. A steady drizzle pattered on the roof and raindrops streaked the windows. But the room was still. Too still.

Juliet's growl trailed off, but she remained alert, her attention fixed on the corner.

"What do you see, Jules?" Gracie teased, her heart pounding and her skin prickly. It was silly to be so alarmed. Though grim, the sun was up and fears of things that went bump in the night should feel silly in daylight.

Slowly, she circled the room, her footsteps soft on the rug. Nothing moved but the swaying shadow arms of the tree outside, yet something unseen brushed against her throat and made her jump. The hairs at the back of her neck stood on end, and she pivoted as Juliet's snarl became a fierce bark.

The big dog lunged at the corner, teeth bared as she snapped her jaws at the empty space. A ridge of fur stood on her back and her shoulders bunched with aggression, confusion adding a viciousness to her bark. A split second later, she heard Analise scream.

Gracie raced for the door; but Juliet tried to get their first and bumped into her legs, knocking her off-balance.

Gracie's feet tangled in the braided rug and she slammed into the wall with a thud that echoed loudly.

Struggling to regain her balance, Gracie raced into Analise's bedroom and found her daughter huddled on the bed, eyes wide and terrified. Both Tinkerbelle and Romeo stood at the foot of the bed barking crazily. Reilly burst into the room a half step behind Gracie. His shirt was off, the top button of his jeans was undone, and his feet were bare.

"What happened?" Gracie demanded, pulling her daughter into her arms at the same time that Reilly asked, "Are you okay?"

Analise couldn't catch her breath, let alone answer and Gracie soothed her, rubbing her back and murmuring calming words. Juliet joined the other dogs on the bed and all three crowded around her, seeking solace, too. A strange, unsettling scent hung in the air and the warmth after her freezing room felt shocking and unnaturally . . . *dark*.

Chloe and Bill Barnes stood at the doorway, looking in with curious eyes. Chloe's turban was gone and her white hair stuck up in thin, frizzy tufts. Behind them, Jonathan tried to peer over their shoulders.

"What happened, sweetheart?" Gracie asked, smoothing Analise's hair back. "Did you have a nightmare?"

Her daughter's face was deathly pale. "I woke up and there was a man standing over me," she gasped, tears on her face, eyes wild with fear.

Gracie shot an accusing glance at the men hovering in the door.

"No," Analise said. "Not one of them. He was big. He grabbed my arm and tried to pull me out of bed."

"He *what*?"

Analise leaned back showed Gracie her arm. Gracie looked for signs of a handprint or redness, but the skin was cool, smooth, and unmarred in any way.

Reilly crouched down in front of her daughter—*their* daughter. "Did you see where he went? Can you describe him?"

Analise's tears came faster. "No. He was just over me when I opened my eyes—this shadow. I couldn't see his face. He was just leaning over me. He grabbed me and when I screamed, he was gone."

"Gone where, Analise?" Gracie asked.

"Gone. Just . . . *gone*."

Gracie met Reilly's eyes, both of them thinking about their own inexplicable visitors. Gently, Gracie patted Analise's arm.

"He was here," Chloe announced, chin up and eyes darting around the room. She heard fear in the old woman's voice.

"Who was here?" Analise cried.

Before Chloe could answer, Gracie stood and blocked the woman's view of her daughter. "You saw someone in her room?" Gracie demanded.

Chloe shook her head. "I can feel his spirit. Can't you?"

"Whose spirit?" Analise whispered.

Fury welled up inside Gracie and she stared down Chloe. "Get out." Chloe looked startled, but Gracie didn't care. "I won't have you scaring my young, *impressionable* daughter this way."

"But—"

Gracie held up a hand and Bill reached for Chloe's arm, pulling her away from the door.

"I'm only trying to help," Chloe insisted.

"Get. Out."

Analise's frightened gaze moved between them. "Does she think there's a ghost in my room? Is that what she means?"

"Don't listen to her, Analise," Gracie said as Chloe retreated.

"You think it was just a bad dream?"

Gracie didn't know and couldn't lie, so she asked, "Do you think it was?"

"Maybe. I was sleeping pretty hard and the dogs didn't bark until I woke up and scared them. They'd have gone nuts if there'd been someone in here."

All three dogs had their ears pinned as they watched their humans with anxious eyes.

"Chickens," Gracie said.

Analise smiled.

Forcing a calm she was nowhere close to feeling, Gracie said, "I was just on my way to wake you up, anyway, Analise. I thought we could head over the doctor's and check on Brendan. Maybe get some coffee on the way. Why don't you get dressed?"

"You think he'll be okay now?" she asked and Gracie heard a guarded note in her voice that was out of place.

"Eddie said his injuries weren't serious. I would think so. We'll call and make sure before we head over, though."

Analise nodded, lowering her eyes before Gracie could read what was in them.

"Don't give what the Chloe woman said another thought. When we get back, I'll ask the others to leave the Diablo."

Analise gave Reilly a sideways glance. He had his back to the wall, arms crossed like a badass. He was sexy as hell, damn him. Gracie tensed when her daughter's contemplative eyes shifted back to her mother and quickly she stood, pressed a kiss to Analise's forehead and said, "Get dressed."

She left on shaky legs and returned to Grandma Beck's room. Uninvited, Reilly followed.

"You're going to Dr. Graebel's this morning?" he asked.

"Unless you know another way for me to retrieve Brendan." The look on his face suggested she leave Brendan there. "Tempting," she answered, drawing in a deep breath.

"You okay?" he asked. "I thought I heard a bang in here before Analise screamed."

"I tripped," she said, flushing. "I guess being here has us all on edge."

Her arms were crossed beneath her breasts and the frigid temperature after the heat of Analise's room brought goose bumps to her skin. Reilly stepped closer and curled his big, warm hands around her chilled arms.

"You're shaking."

Gracie nodded, trying to look anywhere but at his bare chest and the light scattering of hair across it. His skin was the color of honey and the heat from his body tempted her to move closer, to let him fold her against all that strength.

She cleared her throat and looked down, but her gaze caught on the glimpse of white boxers with a pattern of tiny penguins peeping out at the waist of his unbuttoned jeans. Who'd have pictured such boxers on a man like Reilly Alexander? She nearly smiled at the sight and finally, *finally*, her heart began to slow.

"I'm fine," she forced herself to say. "You don't need to stay."

The corners of his mouth tightened and he dropped his hands to his sides. Without a word, he walked away.

Just as she'd asked.

Yet after he closed the door behind him, Gracie had the irrational urge to call him back. The Diablo didn't just have her on edge . . . it had her on the very edge.

CHAPTER TEN

With no small amount of relief, Gracie loaded the dogs and Analise into her car a half hour later and left for Dr. Graebel's. The doctor's house doubled as Diablo Springs' only medical facility. It wasn't that far from the Diablo—nothing in the tiny town was that far— but with the rain coming down in sheets and the wind buffeting her car, it took forever to navigate the few miles they had to go. The three wet dogs in the back and her daughter's tension didn't help, either. With each mile, Analise withdrew a little bit more, and Gracie didn't know why.

"Hey," she said. "You want to talk?"

Analise shrugged.

"Did you and Brendan have a fight?"

Gracie pulled her gaze from the wet road long enough to look at her daughter. Analise opened her mouth but shut it again and shook her head.

"You can talk to me, Ana."

She shook her head again. "Not about this."

"I don't know what *this* is, but yes—"

"You don't like Brendan."

Gracie didn't dispute it, but she did try to qualify it. "It's not that I don't like him. He's just older—"

"Two years. That's it. And don't say anything about dog years, either."

"You're both too young to be so serious."

Analise shot her a resentful look. "Who's the guy at Grandma's?"

The question came from nowhere, though Gracie should have been preparing for it since she saw Reilly standing in the Diablo. Analise was too smart not to notice the sparks flying between her mother and Reilly.

"Someone I used to know," she hedged.

"He's my dad, isn't he?"

She swallowed hard. "Yes."

"You said you didn't who he was. You lied."

"Yes again." Gracie let out a deep breath. "I'm sorry. I had my reasons and I thought they were good ones."

"I deserved to know."

Shame stained Gracie's cheeks. She'd never been reprimanded by her daughter before, especially not justifiably.

"Teenage pregnancy is messy business, kiddo. I love you more than any words can say and if I had the chance to do it over, I would always pick having you. Do you hear me?"

Her voice had thickened and dipped low with the urgency of her feelings. It filled the space between them.

Analise stared at her folded hands, but she nodded.

"Reilly left me when I thought he was going to be there forever. Be there for me."

"He left you when you told him you were pregnant?"

She shook her head quickly. "He didn't know about you until last night."

"Mom," Analise said, shocked.

"I never had the chance to tell him, Analise. He disappeared, and I had no idea where he'd gone or how to find him. By the time he surfaced again, you were five and I was just starting to get on my feet. I hated him, and I didn't think you had the right to know you."

"You didn't act like you hated him last night."

Gracie could feel her face flaming. "He's a little hard to ignore."

"You think?"

They shared a quick smile. Even her daughter recognized what a devastating force Reilly Alexander was.

"Did he recognize me?" she asked softly.

Gracie nodded.

"What did he say?"

"He's not happy that I didn't tell him."

"What did he say about me?"

Gracie smiled. "He said you're beautiful."

"Do you think he wants to get to know me?"

"I think he'd be stupid not to."

"But?"

"Reilly's not the kind of man who sticks around, sweetheart. I just don't want you to get hurt."

She shrugged. "I'm already hurt."

The truth of that cut Gracie to the quick. "I'm sorry. I should have made better choices about you and him."

Analise seemed to consider that in silence. Gracie tried to find a way to soften what she had to say next, but finally, she just came out with it.

"Don't expect too much from him, okay?"

They exchanged another quick glance, and Gracie saw a glimmer of the woman Analise would become in her daughter's hazel eyes.

"You be careful, too, Mom."

"Don't worry about me. I'm on to him."

Analise snorted. "Maybe you better stay off him."

Gracie tried for outrage, but in the end she could only grin. "He does have a way about him."

"Yah. Good genes."

And the two of them laughed for the first time in weeks. For a few moments at least, Gracie thought things might work out okay after all.

* * *

The roads grew more treacherous by the second. They risked their lives for coffee and took the small detour to the run-down Circle K, only to find it closed. Frustrated, Gracie dashed empty-handed back to the car. It smelled like wet dogs inside, but she hadn't even considered leaving them behind with the circus that had taken up residence in the Diablo.

By the time they pulled up to the clinic, Gracie was white-knuckled and stiff from head to toe. Beside her, Analise had grown quiet again.

"I don't think this storm is ever going to stop," Analise muttered, staring out at the churning sky and falling rain.

"It doesn't look like it, does it? I can't remember it ever raining for so long here. I hope it lets up long enough for us to bury Grandma Beck."

Saying the words brought a wash of uncomfortable and unresolved emotions. As if the death of her grandmother wasn't as important as getting her into the ground. But that's how she felt. Now that she had Analise safely with her, she just wanted to collect Brendan, put her grandmother to rest, and get the hell away from Diablo Springs.

And everyone in it, she added silently. *Especially Reilly Alexander.*

She pushed the button to crack the back windows before getting out of the car, knowing the seats would be wet and the dogs even smellier when they got back. The entire trip could be summed up in the same way: one unpleasant thing to counteract a dozen worse.

Dr. Graebel opened his door immediately, looking tired and old. Gracie stared at his familiar face, swamped with an unexpected wave of nostalgia. Dr. Graebel had treated her childhood ailments until she'd left town, and she had the ridiculous urge to throw her arms around him and cry. He gave her a kind smile, a bear hug, and told her how sorry he was to hear about her grandmother. Gracie deserved an award for holding back her tears.

After he released her, he fawned over Analise for a while, embarrassing a smile out of her. Finally, he got down to business.

"Brendan is much better today," he said as he led the way back to the patient room. "You can take him home with you now."

Analise said nothing, surprising Gracie again. She'd said they hadn't fought, but something was definitely amiss here. When she got her daughter alone again, she would work harder at getting it out of her.

Brendan was a gangly young man, tall and rangy with corded muscles and sunbaked skin. He had blond hair and ice-blue eyes. He was a product of harsh raising and hard outdoor work. Not the kind of boy Gracie had ever wanted for her overachiever daughter. She'd tried to keep thoughts about him to herself as much as she could. Obviously, she hadn't done such a great job at it. She remembered how it had felt when Grandma Beck looked down her nose at Reilly, called him white trash . . .forbade Gracie to see him.

She'd driven Gracie and Reilly to plan their escape together. Even though they'd never actually carried it through, they'd come close. She didn't want to push Analise into the same desperate situation.

When they entered the room, Brendan was dressed and sitting in the stiff plastic chair next to the bed, deep in concentration. A white bandage circled the top of his head, and it looked very bright against his deep tan. Bruising seeped out from beneath it, discoloring the skin around his temple and right eye. One arm was in a sling but without a cast.

He looked up, frowning when he saw Gracie, but his expression brightened when Analise stepped in behind her.

"I've been so worried about you," he said, reaching out for Analise's hand.

Analise hesitated before she let him pull her forward. It didn't make sense. Yesterday, Analise had been giddy as she left the house for her clandestine getaway with Brendan. Gracie had noted it but hadn't thought much of it. Her daughter was sixteen, and a lot of things made her giddy, like sleepovers with her bestie. She'd never even considered that Analise might be lying about where she was going.

Brendan tugged Analise's fingers until she stood close and then kissed her on the back of the hand. The gesture seemed old-fashioned, out of character for the boy. The bruises and bandages gave his face an unfamiliar contour. He almost looked like a different kid—man. He was at that age the bordered that both, and it was hard for Gracie to tell.

"Why did you leave me here last night, babe?" he asked.

"They wouldn't let me stay," Analise murmured. "My mom was waiting at my grandma's. She died last night, Brendan. Did you see her out at the . . . that horrible place?"

Brendan looked stunned. "She died?"

"She was out there, and she fell in that pit."

"They should have filled the springs a long time ago," Dr. Graebel said, signing something on the clipboard he held. "Should've brought in workers from Phoenix if our own boys were too scared of a damned hole in the ground."

Gracie remembered hearing that once they had actually imported workers from another town to do the job suspicious Diablo Springs men wouldn't do. Things had gone wrong on the site, though, confirming the rumors that the place was haunted and cursed. Accidents. Faulty equipment. Two men had been killed and others wounded on the first day. After that, they'd all packed up and gone home. The town had erected a fence around the springs, posted warning signs, and called it good enough. Time had worn the fence down, though. She'd seen from the windows of the Diablo how it sagged all around and lay flat in some places. It certainly hadn't kept the kids out.

"I don't even know what happened to us," Analise went on. "We almost crashed right into that hole, too. We got turned around, and we drove right over the edge, Brendan."

Brendan shot Gracie an accusing glance, as if somehow she was to blame for it all. Gracie met it with an irritated, incredulous look of her own. Brendan had brought her daughter here, knowing she'd lied to Gracie about her whereabouts. Injured or not, he was on Gracie's shit list.

His lips curled at the corners. A grin? A sneer? A wince of pain? Gracie couldn't tell, but it bothered her, Made her tense each time he pulled Analise closer. Was she projecting, or did it seem like Analise didn't want to be that close?

Too many things didn't make sense. For the most part, Brendan went out of his way to be polite to Gracie. His behavior now . . . It wasn't *normal*.

"Are you hurt?" he asked, turning back to Analise. He stared deeply into her eyes with touching concern. Even that bothered Gracie.

"I'm fine, I guess. It was scary."

"It was exciting," he teased. "Got our blood pumping."

"It did more than that. I thought we were going to die, Brendan. That hole . . . It's not right. It felt like something was in it."

"You're just freaked out, babe. It's pretty out there. Wait until you see it in the daytime."

"I don't ever want to see it again."

Brendan made a hushing sound. "I'd say you need to. You don't want to be afraid of something like that, do you? Trust me, babe. We'll go see it when the sun's out."

"I don't think so," Gracie said, putting a stop to it right there. "By the time the sun comes out, we'll be gone."

Analise shot her a grateful glance, but Brendan seemed distressed. "I made a mess of things, didn't I?" he said, looking at Analise. "I wanted to surprise you for your birthday, and instead, I just fu— screwed everything up."

"It's not your fault," Analise said grudgingly. "It was a cool idea."

"You think so?"

Analise lifted one shoulder and Brendan stared at her with pleading eyes, and for a moment, Gracie was almost moved. They were young, but maybe he really did love her daughter. Maybe Gracie had let her own past influence her opinion of this kid. Yes, he was too old, already out of school, not smart enough for Ana by far. Not worthy of Gracie's amazing daughter. She'd resented him, wished that Analise would kick him out of her life.

Brendan knew all that without Gracie ever having to say it, but he'd treated her daughter with respect, brought her home by curfew, and never gave Gracie an excuse to forbid Analise from seeing him.

Right up until he'd absconded with Analise and brought her here, of all places. To the one town Gracie never wanted Analise to go to.

As if hearing her thoughts, he shot Gracie a sly look that she didn't understand until he moved his hand to Analise's abdomen and asked,

"What about the baby? Is the baby okay?"

CHAPTER ELEVEN

May 1896
Colorado

I turned slowly. The mountains caged me in a valley filled with scrub in every direction. I had survived the violence of the outlaws, but I would not survive this. I'd left behind the flames that had chased me from my family's burning camp, but I couldn't stop running. The vision of my mother, slaughtered, crushed beneath the burning wagon, unborn baby dead inside her . . . It would haunt me forever. I knew I would always remember her, not as I'd known her alive, but as she'd been in death.

So I ran. I didn't know for how long or how far. The sun had arced across the sky and night had fallen more than once, but time had no meaning to my pain. I didn't know where I was, how to get back to where I'd begun. My only thought had been to flee, like a coward.

I didn't even know if there were bullets left in the rifle I had taken from the wagon. At least I knew how to shoot it, though not with any skill. I even knew how to load it, if I'd had more bullets. But at that moment I didn't care. The knife hung in the pocket of my skirt, sheathed in its heavy leather. It felt like an anchor, pulling me down into the depths of this horror. It banged into my leg as I charged across the desolate valley between the foothills, punishing me for my weakness with every step. My thigh would be black with bruises. I was glad of it.

Dusk hung heavy in the sky again, like a gray velvet curtain with a tiny, intricate pattern of rhinestones glimmering in the weave. I knew later the stars would be like diamonds glittering so bright they hurt the eyes. Where would I be when they came out? Where was I now? I hadn't seen another living soul or even a sign of life since I'd left the camp.

As the silvery light crept over the lavender sky, my eyes caught on a wisp of smoke in the distance that had been invisible to me before. Had I run in circles? If I followed that smoke, would I end up back at the camp?

There would be nothing to find but death, and yet it was a destination. I reached the hilltop and looked down into a wooded valley. Aspen and cottonwood trees grew wide and sprawling in the pocket of lush vegetation. This was not where my family had camped. Pine trees scattered darkly over the foothills, but the grove where I'd hidden was nowhere to be seen. I couldn't see where the smoke came from, but it wasn't from the smoldering ashes of my family. It was a campfire. I smelled food.

The Smith brothers? Had I stumbled across their camp? The taste of vengeance rose up inside me, bitter on my tongue. I wrapped my hand around my daddy's shotgun and, once again, I began to run. I bolted through the trees with branches snagging at my hair and ripping at my clothes, but still I didn't slow.

I could hear voices as I drew closer, but not the deep drawl of any of the Smith riders. These were women's voices.

Confused, I paused. Why would women be out here with murdering outlaws?

In shadowed twilight, I crept closer. I could smell the fire—made of cow pies based on the noxious odor—long before I could see the flames.

At last I was near enough to see them. Three women, clothed as I was in traveling dresses of indistinguishable browns and grays, sat comfortably by a fire. One of the women was Negro, another was a mix of races I couldn't discern—she looked to have been made from golden wax—and a third who had a mane of rust-red hair, pale skin and an Irish lilt.

The Negro and Irish women were sewing as they listened to the golden woman speak. Her teeth flashed white as she smiled. She seemed to be telling a story, and the others hung on her words, pausing with needles poised for the next stitch as she drew the tale out.

Beyond her, another Negro woman, this one large and lumbering and black as the night, moved about the fire. She wore a handkerchief tied around her head and an apron that seemed to glow in this world of black and white. She didn't give the speaker the attention the others did, but she appeared to be listening all the same as she fried bacon and tended something else that smelled heavenly. My stomach growled so loud I feared they'd hear me.

They camped beside a wagon with a tarp strung from the side to posts pounded into the ground. I crouched, watching them, afraid to step into the open. I didn't see a corral for horses or any livestock that might pull the wagon. Were these women stranded? Perhaps victims of thievery? I thought of the Smith brothers again. Had they been here? The laughter I'd heard said no, but people had a way of rising to the occasion when tragedy struck, and they had each other to see them through.

When I looked back to the campfire, the golden woman had finished her story. She sat beside the young Negro woman, who looked, upon closer inspection, much younger than my seventeen. The larger woman still hovered over her skillets, scorched skirts perilously close to the fire, but the redhead was nowhere in sight. Their laughter drifted back to me, waking an ache so deep it hurt. There had been laughter at our campfire each night when Grandma, burdened though she was by her wheelchair, Momma, and I would clean up after our meal.

A snapping twig to my right caught me unaware and I spun around. I was face-to-face with the redhead. She gave a shout of surprise, eyes round as saucers, skirts bunched around her waist, knees bent in a squat. She stumbled backward and fell on her bare behind. Embarrassment rooted me to the spot. I looked away, sputtering an apology.

"Saint Mary and Joseph," she exclaimed in a lilting Irish brogue as she struggled to stand, yanking her drawers up and her skirts down at once. In an instant, the women from the camp had surrounded us.

"Where you come from?" the large black woman exclaimed.

I opened my mouth to answer, but the Irish woman interrupted me. "You're head to toe in blood, lass. What are y' doing out here?"

The big woman had a knife in her hand, the kind my mother used to bone chicken. She waved it at me.

"She trouble. You get, trouble."

The girl I'd guessed to be younger than me pushed forward. She looked no more than fifteen. A light rash of blemishes made a T of her forehead and nose, but it was her luminous eyes and dark lashes that gathered the attention. She would be an incredible beauty when she matured.

"She scairt," she said. She laid a gentle hand on my arm and said, "Don't be scairt. We won't hurt you. I'm Chick."

I stared uneasily from one unfamiliar face to another, afraid to speak.

"She look like somebody been at her with a whip. Somebody after you?" Chick asked.

I shook my head.

"She looks hungry, is what she's looking," the Irish one said.

"Don't be feeding her like no stray dog," the hefty one replied. "Mis'r Tate see you doin' that he'll have your hide."

"That Athena," Chick said softly of the woman waving the knife. From her tone I understood that Athena was the ruler of this small band of women.

"He wouldn't dare lay a hand on her," the woman who looked dipped in gold said, moving nearer to me. Up close, her skin was the color of light molasses and it gleamed in the weak light. I had thought Chick lovely, but this girl—woman—was breathtaking. She shined like a luminary. Her hair was cut very short, almost masculine, but there was nothing male about her curving figure and gleaming beauty. She spoke with fine grammar, not like the other girls.

"Best not let him hear that talk," Athena said, still waving the knife. She glared at me with a loathing that went deeper than our short acquaintance. I didn't know what I'd done to earn it, but I was smart enough not to ask. "He have your hide," she told the golden girl. "Honey or no Honey." Another pointed look at me, as if I had caused some great trouble by stumbling in half-starved and desolate.

"Why don' she talk?" Chick asked Athena, whose expression became harsher by the minute. I thought I'd better say something before she ordered me away.

Swallowing my fear, I asked, "Are you stranded?"

"Stranded?" the Irish one repeated. "No, girl."

"Then where are your horses?"

"Mis'r Tate got them," Athena said suspiciously.

"Do you . . . Have you seen the Smith brothers?"

"Who?" Athena demanded.

"Lonnie and Jake."

"Don' know no Lonnie and Jake. You get hit in the head?"

I didn't think so, but I'd fallen enough times during my mad dash that I could have.

"Why you covered wit blood?" Chick asked, reaching a hand out but not touching me.

I wasn't ready to answer that. I wasn't sure I'd ever be ready.

"My name is Ella," I said. "I'm lost."

The golden girl approached and laid a gentle hand on my arm. "Are you hurt, Ella?"

I shrugged, and tears filled my eyes. I didn't want to cry, but I didn't want to be lost and alone in the world, either. Whether it was wise or not, I couldn't pretend that I was not in desperate need of help.

The golden girl said, "Bring her over to the fire. Let's get her cleaned up."

Even though I wanted that, wanted the fire, a taste of whatever smelled so heavenly, a rest, I couldn't so easily forget the fear and apprehension that I knew would never leave me.

"Why are you out here? A group of women . . . alone?" I heard the words, knew I'd formed them, but hardly recognized the directness, the hard tone. They seemed to have come from a different girl than the one who'd woken up just a few days ago, mad at her father for taking her away from her friends. But I would never be that girl again.

The women looked at each other. No one answered.

I stood my ground, yet inside I was shaking. It was part fear, part anticipation. If they told me they were the Smith brothers' women, I don't know what I would do to avenge the deaths of my family. I didn't think I had the courage to hurt them, but I would not eat the food or lay in the blankets by the fire of the men who had destroyed my life.

The silence stretched. Finally, the golden girl whispered, "What terrible thing happened to you, child?"

Despite my resolve, her kindness and apparent ignorance of the horror that had befallen me was my undoing. "My family—" I hitched in a breath. "Outlaws killed them."

This made Athena pull her neck in turtle-like. She looked around with big eyes as if expecting the outlaws to charge them at any moment. It wasn't an unreasonable assumption. I wasn't certain they wouldn't.

"I thought you were them."

"You thought we was them? What was you gon' do? Kills us?" Athena asked, hands on her hips and scorn on her face.

I raised my chin. "Yes."

That caused looks to pass from one woman to another.

The redhead said, "Sure, and now you can see we're no such thing as outlaws. Why don't you put your gun down, lass? Won't be no need of it."

I followed her glance to the rifle still clutched in my hands. I'd forgotten about it.

"'Less they followed her," Athena said.

They all glanced out at the scrub and brush. "They couldna made it past the Captain," the redhead answered.

This seemed to be enough reassurance for them all. I didn't have such faith in this captain, whoever he was. One man would not stand against the Smith brothers.

The golden girl reached for my hand and guided me closer to the fire.

"That Honey," Chick said softly. "Honey Girl, cause she's sweet and creamy—that what Aiken say."

Chick followed me and Honey Girl, chattering to my back. "The call me Chick, on account I'm small and soft. I told you that Athena; she take care of us." The big woman glared at me so there'd be no confusion. *I* wasn't one of *us*. "And this Meaira. She from Ireland."

The last said in awe. I felt it, too. I knew that my daddy thought immigrants were a sea of trouble that flowed steadily on our shores. My family could trace its heritage back to England, or so he boasted. Our ancestors had come over a hundred years before, which, according to my father, no longer made us immigrants. *We're settlers*, Daddy was fond of saying. The distinction was not quite clear to me, but I was sharp enough to understand that somehow the distinction existed. I imagined for Chick anything beyond the ocean was a wonder.

The woman called Honey Girl had a dark sadness in her eyes, but she smiled at me and gestured for me to sit.

I perched carefully on one of the crates by the fire while Chick bustled over to the spider frying pan propped on the rocks at the edge. She picked up a long-handled fork to turn the bacon, and Athena snatched it out of her hand. I noticed Athena walked with a pronounced limp.

"Don't mess wit my skillet."

"No, Athena, I surely won't do that."

Chick gave her a guileless smile that softened Athena's expression. She gently touched Chick's cheek. "Go on and sit yourself down."

Chick scurried over to sit beside me. Meaira came with a bowl and a rag. She began dabbing at my face. When I didn't wince, she asked. "And whose blood is this if it's not yours?"

I shrugged. I didn't want to tell them it belonged to my mother. I couldn't put my thoughts around the words. Didn't want to conjure the memory. But there it was anyway, hovering just at the edge of my mind. I felt hot tears filling my eyes again, and I clenched my teeth hard to fight them back. I was a coward, not a crybaby. But they wouldn't be staunched. They spilled over and streamed down my face. One plopped onto my hand and mingled with the dried blood there. I must look a sight. The thought made the tears come faster. Meaira put her arms around me from one side and Chick from the other, and the two strange women held me while I cried.

* * *

Later I ate under Athena's fierce eyes. Why she disliked me so, I didn't know. But she watched the horizon fearfully—I assumed for murderers to swoop down on us. I watched for them, as well. I spent a restless night with the women, tossing and turning, starting to wakefulness in the grips of nightmares. Chick was there beside me, her luminous eyes full of compassion. On my other side lay Honey, who set her cool hands on my forehead and murmured comforting words in her sweet tone. Somehow I made it to morning.

Dawn found us back around the fire drinking Athena's coffee. I offered to help with breakfast, and she gave me a withering stare. I didn't know if she resented the implication that she might need help, or if it was just me she took exception to. I thought it was probably me, but I still didn't know why. She made breakfast from last night's meal, and then the camp became a hive of activity. I felt useless in the midst of it and tried to help. Chick kept a steady conversation, telling me that soon Aiken and the Captain would be here.

"Who are they?"

This question stilled all the women. They stared at me, then from one to another, none of them answering.

"A businessman, the Captain is," Meaira began, hesitantly. "You understand?"

I nodded, though I didn't think I did. "My father was a businessman. He was a banker."

This produced another round of stares. "That not the kind Captain is," Chick said. "He work the tables. You know. Cards. He won hisself a saloon."

I raised my brows at this. My father had been a player of cards, although my mother had disapproved. Perhaps if he'd ever won she'd have considered it a business venture, too, but unfortunately, he hadn't been very skilled. He understood the rules of gambling but not the concept of the game. He'd taught me when I was only eight, and by the time I was ten, I could beat him every time. He'd often joked that he wished he could smuggle me in with him. Many a night my entire family had settled around a table with a deck of cards and my daddy's hope that practice would make perfect. For me it had, but for Daddy . . . I bit my lip, knowing he would never learn to win now.

"And Aiken," I asked. "Who is he?"

"He the devil," Athena said, turning her back on me and the conversation.

"The devil," Meaira scoffed. "What will she think? No lass, not the devil. A man of business, as well."

Athena snorted and jabbed a finger at me. "Well, he ain't gon' be happy to see her."

The devil and a gambler who thought themselves businessmen. I still didn't know where the women fit in, but Athena's words inspired them all to move faster in their efforts to be packed up and ready.

It was close to nine in the morning when Honey stood up and shielded her eyes from the bright sun. The camp was tidy, and the women waited in a circle around the low fire.

"Captain's coming," she said.

"Is Aiken with him?" Meaira asked, looking very hopeful about the prospect of the devil's arrival.

"Just the Captain," Honey said. Meaira's disappointment had a pale and shaken air to it. I wondered at her relationship with this Aiken.

I looked but saw nothing of either man. Honey must have excellent eyes or a sixth sense where the Captain was concerned. After a few minutes of staring, I made out a speck on the horizon. Possibly a man on a horse, but how could they be certain it was the man they called Captain?

The declaration of his imminent arrival had a galvanizing effect on the other women, however. They all began to move about with feigned casualness, as if they'd risen on a whim to dust off their skirts or straighten the already neatly stacked crates by the wagon. But the tension hung thick in the camp. Athena clicked her tongue and looked around like a soldier at her troop.

Honey disappeared into the back of the wagon. When she came out, she'd touched up her makeup and changed into a dress that looked very fine for camping. Meaira slouched on a crate dejectedly. I noted the dark circles under her eyes and a grayish cast to her skin. She looked unwell.

Chick fussed with her hair and adjusted her dress over her underdeveloped breasts. Even Athena, though unconcerned with her appearance, busied herself around the fire. She retrieved her skillet from a crate and started cooking. By the time the Captain came into sight, the bacon was popping and Athena began cracking eggs in beside it.

He was a big man riding an enormous horse. The mount was a mottled blend of grays and white with brown mixed in at intervals, as if by mistake. My brother would have known the name of it. He would have run out to meet the rider, hopping alongside as he admired the horse. I swallowed thickly.

The Captain's saddle was worn, dark leather. A workingman's saddle, not a fancy tooled thing like the one my daddy's boss at the bank had. The Captain wore boots and dark pants with a gold strip down each leg. They were faded pale and the cording sapped of color until it looked more lemon than golden. His work shirt was grayed and buttoned casually up over a broad chest. He wore no jacket. The hat on his head was low, keeping his face in shadow.

On the saddle behind him hung a string of rabbits. He untied them and dropped them by the fire.

Athena picked up the string and said sweetly, "Thanky, Captain."

He gave a half nod and backed up his horse. As he turned, the angle shifted and the shadows cleared from his face. For the first time, I saw him full-on. He had eyes the color of the Mississippi River—all muddied browns and swirling greens. Dark, yet glimmering with light and current. I recognized him, of course. He was one of Lonnie and Jake Smith's riders.

I'd seen him once in town. I'd been coming out of the dry goods store as he went in. We bumped into each other, and for a moment he held my arms between his big hands. I remember looking into those eyes, seeing the ebb and flow of the powerful tide of emotion and hot-blooded man-thoughts that swept across his face. I'd felt the sensation of his look as it skimmed over me and lingered on my breasts. I'd never seen a man like him before. He was hard and weathered, his face tanned. He smelled of a fresh bath, and his cheeks had been smoothly shaven but for the blond-gold mustache that curled over his lip.

He'd held me longer than was necessary, and I didn't protest as I should have. My hands were pressed against the hard warmth of his chest and his heart beat steady beneath my palm. My imagination took flight with thoughts of him pulling me tight against the solid breadth of him. Bending me back over his arms as he kissed me. I didn't really know what he might do next. I had an idea of what went on between barnyard animals but no clue how that really applied to humans.

He'd smiled at me then and the look had a hint of devil-may-care. It took my breath away while at the same time making me smile back. His attention focused on my mouth, and it seemed he was as fascinated by me as I was of him. He'd even leaned forward, ever so slightly.

That was when Mama had noticed us. She'd already walked out of the door, pushing Grandma's chair and chattering about the new fabric she'd purchased. She hadn't realized I wasn't at her side.

"Sir, kindly release my daughter," she'd snapped when she turned back to the store where we stood.

He'd dropped his hands instantly, tipped his hat at us both and stepped aside. I allowed my hands to trail his chest as I lowered them. He recognized the gesture for what it was. Even though I'd never been so bold with a man before, I wanted him to know that I liked his touch. I succeeded.

"Outside, Ella," my mother snapped, angrily grabbing my arm. She'd marched me home where my father told me who he was. Sawyer McCready. A Smith rider.

He narrowed his eyes at me now, noticing for the first time that I sat near the fire. I held my breath, wondering if he recognized me, too. He didn't say a word, just cut his eyes from one woman to another as he sat astride that huge horse.

"Captain," Honey said, moving up to his side and setting her hand on his thigh. She had long, slender fingers, slightly darkened at the knuckles but smooth as the rest of her. "This young woman found her way to our camp last night. Her family's been murdered."

Those eyes snapped to me again, and I felt them drilling into me. I inched my hand down to my pocket and eased it in. My father's knife lay heavy and warm against my thigh. It wasn't the shotgun—they'd taken that from me last night— but it would do. My fingers closed on the smooth metal, and I slowly pulled it out, keeping it hidden in the folds of my skirts. He was still watching me, and I knew I would have to act fast before he figured out why I looked familiar.

Hands behind my back, I pulled the knife from its leather sheath and I charged. I'd moved so quickly and unpredictably that no one thought to stop me. It didn't occur to me that they might. I was focused only on one thing—this man who'd helped slaughter my family. One way or another I would be dead soon, either by starvation or murder, but I wouldn't be a coward anymore.

I didn't hesitate as I took a running leap up and over one of the crates on the ground by his horse and hit him square on as he sat horseback. I knocked him off-balance and ruined any angle I had at bringing my knife down in a fatal blow. We fell off to the other side, and my blade glanced his arm. He cursed and rolled with me, the weight of him far too much for me to fight. That didn't mean I wasn't going to try. I kicked and bit and swung wildly with my knife until he got me pinned on my back, both hands captured by one of his. I had the satisfaction of knowing he was breathing heavily as he looked down at me. I stared defiantly back and saw the dawning of recognition.

"Ella," he said.

He remembered my name, though my mother had only said it once. For a moment, this distracted me. He'd remembered my name. But I remembered why I wanted him dead.

"You murderer! They were good people," I shouted. "You killed them. You killed them as they ran." I was shrieking, but I couldn't stop. I screamed at him again and again. "Murderer."

He wrestled the knife from my hand, easily twisting it out of my grip as I cried out with rage. He sat astraddle my body, looking at the long wicked blade I'd nearly skewered him with. His expression crossed between disbelief and anger. I waited for him to bury it to the hilt in my heart—I welcomed it. He looked at me, those muddy eyes cold, and then he backed off and stood. I flipped over and took off running. I heard him curse again and the others scream in surprise. I hiked up my skirt and ran for all I was worth. I didn't know if he was following me or not until he tackled me, sending me sprawling on the ground, my mouth full of dirt and grit.

Roughly, he turned me, lying on me to keep me pinned to the ground. "I don't know what you're talking about," he shouted at me, his face inches from mine. He was hurting me.

"My parents," I shouted back. "My brother. My grandmother. Why? They were leaving. They were leaving."

I was sobbing, hysterical with fear and anger and hurt.

"Go ahead and do it," I told him. "Spill my blood like you did theirs."

"Who are they? Your parents? Who were they?"

The correction caught and silenced me. *Were.* My family had to be spoken of in past tense now. "My father was Conrad Beck."

Sawyer knew the name. I saw it in his face. I waited for him to deny it, though, expecting only lies from the likes of him.

"I don't ride with Smith anymore. Not for almost a year." He stood up and reached down to offer me a hand. "I didn't kill your family."

I didn't believe him. I'd heard Lonnie sit on the witness stand and swear he hadn't touched Louise Franklin, even though more than five witnesses saw him rape her before he'd murdered her. I hadn't believed him, either. Just because I didn't see him do it, didn't make him innocent.

Sawyer offered his hand, but I stayed where I was, glaring my hate. He stared back at me for a moment and then walked away. He had my knife, but my rage was far from gone.

"Get the hell out of here," he said over his shoulder.

That stopped me. I looked around at the same desolate nowhere I'd journeyed through for days without seeing another sign of life. I didn't know where I was now any more than I had last night when I'd stumbled across the women. Where would I go? What were the odds of me finding another camp, another living soul who would help me? My father had taught me enough about gambling to know they weren't good.

Sawyer didn't wait to see what I would do. He showed me his back, which I thought both brave and foolhardy considering I still wanted to kill him. When he reached the camp, the women fussed around him, tending to his wounded arm and bringing him food.

I put my face in my scraped and bloody hands, wanting to sob until all the pain inside had come out. But what good would that do me? I wouldn't stay out here like a hungry dog waiting for scraps. I wouldn't let him see that he'd broken me. Wincing, I pushed to my feet. My knees were as skinned and torn as my hands, and my ribs felt bruised and battered. But my anger fueled my steps. I followed the stream that I'd found last night with a determination rooted deep in my desperation.

The long steps between afternoon and twilight gave me too much time to think. Sawyer's words played through my mind, keeping time with my progress. He said he hadn't ridden with the Smiths for over a year. Was it true? I hadn't actually seen him among the riders who had killed my family. Nor were the murderers with him now. And the women . . . They'd been genuine in their surprise when I'd asked about the Smith brothers.

Sawyer had ridden with them once, though. And if not a murderer, it at least made him a thief. An outlaw, all the same.

The tears I'd refused earlier would be denied no longer. They burned my eyes and slid down my cheeks, but they didn't slow my steps. I didn't know what I would do now, but somehow, quitting would mean that I'd failed my family even worse than when I'd let them die. My mother had always said I possessed an inner strength that would keep me going when times were hard. I hadn't believed her, but now I felt her whisper to my heart, *You can do it, Ella.*

The words of encouragement didn't slow my tears, but my steps became more certain. Maybe I *could* survive this. But all around me only open terrain and encroaching darkness waited. I was scared. I couldn't pretend otherwise.

Sobbing, I stumbled in the widening stream to nowhere and howled with grief and heartache as I plowed determinedly forward. I cried so loudly that at first I didn't even hear the hoofbeats of the approaching horse. It was not until the animal came to a stop abreast of me that I noticed it. Although it was fully night now and only the black silhouette showed, I knew who the rider was: Sawyer McCready. Captain McCready.

I slowed to a stop, staring at the powerful man and horse. My face was wet with tears, my shoulders still shaking with my anguish. But I managed to hold my head up and glare at him.

"I hope you brought my gun and knife since you've sent me out here to fend for myself," I said.

His mouth dropped open with shock. The reaction brought me a flush of satisfaction. Then he said, "*You* attacked *me.*"

"I was just protecting myself."

"Yeah? So was I."

I heard him click his tongue, and the horse came closer. He stopped beside me and looked down.

"You're going to get yourself killed out here," he said, his voice dark as whiskey.

"What do you care?"

In the silence that followed, I bit my tongue. He was right: I *was* going to get myself killed. If a bear or mountain lion didn't decide to make a snack of me, then perhaps Indians or even the Smith brothers would see me dead. But I'd go down fighting, as my daddy used to say.

"I didn't murder your family, Ella, and I'll be damned if I'll have you out here dead weighing on me. I'll take you back to camp. Tomorrow we'll be moving on, and when we get to a town, you can find your way home from there."

My nose was running and I had no handkerchief. Feeling foolish, I lifted my skirt and wiped it. I thought I saw a flash of a smile, but it was gone so fast, I might have imagined it.

"Why would you help me?"

He looked down, shook his head, then met my eyes again. "Because I'm a damn fool. Because I know what Lonnie and Jake are and you shouldn't have had to see it."

The truth of his words made me want to start crying fresh tears, but I bit my lip and nodded.

"You got nothin' to fear from me," he said. "But I won't sit out here all night trying to talk sense into you."

That made me want to snarl back, but for once, I managed to hold my tongue. I looked around at the clustered darkness, the black woods in the distance, the deep valleys between the foothills. Swallowing, I peered into his shadowed face, wishing I could read him. Wishing I knew what to do. How could I trust this man? How could I not?

"Come on, Ella. It's late."

He kicked his foot free of the stirrup and reached down a hand. With a deep breath, I took it.

CHAPTER TWELVE

This was how the morning went.

First Gracie damn near gave him heart failure when he heard her horse-dog barking like a killer was on the loose, and then Analise had topped it with a bloodcurdling scream from her room. They'd both been so shaken up that he couldn't doubt they'd seen something. He'd wanted to scoff at Chloe's claim that a spirit from beyond had been in the room, but he really couldn't.

Especially after what happened later.

Gracie left for the doctor's—without saying good-bye—and the storm morphed into a full-fledged monsoon, which she was out driving in, behind the wheel of a car that was no match for the rising water and gusting wind.

With his daughter.

He snorted. A daughter. Poor kid. The only thing worse than not having a father was having Reilly Alexander for one. Jesus, she was screwed no matter what.

He'd showered and dressed, then came downstairs to find Chloe, Jonathan, and the priest sitting at one of the tables in front of the oh-so dry bar, playing cards and drinking coffee. They seemed like a parody of the many portraits surrounding them. Chloe's dark eyes followed his anxious wandering from window to window, making him even more irritable. She seemed a little shaken up herself. Gracie's sharp reprimand must have done the job.

"Where's"—*Abe the Vampire*—"Bill?" he asked, looking around.

"He's not a fan of bacon, eggs, and toast," Jonathan answered with obvious disdain as he played his card. "He went to the store to stock up on gluten-free products, free-range whatever, and organic vegetables before the roads wash out."

Reilly almost laughed. Bill had his work cut out for him if he thought he'd find a good selection here.

But the mention of the roads washing out worried Reilly anew. He stared out the window, willing Gracie's safe return. At last, he went to the porch to find the rain had finally cooled things off. The wet wind felt good after the sweltering heat inside, and he took some deep breaths, trying to settle down and quit worrying about Gracie. As she'd pointed out, she'd done just fine without him for the past seventeen years. Chances were she'd do fine without him for the next seventeen, too.

That should have made him feel better.

He took another deep breath and went back inside. "I'm going to try opening all the doors upstairs," he said. "See if that gets the air circulating."

Jonathan jumped to his feet. "Want some help?"

"Opening doors?" Reilly asked, glancing over his shoulder as he walked away. "I think I can handle it."

But Jonathan tried to follow him anyway. Reilly turned on him with a hand up before he got too far. "What do you want?"

"Just to talk to you," he said, surprised.

"About?"

"I like music. I was a big fan of your band. You're famous."

Badlands had played the kind of music that resonated in smoky bars with drunks who had too much to forget. Mr. Rogers here didn't exactly fit in their demographic, but weirder things had been known to happen…like Reilly and Gracie Beck ending up in Diablo Springs at the same time.

Reilly narrowed his eyes at Jonathan. "Name one song."

"Dead Lights Calling," he said instantly.

Reilly shot him a bored look. That one had topped the charts and made them a household name. A one trick pony. Ten years after the band had broken up and it still got play time. "Try again."

"Dark Water Gold."

Reilly shut his mouth. That one had never been released as a single. Maybe Jonathan really had been a fan.

"You think it's there?" Jonathan asked.

"What?"

"Gold in the old springs. That's what the song's about."

The tension drained out of Reilly and he laughed. "That's not what it's about."

"Treasure's calling me from under it all..." Jonathan sang off key.

Reilly had written Dead Water Gold years before his brother shot himself. Now he wondered if he'd known even then. A darker song had never been put to music.

"It's about suicide, Jonathan. The treasure is the joy of having it all over and done with."

Jonathan's face went slack. "That can't be true. It's such a beautiful song."

Reilly laughed again. "Okay. You got me. It's about buckets of gold in a dried up hole."

Flushing angrily, Jonathan went back and sat at the table and Reilly felt like an asshole. The guy was harmless, wearing a wounded expression and a baby-blue sweater he had to be roasting in. As ridiculous as it felt, Reilly probably was the most famous person he'd ever met and he'd just treated the guy like crap.

Christ, he needed to get out of here. Without another word, he turned and headed for the stairs again.

As Reilly passed through the entryway, he caught sight of an iron doorstop shaped like a hound taking a piss. He pulled it from the corner and used it to prop open the front door. Rain whisked in on the damp wind, but the cold air was worth it. Upstairs, he opened all the bedroom doors and immediately felt the chill pouring out of Gracie's room and into the hall. Pleased, he turned to head down again but a tickle danced over his spine a second before he heard the whisper of the first door closing.

He spun in time to see the second door swing shut and watched as one by one, they all closed. Frowning, he went back to Gracie's room and opened the door again. He used a stack of books he'd found on the dresser to prop it open before doing the same to the others. Yet again, each door clicked shut before he made it down the first few steps.

More annoyed by the mysterious draft working against him than anything else, he went back to the hall, expecting to see piles of books toppled onto the landing in front of each doorway.

That's when shit got weird.

The hall was uncluttered, dim . . . quiet . . . and for the first time, Reilly felt uneasy. An air of expectancy hung in the hushed corridor . . . unnatural and somehow unmistakable. It followed him as he retraced his steps to Gracie's room, squirming beneath his skin, seeping in his bloodstream. He had to fight the urge to keep looking over his shoulder.

The knob on Gracie's door turned easily, and the door swung back on silent hinges. The books he'd used to prop it open had returned to the top of the desk where he'd found them.

"What the fuck," he muttered as he checked the other rooms and discovered all the things he'd used to hold the doors open had settled back in their original places.

Eyes narrowed, he surveyed the hallway, the vacant rooms. He even looked in the closets. Nothing moved, nothing jumped out and said, *Boo*. Determined now, he dragged the heavy nightstands from each room in front of the doors and wedged them in the doorframe to hold them open. Satisfied, he backed down the hall, gaze shifting left and right as he watched for movement.

The doors gaped at him, trapped by the bulky furniture. They wouldn't be closing this time. He was grinning as he started downstairs.

He almost made it to the ground level before he heard the rapid *boom-boom-boom* of the doors slamming with such force the whole house seemed to shake.

He froze, turning disbelieving eyes up as the front door banged shut behind him. He looked down. The cast-iron hound was back in the corner. Chloe, Jonathan, and the priest stood at the foot of the stairs, watching him.

"Guess we have a ghost," he said lightly, like he wasn't just a little freaked out by it.

Chloe lifted her chin, vindicated. "Was there ever any doubt of that?"

"I'm joking."

"I'm not."

He was saved from answering by the sound of a car outside. "Not a word about this to Gracie or Analise, got it?"

"You think you can hide a haunting, Nathan?"

With an angry, dismissive glance, he hurried past them and out to the porch in time to see Gracie's car turn the corner, splitting the flood waters on the street into geysers that sprayed four feet high on either side. She wasn't driving fast, but the car was too low, the water too high. A gust of rainy wind hit the vehicle just as the tire hydroplaned and the car spun into the ditch on the other side of the road.

With a muttered curse, Reilly charged off the porch and into the downpour. He reached the car as one of the back passenger doors popped open. A blond kid with eyes like glacial ice and a bandage on his head crawled over the seat and out the door. He reached in and caught Analise's hand, helping her scramble out of the tipped car. That had to be the boyfriend—*idiot*—who'd brought Analise to Diablo Springs in the first place.

Reilly opened the front side door and saw Gracie fighting gravity to get over the gear shift and out of the car. He reached in and helped her climb the steeply angled seat and escape. They'd have to tow the car out once the storm passed.

She was shaking, and for once, she didn't push him away. The dogs leaped out with no trouble, all but the little dust mop Gracie called Romeo. Reilly reached behind the seat and caught him by his scruff. The little beast tried to bite him, but he finally got it out. They were all drenched by the time they reached the front door, but no one appeared to be injured.

"Thanks for the help," Gracie said, taking the little dog from him and tucking it against her body.

Her face was pale, her eyes shadowed. Her ponytail drooped and dripped. The rain had made her shirt nearly transparent, and the lacy bra he'd guessed at when he'd first seen her last night showed through all too clearly. Her nipples pressed hard against the wet fabric, pebbled by the cold. He made himself look away only to find Jonathan had come out and was unabashedly staring at her breasts. Reilly caught the other man's eyes with a look that should've drawn blood and moved his body between them, shielding her from Jonathan's sight.

"I'm going to go up and change my clothes," Analise said, giving her mother an anxious look.

"I'll come with you," the blue-eyed idiot said with a smile that grated on Reilly's stretched nerves.

"She can change her clothes by herself, Brendan," Gracie told him in a hard voice.

"It's a little late to worry about me being alone with her, isn't it?" Brendan answered cheerfully.

Reilly liked him less by the moment.

"Mom," Analise said when Gracie opened her mouth to retort. "He needs dry clothes, too. Besides, I don't want to go in that room alone."

Some silent communication passed between the two of them. Gracie looked like she still wanted to argue, but in the end she said nothing. Analise was right; they all needed dry clothes after being out in the storm. But that wasn't why Gracie gave in, and Reilly's guess was that it didn't have a lot to do with being afraid of ghosts, either.

Gracie didn't look surprised to see Reilly waiting outside her room when she opened her door after she'd changed her clothes. She didn't look sorry, either. He tried not to make too much of that, but he'd never been that great at listening to his own voice of reason.

When they passed Analise's room, she paused. "Is he still in there?" she whispered softly.

Reilly nodded. He'd thought about butting in and telling the kid to keep out, but he had no right and he doubted anyone would appreciate his interference.

"Why don't we go downstairs and I'll make us some coffee?" he suggested.

Gracie hesitated, but only for a moment. "A cup of coffee sounds like heaven."

Her horse-dog thought that was a great idea, too, and nearly tripped her in its effort to get down the stairs before them. Reilly caught Gracie around the waist a second before she fell.

"Juliet," she scolded while a blush traveled up her throat. Her gaze snagged his, and he felt like a kid himself, nervous and excited. Frowning, he made sure she had her balance and stepped away.

"What kind of dog is that, anyway?" he asked.

"A rescue dog. Actually, all three of them are from shelters. Juliet and Tinkerbelle are part Great Dane and part . . . well, I'm not entirely sure what else. Even Romeo is a mutt, but don't tell him. He'd be horrified if he knew his daddy was Chihuahua."

Reilly smiled, remembering how much he'd loved her sense of humor. She glanced up, caught him staring and he felt himself blushing. Christ, he needed to hit the road before he got in any deeper.

Chloe, Jonathan, and the priest were still paying cards when they came back. Reilly caught Jonathan eyeing

Gracie's chest again, but the older man about-faced when he realized Reilly had seen him. Gracie ignored Chloe and her bright-eyed curiosity.

In the kitchen, she shook her head. "I don't like that woman."

"She's definitely . . . different."

Gracie almost smiled. "What's been going on here?"

"You might want to sit down for that," he said, opening cupboards until he found the coffee.

"Is it bad? I've had enough bad for one day."

He gave her a searching look as she pulled out a chair and sat at a worn butcher-block table. He set the coffee to brew and took the seat beside her.

"Something happened when you went to pick up the kid?"

It wasn't really a question, even though he posed it that way. Obviously, something had happened.

"Analise is pregnant," Gracie said softly.

"What?"

She nodded miserably. "I can't believe it. I've spent my whole life trying to raise her right, trying not to make the same mistakes my grandma made with me. Trying to keep her from making the same mistakes I made. Yet, here we are, in the exact same place."

Gracie covered her face with her hands, took a deep breath. When she looked at him again, her eyes held such dejected disbelief that he turned her chair and pulled her closer, bracketing her knees with his legs. He looked her in the eye and asked the question that had been bothering him since he'd seen their daughter for the first time. Since Gracie had told him her grandmother had thrown her out, pregnant and sixteen.

"Why didn't you wait for me, Gracie??"

Gracie lifted her chin. "Why didn't you take me with you, wherever it was you went? That was our plan. Why didn't you tell me you'd changed your mind?"

He should have expected it, but surprise made his breath catch somewhere low in his chest and he couldn't seem to move it any further. A hot, panicky feeling washed over him. He realized he was scared that she wouldn't believe the truth when she heard it. And he hated how badly he wanted her to understand.

The coffeepot belched, and Reilly used the excuse to escape her perceptive gaze. She didn't let him get far, though. She followed him, taking the cup he offered and positioning herself in front of him at the counter.

She sipped at her coffee. Waiting.

"Matt," he said at last. "I didn't change my mind. Matt changed it."

Her laugh held little humor. "Of course. Matt always came first."

"It wasn't like that. Not this time. It was about you."

"That's not new, either, Reilly. He knew I didn't return his feelings."

"Yet."

She raised her brows.

"Matt didn't see things the way most people do. He didn't trust what he saw, so you telling him *no* . . . That didn't mean much to him. In his mind, it just meant he had to try harder to win you."

Her eyes searched his. She opened her mouth as if to respond and then shut it again.

"I didn't know how bad things were, though. Maybe I didn't want to know."

His reluctance made his words thick. Because pretty soon he would get to the point where he'd have to say things that would hurt her. Even though he was still pissed off about everything that had happened after, about the fact that she'd never told him he had a daughter, he didn't want to hurt her.

"I told him about us," he said with a shake of his head. "We said we weren't going to tell anyone, but I couldn't just leave him. Not like that. So I told him we were going to run away together."

The words sounded so immature, so After School Special. But she sucked in a breath and slowly let it out.

"Reilly," she said on the exhale.

He cleared his throat. "Yeah, I know it was stupid. I knew it the minute I did it."

"What did he say?"

"Nothing. He put his fist through the wall and walked out the door. I didn't see him again until the night before we were supposed to leave."

"Where did he go?"

"I didn't know, and I didn't care. I was so fucking relieved, Gracie. A part of me hoped I'd never see him again. My own brother."

Those words hurt to say out loud, especially now, when he never would see him again.

Gracie set her cup on the counter and stepped closer to him. "You weren't responsible for Matt, Reilly."

He laughed. "See, that's where you're wrong. I was always responsible for Matt. But back then? All I could think about was you and me, getting out of here. Starting a new life away from all the crap in my old one."

"That's all either one of us could think about," she said, lowering her lashes so he couldn't see the hurt he heard in her voice.

"I came home from work late that night before we were supposed to go and found him on the porch waiting for me. I was packed and ready, but there he was, just sitting in the shadows. Waiting. I could hardly see him at first because the sun was down and the porch light hadn't worked for years. Wasn't until I got closer that I realized he was covered in blood. *Caked* in it. His hair, his lashes. Fuck. It was everywhere."

"Whose blood?"

"When I asked him, he couldn't remember. He was so whacked-out, he barely knew who he was. He kept babbling about people I'd never heard of, and all I could think was that he was going to fuck everything up. My brother looked like he'd walked out of a chain saw massacre and all I cared about was me and you and how he was going to screw up our plans."

"So why did you let him?" she asked, her voice small, distant.

"I didn't have a choice."

"There's always a choice."

He shrugged. "There's not always a right one."

Their gazes locked for a long moment. He thought about stopping right there and heading for the door. Because really, what would it matter to Gracie what had happened next? He'd had his chance with her. She'd said it loud and clear.

"I figured he'd hurt somebody," he heard himself say. "Maybe killed somebody. He made me think it was you."

He tilted his head back and stared at the ceiling. He couldn't look into those pretty eyes and say the ugly words that haunted him to this day. "He took the time to tell me every step, every detail of how he'd raped and killed you. He was crying the whole time, great big tears smearing all that dried blood into a mess. He looked like a monster."

Gracie took a step back and braced herself with a hand on the counter.

He turned to stare out the window. In the silence, he watched the deluge pouring from the sky, gushing from the gutters. The world had become a smeared and sooty brown, and his thoughts followed the runoff-carved rivulets across the hard desert floor, racing toward the ruins of Diablo Springs.

"I took off for your house. I ran the whole fucking way, Gracie. It was what, a hundred and eight outside? I still ran. I can remember the fear making my heart hurt. The sweat in my eyes. I got there just as you and your grandma got back from the store. You were telling her about your day, who you'd talked to at school and she asked you about me. At first I was so damn happy to see you, I almost grabbed you right then and there. If I could've caught my breath, I probably would have."

"I never even saw you."

"No. I heard your grandma say she wanted you to stay away from me because I was trash and I'd make you trash, too. She said I'd drive to your death, just like your father had done to your mother."

"She would've said that about any boy I liked. She was obsessive when it came to that particular topic."

"But she was right, Gracie."

"No, she wasn't."

He turned on her, suddenly angry. "Are you listening to me? Matt didn't have your blood on his hands that day, but he could've. He might've. Eventually, he *would have*."

He stared at her, the stark truth in his eyes. He saw the moment she heard it, the instant she really *heard* it.

"If I'd left with you the next day, sooner or later, he'd have hunted me down and he would've done all those terrible things he described. To you, Gracie. He would have done them to you."

She shook her head, but not in denial.

"I couldn't let him near you ever again."

"So you just left without a word? Why didn't you tell me, Reilly? Why did you let me believe you'd just left me?"

"How could I tell you that? *I* barely understood and he was my brother."

"You didn't even try to explain."

"And let you talk me out of it? Watch you cry when I still left?"

"I cried anyway."

"You don't get it. I didn't want to leave you, Gracie. I wanted to marry you and live in that fairy tale you'd convinced me we could have. I'd have let you change my mind."

Her eyes glittered, but she didn't cry now. She held her lip between her teeth and shook her head.

"And my brother would have killed you."

She cleared her throat, but her words still came low and thick. "For weeks, I waited for you to come back. I went to the sheriff, Reilly, and reported you missing. When he told me you and your brother had skipped town . . ." She shook her head. "You should have told me the truth. Left me a note. Something."

Reilly set his mug on the counter next to hers. "I should have. I've spent years wishing I would have."

Wordless, she stared at him while he tried to decipher what he saw in her eyes. He felt open and raw, and the survival instincts that had kept him alive all the hard years between then and now urged him to shut down, get out.

"We were gone about six days before he tried to kill someone else. I'd thought if I could just get him out of Diablo Springs, it would fix him. I realized that wasn't going to happen. I realized that even if it did, I'd be too broken to care, because without you, there wasn't much I liked about me. I decided that you were more important than he was."

Reilly's voice hardened with the memory of what came next.

"So I got him drunk and got him to tell me whose blood he'd been wearing the night he came home."

"Whose was it?"

"A stranger. Some poor woman who'd been unlucky enough to meet my brother in a bar. He'd raped her. Murdered her. Thrown her body in the springs. And he was jonesing to do it again. I waited until he went to sleep and called the cops. The body was easy enough to find once I told them where to look. They never identified her, though. No one ever came forward to claim her. She was just some lost soul he killed."

"I don't know what to say."

"Yeah, I know how you feel. It took some time to take care of things. Matt . . ." He shook his head. "He cried when he found out I'd turned him in. I still hear him sometimes."

Gracie stared at him, her eyes such a closed book that he had no idea what she might be thinking. He pushed away from the counter and faced the back door, looking out at the storm. Feeling it bluster inside him.

"I came back after that, and your grandmother wouldn't even open the door. I found out from Charlie, down at the Buckboard, that you'd quit your job and gone to live with relatives somewhere east."

She cleared her throat. "We don't have relatives in the east, or anywhere else that I know of."

Obviously, Carolina had wanted to make sure Reilly never found out where she'd sent Gracie.

"I didn't think you were ever coming back," Gracie said. "By then I figured out I was pregnant. I told my grandma—there was no else to tell—and she packed me up and shipped me to San Diego to live with an old friend I'd never even heard of before. Mrs. Graham, an elderly woman who used to stay at the Diablo, back when she was young. I didn't have a choice about any of it."

"Your grandma didn't tell you I came looking for you?"

Gracie shook her head. "I called her every week, and every week she made a point of telling me I needed to move on. You were gone and never coming back."

"What a bitch."

"I wrote to my friends, though. I told them where I was. You could have come for me. I used to lie in bed and pray that you would."

"Not a soul knew where you were, Gracie. I asked. I'd just put my brother in the fucking penitentiary so I could be with you. Believe me, I asked. I couldn't understand how you gave up on me just like that."

She didn't say anything. Reilly glanced over his shoulder. "All those letters you wrote . . . Did anyone write you back?"

"Not even Grandma Beck. After a while, she quit calling or answering the phone. When the baby was born, she sent fifty thousand dollars and told her friend to take care of us, but Mrs. Graham died a couple years later. I was eighteen by then and there was enough money left for us to make it on our own . . . we moved away and it's been just the two of us ever since ."

"Where'd your grandmother get that kind of money to send?"

Gracie shook her head. "All I know is that you left and the whole world turned its back on me and my baby."

Reilly moved to stand in front of her, staring down at her bent head. The scent of her wrapped around his senses and bypassed his brain. He'd been with dozens of women since he was the teenaged lover of Gracie Beck, but he'd never forgotten her. He'd never had a woman get under his skin so quickly and completely.

Years separated him from their last kiss, but it felt like yesterday, and he wanted to press his mouth to hers like he wanted his next breath. But what scared him was the knowledge that his feelings had nothing to do with the scalloped lace he could almost see outlined beneath her cotton shirt or the history that would always bind them together. It had to do with the here and now, with *feelings* he barely understood himself. And the fact that she hadn't turned away even after he'd told her the most horrifying truth she would ever hear. She didn't look at him like he was something she'd scraped off her shoe.

Slowly, he cupped her face, the feel of her soft skin almost painful against his callused fingers. She was everything good and pure, and he was the last thing she needed in her life.

"I'm sorry," he said against her lips.

She made a sound in her throat, protest and surrender all wrapped in one confounding moan. Her hands flattened over his chest, fingers spread, his heart captive beneath her touch. Her short upper lip fit perfectly between both of his, and her mouth clung when he took it. They'd learned to make love when neither had been old enough to appreciate the fleeting preciousness of such a thing. Now the need to have that closeness again made him deepen the kiss, part her lips, and taste the sweetness of her mouth.

Her fingers curled into the fabric of his shirt, holding tight as she returned his kiss with lips and teeth and the soft brush of her tongue. He pulled the band from her ponytail, and her hair cascaded into his hands, soft as satin, damp from the rain. She arched into him while he ran his fingers down the curve of her spine, pulling her hips against his, letting her feel how much he wanted, needed her. He wanted to lay her down on that butcher-block table and make her his once more.

She turned her head and said his name.

He heard the withdrawal in her voice like a shout in a quiet room. Instantly, he dropped his hands and stepped back.

Her hair was tousled, her lips swollen, and her eyes filled with bewilderment. Every instinct inside him told him to run. Who cared if that made him a coward? In the end, she made the decision for him and headed for the door.

The horse-dog paused to give him a strangely compassionate look as it followed her out of the kitchen, but Gracie didn't even slow down.

CHAPTER THIRTEEN

May 1896
Colorado

The ride back to camp with Sawyer would be imprinted in my memory forever. My emotions had been drawn and quartered, until I didn't know what feeling went with what part of me. I sat behind Sawyer on his powerful horse, lulled by the rolling motion of its gait, my face pressed into his back. He smelled of horse and sun and river-washed cotton. Familiar smells that mingled pleasantly with his own unique scent. Against all reason, I was comforted.

My tears had doused my bloodlust, and I began to think that I'd acted out of judgment rather than rationale. I hadn't seen Sawyer with the Smith brothers, and he would have been hard to miss on his enormous horse. And why would he be riding alone now if he was with them? More to the point, why wouldn't he have simply killed me when I'd attacked? He'd have witnesses to verify he'd acted in self-defense should it ever come under the scrutiny of the law. But he hadn't taken my life. Instead, he'd helped me.

My arms were around his waist, and only the anchor of his solid body kept me from sliding to the ground. His chest rose and fell with his steady breathing. His voice was gentle when he talked to the horse, but he didn't speak to me, nor I to him. What would I say? Perhaps I was wrong to have tried to slit your throat? Thank you for not cutting mine?

When he deposited me back at the camp, Chick and Meaira were there to help me. Honey brought me food. Athena fussed around Sawyer and then cared for his horse. I heard his deep "Thank you" and the hint of a smile in her "Welcome." I'd only heard her use that tone with Chick. After he'd eaten, Sawyer took his bedroll and moved to the other side of the fire. The rest of us slept beneath the tarp by the wagon. It seemed exhaustion took all of us, or maybe it was the sense that we weren't alone this night, that there was someone to watch over us. Ironic, that the someone was Sawyer McCready. When I awoke the next morning, he was gone.

* * *

We ate a cold breakfast of biscuits and bacon and then finished packing the camp again to move out. Athena complained the whole time about how I'd caused unnecessary work and grief. In her eyes, I was an ungrateful girl who'd tried to kill their benefactor.

They didn't speak of Aiken Tate this morning, but they had plenty to say about the Captain. As far as they were concerned, he was better than the second coming and twice as dependable.

I still didn't know who exactly the other man, this mysterious Aiken Tate, was, and I could only guess at his relationship to these women. Where had he been all this time? Meaira paced and watched the horizon with a desperation I only partly understood. We were stranded with a wagon and no horses. Evidently, Aiken was expected to bring them. But it seemed she was anxious about more than that. She was agitated and irritable, snapping at the others for no reason until, at last, she stalked off to sit by herself. After awhile, Honey joined her. I didn't know what had happened to have her so upset.

Chick went to work on a party dress she'd been sewing. She was very proud of her efforts, but her skill didn't quite match her enthusiasm. Darning and sewing the family's clothing had been my chore since I was ten, and I could stitch a suit of armor if the need called. I feared that her feelings would be hurt should I offer to help, but she was more than happy to let me fix her clumsy stitches and embellish her gown. The cotton fabric was not so fine as the cut and style of the garment, but the dark-rose color would look lovely against Chick's skin.

"Where will you wear such a dress?" I asked her as I stitched tiny beading to the gathered bust.

Chick turned her round eyes on me, considering before she answered. After a moment she lowered her voice and said, "Athena say don't tell you our business."

"This dress is your business?"

Chick shook her head. She leaned forward and spoke softly. "It what I wear when the men come."

I tried to keep my expression blank, but my surprise must have shown on my face. Chick looked for Athena and saw her down by the river, bent over her washboard. Honey and Meaira sat on a small rise not far away. Watching for the Captain or Aiken, I thought.

Satisfied that no one could hear, Chick said, "You cain't tell I said."

I shook my head. "I won't."

"We's fancy girls." She gave a nod, her expression prideful. "Not yet. Now we work the fields, wherever Aiken tell us."

I didn't know much about fancy girls, but I'd never thought of them as field laborers. I said as much.

Chick laughed, covering her smile with her hand as she did. "I mean we's *in* the fields, not working them."

I still didn't understand, and I felt embarrassed and dense under her knowing eyes. I was older than she was, but not so world-wise.

"Aiken, he take us from place to place. He got us, but he don't have nowhere to put us, see? Not anymore. Used to be we was in Atlanta, but Aiken got runned off. Now, sometime, we not even in a town. Just someplace where men be."

There was no hiding the horror I felt at her words.

"Ain't so bad," she said. "He gots a tent and the men is nice. Usually." She looked down, picking a long blade of grass and pulling it apart with her fingers. "Sometime they's old," she said. "Sometime they smell even though Aiken make 'em take a bath."

"Why do you do it, then?" I asked.

"What else I gon' do? It not as bad as working cotton. My momma did that. She die 'fore I was ten. Aiken take me in then and I do dishes and scrub floors 'til I was older. Some nights my hands be bloody from it."

"And now . . . Aiken is . . . ?" I didn't know how to word it.

"He own us."

"Slavery isn't legal anymore, Chick," I said, thinking perhaps it was possible she didn't know this.

"Murder neither, but it still get done."

Her words brought forth a rush of images. My grandmother's broken wheelchair . . . My brother. Chick squeezed my hand, pulled me back to her.

I said, "Why don't you run away?"

Chick looked at me, and her eyes were much older than her years. "I got no place to go." She shrugged. "Nothin' better waitin' for me later. I can do this here, elst I can do it in some town for someone else who maybe treat me worse. I don' want to work no crib."

I didn't know what she meant.

"See, the old whores, they's in the cribs. That what they call the place they work.—cribs. They nasty, but once a whore get used up, that's all that left of them."

"Is that—this kind of work—your only choice?"

Chick shrugged. "Athena, she used a work all day, half the night for people who barely gave her enough to eat. Least here we goin' somewhere. We ain't hungry. We better off than most."

I didn't know what to say.

"'Sides, I like it when they choose me. The young ones always do. Me and Honey. They likes us best."

Again, I knew my face had betrayed my thoughts. Chick dropped her gaze and spoke to the ground between our feet.

"Athena say you cain't know how things is for us. She think you look down on what we do. Think us trash."

"No, Chick," I said, touching her hand. "I don't understand it, but I could never think anything but good of you." And it was true. Chick was sweet and kind, and despite what I'd just learned, I thought her innocent. Someone who needed to be taken care of. But that was foolish of me, I supposed. It was I who was naive and needed to be cared for.

"You ever work for someone?" she asked.

"For my family but not for anyone else."

"Folks treat their dogs better than a person who need help. Just cuz we ain't slaves don't make us people to them. Aiken, he ain't good, but he better than a lot. And things gon' get lots better soon," she said fiercely. "Now Captain 'round. He give us a place. He take care us."

"Does he . . . own you, as well?"

She shook her head. "I wish he did. First, he didn't want nothing to do with us, but Aiken, he smart. He show him we be good for the saloon. We be real good. He talk Captain into being partners"

"How?"

"Don' know. Honey, she think Aiken trick him. She think Aiken cheat him. She say Captain a good man. Not the kind to join the likes of Aiken Tate."

"If he wasn't above joining Lonnie and Jake Smith, I don't think his standards are as high as you imagine."

"Honey smart. She say he good, he good."

If I was honest, a part of me agreed.

I asked, "How about the others, Chick? How did they come to be with Aiken?"

Something over my shoulder caught her attention and froze her expression into wide eyes and open mouth. I looked. Athena stood right behind me. Her eyes seemed to blaze with anger as she looked from Chick's guilty face to mine.

"He comin'," she said.

I turned around and looked to the horizon. Honey and Meaira did the same. Meaira stood, wringing her hands as she watched. There was a hunger on her pale face that confused me. She looked feverish. The others didn't seem to notice, nor was there welcome in their seeking eyes or any of the caged excitement that had preceded the Captain's arrival.

Honey stopped in front of where I sat. "I hope you don't plan on attacking Aiken like you did the Captain," she said.

I shook my head.

"That's good. You don't want to cross Aiken Tate."

I set Chick's dress aside and stood, joining the uneasy vigil that awaited his appearance.

"You do what he tell you," Athena said, her voice dark as molasses.

I'd prepared myself for a man larger than Sawyer, more menacing than ten Sawyers. But Aiken Tate was a petite, dapper man. He had bright, blue eyes and a smatter of freckles across his nose. He wore a small hat perched jauntily on his head and a three-piece suit in gray pinstripes. He was dusty but looked more a businessman than the devil I'd been warned about.

On a lead attached to his saddle were two other horses that looked to be of stock breeding. Work horses. It made no sense to me why he took them rather than leave them with the wagon, but I had to assume he had a good reason for what he did.

He swung off his horse, and Chick dutifully went to take the reins. Athena had a plate of biscuits and bacon waiting and hurried to serve him. There were no niceties accompanying her efforts, however. Just as there was no string of rabbits for her stew.

Aiken's gaze buzzed over and lighted on me like a bee to a flower. "Well, well," he said, smiling to show a mouthful of crooked teeth. Still, there was something vaguely charming about the lopsided smile and the sparkling blue gaze. If it weren't for the apprehension that seemed to flutter between the other women, I might have liked him on sight. "Who are you?" he asked.

My mouth was dry as I answered. "Ella Beck."

"Ella. That's a pretty name for a pretty lady."

His voice wasn't deep like Sawyer's, but it was pleasant. Everything about him was pleasant. "What brings you to our humble quarters, pretty lady Ella?"

"I'm lost. Saw— Captain McCready has agreed to take me to the next town with you."

Aiken's smile widened. "The Captain's a good man." He looked around, then asked, "Where is he?"

Meaira stepped forward, laying a hand on Aiken's arm. "He said he'd ride ahead and meet up with us tomorrow. He said we should start as soon as you got here. Did everything go okay in town?"

There was something in the intensity of her gaze that I couldn't decipher. Aiken ignored her question as he moved to sit on the crate and eat. I realized that, though at first sight I'd thought him a small man, my impression had been erroneous. He gave the illusion of being slight, but in fact he was of solid build.

Meaira followed him like a dog expecting scraps. "Aiken?" she said, her voice edged with need. "Did . . . Do you . . ." She couldn't seem to get it out. Aiken gave her a few more tortured seconds of trying before reaching in his pocket and pulling out a small bottle.

He held it out, but when she reached for it, he pulled it back. "You have to make it last," he said.

She nodded. "I will. I promise. I will."

Her eyes fixed intently on the bottle. He held it away for another moment before handing it over. Meaira's smile lit her face. "Thank you, Aiken."

Athena said, "Everything ready for us to go." and gave Meaira a look I didn't understand.

Aiken nodded. "We got a good twenty-five miles to go today. There's a boomtown sprung up between here and Diablo Springs. I hear they ain't seen a woman for months out there. We'll be more'n welcome to settle in beside them all." He nodded at Athena. "Get the wagon harnessed and let's get a move on."

I saw Meaira disappear into the wagon. After a few moments, she came out again. As I moved to help with the last of the crates, I watched her. She seemed strangely disoriented.

"Laudanum," Honey said from beside me. "Aiken keeps her stocked."

As if hearing us, Meaira hung her head and turned away.

We moved out within the half hour. Athena drove the team from the wagon. The rest of us walked alongside. Aiken rode up ahead, leading the way and keeping the pace.

When my family left home, I'd walked then, too. After the first week, my legs had become strong and my body had adjusted to the toil. We'd had to strap my grandma to the back in her chair because the terrain was too rough for her to wheel over. I'd trudged along beside her, describing the scenery for her as we moved forward. She would comment on my description after we passed. It became a game for us, me stretching my mind for new ways to say *green* or *wide-open* or *breathtaking*. Grandma trying to envision it from my narrative alone.

Thinking of it now brought a lump to my throat, and the grief that I'd yet to acknowledge swamped me. I didn't cry tears, but I mourned with every step. I'd lost my entire family. I was alone in the strange world, heading into a future I couldn't imagine.

It was early afternoon before Aiken allowed us a break. Athena started a fire and warmed last night's beans, but there was no room for hunger in the blackness of my soul. I took water and moved away from the others. I felt Aiken watching me with his bright eyes, but he didn't say anything. When we moved on again, I fell in step, but I was numb and silent. I'd escaped the Smith brothers, survived the wilderness on my own for days, faced off with a man to be reckoned with, but now that I was somewhat safe, I wanted to give up. I wanted to lie down and die.

Hours later, it was Honey who came up beside me and handed me a biscuit with a nonchalance that had me accepting before I realized it.

"I used to want to die," she said softly.

I took a bite of the biscuit. It was old and hard, but my stomach rumbled gratefully as soon as I began to chew. "Do you still want to?" I asked. My voice was scratchy.

"Naw, not anymore." She turned those chocolate eyes on me. "Surviving is all a person can control."

There was a twisted logic in what she said, more in what she didn't. If I gave up now, the Smith brothers would have succeeded in wiping out my family, and succeeded with my blessing.

"I miss my people," I said.

"Me, too. But giving up won't get them back."

How she knew what I was feeling, I didn't know, but I felt kindred to her and was grateful for her words.

"Captain says he'll make sure you get to town safe. After that, you decide what happens to you. Give up and you let them Smiths own your soul. Your momma wouldn't have wanted that."

No, she wouldn't have wanted that at all.

She left me then, to finish my biscuit and make up my mind. In the end, there really wasn't a choice. I picked up my feet and joined the others.

CHAPTER FOURTEEN

May 1896
Colorado

The boomtown was more a grimy gathering of tents and lean-tos than anything like a township. They camped close to the shores of a river with the refuse of the makeshift settlement scattered all around them. In total, I guessed there were about thirty tents. The wagon's wheels sunk in thick mud as we rolled in, and it caked our horses' legs. We hopped onto the wagon in an effort to keep our shoes from being sucked off our feet. Filth had never known such luxury. I had never known such filth.

There were no buildings constructed, but a tent with one side open was clearly functioning as a saloon and another as a place to eat. A Chinese man stared out as we passed, watching us suspiciously. The saloon brimmed with dirty, drunken miners, hooting and laughing as they indulged themselves in liquor. One man stepped out and urinated in the middle of the street. When he saw us, he stood holding himself in one hand, a startled grin on his face as he waved with the other. He slipped in the mud as he hurried to tell the others what he'd seen.

The stench defied my powers of description. It was apparent that man and beast alike used whatever space was available to relieve themselves. The remains of meals past littered the widening path of mud that bisected the row of tents. Bones and skinned carcasses lay in between. A few dogs ran beside us, barking and snarling.

I looked at Honey, but she wouldn't meet my eyes. Chick stared out with a blank expression. Meaira watched as if through a cocoon of her own making. What must they be thinking? What must they be feeling, knowing what the night had in store? How could they . . .

Aiken stopped his horse and spoke to a man who'd flagged him down. I heard the word *bath* and the man looked as if he'd been slapped. Aiken conversed with him for a few moments more before riding away.

"He told them," Meaira said, staring at the squalor with a placid expression.

"Told them what?" I asked.

"He makes them bathe first," she said. "They won't be liking it, but if they want their pleasures, they'll be doing it."

I was overwhelmed with relief, though I wouldn't be one that had to endure their foulness. I couldn't bear thinking of sweet Chick, lovely Honey, or dazed Meaira, mauled by any of these disgusting barbarians.

"Is it always like this?" I asked.

Chick shook her head. "No. This bad."

Aiken moved us to a clearing upwind that had not been contaminated by waste. In the growing darkness, we

165

set up our camp. This time, though, we added a canopy, anchored by four corner poles with one in the middle that held the canvas up like a spire. Long sides flapped in the wind and brushed the ground.

No one had spoken since arriving, and the silence rode heavy on the air. The other women avoided looking at me, but I was acutely conscious of their thoughts. A part of me wanted to shout, to stop what we were doing. I wanted to herd the women back into the wagon and rein the horses into a gallop. But none of them seemed as concerned with what the night held in store as I was. According to Chick, they did this by choice, and though they'd told me Aiken was the devil, it didn't seem to me that he'd threatened them in any way to get them to participate in the upcoming festivities. I assumed they would be paid for what they did, but what price would be enough?

A table with folding legs came from the wagon to be set up in the center of camp. Meaira and Honey opened chairs around it. Four thin, rough mattresses that I'd not seen before came from a trunk. Athena beat them with her broom and laid them out in the tent.

It was fully dark by the time Aiken declared himself satisfied with our work. We could hear the men in town brawling at the river as they took turns bathing in the muddied water. I didn't know how clean they would be once they arrived at the camp. I hoped for the others' sakes, the men used soap. Two who were very eager had been scrubbed and waiting for nearly thirty minutes while we finished setting up. They stood like schoolboys in their

Sunday best, hair slicked back, faces clean. Clothes brushed, if not clean or fine.

A light breeze moaned through the night before dancing across our camp to catch at the billowing sides of the tent. Inside, hanging panels had been strung up to divide it into compartments, each with a pallet on the ground. Athena opened a chest and sheets came out to cover the sagging, stained mattresses. Then the girls turned attention to each other, fixing hair and making up. I sat numbly to the side, wondering what I would do once it all began.

Aiken whistled as he shuffled cards at his table and dealt a hand of solitaire. A cigar hung from his lips, the smoke drifting up on the night air to mingle with the other scents. I dreaded the rest of the night, but the waiting was painful in itself.

"Are you ready for us?" one of the scrubbed schoolboys asked.

Aiken flicked a glance over the camp and then nodded. "Yes, sir, we are ready."

Aiken shook both their hands, ushering them forward. The two were young, younger than I even, and they were eager. Without ado, they asked how much for a tumble. Aiken looked surprised. He proceeded to talk the two young men into circles for a few minutes, denying that the girls would even consider selling their bodies for money. They were young, chaste girls who'd had their share of bad luck, but he, the good Samaritan, was taking them to San Diego where they would enter a life of servitude for the

Holy Church. I watched Aiken with a sick fascination as he weaved his tale like a web around them. The men were obviously distressed to think of the beauties becoming servants of the Church, and they did their best to convince Aiken it was a mistake. One even offered to marry Honey and relieve Aiken of his burden.

Chick leaned close to me. "He do this every time," she said.

"Why?"

"You see."

After he'd worked them up, he found out what they were willing to pay and then offered to make an exception, allow the boys private time to converse with the girls for a price that was two dollars less than they'd offered.

"I'm a charitable man, and I can see how you are both fine young gentlemen who wouldn't think of hurting my girls. I can see where you are pained by the rigors of life. Is that how it is?"

A penny wouldn't rattle in either of their heads, but they nodded and tried to look as if they understood what he was saying.

"I will take your money, but only to put it to the good of feeding and clothing these fine, upstanding women. Now who is it you would like to . . . speak to alone?"

They both pointed at Honey, then, seeing each other, one switched and pointed to Chick.

"Now I can't let those two beauties go for such a pittance. Why not Athena? She's older and won't miss the flower of her innocence."

Of course this wouldn't do. I watched numbly, filled with disbelief as the maestro of manipulation worked his magic. Beside me, Chick smirked.

After much conversation, during which Aiken dazzled them with his use of the English language while keeping them in a befuddled act of negotiation, they seemed to reach an impasse. Aiken drew it out even more until at last the two men "convinced" Aiken to take their money— nearly double what they'd originally offered—and Aiken called Honey and Chick over.

He introduced the girls and, in a fatherly manner, handed them off in kind to the young men.

Honey didn't look at any of us as she led hers into the tent. Chick smiled shyly at her partner, who turned a dark shade of red. I heard him say it was his first time as she took his hand. She told him not to worry, she knew what to do.

Honey's boy was nervous, and she had to work at his confidence. Her voice soothed and drifted out of the flapping walls of the tent. Chick's partner was eager and quick. She'd returned to her seat before Honey's had even begun. I wondered if Chick's young man would feel cheated, but the look on his face spoke of rapture. I thought I might be sick. But others had already arrived and they crowded around, eager to be chosen. Athena and I sat off to the side, each silent until even she was called upon to perform inside the tent.

Our campfire became a beacon, and the men gravitated toward it. Not all came for the women. Some came for the cards that Aiken dealt, others were too drunk to be more than just curious. Some tried to beg and borrow enough to visit with one of the girls. Some tried to win the fee gambling.

While they waited for their turns, Aiken entertained them at the card table and proceeded to cheat at faro. From where I sat, I could see the extra cards he'd hidden beneath the table. He was quick and skilled, and I might not have recognized his game had I been on the other side of the deck. He let them win most of the time, and as the perfect host, he ordered Athena to bring his whiskey when she emerged from the tent. He charged heavily for the honor of sharing his bottle, but no one seemed to mind. Sounds of grunting and the musky scent of carnality carried on the hot breeze, which lifted the edges of the tent like skirts and afforded quick peeks into the goings-on inside. I could smell their arousal and sense the excitement buzzing through the men.

I'd been in the shadows, tucked as far away as I could get from everyone else, but when Athena began to serve drinks, someone noticed me.

"I'll take her," a man with short black hair and clean-shaven cheeks said, pointing at me like I was a horse in a corral.

Aiken cocked his head to look at me, and I held my breath for a moment. "Sorry, sir. She's not one of the girls," he said.

"She looks like one to me."

"She is a beauty. Can't say that I've ever seen so fair a face. But she is from a finer breed than my others."

"That's what you said about them, too," another man interjected. "You's just saying it so as you can charge more."

Aiken's smile made my skin crawl.

"Were that the truth, sir, I would have you call me out. But I'm willing to wager this young lady is of yet untouched. What price can a man put on such virtue?"

I jumped to my feet. "I'm not for sale."

"No, dear, for your price would be far more than what any man here could pay."

"Who are you to say what we can or cain't pay?" the first man asked. "I got a bag full of gold in my pocket and a mine that's spittin' out the nuggets."

"He do," a voice agreed. "I seen it with my own eyes."

"I am not for sale," I repeated.

Aiken said, "You heard the little lady. She will not give herself over to the likes of you."

His words were inflammatory, and he knew it. Offended, the man said, "I'm as good as any man. Better than most. I'm good enough for her."

"The lady says she's not for sale," another said.

"She thinks she's too good. I'll show her ain't no woman too good for me. I'll make her come around."

I saw the warring mixture of excitement and disgust on the face of the man who'd spoken on my behalf, and I understood what was happening. I'd become a challenge.

"I think she'd like me better," a new voice said, and a big, burly man stepped through the crowd.

"She ain't gonna get the chance to know. She gonna want only me after she had me once."

"I am not having anyone," I said clearly. "I'm lost, and the Captain has promised me safe escort to a town."

"She's a spitfire all right," Aiken said. "It'd take more than one man to tame her. It's a shame she's not willing to let a single one try."

I watched with horror as the idea of it went from one to another. Honey, Chick, and Meaira were in the tents, and the gusting breeze brought more than quick glances at their activities. It scented the air. I was young, but I knew nothing was as dangerous as a mob of men. My daddy had told me stories that had made my blood run cold.

The black-haired man shook his head and walked away, but the other men moved in closer. I thought quickly. I picked one out of the crowd who looked to be unsure. "I could be your sister," I said to him. "Or yours," to another.

My words hit some of them like cold water, but before I could feel relief, the burly man pushed through and said, "You couldn't be mine. She's got a face like an ass."

Laughter burst out all around him and then enthusiastic talking. I tried to force my point again, but no one was listening to me now. The burly man moved in and took my hand. "I'll be as gentle as you let me be, darlin'," he said to the delight of those behind him. Another man leaned in and told him to loosen me up good.

I didn't wait for what came next. I began to fight. I hit and scratched and kicked and pulled and screamed. Honey rushed from the tent at the sound of my voice and turned on Aiken.

"You can't do this," she said, eyes wide.

"I told them no. I told them twice she was a lady."

I twisted and bucked in the burly man's arms. It looked like I might get help from the crowd, but those who moved forward were held back by those who wished to be next. I couldn't believe what was happening. Had these men lived like animals for so long, they'd ceased to be part of humanity as I knew it?

The man who had me in his grasp nearly made it to the tent with me screaming and struggling for all I was worth. He didn't wear a gun, but my hand brushed a knife at his waist. I tried to reach it, I tried to pull it free, but he trapped my arms, smiling grimly as he hauled me closer. Honey was there, working at his grip to pry me free, begging the man to take her instead, telling them all they could have her if they'd just let me be. But no one listened. My struggles had become a point of fascination. I could see it. None of them were able to look away. I screamed, though I knew it would do no good. It was all happening too fast. It seemed hours since he'd grabbed my hand, but only a few seconds had passed. If I could just slow him down . . . It was then that a horse charged into camp.

From the corner of my eye, I saw the rider, a man nearly as big as his mount. Though his face was in shadow and his clothes covered in dirt, I recognized Sawyer

McCready immediately, and I cried out his name. A part of me acknowledged that I was praying for rescue from a man who was possibly as disreputable as Aiken, but I only knew that I was glad to see him. He pulled his gun and fired into the air.

The sound echoed loudly, and a sudden, stunned silence fell over the small crowd.

"Captain," Aiken exclaimed, pushing out of the throng to stand beside Sawyer's horse. "I am powerful glad to see you."

Sawyer ignored him and spoke to the man who held me captive. "Let her go," he said.

The burly man stared Sawyer down. Having fought to capture me, he wasn't going to set me free on command. "She's mine," he said.

"I'm not yours," I said.

"Let her go," Sawyer repeated. His tone was low, his words hard.

The man hesitated and Sawyer leveled his gun. For a moment, no one moved, and then slowly, his hands loosened. I jerked free of him, and Honey gathered me up, pulling me out of reach before he could change his mind. But I was too angry to just crawl away. I turned on him, slapped his face, not once but twice, staring at him like the trash he was. I saw something flash in his eyes. Something that spoke of a man who might once have lived inside him, a man who would have been shamed by what he'd done. Then it was gone and he struck me back. The blow knocked me sideways, and I staggered. Only Honey kept me from falling. White spots mixed with red danced behind my eyes. Sawyer's gun was cocked before they cleared.

"Fool," Honey muttered as she dragged me away. I didn't know if she meant me or the burly man.

Aiken moved in closer to Sawyer and spoke in low tones. Sawyer listened, watching the crowd with his gun still in hand. After a moment, he nodded. Aiken faced the men, his crooked smile flashing.

"Drinks on me, boys. Let's get back to having a good time."

And just like that, it was over. I couldn't believe it. The men moved away, and Honey sat me down on the crates. I was shaking, and I was terrified.

"Honey, there's still business to do," Aiken said, his voice steady and commanding. "Don't want the boys restless, do we now?"

"You'll be okay here," she said to me, though I didn't think she believed it any more than I did. She stood, and a moment later she led the burly man into the tent. I clenched my eyes against the sight.

Someone touched my shoulder and I jumped, opening my eyes again. Sawyer squatted down in front of me. His fingers were gentle as he tipped my chin and stared at my face. My cheek throbbed, and my eye was swelling shut.

"You're going to have a shiner," he said. But his voice was not steady, and I sensed that the sight of my battered face upset him more than he'd like to admit.

"Thank you," I said. "Thank you for helping me."

He nodded once and stood. I looked up the long length of him, and though just yesterday I'd tried to plunge my knife into him, right then I wanted nothing more than to be in his arms. As contrary as I was to think it, I wanted him to shelter me from this barbaric world that had somehow become mine. I watched the swirling colors in his eyes as he listened to my thoughts. It seemed he might reach for me, answer my silent request, but Aiken chose that moment to approach.

"Captain," Aiken said, clapping him on the shoulder. "Lucky for us you showed up. A mob's an ugly thing. There was no backing them down."

He stared at me when he said it, and I recognized the threat in his eyes. I looked to Sawyer who was nodding. He believed Aiken.

"You pushed them to it," I said fiercely, locking eyes with Sawyer. "He encouraged them, told them they'd have to fight me to get me to surrender."

"Fight both of us," Aiken said, laughing loudly. The sound filled the camp, and I remembered that I had thought him pleasant when I'd first met him.

"She's understandably rattled by what happened, Sawyer. She's confused. I never would have done such—"

At that moment, six men on horseback rode in at a gallop, stopping Aiken midsentence. They pushed through the small crowd of miners without care of who might be in their way. One man jumped just in time to avoid being trampled.

"Is this a party?" one of the riders asked. "Thought I heard a gun, but it sure looks like a party to me. I don't recall getting my invite, though."

I recognized the voice and turned my head to gaze at him full-on.

"I said, is this a party?" Lonnie Smith repeated. He had his gun in his hand, and the dried blood of my family still smeared on his clothes.

CHAPTER FIFTEEN

Gracie was shaking when she walked out of the kitchen, her emotions so twisted that it hurt to breathe. So many nights she'd cried herself to sleep. She'd raised their daughter, unable to answer the simple question, *Who is my father?* because she'd known it would be followed by *Why doesn't he want us?* and the pain of not having an answer that would satisfy either one of them.

Well, now she knew the truth, but it didn't make her feel any better.

Chloe and Jonathan still sat at one of the round tables, but it looked like the card game had ended. Bill stood behind the bar with grocery sacks stacked in front of him. She glanced at the bags before meeting his eyes.

"It looks like we might be stranded here for a while," he said apologetically. "I didn't want to disturb you when I put them away."

"Thank you," she said, blushing. Wondering how much of her conversation had been overhead by the ever-inquisitive Chloe.

The swinging door opened with a little more force than necessary and Reilly came out. He didn't even look at Gracie as he crossed to the stairs and took them up. He was angry. Gracie realized so was she. Angry at him for circumstances he couldn't control. Angry at him for not doing a better job controlling the ones he might have.

Most of all, she was angry at herself for feeling all the mixed-up—messed-up—*longing* that made it impossible to pretend that anything else mattered.

She took a deep, shuttering breath. A logical side of her said Reilly truly had made the right decision all those years ago. Matt was more than a bad seed; he was the whole damn orchard. He wore his hostility on the outside, a snapping turtle with an impregnable shell.

He'd started watching her when she was thirteen. She remembered the unsettling feel of his gaze tracking her. After school. After work at the Buckboard where she was a hostess on Friday and Saturday nights. Outside her house.

Reilly had told him to stop, but he'd only succeeded in making Matt more furtive. Reilly's brother had been the reason for their plan to run away. Her grandmother had been the motivator, and the passion of young—stupid— love had been the catalyst.

She shook her head, only marginally closer to understanding everything that had happened. For a moment, she stood undecided beside the bar. She didn't want to join Chloe and Jonathan at the table, but the thought of being idle upstairs left her chilled to the core. With a stiff breath, she looked around at all the unfamiliar paraphernalia that Grandma Beck had accumulated. She didn't even know what do next. Grandma Beck had cut

Gracie out of her life, and it was a safe assumption that she'd cut her out of her afterlife, too.

But Gracie and Analise were her only living relatives. Where would all her grandmother's things go if not with Gracie? Who would settle her affairs?

With Juliet on her heels, Gracie returned to the kitchen and opened the door that led to the basement. For as long as she could remember, Grandma Beck had used the landing to store empty boxes and old newspapers. She still did. Even if her things went to charity, they would still need to be packed, and Gracie had time on her hands. Perhaps it would give her some insight into the woman she'd hated almost as much as she'd loved.

Grabbing a stack of papers and an empty box, Gracie started upstairs. She passed Analise's room on the way and paused, listening for signs of life. She'd expected Ana to return downstairs after changing, but she and Brendan hadn't emerged since coming back from the doctor's.

She put the packing supplies in the bedroom and went back to Ana's door. She knocked softly, her head close to the wood panel as she listened for a response. Nothing. Not even the dogs barking, and they usually couldn't resist such an opportunity to raise the roof. At Gracie's feet, Juliet cocked her head and gave a low whine.

She tried the door. The knob turned easily; it wasn't locked. But the door didn't budge when she pushed. Gracie put some muscle behind it, shoving hard while a sizzling drop of panic hit her stomach and flared.

She tried again, using her shoulder now while Juliet made a deep, hushed, motor revving in her throat. Not her usual warning of danger, but a low signal of fear.

"Damn it," Gracie breathed as cold sweat broke out over her skin.

Suddenly the hall felt close, dark and thick with something she felt but couldn't see. Like a corrosive mist, it coated her flesh and began to burn. She shot a look over her shoulder. All the doors were closed. No one was standing just behind her, hot breath on her neck. So why did it feel that way?

She gave Analise's door a last desperate thrust, and it swung back with unexpected ease. Gracie stood on the threshold, staring at the serene picture her daughter and boyfriend presented, struck by a deep, inexplicable fear inside. Analise and Brendan lay on top of the purple comforter, arms around one another, both fully dressed. She could see the uneven rise and fall of their chests, the lax expressions on their faces. Sleeping, like the children they were.

Nothing scary about that.

Gracie's gaze moved through the room, searching for the threat she still felt. Tinkerbelle and Romeo huddled behind the beanbag chair, tucked up under the hanging bookshelf.

Hiding.

Gracie knelt down and made a clicking sound with her tongue to coax them out. The dogs swiveled their ears and whined but neither moved. Juliet had remained in the hall.

181

She woofed softly, and the whining stopped. Gracie didn't understand it. She didn't understand where her own fear came from. Nothing in the room had changed since she'd walked in with wonder last night, so what had her on edge?

Quietly, she moved to the bed and looked down. Brendan held her daughter in a gentle embrace, her head on his shoulder, her fingers curled at her check. They looked like a snapshot of young, sweet love. Nothing scary, here.

Tinkerbelle and Romeo watched her from behind the beanbag. Both had their ears pinned, but neither one bolted for the door. They wore the same expressions when they'd been busted eating trash, so Gracie wasn't positive she could make anything of it now.

No closer to figuring out what was bothering her, she left the room, using a round stone she'd found when she was eight as a doorstop. She felt better with it propped open, and the strange, dark feeling eased. By the time she'd moved a few steps away, it had faded altogether, making her think she'd imaged it. This whole place seemed to have that effect on her.

The room Reilly had claimed was directly across the hall. She hesitated outside it for a moment before finally gathering the courage to knock. After a few seconds, he yanked his door open and stared at her with an aloof expression.

"What do you want?"

She wished she knew. She stared past him to the bed where his duffel sat open, his things obviously going in

182

rather than out. The unsounded feeling of unease shifted to one of all too familiar disbelief.

"You're leaving," she said.

Instead of answering, he moved to bed, shoved a toiletries case inside the duffel, and zipped it up.

"Have you looked outside, Reilly? In case you hadn't noticed, you might need an ark to get out of here. You saw what happened to my car, and that was hours ago."

"I drive a Jeep."

"And that makes you invincible? Or are you trying to get yourself killed out there?"

They stared at each other across the room, separated by all the years of anger and a lifetime of loss. Yet their past, bound them just as completely.

"And what about Analise? You just going to take off on her without a word. She figured out who you are."

He paled and shook his head. "I did you a favor when I left the first time, and I'll be doing her one by leaving now."

"Whatever helps you sleep at night," she said, rolling her eyes.

She'd told Analise not to expect too much. She should have told herself. She turned to go when a box wrapped in clear plastic caught her eye. Young's Mortuary was etched on the side.

"Is that . . . Are those Matt's ashes?"

His narrowed gaze moved to the box and back to her.

"You said he died months ago," she went on.

"So?"

"Have you been carrying them around all this time?"

"What's it to you?"

"Nothing, except it gives emotional baggage a whole new meaning. For the love of God, Reilly, is there no limit to what you'll do to avoid unpleasantness?"

He took an angry step forward. Juliet had flopped on the floor. Now she looked up to let him know she was watching him. Reilly didn't seem to care. He took her shoulders between his hands and glared into her eyes.

"Unpleasantness? Sweetheart, this is hell."

Did he mean being here? Being here with her? Or were they still talking about Matt? She searched his eyes, finding a different answer altogether.

"You're afraid," she said.

"I'm not afraid. I'm pissed off. I just want to leave this behind. All of it."

"But that's not what's going to happen. Once you lay Matt to rest you're going to have to deal with everything you've been using him as an excuse to avoid."

"Like you?" he said softly. "Like the woman who didn't think I should know I was a father?"

She pulled back, stunned at the speed of that arrow. Wounded by how deep it sank.

"You gave up your right when you left without a forwarding address."

"Did Analise agree with that? I didn't know I had it to give up, Gracie. I left thinking I was protecting *you*, not abandoning my family."

"And what are you doing now?"

184

The pain in his eyes stopped her next words, though she'd had this conversation in her mind a thousand times. Over the bitter years, she'd honed snappy comebacks and searing zingers that would hurt him. Make sure he knew just what a disappointment he'd been. But now she knew the truth.

"We were both wrong," she said at last.

Reilly let out a deep breath and released her. "Doesn't matter. Like you said, we had our chance to be something together and we blew it."

"So you're going to drive out of here in the middle of an apocalypse and never look back? All that proves is that telling you about your daughter wouldn't have made a damn bit of difference. You'd have left us anyway."

He stared at her, speechless. She let out a breath.

"Don't look at me like that. I'm not going to throw you under the bus, but I won't lie to her for you."

Still, he didn't speak. His eyes were hard, his jaw tight. She had no idea what he was thinking.

"I've hated you for years, Reilly. *Hated* you. I used to dream of this moment. Confronting you. I thought I'd feel triumphant. Justified." She shook her head. "Now that we're here, I don't know what to feel. I just know I don't want you to go. Not like this."

"Why?"

"Because if you do, we'll be stuck in this place."

"Diablo Springs?" he asked frowning.

"In a way, yes. We need to move on. We've been trapped in this limbo for seventeen years. I can't walk away without knowing that we've changed that."

Reilly stared at her. In his eyes she saw a thousand feelings. They merged in the flecked blues and browns of his hazel eyes and became a wall, locking her out.

"I moved on a long time ago," he told her in a voice that hitched with contradiction. "Sorry I left you behind."

Anger welled up inside her, so fierce that it blinded her. Heat snapped in the air between them and sparked all around. "It's like you believe your own bullshit, Reilly. But I never have. Even when we were just kids, I saw through it. You don't like to feel. I get that. Feeling sucks. It is what it is, though, and you feel this. I can see that you do. I can see what you are, and it's not a man who only knows how to walk away."

He laughed softly, unconvinced. "I wish that were true."

"Which part?"

"The bullshit *is* who I am, Gracie. You've always seen what you wanted to see. I've never been part of the fairy tale. It's never been who I am."

"That works two ways. You think you're going to have to save me. You thought so then. You probably still think so. Guess we're both idiots."

"Guess we are."

They'd moved closer. Gracie wasn't sure when, but suddenly her heaving chest met his. Her head was back so she could see his face. He stared down at her with hooded eyes and that same yearning that had driven her crazy since the very first time she'd realized that Reilly Alexander had noticed her. It urged her to hold on to this moment. If she let it go, she'd never have another chance. It might be the epitome of stupidity, but she wanted that chance.

As if reading her mind, Reilly whispered. "What the fuck do you want from me, Gracie? I'm only going to disappoint you."

"Maybe."

Surprise darkened his eyes. Uncertainty shadowed them. Gracie didn't give him the chance to make a decision—wrong or right. She took his face between her hands and kissed him. Earlier, in the kitchen, too much of their past had been churned to the surface. She'd needed a moment to let it settle, to let the doubts sift to the bottom so she could see what was important.

Reilly had done what he'd thought best. So had she. They'd made the decisions of teenagers—the same age as the two *children* who slept across the hall. Using those choices as a measuring rod now would be as foolish as the choices themselves.

Besides, through it all, in spite of it all, there was still this—the fire, the passion that led them to her pregnancy in the first place.

And she missed it, that consuming need no other man had every inspired. Even the relationships that had seemed to have a future hadn't come with the kind of passion that she felt in that moment, with Reilly.

Tomorrow the storm might be over and the harsh face of reality would be waiting. Reilly would probably still leave. It's what he did, and the hard truths they'd shared didn't really change that. But this moment wouldn't be one of their many regrets.

His kiss tasted of surprise and expectation, and she suspected that the whole list of rationalizations that she'd just completed also played in his head. He caught her bottom lip with his teeth, teased her mouth with his tongue. He stole her breath and replaced it with his own.

His stomach muscles tightened when she lifted his shirt, and he muttered something darkly carnal against her lips after she'd stripped it off him. She didn't know what he'd said, but her body did. She arched against him, and shedding clothes became a dance they did together, their bodies in harmony, their hearts beating out a driving rhythm.

He cleared the bed and then lowered her onto the mattress, the heavy weight of him following her down into the softness. She groaned at the feel of him as she wrapped her arms around him and held on. He rested his forehead against hers, their breaths pooling between them as their bodies aligned.

He kissed her mouth so slowly and deeply that she lost herself in the sensation, the taste of him, the scent of his skin. It was familiar and new at the same time, so exciting she could barely breath. His lips moved to her throat and down to her breasts, and her body arched into his touch. He kissed her everywhere, his tongue a soft friction against the underside of her breasts, on her nipples, at the vulnerable hollow below her belly. His fingers began some magical spell over the sensitive flesh between her legs, dipping, rubbing, pushing her to a place she hadn't truly been since the last time he'd touched her so. When his mouth joined their efforts, she had to turn her face into the pillow to muffle her moans.

"Jesus," he murmured against her, tongue insistent, lips and voice catalysts.

She came so fast it stole her breath and made her cry out into the pillow. He held her through it, his touch gentle against the sensitized skin. Then he was kissing her again, the length of him hard against her thigh. She wanted him inside her so badly she almost begged.

"Gracie," he breathed. "I'm sorry."

"Why?" she asked, so dazed that speaking took effort.

"I don't have a condom." His laugh held irony, his breath soft against her shoulder.

"I'm on the pill."

"Thank fuck."

He shifted and entered her in one smooth thrust that nearly made her come again. He cupped her head and held still for a moment while their bodies adjusted to the sensual intrusion. He muttered something in her ear that excited her even more. He started a steady rhythm that filled Gracie with heat, made her boneless and needy. She rolled when he did and found herself straddling his hips, looking down at his beautiful features. She kissed his chest, using muscles she didn't know she had to rock against his hips and bring him deeper into her body.

He sat up suddenly, sinking into her, gripping her thighs and helping her lift and come down. The shift in angle pushed her to the edge and then hurled her into a sparkling oblivion as pleasure rushed through her, turning her into a flame that burned too hot.

Reilly pressed his mouth to her shoulder as he shouted low and soft. His body pulsed with his release and Gracie's clenched around him, holding tight, wanting to stay like this forever.

He eased them both back on the bed, still inside her, still hard. Without a word, he started all over, and Gracie joined him in the dance.

Chapter Sixteen

May 1896
Colorado

I stared at Lonnie Smith's face and I was struck still by the rush of my hate. There was no questioning what he had or hadn't done. I'd seen it with my own eyes. Seen him laugh as he murdered my father in cold blood. Seen him slaughter my little brother and then calmly sit down to eat my mother's stew. I felt as if time slowed to an unbearable measure. I saw a spark pop from the fire and hover in the air. Beside me, Sawyer stood alert but still.

Aiken moved to his seat at the card table, his smile as oily as the gleaming black hair on his head. "Welcome," he said.

But in response to the weapons drawn by Lonnie Smith and his riders, the rough-and-ready man sitting to Aiken's left had drawn his gun and pointed it at Lonnie. I saw others move their hands closer to their weapons.

Lonnie swung the barrel of his pistol to the man's chest. "Don't be a dummy," he said, smiling to show tobacco-stained teeth. "Drop your gun right there by your feet."

The man shook his head. "No, I don't believe I will."

"We don't want any trouble here," Aiken said. "Why don't you put away that pistol and come down for a drink? We're all friends."

Lonnie's smile was cold and condescending. I looked to my right and saw Sawyer standing close, hand resting lightly on the butt of his gun. On his saddle was a rifle. He looked me in the eye, letting me know he was watching me. I searched for the same cold-blooded ruthlessness that gleamed from Lonnie, but I saw none. Just warning. With his eyes, he told me to keep my head.

"You all look good and friendly," Lonnie said as he scanned the campsite and tent.

Behind him, another man stepped down from his horse. And then two others. The riders who had killed my family. They all had their weapons drawn.

"Why don't you all come on out in the light where I can see you?" Lonnie called in the direction of the tent.

My rage swelled inside me until I didn't think I could control it. Sawyer reached out and took my hand. He used it to haul me back, and then he stepped in front of me.

"I said, come on out," Lonnie repeated, raising his voice. One of his riders went to the flapping white tent. He pulled up the side revealing the bare behinds of two men who'd been so engrossed in their pleasure, they hadn't heard or noticed the intrusion. Laughing, Lonnie's man jabbed the butt closest to him with the end of his rifle hard enough to make the man squeal and turn in outrage. When he saw all the guns pulled and aimed, he scrambled off

Meaira and struggled to get his pants on. When he reached for his gun, Lonnie fired at it and sent the weapon dancing across the dirt.

Hands in the air, the men in the tent joined the circle made by the Smith riders. Meaira, Chick, and Honey remained where they were, barely dressed as they huddled on one low pallet, looking out of the open tent with fear. I couldn't see Athena, but I knew she would be close-by.

"You girls just stay right there," Lonnie said, grinning. "We'll be with you in a moment."

Lonnie turned his attention back to the cluster of men standing at the makeshift card table. He gave Aiken's solicitous face a dismissive glance and moved on to the next man. He stopped when he reached Sawyer. I saw him stiffen, saw the tautness like a fine sheen that went down his body. I felt the beat of it vibrate through Sawyer.

"Didn't expect to see you here, McCready," Lonnie said.

"I could say the same."

Lonnie's eyes flicked to me and I braced myself for recognition, for he had seen me with my family the day my daddy testified against him and his brother. Sawyer's tension matched my own until it was painful to stand so still. Lonnie's cold eyes stayed on me for a moment that seemed to last forever. Suddenly, he smiled. "I don't believe it. I just don't believe it. Boys, boys, looky here. Look who we found. Looks like we hit the jackpot."

His brother and men stood with guns pointed, waiting for their orders.

Lonnie leaned forward in his saddle and said, "You'll be coming with us, Miss Beck." He gave Sawyer another challenging look, noting that he stood close to me, noting that his gun was not yet aimed. But when he spoke, it was to Aiken. "Push that money out to the middle of the table," Lonnie told him. "Jake will be happy to relieve you of it, as well as of the little miss there."

Again, time seemed to move slower than possible. I saw Aiken's face tighten. Knew in an instant that he would not surrender his winnings. The same knowledge passed over Lonnie's face, and for a moment, he looked away from me to level the barrel of his gun at Aiken's chest. I didn't wait for him to do more. I lunged forward, grabbing the gun from the holster of the slack-faced man standing nearby and turning it on Lonnie. I pulled the trigger without hesitation, and the gun blasted in a sound that sucked all other noise from the air. It bucked me backward just as another gun fired. I saw cards and money sail through the air, and it only took a second to understand that Aiken had fired through the table at Lonnie, who was already dropping from the saddle, but I didn't know if he'd been shot or was taking cover.

I saw another man stagger, clutching a red stain that spread with hypnotizing speed across his stomach as all around me guns went off like firecrackers on the Fourth of July. Gun drawn, Sawyer shoved me hard to the ground, but he was too late. A red-hot pain sliced through my shoulder and I knew I'd been shot. I screamed as the ground rushed up at me, and then my head hit something hard and all went black.

* * *

I woke to utter silence, the kind that comes only in the deepest hours of night. But it wasn't night. I could tell by the coolness of the air and the freshness of the breeze that it was near dawn. I looked around, not recognizing where we were. The last I remembered, we set camp by the river. The miners' tent town had been close enough to see but far enough not to smell. We were no longer near it.

I raised my head, looking around at the unfamiliar terrain. We must have moved. I frowned. Why had we moved? And then it all came rushing back. The Smith brothers, the men, the gunshots.

I sat quickly, and pain sliced through my shoulder and tried to split my head. I winced, putting one hand to the lump beneath my hair while I stared at the thick bandage wrapped around my bloodstained shoulder with shock. I'd been shot. Carefully, I pushed to my feet, pulling the blanket I'd been covered with around me. I stood. My legs felt shaky and my stomach none too strong, but I didn't fall over. That was good.

Beside me, the other women slept in a row under the tarp that stretched from the wagon. There was no tent, no pallets, no sign of the violence of last night. I staggered to the water barrel strapped to the back of the wagon and got a drink. The horses were tied up not far away. That meant that Aiken was still near. And what of Sawyer? As if in answer, I heard a shuffling behind me and turned to see him by the fire.

He was dressed in the same clothes he'd worn last night, but his hat was off, revealing golden-brown hair that looked darker in the predawn glow. He didn't look as if he'd slept, and his beard was heavy on his cheeks.

He watched me as he rose, and I saw him wince. There was a dark stain on his sleeve. I was not the only one to be wounded last night.

Without a word, he rolled his blanket tightly and tied it to the back of his saddle.

"What are you doing?" I asked.

"What's it look like?"

"Like you're packing."

He lifted the saddle skirt and adjusted his cinch, ignoring me.

"What happened last night?" I tried again.

He paused, running a hand down his horse's neck. The animal gave a low nicker and tossed its head.

"What happened last night?" he repeated softly. "To start, you blew a hole the size of a dinner plate through Lonnie Smith. Guess you won't have to worry about him anymore."

I caught my breath as the memory rushed in, with it the smell of blood and gunpowder and fear that still clung to me. I steadied myself against the wagon.

"I killed him?"

"Wasn't that what you were trying to do?"

Yes, I'd wanted him dead; I'd wanted it so badly, I'd pulled the trigger without thinking beyond the act. And I wasn't sorry he was dead. He'd deserved to die for what he did to my family. Justice had failed to make him pay for his crimes, but I hadn't. I wouldn't shed tears for ridding the world of the likes of Lonnie Smith.

"What about everyone else?" I asked.

Sawyer shook his head. "Can't say who shot who, but five men are dead for it. Two of Smith's boys, three of the miners. Dead. All of them."

"What about Jake Smith?"

"Last I saw he was riding hell bent for leather. Don't know if he'll be coming back."

The blood drained from my face. It left me dizzy and swaying. Lonnie's brother would be out for revenge.

"Your shoulder hurt?" he asked, nodding at the bandage.

"I was shot," I said, as if he didn't know.

"Barely. Flesh wound. Shouldn't give you too much grief."

"How about you?"

He shrugged. "I'll live."

I nodded, watching as he filled his saddlebags then moved to the other side of his huge horse.

"Where is Aiken?" I asked at last, though I really didn't want to know.

"Took off as soon as he saw what he'd done. You weren't the only one out for blood last night."

His voice was mired in sarcasm, and yet I heard something else there. A note of admiration, an understanding that I would be changed by what I had done—no matter what my reasons—a bit of awe at my tenacity. I deserved none of his regard, and yet I thirsted for the reassurance it gave me.

But as I watched him continue to pack his horse, it occurred to me just what he planned.

"You're leaving?" I said.

He gave me a cold and steady look. "We left five dead men back there, and I'll be damned if I'll take the fall for killing I didn't do."

"So you're going to just leave us here? Just like that?"

"Just like that," he answered.

I looked around at the great nothingness. We could be anywhere. "You know we'll probably die out here."

"I know nothing of the sort. I watched you blow a man into eternity last night. I don't think a few days in the wild will get the best of you."

I sucked in a sharp breath and pulled the blanket more tightly around my shoulders. Tears stung my eyes. "I did what I had to do."

"I'm a firm believer in that motto. I think I'll do the same now."

"But . . . but you could take us with you . . ."

"With me? Why? So you can scalp me in my sleep? I'll be perfectly honest, before—" He shook his head. "I didn't think you had it in you. But now I know different."

"No, I'm not . . ." What? A murderer? "You didn't see what they did to my momma, my grandma, my daddy . . . my little brother. You didn't see." My chest was tight and painful from holding back the tears I refused to shed. He stood, staring at me like I was a unique species of bug. As if he couldn't decide whether to stomp me into the ground or capture me in a jar.

I was breathing heavy with the effort to rein my emotions. He watched me, shifting his weight, looking as awkward as I felt. At last I managed to say, "You're going to Arizona territory. To take over a saloon."

"How do you know that?"

"I may be crazy, but I'm not deaf."

He snorted at that, stopping the smile before it reached his lips.

"You aren't coming with me so don't bother to bat them pretty eyes and ask. Sure as hell there's a posse already forming up, coming looking for us."

"So you'll just ante us up to them. Is that it?"

"You're a bunch of whor— women stranded in the middle of nowhere. They'll follow your tracks easy enough, but they won't think you had anything to do with it. Tell them Lonnie did the killing. Tell them the miners started firing blind. They'll believe you."

"A bunch of whores?"

"I didn't mean that. I know you're not a whore."

"But for the grace of God I'm not. What do you think Aiken had in mind for me when you rode up last night?"

Sawyer swallowed as I locked eyes with him. If he hadn't arrived when he had, if the Smith riders hadn't appeared . . . Just a few more moments and I'd have been the strongest man's prize. I let him see that in my face, see how terrified I'd been, and I knew it bothered him more than he cared to admit.

"I don't owe you anything, lady. I'm real sorry about your family. But you got your pound of flesh. Lonnie's every bit as dead as they are now. I never had nothing to do with what they did, though. I'm no killer."

"But I am."

He squatted down to clean his horse's feet. "Only if that's how you're going to see it. From my point of view, I saw Lonnie get shot by one of the miners."

I looked over my shoulder at the sleeping women. If he left us here, it would be my fault. The sun peeked over the horizon in a blaze of muted gold. Only scrub and cacti stretched as far as the eye could see. No river to follow. No game darting in the trees. No trees at all. And what if Jake found us instead of the posse? I'd killed his brother, and he wouldn't let that go. He'd hunt me. And he'd do more than kill me when he caught me. He wouldn't spare the others, either. I took a deep breath, trying to hold back my panic.

"We could help you." The words were out before I'd considered them, but it was true. We could.

"Help me? Into an early grave maybe."

"What's a saloon without women? I thought Aiken had convinced you that you needed them."

"You bartering out their flesh these days?"

"At least give them the choice. Give them the chance. They've been doing whoring to save their lives. Maybe they've been doing it because they didn't have a choice. But if they knew they were working toward freedom . . ."

He looked at me from where he crouched down, inspecting the hooves of his horse. I stared back, trying to make myself appear earnest, beseeching . . . obliging.

"They would work for you, Sawyer. They think you're a good man."

His eyes narrowed as he watched me. "What about you?" he said at last, and his voice was low and deep. It made something in my belly tighten.

"What do you mean?"

"You think I'm a good man?"

Dry mouthed, I nodded. He made a derisive sound that mocked me. He didn't believe it.

"I can't see you taking on customers," he said.

I hadn't meant that I would, but I saw from his face how hypocritical that made me. I was trying to keep us alive, but I was using their bodies for payment.

"I'll do what I have to," I said, wondering where the fierce words came from. Could I, would I really? I couldn't say what I might have done had the burly man hauled me into that tent. To survive, would I have complied?

Sawyer watched my thoughts flash across my face. Then he stood and approached me, his steps slow and measured. I thought of a wolf, moving silently through the underbrush. What was I doing negotiating with this outlaw? He'd helped me last night, but what made me think I could depend on him? He was no gentleman, no knight in shining armor.

A shiver went through me, sending a fine tremor up my spine as the wind teased a strand of my hair across my face. His hand beat mine to brush it back.

"I don't believe you," he said.

I turned defiant eyes up to meet his. It mattered not that I didn't believe me, either. I knew I couldn't let him leave us out here, miles from any sign of civilization, prey waiting to be taken. I had brought this on these women who had taken me in. I was responsible for their being stranded. Yes, they'd been at Aiken's mercy before, but even he couldn't compare to dying of thirst and hunger. That would be our fate out here in the middle of nowhere with barely enough supplies to last a week. That or Jake Smith, who now had the murder of his brother to add to his reasons for vengeance. I'd seen what he'd done to my family. I could only imagine the torture he could inflict on us.

I lifted my chin, showing Sawyer that I would not back down. I would face him and any other man.

"You'd bed a man for them," he asked, his voice tight and dangerous.

He was testing me. I swallowed and nodded. "For us. If it meant you'd see us safely back to civilization."

"What if that man was me?"

My eyes widened as he stepped closer still. The hand that clutched the blanket around me was white-knuckled, but I didn't back up. If I gave an inch to him now, he would ride off and leave us. Just like that. I felt my breath coming in short bursts, but I didn't move, even when his hands settled on my arms.

"What if that man was me, Ella?"

I tipped my head back so he could see my determination, but the sight of those hazel eyes so close, so turbulent, and filled with swirling need, wiped the rebel from me. I watched as if hypnotized as he lowered his face—watched and did nothing to stop him. His lips touched mine, and the shock of it went through me like the bullet had last night. Only pain didn't follow. Heat did. It raced through my veins and lit a fire within me, burning like it had that day so long ago in town. My world had been different then, but not the sensations he caused. Not the spiraling tightness inside me.

A part of my mind spoke in warning, even as my body responded. Suddenly, life had come so close to the edge of death that right and wrong no longer seemed valid. I'd killed a man last night. This morning I was in another's arms. It didn't seem real, and yet every touch, every sense told me it was more real than anything I'd ever experienced.

Sawyer tasted of power and potency. He'd drunk coffee with sugar and it was on his lips, hot as the feelings moving inside of me. My hands let loose the blanket, and it slipped to my feet as I moved my arms up the wall of his chest to wrap around his neck. It never occurred to me to push him away.

His hands slid across my back to the curve of my spine, and he hauled me up hard against him. His mustache was soft against my skin, and his mouth felt like heated satin. His tongue touched my lips, teasing and insisting until they parted and I opened for him. He deepened the kiss, moving his tongue against mine in a caress more intimate than anything I'd ever known. Low inside me everything became hot and liquid. I curled my hands into his shoulders and held on as I rode the wave of feeling that washed over me.

When his hands began to roam again, I didn't protest. My body became a stranger that welcomed any touch he offered. His fingers slid up my ribs and then closed over the soft flesh of my breasts. I caught my breath and held it as awareness emptied me of everything but feeling.

The sound I made stilled him, and for an instant, we were like statues, frozen in a moment of intimacy. Then slowly, he lifted his head and looked into my eyes. I saw wonder and need in the deep flecked swirls, but then it changed and became something else. He pushed me back roughly, glaring at me as his chest rose and fell with his labored breathing. I staggered and caught my balance, looking at him with hooded eyes. I knew my lips were as red and full from his kisses as his were from mine. But the look he gave me was angry, and I felt the need drain as red heat climbed my neck.

"I don't need a whore," he said coldly.

The words whipped through me, and I couldn't conceal the sting they left behind. I wanted to hide my face from him. I wanted to snatch up the blanket and huddle beneath it so he couldn't see me. Once again I lifted my chin and stared him in the eye.

He turned his back, picked up one of his bags, and threw it across the camp with a low rumble of anger. "Damn it," he growled.

The muscles in his shoulders bunched tightly as he cursed more under his breath. But I wasn't afraid. It was foolish to believe, but I sensed that I was winning. He quieted, shook his head, and made a sound of laughter, though nothing was funny. Finally, he turned around and looked at me, still shaking his head.

"Wake 'em up," he said. "Before I change my mind."

CHAPTER SEVENTEEN

May 1896
Colorado

I was trembling as I moved to the slumbering women and bent to gently wake them up. When I reached Athena, her eyes were wide and black in the glowing light of dawn. She stared hard at me, backing me up as she sat.

"You think you in charge of us now? That what you think?"

"No—"

"No? You makin' deals wit Captain for us. I hear you. What happen to killin' him? You sure changed from killin' to kissin' quick enough."

"What you talking about, Athena? Who kissin'?" Chick asked.

"Ask her," Athena said, bottom lip protruding and eyes hard like ball bearings.

I looked at the expectant faces, some still heavy with sleep, some wide-eyed and waiting.

"Look around you," I said. "Do any of you know where we are?"

Chick frowned and shook her head. "We never do."

"But you always have someone guiding you."

"Or dragging, more's the like," Meaira said.

"She gone and tol' Captain we work for him," Athena said.

Meaira's head snapped back.

Honey said, "Is that true?"

I caught my lip between my teeth as I nodded. "Aiken is gone, and even if he does come back, I don't think any of us wants to be here. The Captain was saddling up; he was going to leave us. Leave us here with nothing but a wagon, a horse, and a good wish. At least if we go with him, we'll end up at a town. Someplace we can find our way home from."

"This wagon my home," Chick said.

"She tell him we his," Athena said.

"You'd planned to go when Aiken was taking you," I told them. "The only difference now is we go with the Captain. You think he's a good man. Honey, you said he was, didn't you?"

Honey nodded, watching me with narrowed eyes.

I shrugged. "You've been doing . . . what you've been doing for Aiken and you haven't gotten anything but more of the same for it. Isn't that right?"

"That's right," Honey said.

"With Sawyer—the Captain—you'll have a choice. You'll have a chance to make some money. Money that can help you start over if that's what you want."

"How 'bout you?" Athena demanded. "What choice you get?"

I held my head up. "The same as you."

"You gon' work for Captain?" Chick exclaimed.

"She gon' work under Captain. She kissin' up with him."

Honey's eyes rounded. "You were kissing the Captain?"

My face was burning, but I nodded. "I had to prove I meant what I said. I told him we would be an asset."

"He know we got asses."

Meaira snorted. "That he does."

"Well, now he knows I have one, too."

"And you gon' use it?" Athena said with disdain.

I thought I might throw up. I found myself repeating my words to Sawyer. They tasted no better with time. "I will do what I must to survive."

They exchanged glances in silence.

I was banking that somewhere in Sawyer was a man whose honor wouldn't allow him to use me that way. I was betting that he'd put me on the first train east. But where would I go? I had no family. No money. All I could do was return to Alamosa and give myself to the charity of the people there. I thought they would take me in, but what if Jake Smith decided to hunt me even there?

I shook my head. I couldn't think about that now. I needed to get beyond this moment, this day, this problem.

"We need to hurry," I said. "He'll leave us if we're not ready."

They jumped up and began gathering things together. By the time Sawyer had returned from watering the horses, the women were up and ready. He gave them each a steady look, ending with me.

"I'm not your babysitter," he growled at them. "I'd as soon as part ways here. Any of you want that, you just say so."

"Ella say you gon' let us work in your saloon and keep some of our money," Chick said, her voice high and thin and clear.

Sawyer looked at me with an expression of such disbelief that I might have laughed.

"That's right," he said. "If that's what you want."

I was as surprised as they, but I didn't let it show.

"But there's no guaranteeing Aiken won't be in Diablo Springs by the time we get there. If he is, you're on your own."

He gave a nod that spoke the rest. I could see from their faces that none of the women needed it spelled out. They'd said it themselves: they belonged to Aiken. Sawyer wouldn't fight for their freedom. That they had to do alone.

Sawyer's eyes lingered on me for another moment, and just that one look brought a fresh wave of awareness to me. An anticipation I was ashamed to feel but couldn't deny. How I'd gone from wanting him dead, to begging for help, to hoping for his touch, I didn't know. But there it was.

He tossed Athena the harness. "You gotta earn your keep, though. Not waiting for none of you. You fall behind, I leave you."

The last he directed at me. He couldn't have been much clearer than that. Once again, he didn't need to be. We all understood.

"Would you like some breakfast before we go, Captain?" I asked sweetly.

He stood, hands on his hips, looking as if he wanted nothing less.

"And some coffee," Honey said with her pearly smile. "A man needs his coffee in the morning."

"You sit by the fire, Captain. Just go on," Chick said. "Athena and me, we get the horses ready. We get it all ready. Ain't that right?"

Athena was still glaring at me. "What *she* gon' do?"

"She gon' take care of Captain's breakfast. Make sure he don't need nothing."

I swallowed. "That's right. I believe we still have bacon, Captain. And biscuits. May I bring you some?"

He looked as if he'd been poleaxed. "You going to shoot me with my mouth full?"

"What would be the benefit of that? We need you, Captain McCready."

I couldn't make out the words he said under his breath, but I was sure they were curses. Reluctantly, he let Chick take the saddlebags from his hands, and Meaira and Honey set about packing things up as I prepared a quick breakfast, served without hesitation.

CHAPTER EIGHTEEN

May 1896
Colorado

With Sawyer hurrying us, we left just as the sun rose up over the horizon in a brilliant shower of reds and gold. It chased back the violet of predawn with a radiance that brought hope. Still, we could not ignore the anxious watch Sawyer kept at our back or the way his gun stayed close at hand. I was worried too. Though Lonnie Smith had been the leader of their gang, Jake was the one most feared. I was sure it was Jake who had violated my mother before shooting her. I was sure he wouldn't hesitate to do the same to me or the others.

Chick drew near me and paced me in silence for a while. We had yet to speak of what had happened last night. I didn't want to talk about it now, but I could see she wouldn't let it go.

"Thems last night was who got your family," she said.

"Yes."

"They done shot holes through everything. We's lucky we was low. Your shoulder hurt?"

"Not much."

"I's glad you get Captain to take us. Athena, she just mad. She just mad 'bout a lot of things. She glad, too."

I glanced back at Athena on the wagon bench, stern and straight and looking like she might not have ever been glad about anything.

"I wish Aiken got shot," Chick said softly.

I had to agree, though not out loud. Justified or not, I had enough blood on my hands without wishing for more.

Honey stepped in time with us. She smiled at me and said, "That was brave what you did."

"I didn't even think first. All I knew was what I'd seen him do to my family." I looked down. "I've never killed anyone—anything—before. Not even a chicken."

Honey took my hand in hers. Chick took the other. "You did what you had to. That's not what I was talking about, though," Honey said. "What you did with the Captain. It was brave. But don't worry, Ella. You won't have to make good on it. I'll see to that."

"How?" Chick asked before I could.

"I'll do her share."

"Me, too," Chick immediately agreed.

"I can't ask that," I said. "I made the bargain."

"You didn't ask. And you don't have a choice. You find yourself something useful to do when we get there, and I'll take care of the rest. Something that doesn't involve the men. Can you cook?"

"Not like Athena. And I don't think she'd let me in her kitchen anyway."

Honey nodded.

"I can sew."

"She good at that," Chick said.

"And I know cards." The last was true, but surprising to be offered as a skill. Though as soon as I said it, I realized it might be my salvation. I could play as well as any man.

Honey raised her brows. "Can you deal?"

I smiled and nodded. "I'm quite good, actually."

"Let me tell the Captain," Honey said. "I'll tell him tonight."

Something in the tone of her voice implied the conversation would take place under intimate circumstances. A stab that could be nothing but jealousy hit me at the thought of Sawyer and Honey locked together. Of his lips on hers, of his tongue tasting her the way he'd tasted me.

When I looked back at Honey, she was smiling. "Like that, is it?" she asked softly.

"Like what?" Chick wanted to know.

"Don't worry yourself. I see the way he watches you. Even when you're trying to stick him like a pig."

I knew my face had turned an ugly shade of red.

"Like what?" Chick said again.

"Like things are looking up for us, Chick," Honey said. "Maybe Aiken will get lost or shot somewhere."

Chick giggled. "I say my prayers."

The sun felt good on my skin, and the companionship of Chick and Honey warmed my heart. I was moved by their generosity and caring.

"Honey," I asked, "how did you come to be here?"

Once, the question might have held a hint of censure. Most likely, that note of disapproval had been there when I'd asked Chick, but just this morning I had joined the ranks of those whose fate was decided for them. I understood that choice did not always make itself available.

It took a moment for Honey to answer me. She looked down at her feet as she gathered her thoughts.

"I'm sorry," I said. "It's not my business."

"You have a right, I think," she said. "You may wish you hadn't asked, though, once you hear it."

She seemed to be waiting for something, and I nodded. She nodded back, as if we'd sealed a pact.

"Used to be I lived with a white family. My grandma had been their slave, though they were kind and fair. When my momma was born, they raised her with their daughter. And when Miss Hazel grew up and got married, my momma went with her. Even after the war was over, my momma and daddy kept working for them. I was born the same year Miss Hazel had Elizabeth. Elizabeth and I were brought up like sisters. We shared everything. When her tutor came to teach her, he taught me, too. I loved her, and she loved me."

Honey's voice was low, and it seemed to vibrate with pain as she spoke. Chick and I stayed quiet, waiting for her to continue.

"Miss Hazel died when I was twelve. She left my momma and daddy part of her land to work for their own and a house to live in. Her husband, Mr. Walton, asked my momma if she would let me stay with him and Elizabeth. She agreed, and I was happy to stay. Mr. Walton used to take me and Elizabeth everywhere. We were like dolls that he'd dress up and parade around. He never got over losing Miss Hazel, but he poured all his love into me and Elizabeth. I remember once we went into a restaurant and they wouldn't serve Negroes. I told Mr. Walton I'd wait outside, but he wouldn't hear of it. He was like that. I was a person to him."

She grew quiet, and I thought perhaps this tale was too painful for her to continue.

"We were in Atlanta where Mr. Walton had frequent business when Aiken saw me."

"I remember," Chick said. "First time he lay eyes on Honey, he say, *I gon' have her.*"

"How old were you, Honey?"

"I was fourteen. He arranged to meet with Mr. Walton and then casually commented on his beautiful daughter and his Negro. Mr. Walton took offense right off. I was not his Negro. I was his daughter's cherished friend." She paused. "Aiken talked circles for a time, trying to find out just how it was. He figured Mr. Walton was doing dirty by me and using Elizabeth to hide his deeds. But Mr. Walton was a pure man. I've never met another with such honor. Aiken offered money for me, and Mr. Walton told him I wasn't a possession to be bartered or sold."

"I 'member Aiken come back and he so mad he spittin'," Chick said.

215

Honey looked down. "I don't think I slept right until we left Atlanta. I knew, even then, that Aiken wouldn't take *no* for an answer. A few weeks later, we returned to Atlanta and it was as if Aiken had been lying in wait for us. Once again he approached Mr. Walton and made pleasant small talk. He then invited us to dinner. He said his sister was in town, and it would give him great pleasure to entertain us. He felt badly for causing offense, so he said, and wanted to make it up. Mr. Walton was too polite to decline, though I knew he would have liked to."

Chick squeezed Honey's hand gently.

"We met at a restaurant and had a fine dinner. Aiken's sister was quiet and subdued. She seemed almost unaware of us and barely touched her food. Later I would learn her name was Meaira, and she was not his sister. I've seen her many times after her dose of laudanum, but she's never been as gone as she was that night."

"I don't understand," I said.

Honey went on as if I hadn't spoken. "The next day Elizabeth became ill. We called the doctor who couldn't determine what ailed her. Her lips turned a dark purple and her skin so white she seemed to glow. I stayed by her side, but there was nothing I could do. She was taken by fits and then she died."

The silence that followed those words was deafening. "What did she have?" I asked.

"The doctor couldn't determine the cause. Mr. Walton was stricken with grief so deep he could not get up in the morning. I tried to tend to him, but he refused all comfort.

He wouldn't take food or water. Within a few weeks, he too was dead."

A sick feeling came over me as I listened.

"I returned to Raleigh, where the Waltons and I were from, to bury them both. Aiken came to the funeral. He told me then that he would have me, and I realized what he'd done to my Elizabeth. I accused him, but I had no proof. The doctor had seen no wrongdoing. I was a Negro woman in the South accusing a white man of murdering my friend."

She shrugged as if nothing else needed to be said. In truth, nothing else did. My horror was so overwhelming I couldn't have responded anyway.

"He told me I would regret not taking his offer. I told him I would not." She looked down, and I saw tears in her eyes. "The next morning we found my nine-year-old brother's body on our porch. He'd been dragged by a horse until there was nothing left of him to recognize but the shoes on his feet. I have five other brothers and one sister. When Aiken came again, I went."

CHAPTER NINETEEN

Gracie dozed in Reilly's arms for awhile, lulled by his even breathing. He'd fallen into the kind of sleep that made her think of the shadows under his eyes and the exhaustion she'd seen on his face. She suspected it had been a long time since he'd really slept.

Her body was sore in places she'd forgotten existed, and she wanted to stretch like a cat and snuggle into his warmth and sleep as well, but fear of being caught in Reilly's bed—naked, no less—kept her awake. The last thing she wanted was for Analise to awaken and come looking for her.

Face aflame at the thought, Gracie carefully eased from his side. Reilly shifted but didn't wake, thank God. Now that the heat of the moment had passed, doubts began to crowd in, and her brain—which had disconnected the moment they'd kissed—began a barrage of reasons why his bed was the last place she should be.

Quietly, she searched for her clothes and dressed. Juliet watched from the door where she'd been asleep, too, and lumbered to her feet when Gracie tried to open the door.

The hall outside was as silent as it had been when Gracie had made the monumental decision to knock on Reilly's door. She crept to Analise's door and peeked in. Both Analise and Brendan were still sleeping. Tinkerbelle and Romeo still lay behind the beanbag. Their heads popped up but neither moved.

Alone but for her sentry, Juliet, Gracie tried not to think too much about anything as she entered Grandma Beck's room. Especially Reilly and what they'd just done. That was hard to do when his scent was on her skin, tantalizing and mysterious as the man himself. She kept discovering a tremulous smile on her lips and misplaced hope in her chest.

She caught sight of herself in the mirror over the heavy dresser and stared, hardly recognizing her own reflection. Gracie Beck may have been a foolish young girl, but she'd grown to a responsible, if staid, adult. Not the kind of woman who jumped into bed with a man she hardly knew—regardless of their history. But she had, and despite her misgivings, she was pretty sure she was glad she'd done it.

"It was just sex. Nothing more," she said under her breath.

But she couldn't align the words *just* and *sex* in the same thought with Reilly. Everything about him exceeded *just*. He could light her up with *just* a glance and she'd still be burning hours later.

After all this time.

And now that she knew he hadn't abandoned her, all those self-defense mechanisms she'd fostered were failing. He'd been protecting her. If Grandma Beck had told him where she was, he would've come for her. But her grandmother had lied to them both. And Mrs. Graham, who'd taken her in and cared for her, had obviously been an accomplice, stopping her mail from coming or going. How else could she explain why no one knew where she'd gone? Why no one had written her back?

She sighed, fishing her cell phone out to check the time, wondering how different her life might have been if Reilly could have simply texted her back then instead of relying on house phones and the post office.

She needed to call Young's Mortuary to find out when her grandma's body would be released and arrangements could be made for her burial, but there were still no bars, no signal of any kind, on her phone. She'd also need to call Mr. Lassiter who handled all the legalities of the Diablo. He was the only lawyer Grandma Beck had ever trusted, so Gracie couldn't imagine that she'd used anyone else for her will.

She also needed to get a tow truck out to haul her car out of that ditch, but the booming thunder and torrential rain mocked that idea and told her it wouldn't be happening anytime soon. She wouldn't risk driving in this weather, anyway.

She took a deep breath and slowly let it out. The box she'd brought upstairs earlier waited on her bed beside the stack of newspapers. Faced with going downstairs and having to deal with Chloe and her consorts, making funeral arrangements, or staying here and packing Grandma Beck's possessions, she decided to go with the latter. Maybe it would give her some insight into the enigma who'd been her grandmother.

She had her back to the door when she heard a tentative knock. She turned, heart thumping as she braced herself to face Reilly, but it was the priest she found hovering just at the threshold with an apologetic look on his face.

"I'm sorry to disturb you, Ms. Beck, but I wondered if I could speak with you for a moment?"

Gracie nodded, but her reluctance must have shown on her face.

"I won't keep you from your packing," he said. He had a kindly smile and warm eyes. Had he not arrived with Chloe, Gracie might have liked him on sight. He came in, turned the straight-backed chair at the desk around, and sat. "I wanted to offer my services."

"I'm not a very religious person, Father. I don't need—"

He held up a hand. "Call me Michael. I am not ordained by any church. I am a man of God, though, and I wear this collar to remind myself of that." He looked around him for a moment, as if unsure how to continue. Juliet padded over to him, sniffed his feet, and then flopped on the floor, completely at ease with his presence. Michael reached down and scratched her behind the ear before continuing.

"My father was a Baptist reverend and my mother an Episcopalian priest," he said. "There were always heated conversations in my house about theology and worship, but never about some things. Never about faith or God. And it was a given in my house that people like Chloe Lamont, people with psychic abilities, were nothing more than heathens. The devil's children. There were no exceptions. When I realized that I was one of them, that I had those same abilities, I believed that made me an abomination. While I don't often see eye to eye with her, Chloe taught me that we have a gift, not a curse. She helped me come to terms with what I do while still considering myself worthy of God's love."

Gracie didn't know why he was telling her this, but the gentle sincerity of his words kept her quiet and listening as she wrapped frames in newspaper and put them in the box.

"You see," he said, "my gift is that I can see things that happened a long time ago. And sometimes I see things that haven't happened yet."

She looked up. "And this is the service you're offering me? I appreciate the gesture, Michael, but I've had a glimpse of my future. I think that's all I can take right now."

"The baby?" he said.

She nodded, beyond questioning how he knew.

"Ms. Beck, there is a reason why Chloe has come here."

Evidently.

"She tells me she wants to end a cycle, a curse that has been on her family and yours for over a hundred years."

The curse. Yes, Gracie knew all about the curse. Her grandma had lived in fear of it. It had warped her sense of reality in the end. The curse had been part of her reason for sending Gracie away until the baby was born. No doubt, the curse was the reason she'd cut off all contact with Gracie afterward.

"I see you know what I'm talking about."

"My grandma believed all the women in our family were cursed. She thought sending me away was the only way to save me and the baby."

"Because the curse is connected to Diablo Springs?"

She lifted her shoulder. "She was never sure. She was afraid to stay and she was afraid to go." Gracie gave him a sad smile. "She believed my mother's soul was trapped in the springs where she died. She didn't want to leave her."

Michael listened with rapt attention.

"Crazy, huh?"

"On the contrary. But I think there's more to it. I would like to know what that *more* is, before I become a participant in it."

His quiet reasoning soothed her stretched nerves, despite the controversial subject. If she was honest, Gracie had to admit he intrigued her.

"You think you can tell me why my grandmother was so convinced it was true?"

"I would be honored if you'd let me try."

Gracie hesitated. "What do I have to do?"

"If you would allow me to touch you—just your hand—and also an object of this house? Something your grandmother owned, perhaps? One of these pictures?"

Gracie had found a small snapshot on the dresser. In it, her mother held an infant Gracie, with Grandma Beck standing just at her shoulder looking down at them both. Even then, she looked worried. Gracie swallowed a lump of emotion and handed it to Michael. "Will this do?"

"Yes." He indicated the bed. "May I sit?" At her nod, he settled on the edge and carefully removed his gloves. Then, with a shy smile, he lifted the picture in one hand and reached for Gracie's fingers with the other.

She didn't know what she'd expected, but the soothing warmth calmed her. She sat beside him and watched his face as he closed his eyes and let the silence stretch until Gracie should have been uncomfortable, but in his stillness was a sense of something coming. Something that snapped into focus as he began to speak in a rapid, stream of consciousness flow.

"Her name is Carolina, and she's at a funeral. Her mother's funeral. Ella? Yes. Carolina is Ella's daughter.

She's crying, but inside she's relieved. She's glad her mother is dead."

"Why?" Gracie asked.

Michael went on as if she hadn't spoken, and Gracie realized he'd put himself in some sort of a trance.

"Ella was always fearful. Superstitious. She kept such a tight watch that Carolina was afraid to breathe sometimes. She was crazy. That's what she's thinking. Her mother was crazy. Even on her deathbed, she'd been screaming about a curse. A family curse. A man named . . . Jason . . . Macon . . . Aiken? Yes, Aiken. Carolina is frightened. Ella said he was in the Dead Lights. He didn't stay dead. He didn't stay dead."

Goose bumps covered every inch of Gracie's body. Who didn't stay dead? Who was Aiken? What was he talking about? Michael's voice rose and fell, becoming more strained as he spoke.

"She's in the Diablo now," he said. "She doesn't think of Ella anymore. She's forgotten that he didn't stay dead. Business is good." A strange smile curved his lips. "Oh," he said. "She has famous guests. Eleanor Roosevelt is here. She's thinking that the president's wife is sleeping in a room once used by prostitutes, and it makes her laugh." The smile dimmed. "There's a man now. His name is Jimmy, and she likes him. He wants to marry her. She is happy. Happier than she's ever been. He tells her about another place . . ."

Michael paused. Gracie could see his eyes moving beneath his closed lids. It was like REM, only he wasn't asleep. He still held her hand, his fingers warm and dry.

"Glenwood Springs," he said triumphantly. "He tells her about Glenwood Springs and how business is booming there. He wants to expand. He wants to make the Diablo like that. There's to be a wedding . . . and a baby. Jimmy's baby. She's so happy. Happy. She's making wedding plans . . . but . . ."

His pause stretched, and Gracie waited impatiently, wanting to press him but knowing it would do no good.

"Chloe is here now."

At first she thought he meant Chloe was in the room with them, and she glanced over her shoulder, expecting to see the old woman. But then he began speaking again.

"She's come to warn Carolina. She . . . Chloe says there's a curse and a man who didn't stay dead. There's a curse. We're cursed. Carolina wants her to leave. Go away . . . go away . . . She's at a funeral again. Jimmy is dead now. The springs . . . underground caverns . . . dynamite. An explosion . . . it opened up a cavern and the water moved underground. Disappeared. Jimmy went with it. Dead. He's dead. Dead Lights. The Dead Lights come. Every night they come. They're looking for something. He's looking for something. Has to find it. Has to find it. Looking for . . . someone . . . It's his. She's his. Dead Lights. Dead Lights. He didn't stay dead. It's true. It's true. Everything Ella said. He's looking for something. Searching. The curse, the fear. He—"

"What's going on?" Jonathan asked, stepping into the room and scaring Gracie to death. She jumped to her feet with a yelp, yanking her hand out of Michael's light grasp. The trance he'd been in was broken instantly. He bounded out of the chair, the picture frame he'd held slipping from his hand and falling to the braided rug at his feet. Gracie bent to pick it up, feeling dizzy and frightened.

"What are you doing?" Jonathan asked, staring back and forth between them.

"Talking," Gracie said, like they hadn't acted like guilty children. "Did you need something?"

"No. I didn't mean to interrupt. I just heard you say you were looking for something, and I thought I could help."

"I appreciate that," Gracie said, forcing a smile. "But no help needed."

Beside her, Michael had gone very still. Jonathan eyed him curiously.

"I know a lot about the history here," he said. "If you're interested."

Gracie nodded noncommittally. Michael snatched up his gloves and hurriedly pulled them on.

"Maybe later, Jonathan. Right now I'm a little busy with grandmother's things."

He gave the box an surprised look. "She left everything to you?"

There was no censure in his tone, yet there was something sly in the question, like he knew something she didn't. Maybe he did. Grandma Beck might have bequeathed all her worldly possessions to her caretaker for all Gracie knew. She resented his intrusion, though. She kept her expression blank and gazed steadily back without answering his impertinent question.

"You won't find what you seek," Michael said softly.

Gracie wasn't sure who the statement was directed at, but both she and Jonathan gave him a startled look.

"What do you mean?" she asked.

"Some things aren't meant to be found."

With that, he bowed his head and took a step toward the door.

"Did you learn what you needed to, Michael?" Gracie asked before he stepped through.

"I did."

She wanted to ask specific questions but not in front of Jonathan, who seemed as astute as stone when it came to the nuance of rejection.

"I need to study some of my documents," Michael said. "I'll come find you later."

"What documents?" Gracie asked.

Michael blushed. "I'm endlessly fascinated by the past, Ms. Beck. I carry a piece of it wherever I go." He smiled but his kind eyes held concern. He nodded, leaned in, and said in an undertone, "In the Dead Lights."

She nodded, though she wasn't sure why. With another courtly bow, he disappeared down the hall.

"He's a strange one," Jonathan said.

"He's a very nice man."

"No offense intended," Jonathan said, blushing. "Do you need some help in here?"

"Thank you, no. I think I just need some time alone."

At last he seemed to take the hint. Nodding, he closed the door behind him and left Gracie alone with her troubled thoughts.

CHAPTER TWENTY

Reilly woke up alone. For a moment, he lay in the shadows, vacillating between relief and disappointment. Even when he'd been deep inside Gracie, so caught up in her that he could barely breathe, a voice had been warning him not to get too comfortable. She'd come to her senses and be gone before he knew it.

He just hadn't realized how soon *soon* would be.

"Fuck," he whispered, rubbing his hand over the shadow on his jaw. He exhaled heavily and got up, got dressed. In the bathroom, he took a quick shower, hoping that once he washed her scent from his skin, he'd be able to banish her from his head. No surprise it didn't work. He avoided his own gaze in the mirror as he brushed his teeth, just as he ignored the questions circling in his thoughts.

What did it mean, making love to Gracie? What did he *want* it to mean?

In the hallway, he paused, giving the closed doors a dirty look. The house was so still that he could hear his own heart. Where was Gracie now? In her grandmother's room? He thought about searching her out, but they'd come together with so much unsaid between—and now, the unsaids had doubled.

His stomach growled. He'd scrounged something to eat this morning, but that seemed like years ago. The hope that the bags he'd seen Bill bring in early held food pulled him downstairs. He hadn't gone far before a familiar scent made him pause and sniff the air. Roasting beef, fat crackling in the heat, spices baking until they released their perfumes. His mother hadn't been much of a cook, but she could cook the hell out of a pot roast. He started to follow the smell when the nimble fingers of disquiet traced down his spine, making him pause. Brows pulled tight, he tried to isolate the source of the unease.

Nothing was moving around him, no doors swinging insidiously shut. Yet, it was there, that sense of foreboding. Frowning, he continued down the stairs. The smell was stronger down there. It made sense; he was closer to the kitchen. Only now he noticed something sweet in the aroma, something that didn't belong.

He paused again on the first floor, trying to place it. Chloe sat at one of the tables, looking old and weathered. She watched him with her dark, knowing eyes.

"You cooking something?" he asked.

She shook her head and pursed her lips.

"Who is?"

"No one."

He hated that the subdued answer made him feel like ants were crawling over his skin. "You don't smell that? It's roast."

"I smell it."

A nervous tick twitched her eye, cracking her airtight facade. Surprised at how it shook his composure, Reilly passed her on the way to the kitchen. Though the rest of the house had finally cooled somewhat, it was warm in here, the scent of roasting beef overpowering. Suspiciously, he opened the oven door. No hot blast and thick aroma wafted out. The oven was cold and empty.

There wasn't a Crock-Pot tucked away on the counter, either. Nothing to explain the mouthwatering scent anywhere.

"Nathan." Chloe's voice came from behind him, almost scaring him out of his skin.

His spun to find her standing at his back. "Jesus, quit creeping up on me like that."

"It started about an hour ago," she said. "I thought I was the only one who noticed it."

"This is an old building. Maybe the rain is letting some of its odors out."

Chloe almost smiled. "You're quite accomplished at justifying things that can't be explained."

"Yeah, well, I've had some practice."

"If you're hungry, Bill was kind enough to bring back chicken. It's in the refrigerator."

"Thanks."

Reilly opened the fridge and saw a two king-sized buckets filled with fried chicken on the top shelf. He recognized the logo on the side. Diablo Springs was too small for a big chain grocery, but the market down the street had a deli and made great fried chicken. He snagged a piece, grabbed a paper plate and napkin from the holder on the counter, and went out to one of the tables. Chloe trailed him like an annoying toddler at a family reunion.

"May I talk to you for a moment?"

"Is that a rhetorical question or do I have a choice?"

"Are you always so rude when you're frightened, Nathan?"

"I'm not *frightened*. And don't call me Nathan."

"I'm sorry. I know it bothers you, but when I see you, the name is always in your mind. Did you know that?"

Reilly finished the chicken, wiped his hands and fingers, and leaned back in the chair, resigned to her conversation.

"You hate it because it was your father's name and you hated him."

A deck of cards sat in the middle of the table. He reached for it and began to shuffle.

"And now you resent me, because I've made you see it."

Eyes narrowed, he looked up, and his gaze locked with hers. "Chloe, what do you want?"

"I want to know when your brother Matthew began to change."

She stood poised on the other side of the table, as though she might run if the conversation turned south, which it very well could. She looked frailer than she had just last night. And older. So much older.

"You okay, Chloe?" he asked gently.

She gave him a weak smile. "The last time I was here, I was younger and stronger. I was able to block them out."

"Them?"

"The voices. Diablo Springs is full of voices, and they all want to be heard."

He started shuffling again, thinking about that. "You talking to dead people, now?"

"Since I was a little girl and my mother died."

He stood up and moved to the bar in a futile search for some booze.

"Try the panel against the wall," Chloe said, pointing.

Reilly moved to the end of the bar and pushed the strip of wall near the corner. He heard a soft *snick* and the panel popped open, revealing a small storage room he'd have never noticed otherwise. Inside, three shelves of dusty bottles stood in wait. Reilly pulled out a bottle of amber twelve-year Macallan scotch and smiled.

"Join me?" he asked Chloe.

"How could I refuse."

He grabbed two glasses from the kitchen and sat down at the table. After they'd both savored the burn for a moment, Chloe said, "Your brother . . . He wasn't always such a monster, was he?"

Way to kill the joy. Sighing, he said, "No."

"But you never understood what happened to him, did you?"

"I understood fine. Life happened. My dad happened."

"And when he killed your father . . ."

Reilly downed the rest of his scotch and poured another. His heart was doing a tango in his chest, and his hands felt clammy. Chloe stared back at him nervously, like a rabbit in an open field.

"Matt didn't kill our dad."

He heard her swallow, but her words didn't hold the same sense of fear her expression did. "Covering up for him has always been a way of life for you, Nathan. You lied to protect him, even though he still had blood on his hands."

"I didn't always protect him."

"But you were the good son. Then you were the good brother. Now it's time to be a good man. Be a hero, Nathan."

He snorted. "You and Bill been out in the back getting stoned, Chloe?"

She gave him another of those leveling looks. He wanted to stride out of the room. He wanted to get in the Jeep and plow through the river-filled roads until he could go no farther. But he couldn't make his legs and feet cooperate. Just as she'd made him bite at her bait and come here, she'd hooked him with her leading questions.

"My father was an abuser, too," she said. She walked over to the picture hanging above the mantel and pointed at it. Each step seemed to cause her pain. How had she aged so much in so little time? Reilly found himself glancing around, looking for Bill. If she keeled over, he wanted Bill around, but for once, Chloe Lamont was alone.

"That is my grandfather," she said, pointing to a man who stood just at the corner of the picture.

The statement blew every other thought out of Reilly's head. Her grandfather? Why would Carolina Beck have a picture of *Chloe's* grandfather hanging in her house? He came to stand beside her, staring at the tidy man in the pinstriped suit standing just shy of the background. His disbelief turned sour as his gaze shifted from the sepia print to the woman beside him.

She watched him as he noted the similarities she shared with the white man in the portrait. The shape of their faces, the small, tucked ears, the pointed chin, the piercing gleam in their eyes.

"He's my grandfather." Her voice dipped. "And he is also my father."

"What?" Reilly asked. "He can't be both . . ."

But even as he said it, Reilly realized that he was wrong. It was possible that he could be both grandfather and father, it just wasn't right.

"You ask yourself, how could a man violate his own daughter? The answer is worse than you can imagine. In his mind, my mother was an animal, as was her mother. Animals do not have the rights of parentage. They have no rights at all."

Reilly didn't know what to say, but she didn't seem to expect a response.

"He was old when he came for me. But his hate and anger had turned him into something stronger than a man half his age."

It took a moment for Reilly to register what she'd just said. *He was old when he came for me.* The bastard had impregnated her grandmother, her mother, and he'd gone after Chloe, too? It was sick beyond his understanding, but he didn't think for a moment that she was lying. The raw shame in her voice was too real.

"I was a young woman, still in school when it happened. It killed my mother, knowing what he'd done. Eventually, she died of her despair."

A logical part of Reilly wanted to argue that someone couldn't die of despair, but the night he'd stood in front of the mirror and shaved his head, his own anguish had felt great enough to kill him, hadn't it?

"Why are you telling me this?" he asked.

"Hear me out. Please."

Reluctantly, Reilly nodded.

"For generations my family has told stories about this man." She pointed at the picture, revulsion on her face. "We thought he was dead once, but it was merely a fool's hope. My mother believed he couldn't be killed and that he haunts our family still. Carolina Beck also held this belief."

Reilly looked at the picture and back at Chloe. He didn't know what to say.

"My grandmother lived in this very place. Here, at the Diablo."

Her pause felt more than weighted. It felt of things he couldn't understand, things she didn't want to explain. The heaviness of it filled the stillness until it seemed like sand, shifting, but so dense it threatened to crush them.

"Why are you here, Chloe?"

She moved back to the table and sat down with an exhausted sound. Age hunched her shoulders and darkened the crescents beneath her eyes. When she spoke, it wasn't to answer his question.

"Even before I understood what there was to be afraid of, I knew my mother was frightened. It was in the way she'd watch the horizon, the way she'd check the locks after dark during a time when people didn't lock their doors. It was in the shadows of her eyes. We were like animals in a cage, trapped by our own fears. Our family stories told of how we'd tried to get away from him and how he always tracked us down and made us pay." She looked at him. "Do you know what my mother's name was? Misery. They named her Misery. She was a child born of pain, and my grandmother wanted her to always remember that."

"That doesn't make sense."

"No, it doesn't. Sometimes sense cannot be made from violence. You, of all people, should know that."

He nodded in acknowledgment, but he couldn't quite meet her steady gaze. Quietly, he splashed more scotch into both their glasses. Chloe gave him a weak smile and downed hers.

"He still plagues my family. I believe he plagues Gracie's, as well."

"Plagues? He can't still be alive?"

"Can't he?"

"If he was old when you were a girl, then he'd be over a hundred, hundred and twenty by now."

"His body, yes. Not his spirit."

"You're talking about ghosts, again."

"There *is* another world, Nathan Reilly Alexander, and it exists within our own. My gift, my curse, is that *I feel* the spirits around me. Sometimes I can help them find the resolutions they seek. Sometimes I can only suffer alongside them."

He glanced at the kitchen. He could smell the potatoes and carrots roasting alongside the meat, now.

"I have visions. Terrible visions. I *saw* the murder of Gracie's mother."

"She fell into the springs, Chloe. Hardly murder."

"In the middle of the night? Why would she be out there, in a place everyone in this town fears?"

He said nothing. More disturbed than he cared to admit, he glanced at the picture again. He could feel Chloe tightening the threads of her tale, and he knew that somehow he'd end up at its center.

"Diablo Springs has been haunted by evil for years, Nathan. Your people talk of the Dead Lights as if they're some phenomena of steam and moonbeams. But no one mentions all the bodies in those caverns. You know there are many."

He knew. It was probably chock-full of dead bodies. But evil spirits . . .

"My, that roast smells delicious," Chloe said.

"Old houses smell. Damp brings it out."

"Of course. What else could it be?"

He turned his back on the picture. "Cut to the chase, Chloe."

"Three months ago yesterday, my mother came to me in a vision."

She watched him closely, watched a reaction he couldn't stop sweep across his face. Three months ago yesterday, Matt died.

"Every night since, she has come. Last night she was joined by Carolina Beck. Nathan, your Gracie and her daughter are both in danger."

"Because of your visions?"

"Because it's *true*," she cried, anger making her voice sharp. "Do you think I *want* to be here? I have tried to forget this horrible place my entire life."

The throb in her voice struck Reilly deep. Hadn't he tried to forget Diablo Springs in the same way? Hadn't he found a way to survive by wiping his memory of everything that had happened prior to his leaving here? It wasn't that he forgot; it was that he didn't choose to remember. And being back now was like peeling the scab off a festered wound.

"I came because I want to stop *seeing* Diablo Springs. I'm an old woman. I want to know peace before I die. Now I ask you again, when did your brother change?"

Reilly didn't even have to think about it. Matt changed the night their father had beaten their mother to death. The night Matt had returned the favor.

He wished it weren't so easy to play the memory in his head, but something like that you never forgot. After their father was dead, he and Matt had shoved his body behind the wheel of his old Grand Prix and rigged it to drive right into the springs. For weeks after, every time he closed his eyes, he saw those taillights wink an instant before they plunged down into that pitch-black hole. He could still here the boom and screech of metal twisting.

As they'd stood watching, the clouds had shifted and the moon broke free. Reilly had looked into his brother's face then, and he'd seen it. He'd seen the change. As if some kind of exchange had been made. A deposit. A withdrawal. His dad for his brother.

Reilly knew what came next. He knew he wouldn't be able to stop Chloe from prying deeper any more than he could have stopped that night from happening. He stood and strode to the window, staring out at the storm.

He said, "Why are you asking me questions when you know the answers? Who wouldn't change after what we saw, what we lived through?"

"You didn't."

"The hell I didn't."

She braced herself against the back of a chair as she faced him. "I know what's in your heart, Nathan. I know you yearn to remember your brother as a good man. You don't blame him for your father's death. The law was willing to believe your story; this town was willing to turn a blind eye to what was obvious because they knew your father and they'd done nothing to help you boys or your mother against him. But after that . . . after that, Matt changed. He wasn't a monster before, but he became one, and you couldn't protect him anymore. Wouldn't you like to know why? Wouldn't you like to release his spirit from the guilt of this world? Wouldn't you like to release yourself from the feelings of failing him?"

Reilly swallowed around a lump of emotion. He didn't answer. He didn't move a muscle. He couldn't.

"Do you know why your father beat your mother?"

"Because he could."

"Yes, because he owned her. And nothing in this world would ever change that. If she'd left him, he'd have followed. No matter where she went, he would have found her."

Reilly stared at a point over her shoulder, fighting to keep the tide of his feelings from spilling over. Spilling out.

"My grandfather felt the same about these women," she said, gesturing to the picture again. "He still does. You've recognized the woman in the middle, haven't you? You see the resemblance between her and Gracie. She's Gracie's great-grandmother, Ella."

"If you say so."

"She's the one he wants."

"Well, that should make it easy then. She's dead, he's dead. Let him have her."

The look on Chloe's face made him regret the words as soon as they were spoken. "Would you condemn your *brother's* soul to hell so easily?"

She didn't wait for an answer. He supposed his expression was answer enough. If he could save Matt's soul, he'd do whatever it took.

"There are only women in the Beck family. You've noted this, I'm sure. Each generation is another chance for my grandfather to have his precious Ella." Hatred flashed across her face. "He lured Gracie's mother to the springs. He lured her daughter there, too. *Your* daughter."

His daughter. On the heels of the thought came a rush of protectiveness that stunned him.

"I told you last night, *you* are part of the story. And I gave you the excuse you needed to come. I'm here to end the cycle, Nathan. I'm here to send my grandfather to the other side."

"How?"

"There are two reasons why he won't leave. The first, as I've told you, is Ella and her lineage. He considers the Beck women his possessions. He wants them back."

"And the second reason?"

"He's searching for something. Something lost. Again, something he believes belongs to him."

"And what is that?"

She looked guarded for a moment. "I don't know."

"I think you do."

"That's because you don't believe what I'm telling you. You're looking for a concrete *thing* that will explain it all in a tidy way."

Fair enough. "So how do you plan to accomplish the ending of this cycle?"

"I want to do a séance, Nathan. Tonight. I need Gracie and Analise in my circle. And you. We are all connected in ways I don't understand. My mother, your brother, Gracie, and now Analise. I have to know what happened. I need to see the past so I can protect against the future."

Reilly laughed. "Are you out of your fucking mind? Even if I believed everything you said—which I don't— I'm not going to be part of a *séance*. And your kettle's cracked if you think Gracie will stand for it."

"She will if you ask her."

"Which I won't. There's a lot of history between me and Gracie, Chloe. None of it inspires the kind of faith in me you're imagining."

Chloe's smile was resigned. She shook her head and took a step away. Like magic, Bill chose that moment to appear, and Reilly had to wonder how long he'd been listening. Mr. Rogers chose that moment to make his way down the stairs, too, looking surprised to find them there. He was a shitty actor. He'd probably heard the whole damn thing. Suddenly royally pissed off, Reilly splashed more scotch into his glass and gave the caretaker a look that said, *Open your mouth and lose some teeth.*

Chloe leaned heavily on Bill as he led her to the stairway. "You don't have to believe in me, Reilly, but think about what I've said. If I'm right, it could bring closure to years of pain. And if I'm wrong . . ." She shrugged. "Think how good it would be in your new book. The atmosphere alone would be mesmerizing. And should

I prove true and raise a spirit or two, my, my, wouldn't that be something."

Oh, she was manipulative. She cast that hook effortlessly and snagged him with her sly lure. But he didn't bite. Chloe stared at him for a moment, surprise widening her eyes just a little. She thought she'd have him that easily. What made him angry, though, was the desire to sink his teeth into her bait. She was right. Without him even being aware, the structure of a story had been building and linking in his head, and now he saw it, standing like the wooded framework of a house, waiting for the walls, the windows, the paint. It was huge and precise. And if she delivered on a séance tonight, and he could capture that in words and mood . . .

"You've let her down before, Nathan," she said, her eyes now sparkling with an inner knowledge he resented even more. "What if I'm right? What if this time you could help?"

"Help with what?" Jonathan asked. He moved to the table and eyed the bottle. "Where'd you find that?"

Angry, Reilly swiped the bottle off the table and moved away, the smell of roasting meat so strong it was sickening now.

"You cooking something?" Jonathan asked innocently.

"Get the fuck out of my face," he snapped.

Jonathan raised his hands and gave a shaky laugh. "Sure thing, Clint. Just don't shoot me."

Jonathan muttered something about *assholes* and headed into the kitchen. Finally alone, Reilly turned back to the mantel and the picture. He stared at it, seeing more than he had before. From the start, there'd been no missing the resemblance between Gracie and the woman seated in the center of the picture. That alone had dominated his attention. Now the tidy man in the background became a young, pasty version of the woman who'd just left.

But as he stared from one face to another, he saw more. Beside the pinstriped suit was another man, one nearly concealed by the shadows and the smoke. Reilly moved closer, staring into the man's face, prying his features from the faded picture. Like an optical illusion where the image is hidden until you stare at it long enough, the man's face jumped into focus. Reilly took a step back. Then another. But now that he'd seen it, he couldn't *unsee* it no matter how hard he tried. Couldn't believe it, couldn't dismiss it.

That man looked like someone else who'd been gathered here in this throwback saloon in this ghost town that wouldn't quietly fade away.

That's man's face looked very much like the one superimposed on the glass that covered it. That man looked like Nathan Reilly Alexander.

CHAPTER TWENTY-ONE

June 1896
Arizona Territory

We'd been on the move since daybreak, following the sun as it arched across the sky. Sawyer kept us off the road, though how he navigated through the great openness I'll never know. He seemed certain we were heading in the right direction, however, and none of us thought to question him. He could have led us to hell and we'd have followed.

I spent much of the time mentally replaying the kiss he'd given me, blushing at my own detailed memory. Inside, I was knotted up by recollections of the way his touch had moved me, had made me respond to feelings I didn't even fully understand. It was as if I had two minds, one that kept me on this path and moving forward, another that wanted only to return to his arms and be held and kissed and awakened to the wonders of flesh.

My face grew hot again. I tried not to think of the way our passion had ended or the sting of his cold words. *I don't need a whore.* Well, I wasn't one, but I'd offered myself as if I were, hadn't I? I thought about this and wondered if perhaps I'd confused him as much as he'd confused me. I thought he'd pushed me away because I was acting like a whore, but as I examined each nuance of those moments together, I began to see another possibility. When he'd pulled back and looked at me, I know I saw the same startled ardor in his eyes that must surely have been in my own. But what had he been thinking? I'd just told him I would join the girls in their profession. Had he imagined that I was playacting while I was in his arms? Pretending to be carried away by the tide of needs that pulled us together? Performing to prove my point?

It would explain his anger and his cruelty. He had no way to know that the desires he'd fanned inside me had managed to completely disable my brain. There hadn't been a thought in my head beyond what I would feel next. Even as I considered all of this, I acknowledged the ridiculousness of it. So what if we had both felt the same consuming passion? Nothing could come of it. Sawyer was not the kind of man a banker's daughter settled down with.

After we rested the horses and ate, Sawyer slowed our pace. I hoped that meant he felt we were safe from whoever might be following, but I knew that was a child's way of thinking and I no longer had the liberty of comforting myself with falsehoods. My world revolved around harder, colder realities now. I had killed a man, and though I felt fear when I thought of it, I did not feel shame. Lonnie Smith deserved my bullet, and should I be found by a posse, I wouldn't deny it. If it was not for Jake Smith, who I was certain was hunting me now, I would turn myself in and face the consequences rather than live life on the run. But I wouldn't bring peril or the unwanted eyes of the law into this makeshift family of mine. I had put Sawyer McCready in danger twice now—once when I tried to kill him myself and then again when I'd shot Lonnie Smith.

A strange bubble of laughter rose in me. It would be a justified irony if Sawyer were as afraid of my violent nature as I was of his shady past.

I looked for him ahead and found him riding not far away. He was watching me from beneath the shadows of his hat, and my face grew hot imagining he could read my mind. He looked away and so did I, but many times after, I found his gaze on me. Many times I found mine on him, too.

We didn't speak until midafternoon, when he dismounted and fell into step beside me. Startled, I looked around and realized I'd been moving fast and I was a good distance ahead of the others. I hadn't been aware of it.

"How's your shoulder feel?" he asked.

"Sore, but not unbearable."

"Athena did a good job patching you up."

"Athena did?" I asked. My voice betrayed my surprise.

He raised his brows in question. "Athena's a good woman."

"I know. I just didn't think she liked me much."

He grinned. "I don't think she's so wild about me, either."

"Oh, but she is," I argued. "I've never seen her so warm and friendly around any of the rest of us."

I think he was pleased, but he didn't say as much. I liked him better for his words about Athena. It's easy to care about people like Honey and Chick and even Meaira. But it took character to find the good in someone who looked at the world through her anger.

We walked in silence for a few moments. Our feet made a soft thump against the hard ground. In the distance I saw a coyote race across the rugged terrain. Sawyer saw it, too, and quietly tracked its path until it disappeared. I saw in his eyes a kinship with the predator, in the simple act of hunting to survive.

I cleared my throat and looked away. I needed to break the silence. I asked, "This town where your saloon is, this Diablo Springs . . . Have you been there before?"

"Nope."

"Did you know *diablo* means *devil*? Why is it called Devil Springs?"

Sawyer shrugged. "The man who sold it to me—"

"Lost it to you in cards."

"That's right," he said, looking at me out of the corner of his eye. "Lost it fair and square. He said that some people think the town is cursed."

"Why?"

"Used to be Apache land, but they got run off."

"And they cursed it?"

"That's what they say. Others say it was named because of the hot spring. Hot-hell-devil. That's how they named it."

"A natural hot spring? I've heard of them."

"He said the town wasn't much yet, but it's growing like a weed. The more he drank, the more he talked. He had big plans. Not sure what we'll find when we get there, though."

I hoped for the best and he must've seen it on my face because he grinned.

His mouth caught my attention and brought a rush of memory. I could still feel how my heart seemed to stop somewhere between beats as he stepped closer. How my breathing ceased as he trapped me in his gaze and held me tight. His voice had been low, low enough to brush against my senses like suede against my skin. The greens and browns of his eyes had darkened, like water with a deep undertow.

"You feeling sick?" he asked.

"No. Why?"

"Your face got red all of a sudden. You feel all right?"

"I . . . Yes, yes, I'm just warm."

"You can ride," he offered, hooking a thumb at his horse.

"You'd give me your horse?" I said.

He frowned. "Not to keep."

His seriousness made me laugh. "I didn't mean to keep. I just . . . We haven't actually been friendly."

His gaze made an imperceptible shift to my mouth, and I read his mind this time. For a moment, we'd been more than friendly.

What if he took me up on my offer? What if there was no "what if" in that question? He'd made it clear the women were all a burden. He didn't want us and he damned sure wasn't doing us any favors. We'd be expected to work for our keep. That included me. And if he came to me, what would I do? I'd committed us all to this path.

I squared my shoulders. I had not been raised to sell myself to a man, but I had not been raised to let another shoulder my burdens, either. I peeked up at Sawyer through my lashes. Although if I was honest, was the burden as heavy as I thought?

I realized he'd stopped walking and was looking from me to his horse.

"No, thank you," I said, more forcibly than I'd intended. "I will walk."

Sawyer frowned at my sudden rigidness, and I saw our friendly camaraderie vanish. I was both happy and sad to see it. I would be smart to keep my distance from Sawyer McCready.

* * *

The first thing I noticed about Diablo Springs was the filth.

I'd become adjusted to the thick layers of dust, sand, and grit many days ago when the trees and grasslands had become a faded memory, replaced by low scrub, spiky yucca, and short barrel cacti that wore rings of bright-yellow fruit on their tops. There were also towering green man-shaped cacti with hats of tiny bell-like blossoms. Sawyer called them saguaros and told us they were the smartest plants alive. They stored water in their tall trunks, and when the wind blew them off-balance, they'd grow an appendage to straighten themselves out. We saw clever little birds living in holes they'd drilled in the meaty flesh of the giants. Sawyer said if you ever got lost in the desert, the liquid in the cactus's skin could keep you alive.

After we climbed into the foothills, Sawyer consulted a hand-drawn map and then we found a trail, which led us up a steep incline. As the sun rode low in the west, we crested a peak and looked down at Diablo Springs. We were each silent as we viewed the lone street and the makeshift houses and tents sprawled haphazardly in the valley. From our vantage point, I could count five buildings, two on either side of the narrow roadway and the biggest on a rise at the end. It seemed that there were more people walking to and fro than there were residences to house them. The man Sawyer had beaten at cards had been right. Diablo Springs was growing like a weed.

"Ain't as bad as the last place," Chick said with a bright smile.

But it wasn't as good as we'd hoped. Like the other mining town we'd visited, it appeared to be the kind of place where stagecoaches didn't stop. Where men shot one another over cards and urinated in the streets. Where sheriffs were appointed because they were mean, not ethical. Where outlaws felt safe and honest men frightened. And where women were rarer than the ore that was mined. I couldn't make out a single skirt moving in the streets. Perhaps the women were inside, avoiding the mud and filth.

What Sawyer thought of his new town, I didn't know. His face remained closed as he stared at the dirty encampment.

He asked us to climb into the wagon so as not to start a riot when we got there. We jumped to obey. Only Athena could be seen at the reins as our wagon lumbered into town. Still, men stopped to watch us pass as they mingled in and out of the few establishments. From the back of the wagon, I saw the assayer's office, a tent with the word *food* painted on the side, another space selling tools, and beside it, a general merchandise store.

A man was hocking the personal belongings of his partner, who'd been shot the night before, next to a carpenter hard at work on a coffin. Scattered on the hillside beyond we saw grave markers, several of them fresh. The young town was no stranger to death.

The street was muddy from horse urine and droppings, and the town stank as badly as the mining camp had two nights ago. I didn't understand how people could live in such filth, but without women to guide them, I was beginning to think men reverted to bovine behaviors.

"Lord in heaven," I heard Athena mutter.

A large, matronly woman stepped out from a tent and stared. Behind her was a table spread with bread and pies, and as we passed a whiff of something freshly baked overcame the less pleasant smells. Two men sat at a table inside, eating. I felt better knowing there was at least one other woman here, even though her eyes were cold. Another tent like we'd seen in the mining camp ran a boisterous business of selling liquor to intoxicated men. There were few places to sit and most stood shoulder to shoulder, lifting their glasses and watching us pass.

A young man raced out beside Sawyer's horse and shouted to him, "Hey, you the Captain?"

Sawyer frowned. "Who wants to know?"

"Who wants to know?" the man yelled, walking beside him. "Hell, just everybody. We been waiting for you to get here and open the damn saloon."

Laughter came from up and down the street, and Sawyer smiled back.

"Angus told us you'd be here a week ago."

"Well, I'm here now."

"And thank God in heaven. We've been drinking old Hank's piss water. Angus promised the best liquor in the West, and then he never even poured a goddamned drink. How long until you open? I guarantee you'll have a line awaitin'."

"Hate to disappoint you, but there's nothing to drink in there yet. It's going to be a day or two before my first shipment of whiskey is in."

That brought mixed reactions. Some of them cheered for the whiskey, others moaned for the delay.

"Which one of these places is it, anyway?" Sawyer asked.

The young man laughed and said, "Are you blind? It's right there."

From the shadowed interior I saw the stunned expression on Sawyer's face, but I couldn't see where the man pointed. Sawyer thanked him and continued down the street. He stopped his horse at a hitching post in front of a surprisingly tall building, and I understood his shock. It was the biggest building we'd seen from above. It was on a natural rise of sorts, and so it lorded over the other structures on the road, making it seem enormous. Additionally, it was two, possibly three stories high, and built of sturdy wood with a shingled roof. A sign hung over the door with brilliant red letters painted in the hollowed out channels: the diablo springs hotel and saloon.

Though it was nothing more than a wooden building in a town made of canvas and mud, it had a look of permanence about it that was somehow heartening. Steps led up to the railed wooden porch that stretched the length of the first floor. The door was locked tight, and the handles chained. Sawyer pulled a large key from his saddlebag and opened up. Only then did he gesture for us to come out. We were all acutely aware of the eyes that followed us as we emerged from the wagon and went inside. You could feel the excitement charge the street, and it frightened me. I had not forgotten the mob at the mining camp. Sawyer made a show of checking his rifle before carrying it in with him. I was glad of it.

Inside still smelled of freshly chopped wood. The ceiling and walls were rough paneled, but they were even and mounted with care, as if the builder had planned for it to last forever. The floors had the same rough look but compared to the mud, they seemed as beautiful as marble. A plain stair case hugged the wall to the right. Straight ahead was a wide open room with a handful of tables and a bar against the far side.

The bar had obviously been constructed by a person who loved his craft. We all moved to it, as if beckoned. The wood was rich, golden oak and it gleamed like glass. Ornate carvings marked the supports every few feet, and a brass boot rail shone bright as day. Behind the counter, a beveled mirror reflected the five of us standing with identical looks of wonder on our faces. Sawyer let out a low whistle as he surveyed the place.

"You didn't expect this?" I said.

"Hell no. I was half convinced I was going to find a tent and a deck of cards and feel a fool for coming. I had no idea it would be like this. What kind of idiot gambles this away?"

He was so incredulous that I found myself viewing the place through his eyes. I didn't know what a saloon should look like, but if the conditions outside were a measurement, the Diablo Springs Hotel and Saloon was opulent. And it belonged to the outlaw Sawyer McCready.

"How much was wagered when you won this place?" I asked.

"Twenty thousand dollars."

My mouth fell open. I could see the same reaction on the other women's faces.

"Where did you get so much money?" I asked without thought to the appropriateness of the question.

"Won most of it. Had some of it."

The way he said it made me think he was lying. It wasn't my business, but I suspected that Sawyer acquired that money by means of a bank holdup. Wisely, I kept my opinion to myself. But I wondered if we had more than Aiken Tate, Jake Smith, and a sheriff's posse to worry about. As if we needed more.

"Aiken put up what I was short."

He said the last as he headed for the stairs. We followed him up to a long hallway with doors opening along the side walls. There were rooms in all, and inside each was a made bed with a mattress and a small table. The whole place smelled clean and unused.

Sawyer grinned, exchanging glances with all of us. "Looks like we're done sleeping on the ground," he said.

"You mean, we gets to sleep in here?" Chick exclaimed.

"Hell yes," he said.

Chick squealed with excitement. "Can we pick which we want? Cuz me'n Athena we want here, if that awright?" she said, pointing to two doors across from each other without consulting Athena first. Sawyer shrugged. Taking that as a *yes*, Chick skipped in and flopped on her bed. She let out a shout of pure joy. "Soft as a cloud," she said.

Meaira pushed through to the next room and spread out on the mattress. Laughing, Honey did the same. Athena approached the door Chick had claimed for her with hesitant steps, as if she expected to be stopped. She looked back, and Sawyer gave her a small nod. She eased her bulk onto the bed and broke into a smile that lit the room.

"This here nice, Captain."

Sawyer turned and started down the hall. "Which one do you want?" he asked, looking at me as he reached my side.

I know my face turned an awful shade of red. I nodded at the next open door and walked stiffly to it. Sawyer came and leaned against the doorframe, watching me with wolf eyes as I stopped beside the bed.

"Aren't you going to try it?" he asked.

My face grew hotter as I sat down on the edge. The mattress was soft and feather filled. Not hay, not ticking. I smiled and leaned back, more aware of the eyes watching me than the comfort welcoming my body. I turned my head to look at him and our eyes locked for a minute. That look made me glad I was lying down. He made me feel boneless and warmed to the soul.

He pushed away from the door, and I thought he would step in. Instead, he gave me a knowing smile and walked away. I put my hands over my hot face and tried to slow my heart down, but all I could think of was that look and the promise it held.

It didn't take long for us to unpack the few possessions we'd carried in the wagon. I had nothing but my daddy's gun and hunting knife, both of which Sawyer returned to me. As soon as we'd carried the last item inside, there was a knock on the door.

"We're closed," Sawyer called out without bothering to answer it. We heard the knocker hesitate and then walk away. A few minutes later another knock came. "Still closed," Sawyer said. And so it went until after dark when the last of them decided that Sawyer meant it and really wasn't going to open the door that night. I think he would have if there had been any liquor to serve, but the bar was bare. It was hard to believe it had never opened its doors and served a drink before. The men of the town took their thirst and presumably quenched it at Hank's.

We could hear their hell-raising drifting down the street to the other end from where we were. We'd noticed from our bird's-eye view that the tents and makeshift houses sprawled away from the saloon, so we were somewhat isolated on our plateau at the end of the street.

Later, after Athena had made us something to eat and the dishes were done, we girls were upstairs laughing and enjoying our new rooms. Sawyer came to find us.

"I'm going down to the springs," he said to all of us and none of us at once.

"Where are they?" I asked, standing in my doorway.

He walked into my room and pointed out the window. The other girls came in, too, and crowded around. The pools of water were dark in the early night, but the moon was bright and cast a glow on their surfaces.

Chick asked what we were all thinking. "Can we come?"

Sawyer's nod elicited another round of squeals and giggles from us. We all seemed to be drunk on our good fortune to be staying beneath a solid roof, unmolested by the men at least for the night, and to lay our bodies on a real mattress when we went to sleep. It was beyond anything I thought I'd see again.

Happily, we followed Sawyer downstairs and out the kitchen door to the back of the hotel. There were no tents here, no squatters in sight, and I was relieved by that.

"Do you think this is all part of the Diablo's grounds?" I asked.

"It could be. Why else aren't there any tents back here?"

A wooden bridge had been built between the springs and the Diablo, making the short trek easy. As we approached, we could see the steam rising off the pools and smell the heavy sulfur that came with it. The planking continued in a sort of deck around the largest of the pools. If we sat on the edge, we could dangle our feet in the water.

It seemed we all thought of it at once and immediately began taking off our shoes. Sawyer reached down and ran his fingers across the surface.

"I'll be damned," he said. "It's like a bath."

The word *bath* brought up all of our heads. Chick got her shoes off first and hiked her skirts up so she could put her feet in. "Ah, Lord, that good."

"I haven't had a bath in ages," Meaira said. "Not a real one."

She had that hazy look about her that I was beginning to understand went with the laudanum. She gave us all a dreamy smile, and then without hesitation, she stripped down bare and slid into the water.

"Is it deep?" Chick asked. "I cain't swim good. Athena, neither."

"No," Meaira said, and she stood to show them.

That was all the invitation the others needed. They shed their clothes as easily as they had their shoes and jumped in with Meaira. Sawyer watched with interest, I with jealousy. Their sighs of ecstasy filled me with longing. A bath. A hot bath . . .

"Ain't you comin'?" Chick asked, splashing merrily. Her golden-brown body gleamed beneath the murky surface.

Sawyer sat down beside me and took off his boots and socks. As I watched, he stripped his shirt and his pants. His eyes were on me when he reached for his undergarment. Blushing in the dark, I looked away until I heard him splash into the water. I watched with envy as the women frolicked around Sawyer and each other like sleek seals, wet skin against wet skin until at last my jealousy wouldn't be ignored.

I unbuttoned my blouse and pulled it from the waist of my skirt. I pretended that the dark concealed me, but I knew my skin glowed like pearl in the moonlight. I quickly removed my shirt and my skirt. Dressed only in my chemise, I looked up to find Sawyer watching me from the black waters.

He didn't look away when I caught him, didn't pretend to stare at anything but me. I stood for a moment, knowing I couldn't pull that last garment off with him watching me, but I had no other clothes and I would need these to be dry when I came out. At last, I turned my back and stripped the chemise to the ground. For an instant, I stood naked, wrought with feelings and sensations I'd never known. My breath was coming in shallow gasps that at once hurt and excited me. Before I thought better of it, I turned and ran into the water. The look Sawyer gave me as I skimmed the surface rivaled the steam in its heat.

The girls gathered around me, their skin as slick as the damp heat soaking into my body. They had no modesty, no shame in their nudity, and they frolicked like children. Honey swam beneath the surface and, in a flash, Sawyer went under. He came up laughing, sputtering, and launched himself at Honey. The girls screamed with glee and splashed away but the game was on, and before I knew it, I was playing, too. Our laughter echoed off the thick bank of clouds and seemed as foreign as the hot pool of water in the midst of the desert. We shushed one another in case our voices carried to the tents and men in town, but it felt good to laugh. It felt so very good.

Then Sawyer was there in front of me, low in the water so only his head and shoulders appeared from the surface. I watched him move closer, our eyes level with each other. Our breath joined the rising mist and created a cocoon around us. I was never so aware of my nakedness, of his. He swam closer still, watching me with his unusual eyes, only they seemed darker, like a reflection of the opaque surface of the water. The voices of the others seemed to fade in the mist, and it was only me and Sawyer, the shining moon, and a million stars. A light beard covered his cheeks, glinting gold and red in the moonlight. His hair was wet and slicked back from his face, his skin browned by the sun. He was a man who took his shirt off when he worked. My father would have been scandalized by that, but my father was not a survivor.

I caught my bottom lip with my teeth, and Sawyer stared at it like it was the most interesting thing he'd ever seen. His hand came out of the water, and he drifted closer to me. His fingers, warm and rough and wet, slid over my jaw, and his thumb rubbed up against my mouth.

A small sound escaped my lips, a sound I'd never known myself to produce. It was a sound of satisfaction, a sound of need. I'd wanted him to touch me. I wanted more.

As if I'd voiced it all in that one sound, Sawyer moved closer still, until his bare chest touched mine. His skin felt like hot silk. My hands found their way to his shoulders without my being aware I'd made the decision to touch him back. His went to my waist, and in the same movement, he kissed me. His lips were soft and the kiss questioning.

I should have pushed him away, I knew he was not a man to trifle with, but my lips softened beneath his and anything tentative about the kiss vanished. His arms tightened around me, pulling me to the hard muscles of his chest. My legs slipped between his as he held me off the soft bottom of the spring. There was no mistaking the other hardness that pressed against my stomach. But the feel of him sent signals to every part of me, making me want to wrap my legs around his hips and hold on tight.

My own wanton thoughts terrified me and brought me to reason with a rush. I pushed away and swam to the side as fast as I could. I scrambled awkwardly onto the platform and grabbed my clothes, pulling the chemise I'd hoped to keep dry on over my wet body as swiftly as possible.

My skin was hot now, and the damp chill felt good. I was breathing heavily. I tried not to, but I couldn't seem to stop taking a look back. Sawyer had swum to the other side of the pool. I couldn't see his face through the thick steam, but I could feel his eyes watching me. Enticing me. And truth be told, I wanted to return to him. I wanted to touch him. I wanted to feel him and let him show me the mysteries between a man and a woman.

"You done, Ella?" Chick asked.

"I'm overheated. I think I'll go back."

I heard Sawyer's laughter follow me as I fled inside.

CHAPTER TWENTY-TWO

R eilly sat on the porch, watching the rain sluice from the sky and the rivers in the streets become lakes. The water table in the desert couldn't absorb so much in so little time; the earth was too hard, too much like stone. Through the gray shroud, he could see the decaying bridge, railing, and platforms that surrounded the springs. There, the rain guttered down into underground canyons, but it wouldn't be long until those, too, filled and the pools would once again flow with water. It was too much like the resurrection of something long dead for it not to be disturbing.

The Diablo was up on a rise, but even here the water would soon reach its floorboards. It was as if God had a mission to wipe out the entire town.

If only.

He leaned his head back, tossing his notebook on the bench beside him. He'd been writing nonstop for two hours. Not since he'd penned his first novel had a story come so fast. And the words weren't a draft—disjointed thoughts or sketches—they were *pages*. Handwritten pages that could be lifted and typeset. His method might be old-school, but the story was edgy and writing it was cathartic.

It was about Matt, or a version of him that never had the chance to live.

Behind him the door opened, and Gracie stepped out with one of the horse-dogs right behind her. He hadn't seen her since she'd been curled against him, naked, sated, and sleepy.

Wariness filled him as he watched her approach. She looked tired, pale, and every bit as wary as he, but her chin was up, her back straight. Nothing weak about Gracie Beck. And despite everything that weighed on his mind, despite the nagging anxiety that Chloe's revelations had left him with, once again the minute she walked in, he wanted to touch her. He wanted to smooth the worry from her brow, let his hands trail down, over the softness and the curves. He wanted to taste the dark mystery of her mouth. He wanted to put himself out there and see what happened.

God help him.

"Hey," he said in a low voice.

"Hey," she said back.

They stared at each other for a moment while Reilly debated the wisdom of asking her why she'd left his bed. Why she'd come to it in the first place.

Deciding on a safer topic, he stood and moved to her side. "Where you been?"

"Upstairs, packing my grandma's things. Talking to Michael."

"Michael?"

"The priest."

Reilly frowned. "Why?"

"He thought he could help me make sense of what happened."

"Did he?"

She caught her lip and shook her head. "I don't know. I didn't understand half of what he said."

Reilly cocked his head. "But?"

"Well, he knew a lot of names of people in my family—some I didn't even know." She shrugged. "Maybe he was making them up. But he talked about the curse."

The curse. Reilly shook his head.

"Chloe and I had an interesting conversation about curses, as well."

"Why am I not surprised."

"Go figure."

Their gazes snagged again for a hot moment that he felt deep beneath the skin.

"I found some scotch," he said. "Wanna get drunk with me?"

"Is it making you feel better?"

"You make me feel better."

He froze. He hadn't meant to say that, but she gave him a beatific smile that made him glad he had. It was true; he did feel better.

She moved to the small wrought-iron table he'd been sitting next to and took a sip of his scotch. Her lips against his glass made his muscles tighten. He wanted to taste her lips.

"Writing?" she asked, glancing at his notebook.

He nodded, coming closer.

"Is that really why you're here?"

He shook his head. "You know it's not."

She bit her lip, but he could see she believed him.

"What else did Michael tell you?" he asked instead of kissing her, like he wanted to.

"He said my grandfather's name was Jimmy."

"That's better than Horatio."

Her smile pleased him more than it should have.

"I never knew. Grandma Beck never talked about him, and every time I brought him up it made her cry. Michael also talked about another man. Someone with a weird name."

"Aiken?"

Surprised, she asked, "How did you know?"

"Chloe."

She gave him an *of course* look.

"What did he say about Aiken?"

"That he didn't stay dead and he's looking for something in the Dead Lights."

Reilly's gaze shifted to the ruins. "Chloe's version was about the same. She said she came here once, to tell Carolina she was in danger."

Gracie nodded. "She warned her about a man and a curse."

"I feel like I'm in a Hitchcock movie."

"I keep wanting to laugh, but Michael was pretty convincing, and God knows I heard enough about curses from Grandma. I know I'm freaking myself out. I keep feeling like someone's watching me."

"Sorry. I'll try to be more subtle."

She did laugh at that.

And Reilly found himself grinning like an idiot. He wiped the smile away and cleared his throat. "What else did Michael say?"

"Nothing. Jonathan interrupted us."

"That guy makes me want to hit things."

"Why?"

"There's something off about him."

"Compared to all the other normal people here?"

Point taken. "How's Analise?"

"Finally awake. She and Brendan crashed as soon as we got back. I heard them talking before I came down, but they haven't come out of her room yet."

Her frown puckered the skin between her eyes, and she shook her head.

"Tell me about this Brendan."

Who knocked up our daughter . . .

"He's nice enough. He's been on his own since he was fifteen, though. Rough life." She sighed. "And he's devoted to Analise."

"But you don't like him?" Reilly said.

"It's not that. He's just changed the course of her life so radically—how can I not resent him for that? Analise had her hands filled with opportunities and now . . . now she's going to have her hands filled with diapers and baby bottles. She's not even out of high school, Reilly."

He looked at her, not sure if this was the place to butt in or butt out. "Your circumstances were a hell of a lot worse at her age and you still turned out pretty good."

"Appearances can be deceiving."

"At least she'll have you."

And me if you'll allow it.

The thought came from nowhere and nearly choked him with surprise. Did he mean it? Did he *want* that?

She gave him a curious look, like maybe she'd heard his thoughts. She'd always been able to do that, from that very first time they were alone in the library when she'd calmly asked if he was going to think about her forever or just get it over with and ask her out.

"So are we going to talk about it?" he said, shocking the hell out of himself.

Evidently, out of her, too.

"You didn't used to be so direct."

"I didn't used to be a lot of things. Did it mean anything or were you just blowing off steam?"

A flush crept up her face. "Both, maybe. I wanted to prove something."

"That you were right to move on?"

Her eyes were wary again. "That you were just some man I used to know. No one special."

His smile felt brittle, hard edged, and meaningless. "You didn't use to be so cold," he teased, like it didn't matter.

"I didn't used to be a lot of things."

"So what did you decide?"

She stared at him, her eyes the color of the storm thundering around them. Within their misted depths he saw hurt and confusion.

"I'm sorry I never told you about Analise."

He took another step closer to her. He couldn't seem to help himself. "You did what you thought was best. I didn't deserve to know."

"It's hard to remember that now that I know why you left," she said, and he moved closer still. He could almost touch her now. "I wish you'd trusted me with the truth, though. Maybe we could've . . ."

"We couldn't have, Gracie, and that's exactly why I didn't tell you. Because I knew you'd be looking for ways to prove me wrong. But you didn't know Matt like I did."

"I know he loved *you*. He wouldn't have hurt you."

When did he change?

Reilly exhaled, his fingers caressing the silk of her check.

"Did you ever meet my dad, Gracie?"

She shook her head. "Grandma Beck told me to stay away from him. She'd cross the street rather than walk on the same side. He died before you and I became a thing."

A thing. Is that what they'd been? Young love in motion. He'd been obsessed with Gracie. The day didn't start until he saw her. It didn't end until he had to say good-bye.

"He didn't *die*," Reilly murmured.

"He crashed his car in the ruins," she said, frowning. "It was all anyone talked about for weeks. That, and your poor mother."

Reilly stood at the edge of the porch railing. The rain splattered him there, but he didn't care. It felt good. Clean.

He'd been fourteen years old the day he and Matt had come home from school to find that his father had beaten their mother to death with her iron. Her *iron*. He'd been drunk, of course, and in a rage. By the time he'd called the job done—her face, her skull—there was little left but blood and gray matter. Most of that was smeared on his dad's face and neck and hands.

Reilly leaned against the damp pole behind him, not sure if he could keep going. Silently, she came to stand beside him.

"You'll get wet," he said.

"I'll dry."

He nodded once, tried to smile but there was lump in his throat the size of a fist and he couldn't even fake it.

"You know how my dad killed my mom?"

She nodded. Everyone had known. Small towns loved a good bloody drama and Diane Alexander's bludgeoning had been too grisly not to share.

"Matt went nuts after we found her. We came home to all that blood in the kitchen. Dad was passed out, mom dead. I remember picking her up off the floor and then I didn't know what to do with her. I just stood there, holding her, thinking, *What now?* I don't know how long I stood that way before I realized that Matt had the iron and he was turning my dad's head into mush."

"But they found his car in the crater . . . Everyone said he killed himself."

Reilly shook his head. "Not without help he didn't."

When did he change?

Reilly stared at the rain. He didn't want to look at Gracie, didn't want her to see what was inside him as he confessed. "There's bad blood in our family. I wouldn't be doing you any favors by coming back into your life."

Gracie closed the distance between them and took his face between her hands, forcing him to look at her. "Even when I hated you, I didn't believe that."

He slipped his arms around her and pulled her tight, burying his face in the fragrant softness between her neck and shoulder. She held him back, her lips against his throat, his cheek. She said nothing when his hands found the hem of her shirt and slipped under to glide across the warm satin of her ribs up to her lace-covered breasts. There, they stopped, as the feel of her overwhelmed him. No matter how strong she was, here, at her core, there was a fragility that he yearned to protect. She wrapped her arms around him tighter, and the sound of the pouring rain seemed to blend with the pounding of his pulse.

His feelings were a knot of confusion inside him, but he fought to find one that he could ride. He thought it would be desire, but it was something much more important.

She drew back and stared into his face. "You didn't do me any favors leaving me, either, Reilly. I know that you think you did the right thing. I even believe that maybe you did. But it's time to quit making excuses. You want to know if it meant something today? Only if you let it."

Deep inside him, the yearning he'd lived with for far too long rose up and swamped him. She was asking for more than words, and he didn't know how to answer. Not a day had passed when he hadn't thought of her, yet he hadn't tried harder to find her because the man he'd become understood what the boy he'd been never had. He could—he would—lose himself in her. He'd give up what he'd always been and become someone new. Someone vulnerable. Someone she could hurt.

And it fucking terrified him.

He stared into her eyes, saying nothing. She saw it all, though. The shutting down, the withdrawal. He still had his hands on her waist, still held her close enough to kiss, but it was already too late.

She pulled away with a bitter shake of her head, and Reilly wanted nothing more than to call her back. His body reacted before his thoughts and feelings could catch up and talk him out of it. He caught her hand and spun her around.

"That's what I want," he said, his voice gruff as the walls crumbled inside him. "I want it to mean something." He paused and shook his head. "But I don't want to fuck this up again. It almost killed me the first time."

Gracie's eyes shimmered as she turned into his arms and pressed her lips to his, letting her kiss speak for her.

275

Reilly kissed her back with a desperation that shook him. He could almost hear the doors hidden in his heart bursting open, could feel the release of years of pain that had been sealed up behind them. He couldn't get close enough to her. He wanted to strip her of her clothes and kiss her everywhere, savor the taste and feel of her without the barrier of the past getting in the way. He'd been confused, resentful, and inflamed when she'd come to his room earlier. What he'd given, what he'd taken, had come at price. Now, he felt free, and he wanted to just *be* with her, make love to her, let her make love to him.

He lifted his head, stared into her beautiful eyes, and saw a reflection of the avalanche of emotions he was feeling.

"I don't think I ever stopped missing you," she said.

His eyes burned, his throat felt raw. He swallowed, trying to hold it all inside until he could get her alone.

"Let's go upstairs."

"Yes."

It was the best thing he'd ever heard, but at that moment, their daughter stepped out on the porch, and the world shifted again. Gracie tensed but she didn't move out of his arms, and Reilly felt dizzy with relief. He understood the enormity of that small act of *staying*. She didn't mean to let either of them hide away from the choices they'd just made.

He should have known. Gracie had never done things halfway.

Analise's gaze took it all in—her mother's flushed face, her body pressed against his. What did she see when she looked at Reilly? A disappointment? A broken man who'd never be a father?

Their daughter was so beautiful, so like her mother. So like him, in ways he could barely fathom. So undeserving of anything less than the best. Yet, he had nothing to offer but himself. With a deep breath, he met her gaze and hoped that would be enough.

CHAPTER TWENTY-THREE

Analise stood there, looking back and forth between Gracie and Reilly, frowning at them both while a hot blush spread over Gracie's face. She felt like a teenager caught making out instead of a responsible mother, but she didn't move away from Reilly. She could feel his tension, sense his uncertainty about what came next. Gracie knew how hard it had been for him to open up to her and she refused to give him the chance to shut down again. If there was ever going to be a future for them, it had to be in the open. That didn't mean Analise needed details about how he made her heart race, though.

"Reilly and I were just catching up," Gracie said. Analise didn't roll her eyes, but Gracie could feel her disbelief. "Did you need something?"

Analise's gaze darted past her and lingered on her father's face. Gracie braced herself as the two eyed one another.

"So, you're my dad," Analise challenged.

"So, you're my kid," Reilly answered.

Analise's chin came up. It was her defiant look, but Gracie could see the vulnerability around her mouth, the insecurity that lurked in her eyes.

"Your mom tells me you're pretty smart."

Analise shrugged.

"You must get that from her. I'm dumber than a horse's ass."

The corner of her mouth twitched, but she staunched the smile. "I know your music."

Reilly couldn't hide his surprise, and inside it, a hint of his own insecurity.

"I mean, I didn't know it was your music. I mean, I didn't know . . ." She trailed off, blushing furiously. "I play the violin. And the piano. But I'm better on the violin."

A bemused look crossed Reilly's face.

"Maybe I get that from you. That would be cool. A little."

Reilly nodded. "That would be cool. A lot."

Analise grinned shyly. Reilly grinned back. And Gracie's heart swelled so big she was certain it would break.

An awkward silence followed. Feeling overwhelmed with emotion, Gracie cleared her throat. "How are you feeling, Analise?"

"I'm okay, but everyone's looking for the priest."

"Michael? I saw him about an hour ago," Gracie said.

"Bill knocked on our door and said they've checked every room in the house and can't find him."

Reilly and Gracie exchanged a glance. "Well, he couldn't a have gone far," Reilly said calmly. "Not in this storm."

But thirty minutes later they'd gone through every room upstairs and down, and there was no sign of Michael. His bag was still in his room, his bed neatly made, a Bible on the nightstand. But the man himself was gone.

"What about the cellar?" Reilly said. "It's the only place we haven't checked."

Analise and Brendan sat at one of the tables with Chloe and Jonathan. Tinkerbelle and Romeo circled at their feet, picking up on the tension.

Gracie led Reilly and Bill to the narrow door in the kitchen that opened onto a steep stairway. "It's not really a cellar. It's more a crawl space than anything," she said, reaching for the string attached to the bare bulb that dangled overhead. The light came on, illuminating twelve rough wooden steps leading down to a pit as black as ink. "This is crazy. He's not down there."

There was a flashlight in a wall mount by the door. Bill pulled it free and switched it on. Juliet nudged in between their legs and started into the dark. The three were halfway down when the overhead bulb suddenly brightened and then dimmed, brightened and dimmed again. They paused looking up. The kitchen phone began to ring.

"Hold on," Gracie said and hurried up to answer it. But when she lifted the receiver the phone was dead. She tapped the hook switch and listened again. Nothing. Slowly, she replaced the receiver and turned back to the waiting men. "It's dead."

But it began to ring again immediately, and each peal grew louder and louder. At the same time the kitchen lights blinked off and then on. Through the open door she could see the lamps in the front room doing the same.

Reilly came up the stairs and took the receiver from her hand, listened, then hung it up, but it kept ringing until Gracie felt like her eardrums would pop. Reilly pulled the phone off the wall and disconnected the line that went in the back, but the ringing kept on.

"What the . . ."

The bare bulb in the stairway exploded, sending shards of glass in a rain over Bill. And the ringing stopped.

"Mom?" Analise said from the other room. "What's going on?"

Brendan said something in answer, but Gracie couldn't hear over her pounding heart. In the silence that followed, one by one, the lights switched off until the gathering gloom of the late afternoon cloaked the first floor of the Diablo.

Gracie looked at Bill, who stood frozen on the cellar stairs. The hand that clutched the flashlight looked very white against the darkness.

"That was weird," Reilly said.

The understatement caught Gracie off guard. She gave a shaky laugh. "Yeah."

He moved to the door and looked in at the kids sitting with Chloe and Jonathan. "Everyone okay out here?"

Owl eyed, they nodded. Brendan even smiled. Reilly raised his brows at that.

"Stay put. We'll be back up in a minute."

Back in the kitchen, he took Gracie's hand. "You want to wait up here?" he asked.

Of course she did, but she shook her head.

"All right then. Let's see what's down there."

Somehow Gracie managed to take the first step and then another, concentrating on the weak flashlight beam as she followed the two men down.

Chapter Twenty-Four

June 1896
Arizona Territory

I was once again in control of myself by the time the others came laughing up the walkway, and I joined into their easy conversation with a composure that surprised even me. I felt Sawyer's eyes watching and I knew inside he was laughing at me, but I ignored him and went on as if he wasn't there. I still had to talk to him before the evening concluded, and I needed to seem calm when I did so. There were things to be settled before the doors of the Diablo opened for business.

When the others went upstairs, I decided I wouldn't have a better opportunity to speak with Sawyer alone.

I found him at a table with a ledger book in front of him. He looked up when he saw me.

"I'll ask about a stagecoach tomorrow," he said, his tone serious. "Small place like this, it may not come regularly. May not come at all."

A heady mixture of relief and disappointment coursed through me. He intended to help me get home. Home? The notion seemed foreign to me. I had no home. Home, for me, would be where I made it. But the relief that he didn't intend for me to sell my body for him—to him—brought a rush of feeling.

"Thank you," I said. I knew he was right about the stagecoach. I'd made the same realization myself. In the best of circumstances, I would be here for a few weeks. In the worst . . . Well, I wouldn't think of that. Either way, I would need money. I had only one dress, and though all of the girls had generously shared with me, none of them had much themselves.

I knew my parents would not approve of me earning wages in a saloon, no matter how nice it was, but I think even they would understand that my choices were limited. If I could convince Sawyer of my worth, I might save myself the other, more uncertain fate that awaited me.

I took a deep breath, mustering my courage, and went to sit at his table. He looked up, surprised, and then back down to the ledger book. He turned pages and frowned.

"I found this behind the bar. Looks like his accounting for the cost of this place. I can't make much sense of it though."

I leaned across the table. "May I see it?"

"You understand numbers?" he asked, surprised.

"I am a banker's daughter."

It appeared that was good enough for him. He nodded and gave me the book. I studied it for a moment, but it didn't take me long to figure out why the previous owner had gambled the place away.

"He owed," I said. "He owed quite a bit. From the looks of it, he still does. I guess that would be you now. You owe."

Sawyer scowled. "The hell I do."

"Evidently, he sold bits of the saloon to any takers that wanted some. Either you pay them their money or they get a share of your profits."

"It says that?"

I showed him the note written on the pages.

"I knew it was too good to be true," he said.

"No, it's not. When you open your doors, you'll be making money hand over fist."

"I'll need to."

"That brings me to something . . ." I took a deep breath and plunged forward. "I have a proposition for you."

"I think we're past that," he said.

I ignored the baited words and the tone that made me feel hot inside. "I assume you'll have gambling here?" I said.

"Hell, I'm not opening a boardinghouse. It's a saloon. Of course there'll be gambling."

I stiffened my back at his sarcasm and continued. "It may surprise you to hear this, but I know how to play cards."

"It won't be pinochle played at the table."

"I realize that. Truth be told, my father was a gambler."

"Your father was a banker."

"And a gambler. A poor one, as luck would have it, but a gambler all the same."

"And you?"

"I am very good."

My voice made a strange hitch over the double meaning of my words, which didn't occur to me until midsentence. Sawyer watched me with guarded interest.

"I propose that you bank me into a game," I said.

"And why would I do that?"

"Because I will split my winnings with you."

"Seems to me, that's not one of your better propositions. I'm the only one risking anything."

"I know it seems that way, but I promise you, I won't lose."

Sawyer grinned. "Now there's a bet I'd take. If I had a dollar for every man I'd heard say that one, I'd be richer than God."

I chewed the inside of my lip, wondering what I could do to convince him.

"You got something to put up for collateral?" he asked.

I shook my head. "I have only the clothes on my back."

"You willing to wager them?"

Just like that, the temperature in the room rose. The temperature of my blood went with it. Already hot, I felt like steam might rise from my skin at any moment.

"Name the game." My tone was not near so bold as my words, but his smile let me know the meaning was taken. I was playing with fire here, and I liked it.

He leaned back in his chair, letting his gaze make a lazy voyage over my body. "I was down south in Texas not too long ago. Learned a game called Hold'em. Ever heard of it?"

I couldn't have been more pleased. "Yes," I said. "My father played with a banker from Robson, Texas, who taught him. I do know the game."

And it was one I'd had an instant connection with. I understood the strategy and loved the excitement and challenge of it. Sawyer looked suitably impressed, and I couldn't help my triumphant smile. Spurred by the small victory, I grew bolder. Leaning across the table, I asked, "If I am wagering my clothing, what will you wager?"

"Every goddamned thing I own," he said softly.

I looked up, startled and jittery. Excited beyond the game at hand.

He seemed to sense my tension, and he smiled. My heart tripped over itself at the look he gave me.

"How about we each start with two dollars. We'll see how you do?" he said.

He stood, went to the bar, and got a deck of cards from behind it. Then he poured two cups of coffee, added a splash of whiskey from the small flask he carried to his own and sugar to mine. I blinked with surprise when he set it before me.

"Thank you."

Before sitting down, Sawyer counted out some money and laid it on the table in two piles. He took a sip of his coffee and then slid one pile over to me.

"We'll play quarters," he said.

I took the pile of coins, counted them, then stacked them neatly. Sawyer seemed amused by this, but I didn't let it bother me. I knew I had his full attention now as I dealt us each two cards. He looked at his and threw a coin into the center of the table. I called and turned three cards face up. There was a king of hearts, a nine of hearts, and queen of spades. In my hand I had both the ace and ten of hearts. Sawyer bet once more, and I called again. I turned the two of diamonds out, and we bet again. The next card was the five of hearts. I fought to keep my face blank as I studied the cards. He barely glanced at them before tossing another coin in. This time I raised him. His brows shot up, and he assessed his cards again. I took a sip of coffee, smiled when I tasted the sugar, and waited. He looked cool as the day was long, but I didn't think he could beat my flush. He called my bet, and I happily showed my hand. I'd beat his three kings.

His grin held a hint of surprise and a spark of admiration. I pushed the cards his way and scooped back my winnings. He shuffled and dealt, and I won again. The third hand I bluffed him into folding.

As I reached for the winnings, he asked, "What'd you have?"

"A winning hand, Captain."

And with that, I mixed my cards in with the others and waited for him to deal. I won that one, too. He fished another couple of dollars out of his pocket and put them on the table. I relieved him of those, as well.

"Your daddy taught you?" he said when he called and I set down my three jacks to his two pair.

I nodded. "All of us. He so wanted to be good at the game, but his face was open. Always open." I looked down, missing that. "My momma thought it scandalous that he had us playing cards at the kitchen table, but I think she liked it. She wasn't very good, but she laughed a lot when we played. My grandma—now there was someone you didn't want to play cards with. She was lucky, too. The cards always came to her."

By the end of my little speech tears were in my eyes and my throat was thick with emotion. "We thought if we played with Daddy, it would help him get better and he wouldn't lose so much."

"Did it work?"

"No. He didn't have the mind for it."

"He was a banker."

"But he never understood odds, even in his investments. He always believed what he saw, not what made sense."

He raised his brows at that. "And you?"

"You have to ask?"

He smiled at me and shook his head. I counted my winnings and then split them into three piles.

"Here is the two dollars you started me with. And here is half of my winnings."

I'd come out two dollars to the black. He jangled the coins in his hand before pocketing them.

"So," I asked. "Will you bank me?"

"Ella, I will bank you."

I smiled, only realizing then how tense I'd been. A lot had depended on my winning his confidence. If Aiken came back now, I wouldn't be so afraid he would force me into another situation like the mining camp.

"I can balance your books, too," I said.

He looked at the green ledger book and back at me. I didn't have to prove anything to him there. He slid it across the table, and I picked it up. I stood, aware that he watched every move I made with those Mississippi eyes of his. They sent chills down my spine and heat spiraling through my veins.

"It's been a pleasure doing business with you, Captain," I said.

He reached out and caught my wrist in his hand as I moved to step past him. I paused and looked at him questioningly. I thought he was as surprised by his reaching for me as I, though I couldn't have said exactly why I thought that. I looked down at the place where his sun-browned fingers wrapped around my white skin. His thumb moved across the pulse that beat there, and slowly, he reeled me closer. I watched the colors in his eyes swirl and darken, and I didn't fight him.

When I was standing beside his chair, my legs bumping his thighs, he spoke.

"It's not going to be pretty down here, when it's filled with miners and the likes."

"I know, Captain. I never expected it would be."

"A woman like you isn't used to that."

I faced him then. "I would rather see them over a card table than a bed."

He stood and I stopped myself from backing up. Our shift in vantage points brought his body close to mine. I wondered if he could see the bravado of my words.

"Maybe I'd rather see you in bed."

I caught my breath but moved no other muscle. My silence became an invitation, though. He bent down and took my lips in a kiss that sent my pulse hammering against the thumb he had pressed to my wrist. I still clutched the ledger book. He took it from my unresisting fingers and set it on the table. In a movement as fluid as the need dancing over my skin, he pulled my free hand up to his chest and settled it over his heart.

His tongue caressed the softness of my bottom lip and I sighed, opening up to him. He deepened the kiss, and I breathed in his scent as his hands explored the contours of my back, the slope of my spine, the curve of my shoulders. He cupped my face, holding me while he made me dizzy with the sensation of his tongue against mine, the taste of my sweet coffee mingling with the whiskey on his breath. I made a sound in my throat that spoke of the havoc he wreaked on my emotions.

He moved from my mouth to my neck. I should have stopped him, but I couldn't bring myself to do it. His roving hands found the roundness of my breasts, and I sensed the coiled passion in him waiting to strike. I felt the point of no return rush at me from all sides, and I was frightened by it. As if hearing my thoughts, he pulled back and stared into my eyes.

"Ella," he breathed, inches from my mouth.

I looked at him, my eyes heavy with passion, my lips swollen from his kisses. He seemed to forget what he was going to say, and he simply kissed me again and I was lost. I surrendered reason and gave myself over completely.

There was a loud pounding at the front door. Sawyer lifted his head and shouted, "Go away. We're closed."

The knocking came again, hard and insistent. "The hell you are. It's Aiken. Open up."

CHAPTER TWENTY-FIVE

With each step down to the cellar, the darkness became more complete. Bill led them with the flashlight. Next came Gracie, with Reilly close behind. When they reached the bottom, they stood in a huddle, looking at the cramped space. It was no more than a fifteen-by-fifteen-foot area—nowhere near the length or width of the house. The floor and walls were concrete, spidered with cracks, but it looked dry. For the time being, anyway.

"Michael? Are you down here?" Bill called. Not a whisper of a sound answered.

Shelves used to store jars of vegetables, fruits, and jams lined the walls. Thick dust covered everything, though, and Gracie wondered how long ago Grandma Beck had preserved the contents. Years? In the far corner, stacks of old furniture and other junk hunkered in the shadows and cobwebs. The pile looked unstable and some of it appeared to have toppled to the floor, revealing a saddle and a small chest not much bigger than a carry-on suitcase. As Bill played the light over it, Gracie saw a trail of dirt that indicated the items had been dragged out from behind the furniture.

The light played over the area in front of them, but everything beyond it was shifting and obscure. Gracie couldn't stop glancing over her shoulder, convinced the bogeyman was going to jump out at her. Down here, the thunder sounded more ominous and otherworldly. Juliet went in the other direction, cautiously sniffing the sealed jars and dark corners.

Reilly squatted in front of the saddle, running his fingers through the thick layer of dust. Bill and Gracie crouched beside him.

"Close your eyes," he said. "I'm going to blow on it."

When they opened their eyes again, Reilly had cleared a portion of the saddle. It was black with finely tooled leather. There was a silver inlay on the horn and saddlebags hanging over the side. An ancient-looking rifle stuck out from a holster.

They looked at one another. "Strange place to keep your saddle," Reilly said.

"Especially when we never had any horses," Gracie answered.

The lid to the chest stood open, and men's clothes that looked to be of the same era as the trunk and rifle spilled out around it. A small round hat sat on the top of the pile. Bill lifted it. Inside, a white label had been sewn and someone had handwritten a name: *Aiken Tate*.

"Oh my God," Gracie said. "That's—"

Juliet began barking loudly and urgently. The three jumped, and Bill aimed the light at the opposite corner. Gracie tried to make out what the beam spotlighted but the darkness held on to its secrets until, at last, she made out the shape of feet, black pants, and a flashing glimmer of white.

Reilly moved first, taking the flashlight from Bill and running the beam over the corner. Dressed in black, Michael blended into the shadows. He sat with his knees pulled up tight, and his head bent. The gloves were off and his pale fingers looked naked and somehow shocking to Gracie.

"Michael," she said softly. "Are you okay?"

At first he said nothing, and he sat so still that she feared the worst. Finally, slowly, he lifted his head. His face was ashen, his eyes dark pits.

"He didn't stay dead," he said.

Reilly handed Gracie the flashlight and hunkered down beside the other man. Gently he reached for Michael's arm. "Let's get you out of here, buddy."

Michael allowed Reilly and Bill to help him to his feet. It was only then that Gracie noticed the book, clutched against his chest. It was brown, obviously old. On the front the word *Ledger* was embossed in ornate script.

The book her grandmother had been holding when Gracie had seen her in the kitchen on the night she died.

Michael turned his head, and his gaze met hers. His eyes looked like black diamonds in the layered gloom. "He's here," Michael whispered.

Gracie's knees felt watery, but she tried to keep her voice steady. "Let's get you upstairs, Michael."

He shook his head. "He moves within us," he said anxiously, still in that whisper that raised all the hair on her body. "No one can deny him. Not even me." Tears filled Michael's eyes. "Not even me. He came to me. He wants what's his."

He handed the ledger to Gracie like a child relinquishing something he'd been caught with that he shouldn't have. She spotted his gloves on the ground and scooped them up before following the men up the stairs.

Brendan was waiting in the kitchen when they entered, his body unnaturally still, his eyes electric in the murky light. The sight of him made Gracie suck in a breath. Jonathan came in right behind him, and Michael cringed against Reilly.

"He's everywhere," he breathed so softly that Gracie wasn't certain she'd really heard it.

"What were you doing down there?" Jonathan demanded.

"Don't worry about it," Reilly answered, helping Michael to a chair in the front room.

Chloe took one look at his face and hurried into the kitchen for water. Analise sat opposite him at the table, Romeo in her lap and Tinkerbelle at her feet. Her face was almost as pale as Michael's.

"What happened?" she asked.

No one really knew, but Gracie had guessed. Something had drawn Michael to the cellar where he'd found the ledger that was somehow integral to what was happening here. He'd touched it and seen whatever secrets it had to reveal. No doubt they'd been dark, violent and traumatic. He'd withdrawn into himself, his eyes distant, his mind shut to their questions.

Soon it would be fully dark and they'd be trapped in this place with no power. Reilly looked worried and Gracie felt helpless, overwhelmed by the need to protect her daughter without knowing what she was protecting her from.

He's everywhere.

It was a pretty sure guess he meant the one who didn't stay dead. The one who'd wreaked so much havoc on her ancestors and instilled fear of curses in her grandmother.

"I have to know what's happening here," Chloe said desperately. She looked at Gracie. "Don't you see? I can't control what I don't know."

Gracie frowned at her and said, "Sometimes you can't control what you do know."

Analise shifted uncomfortably and Brendan leaned back in his chair, his gaze ever shifting from one to the other of them.

He moves within us..

What was she thinking?

"What's that book?" Jonathan asked.

"Something Michael found," Gracie answered.

"Did he ask you?" Chloe demanded, her fingers wrapping around Gracie's wrist.

"Who? Ask me what?"

"No," Reilly said. "And I'm not going to."

"Ask me what?" Gracie repeated.

"About the séance?" Chloe said urgently.

"Are you kidding me? A séance is the last thing we need to be doing."

"You say this because you're afraid."

"Yes," Gracie said. "I'm scared to death. Michael looks practically catatonic, and we have no idea what happened to him. The water's rising about a foot an hour. We have no power, no way to get out, and it's going to be dark soon. So, yes, Chloe. I am afraid."

Beside her, Analise made a noise that took the anger out of her. Gracie instantly regretted her vehement response as she looked at her daughter's tight and frightened face. What was it about Chloe Lamont that made her so angry? Was it the sense that even though Chloe claimed to want to help, Gracie feared just the opposite? That Chloe would hurt her and her family if she could?

"I want to go home," Analise said, sounding very young and defenseless.

"Me, too, sweetheart."

"I'm scared of the ghosts."

Everything inside Gracie wanted to insist there was no such thing. When Analise had been a child, she'd been afraid of monsters under the bed. Gracie had chased her fears away with a squirt bottle with a few drops of perfume she'd called "monster spray." She wished something so easy could be crafted now, but being here, in a place that seemed to channel the past, with these people who so obviously *believed* in spirits walking the earth . . . She couldn't say, *There's no such thing*, when obviously, there was.

Gracie squeezed Analise's fingers and tried to look reassuring. "Tomorrow the rain will stop, and we'll be able to leave. Tonight we just stick together and wait it out."

"A spirit trapped in this world is never a good thing," Chloe said, her eyes pleading.

"Well, I don't see how summoning it would be any better," Gracie answered.

Reilly shook his head and crossed to the front door, muttering something about the damn storm. He stepped out onto the porch, and like a parade, the rest of them followed.

The front yard was gone.

The short wooden fence that had divided the Diablo from the street was just a shadow beneath the dark-brown water. It looked like a lake had swallowed the street whole—no, not a lake, an enormous muddy river that churned and swirled and slammed into obstacles. White caps raced along with the rising current. Reilly's Jeep had been shoved into a leaning mesquite tree, fifty feet away from where he'd parked. The minivan Chloe, Bill, and Michael had arrived in was gone. The ditch she'd careened into still held her little car, but it was completely submerged now.

"Shit," Reilly said under his breath.

The water rushed the channel of the street, hauling with it the spoils of the storm like prizes raised up to the sky. Branches, a bike, something that might once have been a yard ornament, a lawn chair, a propane tank. And who knew what lurked *beneath* the swift, dark waters? If the rain continued to come down, the first floor would be breached by morning, the cellar flooded by noon.

CHAPTER TWENTY-SIX

There was nothing they could do but wait it out, but standing there, seeing it, made Reilly realize just how dire their situation had become. With a deep breath, he turned to face the others. "Chances of the power coming back on are pretty slim. Let's hunt up some candles and matches. After that, let's sit down and calm down. No more ghost stories."

He gave Chloe a pointed look. She sniffed and glanced away, but no one questioned the quiet authority in his voice. Like scared kids, they huddled together. Except Jonathan. He had disappeared now, too.

Reilly pulled Gracie aside as the others began opening drawers and searching the kitchen for supplies. "Did you see where Jonathan went?"

"Upstairs," Brendan answered.

Reilly shot him a look. He couldn't get a read on the kid. Sometimes he seemed open, confused, a kid on the cusp of manhood with a baby on the way. And other times . . . Other times, Reilly felt like he was looking into the eyes of his father. But Gracie had called Brendan *nice enough*. No one had ever used those words when referring to his dad.

Right now, Reilly saw a scared boy pretending to be a man. Brendan held Analise's hand and tried to comfort her—as he should do. But Reilly didn't want Analise going anywhere alone with Brendan—or anyone else but her mother—until he figured out what the hell was going on in Diablo Springs.

In the meantime, he had some questions for Jonathan, who'd scurried off so fast. He was another who Reilly couldn't quite get a grasp on. He didn't like how interested Jonathan always seemed in Carolina's home, possessions, and family. And the Mr. Rogers veneer just didn't feel . . . authentic.

"I'm going to go up and see what Jonathan found so important to do right now. You okay for a minute down here with them?"

Gracie nodded, and Reilly bent his knees so he could see into her eyes. "You sure?"

"I'm sure."

"I'll be right back. Keep Analise with you. I don't like the idea of anyone wandering around on their own."

"Me, neither."

He stared at her for another moment, overwhelmed by the feeling that rose hot in his chest as her misty gray eyes met his. There were things he wanted to say to her—so many things—and he could tell she had words she needed to speak herself.

He stepped closer and cupped her face with his hands. "When we get out of here, I want to . . . talk. For like a week."

Though worry still shadowed her eyes, she smiled at him. "I'd like that."

"Yeah?"

She nodded. "Yeah."

Not caring who saw, Reilly dipped his head and kissed her. Analise echoed Gracie's surprised gasp, but Gracie didn't push him away. She leaned into him and let her lips soften beneath his. The kiss was brief—way too brief—but it held promise that there would be more than words between them later.

When he lifted his head, he felt something fierce tighten around his heart. There would be much more between them later.

He didn't want to let her go, but the sooner he got answers, the sooner he could return to her side. He took the stairs two at a time and quietly moved down the hall, checking behind the closed doors as he went. No axe killer, no headless horsemen or hovering apparitions waited in any of the rooms. So far so good. He paused outside Jonathan's door, listening to the wind howling and the rain slamming against the exterior walls. The hall held the same, hushed breathlessness that it always did. Cold and damp, shadow filled and guarded.

Reilly had his hand raised to knock when a deep voice came from Jonathan's room, the words muffled as they passed through the door. Who the hell was Jonathan talking to?

Instead of knocking, Reilly opened the door, catching Jonathan on his knees in front of an open box.

"Who are you talking to?" Reilly asked, not waiting for an invitation as he stepped inside and scanned the room.

Jonathan spun around and stared at Reilly in horror. "What are you doing in my room?"

Reilly didn't bother to answer as he walked the perimeter, looking for the source of the prickly feeling that had filled him as soon as he'd entered. No one was here but the two of them, yet it felt like invisible eyes watched his every move.

As he circled, Jonathan tracked him with an affronted expression, moving to keep his body between Reilly and the box on the floor.

"This is my private space," he said angrily. "You have no right to barge in here."

"It's not your anything for much longer," Reilly said, stopping by the closet to face him.

"What's that supposed to mean?"

"Carolina's dead and Gracie isn't going to hang onto this old place. It won't need a caretaker when the wrecking ball is coming."

"She can't destroy it. It's a historical monument."

"If you say so. Who were you talking to?"

"Myself, not that it's any of your business. What do you want?"

"Looking for candles."

Jonathan glared at him. "I don't have any."

"Which is why you should come downstairs with everyone else. The power's out and it's going to be dark soon. Don't want you falling down the stairs."

"Your concern is touching."

"I'm a giver. What have you been doing all afternoon?"

"Organizing," he said curtly.

Reilly moved closer. "What's in the box?"

"Cards," he said, taking a protective step closer to it. "Not that that's any of your business, either."

"Cards?"

"I'm a collector," he said.

The door Reilly had left open chose that moment to shut with a click, and an anxious feeling coiled in Reilly's gut as he stared at it. Jonathan shifted nervously, inching closer to his box as he eyed Reilly distrustfully.

Jonathan said, "You feel it, too."

Reilly couldn't tell if that was a question or a statement, but he did feel it. A sense of something closing in, siphoning the air from the sealed-off room, pulling the walls in tight. Jonathan's gaze darted anxiously around the room.

"What are you afraid of?" Reilly asked, watching him.

"Nothing."

The flaps at the top of his box burst upward with a boom, making them both jump. Reilly had dealt with enough of this house and its slamming doors and exploding boxes. Angry, he leaned forward to see what was inside it and found that Jonathan hadn't been lying.

Hundreds of decks of cards, some boxed, some wrapped in plastic, others bound by ribbons sat in neat little rows. Reilly shot him a confused look.

"You expected china dolls?" Jonathan demanded.

With creepy faces and malevolent eyes? Sure, that's exactly what I'd expected.

"They're not just cards," Jonathan snapped in that slighted tone. "See here? This one . . ." He picked through the box and carefully extracted an ancient decked with frayed corners and a faded riverboat on the front. He held it up proudly. "One hundred and fifty years old. From the South. It's where poker was first played."

Reilly reached for the cards, but something brushed against his ear, making him spin around. Shadows clustered in murky corners and huddled against the floor. Thunder cracked hard and loud while lightning blazed an instant later.

When he turned back around, the cowering man with his box of cards was no longer crouching on the floor. Instead, a different Jonathan stood in front of Reilly, one with hard, flinty eyes and a sardonic smile. One who stared at him with the same merciless expression that Reilly had seen on his father's face a hundred times and on his brother's face the night they'd rigged the Grand Prix to take Dad's body into the ravine.

Suddenly things began to click into place, nuances he'd missed, clues he'd ignored.

When did he change?

He'd always felt the change in his brother that night, but he'd always thought it an emotional turning, a mental decomposition. Now, staring at this transformed man who'd shed his Mr. Rogers benevolence without even removing his sweater, Reilly understood.

His brother hadn't just *changed* and neither had Jonathan. They'd become something more . . . something else. Because what Reilly saw now wasn't human. At least, not anymore.

Jonathan smiled coldly, still holding the deck of cards in his hand.

"Jonathan values this," he said and even his voice was different—longer in the vowels, softer on the consonants. The boxed deck flew across the room and slammed into the wall. The worn cardboard split on one side, and cards spilled out with a hissing sound that made Reilly want to step back. They began to swirl in a stiff cyclone, raising up in a wind only they felt.

At a rapid-fire pace, the cards snapped through the room, hard edges zinging toward his face. He raised his arms, to protect his head as the force sucked them off the floor and shot them through the room.

Suddenly the cards dropped, the air stilled, and a sinking feeling hung in his gut. Jonathan waited for him to look up before speaking. His voice was soft, almost cajoling, and his words eerily understated, but Reilly heard the threat in them even before Jonathan pulled out the long-barreled pistol.

"It's time to settle my accounts."

CHAPTER TWENTY-SEVEN

June 1896
Diablo Springs

A iken pounded on the door again. "You hear me? Open up."

Sawyer looked at me for a long moment, and I wanted to shout, *No, don't open the door*! I was still in his arms, a part of me still seduced by the touch of him. But the sound of Aiken's voice brought fear low in my belly. I knew now what kind of man he really was. Before, I'd thought him cruel and demanding, but I'd not imagined anything that compared to the story Honey had told me. I'd been right to feel that Aiken had orchestrated the scene at the miners' camp. Given the chance, he would do it again.

Sawyer stepped away from me, and I was overwhelmed by the loss of his touch. I wanted him to hold me and make me feel safe, but the insanity of that was indescribable. Sawyer may desire me, but only because I required nothing in return.

He seemed to hear my thoughts and turned a probing look my way before he unlocked the door. Once again I wanted to plead for him not to let Aiken in, but it was too late. He'd already swung the door open, and Aiken swaggered in with a grin.

He was covered in dust and caked with dirt from his small hat to his black boots. He wore the same clothes he had two nights ago at the miners' camp, and he smelled rank as the sullied streets. He looked around with bright interest at the gleaming beauty of the saloon. His expression spoke of how far his expectations had been surpassed.

"Damn, look at this," he said softly.

Sawyer couldn't keep the answering smile off his face as Aiken looked around him with wonder. "Hell, man, we hit the jackpot."

I didn't wait to hear more. As quickly as I could, I headed for the stairs.

"You can't even say hello, Ella?" he asked as I passed.

One foot on the bottom step, I paused. "Hello, Mr. Tate."

"I saw you shot the other night. I was worried about you."

I chanced a glance over my shoulder and then back, "It was not serious. Athena patched me up."

"That's good. Glad to hear it."

"Good night, Mr. Tate."

And I hurried upstairs before he could waylay me again. I found the others clustered in the hall, eyes big with worry. I understood their concern. Just having him under the roof was cause to panic.

"He gon' be mad at us," Chick said beneath her breath. "He gon' see up here how it is and he be mad."

I hoped it wasn't true, but I feared she was right. Aiken had been sporting his girls in a tent and now Sawyer had moved them to a real hotel with real beds. Aiken was too mean and petty not to perceive that as a threat and be jealous. From downstairs, we could hear his jovial laughter as he inspected the saloon, and none of us felt comforted by it. To say he was pleased would be an understatement, and I wondered just how much of the bankroll he'd provided, how much of a partner was he?

We huddled out of sight and listened as he told Sawyer that after the shoot-out he'd ridden a full day before doubling back. He was certain he hadn't been followed, but Athena made a face as he said it.

"He wouldn't know if a bear breathed down his neck," she muttered.

Honey nodded.

He told Sawyer he'd seen Jake Smith riding northwest. "We seen the last of him," he said.

"I wouldn't bet on it," Sawyer answered.

"So where's my girls?" Aiken asked. "You didn't leave them, did you?"

There was an edge to his voice, and I wondered what he would have done had Sawyer left us like he'd planned to do. Sawyer hesitated before telling him we were upstairs.

He'd warned us that if Aiken returned, all deals were off, but we'd hoped it wouldn't come to that. I felt anger at a world that would let a good man like my father be gunned down for no reason and yet let a bad man like Tate cruise through without a scratch. We heard him start up the stairs.

"Go to your room and close the door," Honey told me in a low voice. "Now."

I didn't hesitate to do as she said. Athena gave me a dark look as I hurried across the hall, but she didn't say what she was thinking. I didn't care if she considered me a coward. After hearing Honey's story, I was terrified of Aiken. I didn't want him see me again if I could help it. Before I closed the door, I saw Meaira step in front of the others and hurry to meet him halfway. She had that tight, jittery look about her that told me she, at least, was glad to have him back and expected that he'd have a present for her.

Their voices drifted through to me, but I didn't open my door again. I had secured a means of income with Sawyer, and I held hope that he would keep me from Aiken. But I wasn't certain. Whatever was between us, it was not a relationship I understood. His words spoke something different than his actions, and I couldn't say which, if either, I could trust.

My door had a flimsy lock, which I engaged before moving to my bed. I sat on the edge, listening to the others until at last they quieted. Meaira's room was next to mine and I knew Aiken had joined her in it. I couldn't help but listen to the sounds they made as he took his pleasure from her. It made my eyes fill and my heart feel huge and empty.

311

I knew not what had brought Meaira to him, but I understood that he owned her as completely as he did Honey. I only prayed I could escape this place before he set his sights on me.

* * *

A delivery wagon arrived early the next morning. I heard it creak and rattle down the rough dirt road, and then the driver's boots thudded along the boarded walkway in front of the Diablo. I peeked from my window to see him move beneath the awning to the front door.

I dressed and hurried from my bedroom, just as Sawyer did the same. He'd chosen the room directly across from me, and we nearly collided in the hall. He'd been looking down and fastening his pants as he came out. For an awkward moment, we stood still and stared at one another.

I followed him downstairs as he let the man in and stood out of the way while twenty-five cases of whiskey and forty barrels of beer were lugged into a storage room behind the bar. It seemed an enormous amount, but what did I know? The sort of men who would be filling the saloon might have unquenchable thirsts.

"You traveling alone?" Sawyer asked the deliveryman as he stepped outside.

The man worked a huge wad of tobacco to the side of his mouth, spat a dark-brown stream, and nodded.

"All right, then," Sawyer said. "See you in a few weeks?"

The man shot another stream of brown juice and nodded again.

Sawyer looked at me after he left. "Thought maybe you could hitch a ride, but not if he's alone."

I was quietly grateful that Sawyer hadn't made arrangements for me to travel with the foul man. I feared it would have been trading the fire for the frying pan, and who knew where I'd have ended up had I left with him.

I went to the kitchen and discovered Athena there already with coffee made and breakfast begun. I asked if I could help her and received a glare for my effort. I wondered if I'd ever know just why she didn't like me.

I found two coffee cups and filled them each under her watchful eyes. I wanted sugar, but didn't dare ask. Instead, I carried them back to where Sawyer was.

He thanked me before saying, "Looks like I can open up today."

"Yes, it does."

He nodded, appearing as satisfied as a man could be.

"May I ask you something?" I said.

He shrugged. "Shoot."

"How did you come to be partners with Aiken Tate?"

"We're not partners. Not even close. I owe him payment, not a piece. He gets credit until I pay him back, and his girls can do their work out of here. Once we're square, I get a cut of that."

"You'll profit from the women?" I said.

He nodded, looking at me as if he didn't quite understand the question. I couldn't blame him. I'd promised profit from the women, as well. But how did I explain the difference in the two ventures?

"Do you know much about Aiken?"

"I know he had four thousand dollars in his pocket when I needed it."

"How did he come to have so much?"

"I'd guess he turns a good business."

"But he is unscrupulous, you know that?"

Sawyer shrugged. "He paid up when he was asked. That's what I know."

"The girls are afraid of him," I said. "I am afraid of him."

He turned on me then, a look of frustration on his face. "I'm not their daddy, Ella. I am not yours, either."

"I never said you were."

"I told you already. I'm not here to save anyone. I just want to run my saloon and live my life."

I was stung by the words, though I shouldn't have been. I wanted to earn enough money to go home and get on with *my* life. But I was finding my thoughts more on the way I felt in Sawyer's arms than on the life I would return to. I wanted him to care about what happened to me, but I wasn't ready to say why.

I heard rustling from upstairs, and a few moments later, the others started down. Aiken followed at the end like a caboose. I didn't want to face him. Instead, I turned and went through the kitchen, which was empty for once, and out the back door. I didn't stop until I reached the decking around the hot springs. I took off my shoes and sat on the edge with my feet dangling in the hot water. The day was warm, but not so much so that I didn't welcome the feel of the heat on my feet.

I heard a sound behind me and turned to find Chick lying on the sandy area not far from the decking that surrounded the pool. She was curled into a ball, oblivious to me. I stood and carefully stepped over to where she was.

"Chick?" I said. "What's wrong?"

She let out a yelp at the sound of my voice and scrambled to a sit. Her eyes were red rimmed and her face ravaged by tears.

I sat next to her and asked again what was wrong.

"I cain't tell."

"Why, Chick? What's happened?"

"I cain't tell no one. Not even Athena."

This surprised me. I'd not known Chick to keep anything from Athena. "Is it Aiken? Did he hurt you?"

Chick shook her head, but the tears streamed down her face. Her dress was speckled with their wetness. I no longer owned a handkerchief to give her. She wiped her face with her skirts.

"Chick, I promise I won't tell anyone. Whatever it is. Please let me help."

"Ain't no way to help."

She cast her eyes downward, sniffling as sobs shook her shoulders. I thought she'd never looked younger. There were times when I forgot that she was only fifteen. I pulled her into my arms and let her cry her tears until she was dry. I still didn't know what had upset her so, but I felt her pain. In the short time I'd known her, Chick had become a part of my heart. Her sweet smile and optimism was like sunshine. I wished I could take her with me when I left.

After she quieted, I sat with her in the silence and rubbed her back. I began talking of things that had no importance.

I reminded her of the fun we'd had last night, frolicking like children in the pools. I didn't bring up Sawyer, but my face grew hot just thinking of him and the slick feel of his wet skin.

"I thought Athena gon' box my ears when I dunk her," Chick said, the smallest of smiles curling her lips.

I thought she was going to do worse than that but I knew Athena loved Chick even more than I did. I had yet to learn their relationship, but the older woman watched Chick like a mother would.

"She gon' be crazy when she know," Chick murmured.

"When she knows what?" I asked.

She looked down, plucking at her skirt as she thought about her answer. "You cain't tell."

"I won't."

"I gots a baby in me," she said and then burst into tears again.

I didn't know what to say or do. I sat there, stunned, as I considered what Chick had said. She was with child. In the society I had left, she would have been shamed and ostracized or forced into marriage before anyone found out. But here, in this world, what would happen to her?

"Does that mean you'll no longer have to work for Aiken?" I asked hopefully.

She shook her head. "He keep me goin' 'til I show."

She stopped, and I waited. As the moments stretched longer, I began to feel sick with fear of what she'd say next.

"And after you begin to show, Chick? What then?"

"Then he root it out," she said so softly I had to strain to hear.

I stared at her, not wanting to accept the picture those few words drew. "But—"

"Ain't no but, Ella. I seen him do it."

"You have? But, who?"

"She ain't wit us no more."

I hoped that meant she'd been set free, but I knew it didn't. Even I was not so naive.

"What happened to her?"

"He kilt her. She like Meaira. All she care 'bout was Aiken bring her stuff. That all. He give her the laudanum and then he root around and kilt what inside her. Me and Athena, we try to stop her bleedin' but there no stopping it."

"Perhaps he's learned his lesson," I said, my voice desperate with the need to make it true.

Chick looked at me with pity.

"Why don't you want to tell Athena? Won't she know something to help?"

"She just die if she find out. She know how it be for me. It kill her. I know it kill her."

"But you can't hide it forever. How long do you have until you show?"

She shook her head. "I cain't figure my numbers like that."

"How about the last time you had your bleeding?"

She shrugged.

"Last month?" I prompted. She shook her head. "The month before?"

"It been some time."

I took a deep breath. "You're small, Chick, so maybe you'll be able to hide it until the end, but . . ." But what then?

I wished she would talk to Athena, but she seemed determined to bear this burden alone. All I could do was try to help her.

"You know not to tell Meaira, don't you? I don't think she can be trusted."

"I knows that."

I didn't know what else to tell her, but I had to say something to give her hope. I couldn't leave her out here thinking there was nothing that could be done.

"Give me some time," I said. "I'll think of something."

"Like what?" she asked, eyes bright.

I didn't have an answer for her, but I couldn't let the hope drain from her face. "Maybe we can get you away from here. Maybe I can win enough money to help you go someplace else."

"What 'bout Athena?"

"If you don't want her to know—"

"I cain't leave her. She my sister."

I hadn't known that but it explained so much. I should have guessed it, but there was no resemblance between the two.

"I cain't leave her," Chick said again, more fiercely. "Aiken, he do bad things to hurt her. That what he do. When we bad he hurt Athena."

I frowned. "Are you saying if he's angry with you, he punishes her?"

"Not just when he mad at me. Any of us. Honey and Meaira, too."

I didn't understand the sense of that. Why punish Athena if it was the other girls who had displeased him?

"He don' want the rest of us messed up, see?"

And all at once, I did see the twisted reasoning behind it. And in my mind I could see how it would work. I might risk his wrath on myself, but I wouldn't when another would receive the punishment.

"Why don't you kill him in his sleep?"

I'd said exactly what I was thinking, but until the words came out I didn't realize just how horrible they sounded. Had I changed so much that I could calmly suggest murder to this young, pregnant girl? Apparently, I had.

"We try that," she said, unruffled by my question. "That why he don't sleep there with us no more. Only with Meaira and only sometime. Then he sleep with his eyes open." She widened her eyes in demonstration. "I seen him do it. And he always take the horses so we cain't go at night."

"Did you ever try to run away?"

She nodded, eyes downcast. "He find us. He beat Athena near to death. That why she limp now. She cripple. She cain't run no more. Once we get a boy to help us. Aiken kill him 'fore we got to the next town."

I thought about that and could believe she spoke the truth. Aiken was a lot of things, but a fool was not one of them.

"You think you can help me?" Chick asked. "Cuz I scared, Ella. I scared."

I held her again and rubbed her back as I soothed her. "I'll help you," I said, praying I could make it true. "Just give me time, Chick. A week, maybe two. Can you do that?"

She nodded, wiping the last of her tears away. "I can do that."

Her smile nearly broke my heart. I had no idea how I would help her. I was stranded with no money, one dress, and I was at the mercy of two men I couldn't trust. How in the world would I assist this young woman? I only knew I had to try.

I helped her to her feet, and she gave me a hug. "I lucky you came along," she said fiercely.

I felt the weight of responsibility settle on my shoulders. I had failed my own family, but maybe, just maybe I could find a way out for Chick.

CHAPTER TWENTY-EIGHT

June 1896
Diablo Springs

After breakfast we all helped Sawyer stock the bar, wash the glasses, and wipe down the tables. By noon ,Sawyer declared himself nearly ready to open the doors. Aiken sent the girls up to change. I borrowed a dress from Chick that was snug against my fuller figure and made me painfully aware of the scooping neckline. I felt as if miles of skin showed between my throat and the swell of my breasts. I felt at once naughty and beautiful. Chick emerged in the gown we'd made for her, looking so lovely she was breathtaking. She spun and clapped her hands when we admired her. For a quick second, Athena and I exchanged a glance of understanding. She may never like me, but she knew how much I cared for her precious sister.

As I took my place at a table and began to shuffle cards, I was very conscious of Aiken watching me. I did my best to ignore him, but he wouldn't be put off. All I could think of was Chick and what she'd told me. If I'd been a braver woman, I would have killed him myself.

"What do you think you're about?" he asked, sitting down opposite me.

"Nothing, sir. I'm just waiting for a friendly game. Captain McCready has given me a job. I'll be dealing cards at this table."

Aiken laughed at that. "You got money?" I nodded, but my quick glance at the bar where Sawyer usually stood must have revealed my source. "You got him worked around your finger, don't you?"

"No, sir. I don't believe that's possible."

"What would you say about coming to work for me since you're interested in making some money?"

My sweaty palms made it difficult to shuffle the cards. I didn't know where Sawyer had disappeared to, but I prayed he'd return soon.

"Thank you for the offer, Mr. Tate, but I must decline."

"Ain't no cause to be so formal," he said. His eyes sparkled with humor, and he looked to the unsuspecting eye like a kindly soul making innocent small talk. "You can call me Aiken. The other girls do."

"I'm not the other girls, Mr. Tate."

He smiled and reached out to trap one of my hands beneath his. Once again I was struck by how his fussy attire gave the impression that he was smaller man than he really was.

"No, you're most certainly not the others girls," he said softly, watching me. "You're special. I knew that the first time I saw you."

I tried to pull my hand free, and he immediately released me. "I'm not special, Mr. Tate. Just different."

"I didn't know about your family," he said. "I am heartsick over what happened. You're lucky to be alive."

I glanced up, frightened by this compassionate facade, but I saw no mockery or deceit in his face. In fact, he seemed to be sincere.

"Yes, I am lucky to be alive," I said. "My family was not so fortunate."

"If I had known, I would have fought harder to keep you safe that night. I assumed . . ." He looked embarrassed for a moment, but I was not fooled. "The other girls have stumbled into my life through one means or another. I thought you'd come to me the same way."

It took a moment to catch his meaning. He imagined I'd joined the ranks of the women intentionally. What a fool. "No, sir," I said.

"I know that now. Meaira set me straight last night. She tells me you're too good for me, but not for the Captain."

Startled, I looked up as a wariness settled deep in my bones. I remembered that Aiken had used Meaira to capture Honey. I felt sorry for her, but I didn't trust her not to betray me if it meant Aiken would give her more of her drug. I would watch what I said around her.

"Is that how it is?" he asked. "You belong to the Captain now?"

I belonged to no one, but for once, judgment prevailed over my quick tongue. I was not the Captain's woman, but if Aiken thought it was so, he would tread carefully around me.

"Yes, that's right," I said, feeling the stain of my lie creep up my neck.

His eyes narrowed as he watched me, and I knew he didn't believe me. Leaning back, he gave me a slow, satisfied grin. I braced for him to call me out, but instead, he switched tactics and caught me once more by surprise.

"Meaira said you bargained with the Captain. You bargained my girls."

Now I saw something hard and flinty in the sparkling eyes. I was already on guard, but this made me even more cautious.

"I merely tried to keep them safe."

"You didn't tell the girls they could work for the Captain?"

My mouth was very dry. I tried several times before I could swallow.

"You didn't tell the girls he'd let them keep their money?"

I opened my mouth to answer, but he shushed me.

"Don't lie, now."

He waited for me to say something so I tried to rationalize. "Is it so unreasonable that the girls get a share of their earnings?"

"Now, see, that's what I'm talking about. They never thought of such things before, but now they think they should get something. I feed them. I clothe them. I make sure the men are presentable when they come knocking. That's always been enough."

How could I respond to that? It wasn't enough anymore, and he was a monster to think it was?

"What is it you expect me to say, Mr. Tate?"

He reached for my hand again, and I was not quick enough to pull it away before he caught it. This time, he didn't release at my tug.

"You're a beautiful woman, Ella," he said, his voice low. That ring of sincerity was back, and now it brought a terror I couldn't describe. He gave me a bemused smile and leaned very close. I felt his hot breath at the skin beneath my ear. I could smell his hair tonic and the soap he used. But beneath it, there was something dark in his scent, something that shocked me and made me want to fight free.

"Sometimes when I see a woman, I just have to have her."

"And what if she belongs to another?" I asked when I should have stayed quiet.

"But she doesn't," he said, leaning so close his lips nearly touched my neck.

"I've already told you, Mr. Tate. I belong with Sawyer."

At last he pulled back and leveled those sparkling, blue eyes on my face. "I don't think so, Ella."

"I assure you it is true."

"You believe that, girl. But he won't fight for you. He ain't got it in him to fight for something. He'd just as soon turn you over as do that."

I knew the color had drained from my face, but I kept my chin up. "I don't need a man to fight for me, Mr. Tate. I'm capable of doing that myself."

"You going to put a bullet through me?"

"Are you going to force me to do so?" I asked.

He threw his head back and laughed. "You're a sassy one. I like that."

I didn't want him to like it. I wanted him to think me trouble and, therefore, not worth his time.

"See, you might have gotten away with shooting Lonnie Smith, but you can't just go around killing people and not get caught."

"Can't I?" I said, before I could stop myself.

He cocked his head and said, "No. But some people need things proved to them. I'm sensing you're one of them."

I bit back the challenge that longed to come out. I was smarter than that. I had to be or I would not survive.

"You're thinking hard, girlie. That's good. Because there's nothing you can dream up that I ain't already thought of." He leaned in and murmured, "You don't think Honey's tried to kill me before?"

I hadn't thought her capable of such a thing. She wasn't like me.

"Oh, she has. Ask her what I did. She doesn't try it no more." He winked at me. "You won't, either."

With that, he stood, leaving me sitting at the table, trembling. *He can't just take me*, a part of my mind shouted. There was no need to be afraid. But I couldn't stop remembering what Honey had told me. And I realized that nothing in my short life had prepared me to deal with such a man as Aiken Tate.

As he strolled over to the bar, Sawyer came from the back room with a box of whiskey in his hands. He glanced at me and then did a double take as he noted of my new attire. I felt as naked as I had last night at the springs as that mysterious gaze flowed over my bare skin. The look had a touch and feel that lit something deep inside me and I gave it back, responding from instinct to the desire he roused. For an instant, only he and I existed and the rest of the world fell away. Had my legs not been trembling, I would have stood and gone to him, consequences be damned.

Aiken moved then, breaking the spell that had taken me and distracting Sawyer from his concentrated inspection. Aiken gave me a dark look as he slid onto a barstool in front of Sawyer and lit a cigarette. I shuffled my cards and watched like a nervous bird as he leaned forward and spoke to Sawyer.

Whatever he said made Sawyer look up at him, a frown drawing his brows together. I read his expression and felt the blood rush to my face. Aiken had told him what I'd said. I thought of bolting but couldn't find the courage to move. Sawyer turned his head to look at me once more, and I braced myself for his rejection, but what I saw was not that.

Again, he let his gaze travel from my eyes to my throat to the bare skin above my breasts. The heat in my face spread throughout my body until the spark he'd started burst into flame. He locked eyes with me, and I knew he saw all that I was thinking, feeling.

I'd said I was his woman to protect myself from Aiken. But I realized as I stared back at him, that I wanted it to be true.

Chapter Twenty-Nine

Gracie and Analise sat at a table away from the others, looking at the ledger and listening for Reilly to come back down. He hadn't been gone long, but a feeling of malaise had been tripping down Gracie's spine, and she caught herself looking at the stairs several times.

She turned the page. The ledger was filled with small, precise numbers, aligned in columns detailing the day-to-day business of the newly minted Diablo Springs Hotel. It showed an incredible profit, parsed down to income from gambling, liquor, and entertainment. A shorthand code followed each entertainment entry that neither she nor Analise could figure out until Chloe joined them and peered at the book, too.

"The girls," she said softly.

At their blank look, Chloe pointed to the pictures hanging around them.

"The women were the entertainment."

After that, it made sense. The letter following each entry must be an initial. Gracie came to a new page with Aiken Tate written at the top. This sheet seemed to show Aiken's investment in the business and the daily debits against that. In a matter of weeks, his stake dwindled to almost nothing.

"He was a gambler," Chloe said. "Not a very good one, though."

A sudden crack of thunder startled them all, followed by the deafening roar of the downpour. Gracie tried not to think of the rising water, of the risk that torrential floods posed. The Diablo was old. How much force would it take to sweep it off its moorings?

Gracie looked back at the long column of numbers and turned the page. Each page looked much like the first, some with different names at the top, some dated, all in that neat hand.

Until the next one. The date at the top was August 26, 1896, and though the handwriting seemed to be the same, the penmanship was no longer tight and methodical. Numbers crept from their designated column, some scratched out, others written over with such carelessness it was impossible to read. A few of the columns hadn't been totaled at all. And in the margin, the words, *He's not coming back.*

A sound came from upstairs, and they all tilted their heads back. All but Michael. He sat at the table, huddled in a blanket even though it was still hot inside. His eyes looked dull, his skin gray. He hadn't spoken since his whispered, *He wants what's his. He's everywhere.*

The next page had few numbers, more writing: *A baby is on the way. He's never coming back, but sometimes I feel him. Does that make me crazy?*

It went on like that, little notes scrawled at random. Sometimes they were mixed into the columns of numbers, sometimes they took up the whole page. Most made little sense to Gracie but Chloe seemed to be connecting the dots as they appeared, and she whispered her own narration after reading each entry.

"These are Ella's notes. Look there." She pointed to the word *Misery*, circled with no explanation. "That's my mother's name."

"Your mother was named *Misery*?" Analise exclaimed.

Chloe nodded but was too distracted by the ledger to explain. Bill had found a hurricane lamp in a cupboard, and it flickered on the table. Suddenly, the flame began to dance. All three dogs lifted their heads from where they lay on the floor.

The room felt too still, too silent, and the air too thick. The scent of meat still simmered in the warmth, and the storm was battering against the windows. The candles burning around them seemed incapable of holding back the clustered dark, and Gracie wished that Reilly would hurry up. The feeling of foreboding had been growing by the moment, and she couldn't tamp it down.

Something moved to her right. She froze, her startled scream silenced deep in her chest as the hazy form of a man took shape less than a foot away. Full of fear and surprise, Gracie stared at him as he faded in and out of focus, but she could see Chloe and Analise from the corner of her eye, still bent over the ledger, unaware of him.

"Who's Sawyer?" Analise asked. Chloe didn't answer, never looking up from the page. Bill had joined them, but Michael still sat, staring off into space.

Slowly, Brendan pushed his chair back and stood. He was staring at the man, too.

The hazy man tilted his head, as if confused by what he saw. She sensed a frustration in him and then a pressure that strummed hard against her fear. Cautiously, she got to her feet.

"Where you going, Mom?" Analise asked.

She turned, and the man faded to a dim glow, but on the other side of the room, a hard light began to pulse and grow. Gracie felt something lingering in the shadows, a presence that meant them harm. The two lights took up places opposite one another, flickering with a sinister rhythm, casting shadows in every corner. One of them began to grow and elongate as the other shrunk to a pinpoint. Gracie's heart seized as the bigger of the two became a shape with legs and arms.

"Shit," Brendan breathed.

At last, Chloe and Bill looked up. A second man appeared, this one crystal clear and fully formed. He wasn't much taller than Gracie, and he was dressed in a tie, jacket, vest, and trousers. Though formal, the clothes looked worn and threadbare. A feeling of menace spread out from him, lit from within, as thick and terrifying as the cloying scent in the air. It rolled over her like a dark wave, filled with vengeance, hatred.

A door banged upstairs and all of them jumped and looked up—all but Brendan who stood transfixed in horror as he stared into the black glitter of the apparition's eyes.

Footsteps sounded above until they reached the stairs. At first Gracie felt relief as she saw Reilly's legs coming down the steps. But then she realized he had his hands behind him and his expression was grim.

The apparition beside her hissed and wavered, but a new terror had replaced her fear of it. Jonathan followed Reilly . . . and held a gun pressed to his head.

CHAPTER THIRTY

June 1896
Diablo Springs

The night passed in a blur that left no time to think about Sawyer and what he may or may not be thinking about me. I told myself I was relieved, but I knew it was a lie. And each time I caught my breath and looked up, it was to find him doing the same. Aiken remained at my table through most of the night, gambling with skill but no luck. A rough-voiced miner sat to his right and trumped him at every hand. A smarter man would have left the table, but Aiken seemed determined to be the last player of the night. He nearly was. The men who had burst through the doors in the early afternoon seemed disinclined to leave the same way. They stayed and drank until the drunken rowdiness created a din all around us. For the most part they were respectful around me and the other girls, but I was not fool enough to think that would last once they grew used to our presence.

It was after three in the morning when the last man stumbled from the saloon into the street. Aiken stayed at my table, watching with narrowed eyes as Sawyer locked the doors and pulled out the money he'd collected that night. I stood and brought my winnings to the bar. Sawyer looked up as I crossed, and once again I felt hot from the gaze that traveled my body.

"Made yourself a fortune tonight, looks like," Aiken said amiably, watching as Sawyer sorted through the money.

"Did all right."

Aiken's pockets should have been bulging, as well, but he'd lost his money faster than the girls could earn it. Not an easy feat when all of them, right down to Athena, had been servicing the customers without pause since business had begun. I couldn't allow myself to think of the hours they'd spent upstairs or the exhaustion they must feel right now.

Sawyer counted out the money I'd delivered, took his cut, and pushed what was left back to me.

"You did fine tonight," he said.

"She cheated, is what she did. She's going to get us both shot if she's not careful."

Sawyer's eyes snapped to my face. "I didn't cheat," I said angrily. "You are simply unlucky, Mr. Tate."

His face reddened at that, and I knew I should have kept the last jibe to myself. But he infuriated me. How dare he accuse me of cheating?

"You best check on your own business," Sawyer said, his voice calm but deep enough to tell me he hadn't liked what Aiken had said. He hadn't exactly defended my honor, but I knew he believed me over Aiken and that only added to the jumble of mixed-up feelings inside me.

He pulled out his ledger and handed it to me.

"She doing your books, too?" Aiken said. "A piece of tail like her? She'll rob you blind and you'll deserve it."

I picked up a pencil and forced my attention to the columns. Ignoring Aiken, Sawyer set two glasses on the bar and splashed three fingers of amber whiskey into each. To my surprise, he pushed one in my direction and took the other himself, leaving Aiken out completely. I'd never drunk whiskey, though after tonight I certainly smelled of it. It had been splashed over my hands, my arms, my dress, my neck, and in my hair at least a dozen times.

"I see how it is," Aiken said when neither of us responded to his insult. "You think you can muscle me out, you're wrong. I ain't no fool you can just set off like I don't own a bit of what's what."

Sawyer looked at him then. "You don't own any of it, Tate."

Aiken frowned. "I was good enough to borrow from when you needed it."

"And I'm good enough to pay you back. Nobody's questioning that. You got your girls working under a roof. You got your business. Don't mess with mine."

Aiken looked at me as if I were to blame for what Sawyer had said. "I thought we was partners."

"I never said that. Never did."

"But I was good enough to borrow from."

Sawyer picked up the stack of money beside him and counted out five hundred dollars. I knew we'd been busy, but I'd no idea that he'd brought in so much. When he was done, there were still small satchels of gold and coins piled beside him. I estimated over a thousand dollars had been made in the one night. I, myself, had close to thirty dollars of winnings that were mine. I didn't know how much it would cost to send Chick and Athena on their way, but it was a good start.

Aiken looked at me as if he'd read my mind, reminding me that tickets to somewhere else were not all I needed for them. They would have to disappear, vanish without a trace. How would I accomplish that?

"Aiken?" Meaira called from upstairs. "Are you comin'?"

I'd learned that Aiken kept Meaira on short supply when there was work to be done. I could hear the yearning in her voice now, the raw need to have her awareness dulled. I couldn't blame her.

Sawyer pushed the five hundred dollars at Aiken. "I'll have you paid before the month is out."

"I never said you had to do it all at once," Aiken said, trying to push it back.

"No, but I can see it'll be for the best."

Aiken looked back and forth between me and Sawyer, and I knew he wanted to argue. I knew he liked having Sawyer owe him. I wanted to plop my thirty on top of Sawyer's hundreds, but I knew that the gesture would infuriate Aiken more than anything, and I was smart enough, for once, to restrain myself. I had an idea though. I counted ten dollars from my pile and handed it to Sawyer.

"My rent," I said.

He had a poker face I couldn't fault, and only a flicker of his eyes gave him away. Beside me, Aiken shifted uncomfortably, reminding me of a street dog backed into a corner with a bone.

"Your girls are using four rooms, that right?" Sawyer asked.

Aiken nodded suspiciously.

"You want to pay cash or you want your room and board to go against the debt?"

I saw understanding dawn for Aiken, and with it, anger that crept up his face and stained it a dirty red. "We didn't never talk about rent."

"I could be letting those rooms," Sawyer said, taking a drink of whiskey. "I already got the other two going tomorrow. Won't charge you what I charge them—not by half, but I expect you to keep that between us."

Sawyer's voice rang clear and honest, and I knew he meant it. He wouldn't swindle Aiken, though I wished he would. He took another drink and then played his ace, which I had not suspected he held.

"To show you I'm fair, you can play your cards with house credit until my debt is squared."

This, I saw, was a generosity Aiken didn't expect. It went long in appeasing the insult of paying rent. But what I knew and Aiken did not, was that Sawyer had set a trap of his own making. For Aiken could not resist the cards, nor could he win if he was forced to play by the rules. He'd been cheating at his own table for so long, that he believed he had a gift for gambling. But he was no better than my father. By giving him his bankroll up front, Aiken would play more daringly, and he would lose. I knew it without a doubt.

I felt Aiken's eyes shift to me, and I quickly lifted the glass of whiskey Sawyer had given me and took a small sip. The alcohol burned my throat and set me to coughing. Aiken laughed meanly.

"That's a deal. Against your debt, all of it."

"I'll need your mark before you have any of it."

"I'll give it."

And with another mean glance my way, he turned toward the stairs as Meaira's pitiful voice called out again. He paused as he set his foot to the first riser. "Almost forgot to tell you," he said. "I heard Jake Smith is still hunting for her. If I was you, I'd turn her over before he finds her."

I'd almost brought the coughing under control but his threatening words started me anew. I felt I would choke on the burn the liquid left in my throat and the fear his words seared in my thoughts. Sawyer came around the bar and patted my back awkwardly until the coughing subsided. Tears were in my eyes as I struggled to draw a breath. Sawyer stood beside me until I got myself under control again.

"All right?" he asked.

It seemed an insane question to me when Aiken's words still rang in my ears. Sawyer didn't wait for me to answer. He went back behind the bar, scooped all the money and the ledger into a box, and disappeared into the storeroom. I heard thumping and sliding, as if he were moving something heavy out of the way. I stayed where he'd left me, unsure of what to do next.

He stepped from the back room and I slowly stood. I smoothed the fabric of my dress with nervous hands. I didn't know what he was thinking, but I felt him watching my every movement.

"Jake isn't going to touch you," he said softly.

Surprised, I jerked my gaze from the floor to his face. "What did you say?"

"No one's touching you but me."

In two steps he was beside me. Without waiting to hear my response, he swept me off my feet and cradled me against his chest. My arms circled his neck, and I held on as he carried me toward the stairs. A million thoughts flashed through my head but not one of them was *no*. Not one.

He carried me as if I were a child, and I let him. It seemed like years had passed since anyone had taken care of me or sheltered me from the world beyond, yet only a few weeks ago my father had been alive and watching over my family. How different my life was now. But as I looked into Sawyer's face, I realized I felt no fear. In fact, somehow I'd come to trust him. Whatever happened next, I knew my trust would not be shaken.

He carried me into his room and kicked the door shut. Neither of us had spoken since he'd lifted me into his arms, but words seemed unnecessary. My heart was pounding like the hooves of a stampeding herd, and my dress seemed suddenly four sizes too small instead of only two.

Sawyer dropped the arm beneath my legs, and let me slide slowly down his body, until I was standing in front of him with less than a breath of air between us. The moonlight fell across the floor and turned our world into a silver-edged cocoon where only the two of us and the tension that trembled between our bodies existed. He lifted a hand and placed it on the swell of my breasts. I inhaled sharply at the heat of the contact. Slowly, he moved his hand down, watching my face as his fingers cupped my breast. I couldn't seem to catch my breath, but I didn't care. I only wanted more.

Amazed at my boldness, I leaned into him and raised my mouth to his. My small gesture of surrender, or perhaps aggression, seemed to unleash the need he'd trapped inside. His arms circled me and pulled me tight against his chest, the buttons of his shirt pressing into my skin. I ran my hand through his soft hair and opened my mouth to his kiss. He lifted my feet from the floor and moved closer to the bed. I braced myself for something rough, something taking and unknown. I'd seen glimpses through the tent flaps of what happened next, and I was afraid of it. I expected things to go fast now, for him to act as the men I'd seen had—as if they couldn't believe their good fortune and they wanted to press their advantage before minds could be changed and opportunities lost.

But Sawyer's arms loosened, and I now I feared that he would let me go and I would be the one left with chances ended before they'd begun. Once again my body slid down his until I stood in front of him, the top of my head beneath his chin. I was afraid to look up, embarrassed by my behavior, more so by the lust that surely showed on my face. I kept my eyes fixed on his chest and my splayed fingers. The fabric of his shirt was worn and soft, warm from his skin, which I longed to touch. His throat was golden brown from hours in the sun.

I looked higher at the strong line of his chin and the gold-flecked stubble that had grown since he'd last shaved. His lips were soft and dusky beneath the mustache, moist from my kisses. His face was weathered, creased from squinting his eyes as he looked across a horizon. White filled in the lines that fanned from their corners where the sun couldn't reach. And then I was looking into those hazel eyes of his, and what I saw made my heart somehow stumble. There was the need that I felt in myself, but with it was an uncertainty, not that he wanted me but that I wanted him. I understood instinctively, and it made me feel bold and sure when I had no right, no experience to validate the feeling.

He surely saw the wonder as my emotions played on my face, and then he smiled, a slow, alluring smile that made everything inside me feel hot and pliable, like melting wax. His hands moved up and around from my back to my ribs to just below the swell of my breasts. He moved his thumbs lightly over my nipples, watching my face as reaction went through me. I arched against him without meaning to and slid my arms around his neck, pulling his head down so I could kiss him. His mouth hovered over mine for a moment that was at once exquisite and torture. Our breath mingled and I breathed him in, wanting to keep the scent and taste of him in my memory forever.

And then his mouth was over mine, his tongue against my lips, which parted without hesitation. I'd never known anything could feel like this total surrender. His fingers fumbled with the buttons down my back, but mine had no trouble freeing him of his shirt.

I'd pulled the two sides open and pressed my mouth to his chest before he'd freed the first of the tiny pearl-like fastenings that ran down my spine. He made a sound of frustration and turned me. I reached back and started with the last of them as he struggled with the top. After the first came free the others followed willingly, and before I knew it, he was pushing the shoulders down and the dress pooled at my feet. My heavy breasts swung free from their confines, and I was grateful. His touch had made them swell and feel trapped by the tightness of the bodice. He turned me again, like a doll, and I stood between his large, workingman's hands in only my chemise. He had no troubles with the lacings, and in an instant, he'd loosened them. His hands were indescribably gentle as he smoothed the cotton down until it fell away.

His breath seemed ragged and uneven, and all at once I felt shy after so much boldness. But Sawyer seemed to understand. He slid his hand across my chest and up my throat until it cupped my face. He tilted my chin until I looked into his eyes.

"I've been wondering how to get you out of that since I first saw you," he said softly.

And he kissed me again. My bare breasts pressed against his chest, skin against skin, heat fusing us together. I pushed his shirt off his shoulders, and we pulled and freed and fumbled until we both stood naked. Sawyer smiled at me again, and the look in his eyes spoke of passion and possession. I was his now, and I let him see that he would be mine in exchange. He lifted me in his strong arms and set me on the bed, following me down to the softness of the mattress. It was too late to turn back, but the thought of it didn't cross my mind. I wanted him. I think I loved him. It didn't matter what reasoning or sense belonged to the feelings.

I felt the dark danger inside him. The ruthlessness of a man who lived outside the boundaries of civilization, who slept beneath the stars because walls were too confining. I felt his desire to change that, to become one with a life more gentle, more willing to give and less likely to take. In his own way, he sought after stability here, with the saloon. If not an acceptable way of society, then at least a predictable one.

And I realized that my needs had changed so that I wanted it, too. I couldn't go back to the confines of my old

life. To marry one of the boys back home and live life like
I'd been raised to do. In too short a time I'd changed, and
that forging of a new woman couldn't be undone. I
belonged here now, in the arms of Sawyer McCready, and I
would do everything in my power to stay there.

He didn't ask me if I was sure in my giving. I saw
from the look in his eyes that he knew already. There was
power there, the power of knowing I was his to take, to
love, to pleasure. His hands slid over my body, and my
skin seemed to light wherever he touched. I wanted my
own dose of the heady stuff shadowing his eyes. I ran my
fingertips down his spine as I pressed my mouth to his
collarbone and the hollows beneath it. When I reached his
bare buttocks, I froze for a moment. The intimacy of
touching him here, where the skin was white against the
sun-darkened waist, somehow matched any we'd had so
far. He felt my uncertainty and looked up from my breast.
The cool air where his mouth had been warm and wet
added yet another sensation to the thousands assaulting my
senses in a delicious rush.

For a moment I thought he might ask if I'd changed
my mind. I thought he might play the honorable gentleman
and leave me with my virtue. But when I looked into his
eyes I realized he had no intentions of the kind. His smile
was slow and seductive as he shifted his weight so he lay
right beside me, his chest, hips, and thighs a burning
magnet down the length of my body. He propped his head
up and looked at my nakedness with bold possession.

I was breathing hard and fast as his fingers moved to parts of me that no fingers had touched before. The shock of skin on skin, of the gentle exploration of his fingers, wet from the need inside me, arched my body into his. He watched my face as he touched and teased, and this, I realized, was more intimate, more consuming than the feel of his hands. He stared deeply into my eyes, refusing to let me turn away, refusing to let me hide the tide of emotion, sensation, overwhelming longing that hit me with each gentle movement. When he slipped a finger inside that tight place no one had ever invaded, I caught my breath and moaned.

He teased me until his fingers were slick, watching my face for signs of my needs. I felt raw and exposed and utterly at his mercy. He laid me back and kissed me like I was the beginning, like I was the end. Our hot breath mixed and made me giddy. My skin burned, my body ached for something I didn't know how to ask for.

Sawyer worked his way down my throat, my breasts, his mouth hot silk on my nipples, his teeth nipping just enough to make me shiver. His hands were rough, his touch tender, and his kiss a spark that lit me like a torch.

I didn't understand his destination until I felt the soft swipe of his tongue a second before his mouth covered my sex, and the exquisite feeling of heat and friction brought my hips up and made me cry out.

I was embarrassed and enthralled, captive as he licked and sucked and drove me to an edge I wanted to leap from. He murmured words I was too crazed to hear, and then he slipped one of his clever fingers inside me and I was soaring into pleasure and pain so perfect that I cried out his name.

He smiled when he rose to kiss my mouth, a devastating, knowing smile that made me blush even as I spread my legs for him. I kissed him deeply, my taste on his tongue, and that excited me even more. I felt the rigid tip of him and then the slow, insistent pressure as he moved inside. There was pain, but in some unfathomable way, it was good pain. For a moment, concern darkened his eyes and he held still, watching me for a signal. I took in a shaky breath and kissed him, pulling the breath of him into my lungs as he moved again, long and slow, then deep, then shallow. The rhythm of it excited me in the same way plunging heights and dizzying falls could.

I kept my mouth to his, so he would taste the fear and the thrill of my emotions while I drank the dark mystery he unveiled for me. Our bodies were slick with sweat as he struggled to please me while not hurting me and I fought to drive him beyond the ability to tell. I felt a building deep inside, a pounding of pressure, a swirling of tension that rose up and melted down until I was hot and trembling. My body arched in a dance Sawyer knew well, and he shifted, changing the rhythm of his music to make me writhe and tighten around him until we were both unleashed by the song. I heard my own cry and then his lower moan of release. He collapsed on top of me, his weight welcome in the aftermath of pleasure. I knew then that I would willingly spend the rest of my life seeking another chance to move him this way.

CHAPTER THIRTY-ONE

Jonathan had one of Reilly's arms twisted behind his back, held hard and tight and he pressed the long barrel to the base of Reilly's skull. Every time he moved, the gun dug deeper, and it felt like his arm would snap out of its socket at any moment.

His eyes met Gracie's as she watched in horror. Beside her, Analise stood, confusion and fear in her eyes. They had good reason to be afraid. All traces of the mild-mannered Mr. Rogers had vanished. The Jonathan who held him now was strong and deadly. All Reilly could think was how unfair it was that now that he'd found them, they'd be forced to watch him die.

The two horse-dogs jumped to their feet, teeth bared and barking. They couldn't seem to make up their minds about what to attack, though.

"Call off the dogs or I'll blow his head off," Jonathan said calmly.

Gracie gave a sharp command and the two sat obediently, but they watched with eager eyes, just waiting for someone to make a move on their master.

Jonathan ground the gun point into his skull as Reilly scanned the room, looking for an out—or at the very least an out for Gracie and Analise. He didn't know what would happen next, but he didn't want them anywhere near it.

Two glowing orbs hovered on opposite ends of the room. The smaller of the two pulsed in a slow, stationary manner. The bigger one darted away and Reilly lost sight of it when it moved over his shoulder, but he could see the faces of the people around him, the horror in their expressions. He heard Jonathan suck in a deep breath and slowly let it out.

"There we go," the man said softly, sounding like someone had just shot him full of heroine. At the same time, Brendan slumped into a chair, as if his knees had given out. All the while, the other light pulsed silently, watchful.

Chloe moved like she was in a trance, gliding to stand in front of the others, her face slack, her eyes wide with disbelief.

"Aiken, is that you?" she asked.

Gracie visibly startled at the question. Reilly felt the blood drain from his face. A part of him had suspected it, dreaded it, but until he heard Chloe say the name, he hadn't wanted to believe it.

"Will you speak with us, Aiken? Will you let us end this curse that follows us?"

"What curse?" Analise whispered.

Jonathan—Aiken—whoever it was beneath the older man's skin said, "I want my share."

"Daddy, it's time for you to move on," Chloe said, her voice softer, weaker. Pleading. "What use have you of worldly things? Go in peace. Find solace in the afterlife."

Jonathan said nothing, but Chloe watched him with hope in her eyes. In that instant, Reilly understood that she'd been telling the truth all along. She wanted only to lay her ghosts to rest.

"You don't tell me what to do," Jonathan said in a deceptively soft voice. "I tell *you*. Just because you're old and shriveled doesn't mean I won't work you. You best remember that."

The orb flared, as if agitated by the anger in Jonathan's voice. Bill surged to his feet, glaring at Jonathan with clenched fists. The light grew brighter and brighter until it was nearly blinding.

The dizzying sensation of time slowing to a painful halt swept over Reilly. The walls around them seemed to draw in. The thick scent of smoke, malt, and unwashed bodies joined the heavy aroma of meat already in the air.

"Mom?" Analise said. Her voice sounded small and distant. "Do you hear that?"

Gracie nodded. They all heard it. Music and laughter, faint, like ice tinkling against glass. It came from all around them. Reilly shifted his gaze, looking through the stillness for the source of the sound. Something brushed against his legs, something else teased the sensitive skin behind his ears. The dogs growled and salivated, whining as they looked back to Gracie for a command. She remained rigid, watching Jonathan with all the fear Reilly felt. How could he protect her and Analise when he had no control?

The laughter seemed to grow louder, the smoke now a cloud over their heads. And in the sudden gloom, there was movement—people, just out of sight. Shadows danced against the walls, cast by objects he couldn't see. He felt hands move against his shirt, like a woman's touch trailing up his chest to his neck.

He cursed, but his voice was trapped beneath the thudding of his heart as the imagined caress became bolder and more demanding. The hands skimmed over his abdomen, down below his waist, taunting and seductive and blood-chilling. Christ, what was happening?

In the same instant, all the air was sucked from the room with such force that their clothes and hair rose to the pull. The pulsing light flared and began to move away.

"Follow it," Jonathan said coldly. He pulled the gun from where it pressed against Reilly's head and thrust it forward, waving it at the women. "You, you, and you," he said, bobbing it at each one.

From the corner of his eye, Reilly could see that the revolver had to be at least a hundred years old. The metal gleamed with care and polish. Reilly thought of the cards, so well preserved and carefully stacked. His gaze moved to the spotless saloon, the dust-free pictures on the walls.

He'd been taking care of the Diablo for a long, long time.

Jonathan used Reilly's his shoulder to brace his arm as he aimed the gun at Chloe's face. "I want what's mine," he said.

Without warning, Bill lunged at Jonathan and grabbed his arm. The two men struggled. For an instant, Jonathan's grip on Reilly's arm loosened, and that was all Reilly needed to break free. He twisted and slammed into Jonathan, knocking him to his knees, but the other man was faster, stronger than any of them. He managed to knock Bill backward and swipe Reilly's feet out from under him in one swift move. Before either man could recover, the gun went off with a *boom!* that made Analise scream. Gracie pulled her daughter into her arms as Bill crashed into the wall, blood pouring from the wound in his chest.

Before Jonathan could turn back to the others, Reilly charged, thinking to catch him off guard, but with lightning reflexes, Jonathan twisted around and took aim, looking down the long barrel into the eyes of a terrified Analise.

"I want what's mine," he said. "Or I take what's yours."

CHAPTER THIRTY-TWO

July 1896
Diablo Springs

Two weeks had passed since Sawyer swung me into his arms and claimed me forever. Two weeks that seemed a lifetime of learning. There was no question after that where I would sleep or who I belonged to. The girls giggled among themselves and teased me about the look he'd put in my eye, but I didn't care. I loved him, and though the words were not spoken, I felt he loved me back. What a strange world that had brought me to this place and time.

I had not forgotten about Chick during my bliss, however, though I was no closer to finding a solution to her problem. I worried on it constantly, and each time I saw a man take her up the stairs, I felt sickened. She was too much child to be a woman, too much woman to be a child. When I thought of her fear, I knew it was justified.

I'd done my best to avoid Aiken, but he had done his best to see that I didn't. Each night he sat at my table and each night I beat him at cards, praying as I did that I would break him and force him to move on. He played on credit, still banked against his loan to Sawyer. Each time he drew on it, I made him put his mark on the ledger showing his growing use and Sawyer's diminishing debt. I wondered if he understood numbers enough to know just how much he'd lost at the tables. There was no limit to the betting, and the miners seemed determined to lose their winnings. Many a hand I'd dealt had stakes high enough to make my heart flutter. One game at a table such as this could have reduced my father to a pauper. I had no trouble envisioning the high-stakes hand that had won Sawyer this very saloon I'd come to call home.

I was torn about one thing, though. While I wanted Aiken gone with all my heart, I knew that should he leave, he would take the women with him, and that I could not abide. I tempered my desire to influence Sawyer, if I could, to force him out. There had to be a way to free my friends of his domination.

There were no more than a hundred men living in Diablo Springs when we arrived, but each day more swarmed the small town until their white canvas tents dotted the hillside like boulders from a landslide. Each morning I awoke to the sounds of hammers and picks striking stone like the rhythmic chiming of a discordant bell. The silver was hard to find and slow to be had, but apparently, enough had been mined that others were drawn to the search. I grew accustomed, if not agreeable, to the smell of sweat and unwashed men. It might have been worse if Aiken had not insisted that they bathe before bedding any of the girls. Of all the things I loathed about

Aiken, this one redeeming characteristic went far on his short list of good qualities.

Ever the entrepreneur, Aiken set up a tub in a tent beside the Diablo and charged two dollars for a bath. The men could have easily bathed for free in the warm springs, but I'd learned that in addition to being a superstitious lot, most of them were afraid of the water. It seemed that legends about the "devil springs" surpassed even those about the silver to be found in the surrounding mountains. I had heard that the springs were haunted, cursed, damned. I had yet to see evidence of it with my own eyes, and for me it would always be the wonderful place Sawyer and I escaped to in the early hours of the morning when the smell of smoke and the layers of spilled whiskey were too thick to take to bed. Though, I will admit that at times I felt the mist swirl like a phantom and I was glad not to be alone there.

Even Aiken was afraid of it. Once I'd heard Meaira try to tempt him out, and he'd refused with a vengeance that betrayed his absolute terror. Later, I'd learned that he couldn't swim, but it still seemed to me that his fear went deeper than drowning.

Whatever the reason, few would go near the springs and so they washed themselves in Aiken's bathing tent, using water many times over until I wondered how it could clean anyone. Athena's job was to watch them and make sure they used soap, especially in those private areas. When the water became more mud then liquid, she would dump it and start fresh. I didn't envy her the work, especially knowing that her chores didn't end there or in the kitchen, because she was used by the worst of them in the bed, as well. I couldn't imagine her exhaustion and my heart was sick for her, but she wouldn't appreciate my sympathy so I didn't offer it. When she would allow, I assisted her with the household jobs, but usually my help was rejected.

One day a man came and took our pictures. He gathered us up and arranged us like jewels in a setting. He came back later and showed us our likeness frozen forever behind glass. Sawyer bought the picture and hung it on the wall.

Each night, as the wee hours of morning came and went, business at last began to dwindle. The last man stumbled down the stairs looking as if he'd ascended from a part of heaven only he could know, and the last drunken miner was carried from the saloon and laid out on the boardwalk until he woke and found his way back to his tent.

I'd been particularly lucky of late, and even after Sawyer's cut of my winnings, I thought I just might have enough to get Chick and Athena away from here. But where would they go? How would they live afterward? And what if Aiken chased them down? From everything I knew about him, he wouldn't let a possession of his go so easily, and that's what the girls were—his possessions.

All this I thought of as the night wound down and Sawyer locked the door behind the last customer. As usual, he wiped his bar with the pride of ownership and then went to the storage room where he kept his money chest. Aiken watched him go with an expression I didn't like.

I stood, intending to follow Sawyer and speak with him. I had yet to confide in him about Chick's secret, but I knew I would need his help. Besides, there were other issues to discuss before we retired for the night and the words exchanged between us became those sighed over our naked bodies.

Aiken stood when I did, though, and moved close enough that his legs brushed my skirts. I was wearing Chick's dress again, and I was acutely aware of the tight, swooping neck and all the bare skin above it. I knew Aiken was, too.

"You sure smell sweet, Ella. Must be all them winnings. What you going to do with them?"

"That's none of your concern, Mr. Tate."

"Oh, but it is. I think you've got something up your sleeves, or maybe down here." He ran his finger over the neckline of the dress, touching the tops of my breasts in a slow, unnerving stroke. I slapped his hand and took a step away. He followed, standing too close. Sawyer was still in the other room and I was alone with Aiken. I tried to keep my wits about me. It wouldn't do to show this man fear.

"The Captain will not like your touching me any more than I do, Mr. Tate. Please keep your hands to yourself."

I heard the rustle and thump as Sawyer moved some heavy object—a sound I heard each night when he put up the money he'd made. I knew Aiken heard it, too, and had surmised that Sawyer was hiding his profits in the store room. This was something else I planned to discuss with him.

"Sounds like the Captain got a little hidey-hole back there," he said, smiling. "How about you girl? You got yourself a hidey-hole? You think you're smart enough to keep it from me?" He reached for me again, this time skimming his hand up my chest to my throat. I had only a second to guess his intentions and then his fingers were tightening, blocking off my scream before it could escape.

"I know you're thinking you can force me out. I know you talk against me to the Captain at night when he's fucking you. But ain't no one makes me do what I don't want. I'll leave you for dead and won't no one care. You hear me?"

I couldn't move or speak to disagree. I could barely breathe and my fear worked against me, lodging in my constricted throat until I saw spots behind my eyes. I tried to pry his fingers away, but he was strong, much stronger than he looked, and he was furious.

"See, I know all about the Captain. I know what kind of man he is. You think he wants you forever? You think he'll fight for you?" Aiken breathed in my ear. I felt his mouth against the skin there, and I shuddered with revulsion. "He won't. He's not a man to fight for what don't come easy. You keep your legs spread and your mouth closed, he'll keep you fine. You talk against me and my girls, and I'll make you dead and he won't do a thing about it."

With that he shoved me away and started up the stairs. I leaned against the bar, breathing heavily, feeling his threat roll over me. He'd hit upon my uncertainties with deadly precision. Would Sawyer fight to defend me? Did he care more for the convenience of my body than he did who I was? If I told him about Chick and her baby, would he help us? Or turn us away? I realized the answer that formed in my head was more telling than anything. I didn't really know what Sawyer would do.

I had only a moment to pull myself together. I looked in the mirror behind the bar. Only a slight red mark showed where Aiken had gripped my throat. I felt as if I should be black and blue, though.

Sawyer emerged and smiled when he saw me, gave me a playful spank.

"What are you thinking on so hard, Ella?"

I was thinking that I was out of time. That Chick had only a week or two before her condition would be visible to all. Already I could see the swell of her belly and the heaviness of her breasts. Had Aiken not been so busy tormenting me, I was sure he would have noticed by now. I wondered that the others hadn't seen it, but then I knew how exhausted Athena was and how Chick took care to wear her loose gowns when she was with everyone else.

"I was thinking about banks, actually," I said.

He laughed. "You thinking on a holdup?"

I forced a smile. "Not exactly. But I do think you're asking to be robbed by stashing your money in the storeroom."

He looked stunned for a moment, as if it hadn't occurred to him that anyone noticed what he did each night. I was willing to wager that every one of the girls knew exactly where the money was kept. Yes, he locked it up, but locks could be broken.

"You need to put your profits in a bank, Sawyer, or you risk losing all of it."

My legs still felt shaky, so I moved to a barstool and turned it so I faced him when I sat. Sawyer crossed to me and leaned one hand against the bar on either side of the stool. The position brought his face close to mine. I could see the flecks of gold and amber in the depths of his eyes, and I could smell the scent of soap on his skin. I wished he were my husband and this, our business that we would grow together. I wished there were no danger. I wished for a dream.

"You remember who I am?" he said softly, those beautiful eyes crinkled with a smile.

I remembered. He was an outlaw who'd robbed banks until his gang turned to murder.

"I don't trust banks," he said.

"Keeping your money here is like declaring the Diablo a repository. It's foolish."

He considered what I said.

"Maybe you're right."

I was surprised by his agreement, though we both knew I was right. I'd seen the desperate sort that came through our doors. There was no law out here. It would be only a matter of time before my words became prophesy.

He grinned at me then and scooped me off the chair into his arms. "You worry too much, Ella."

Did I? Or was it that he didn't worry enough? He carried me up to his room and closed the door. It seemed I couldn't get enough of him nor he of me, but my thoughts tonight were too heavy. Did I dare tell him about Aiken's threats? Did I dare not?

He sat down on the bed and pulled off his boots and shirt, looking at me quizzically when I simply hovered beside him instead of undressing. He tugged at my sleeve and raised his brows in question. "You going to sleep in that?"

I shook my head. "Sawyer, if I was in trouble, would you help me?"

"I've been doing that all along."

The simple truth of it bolstered my courage. Yes, he had. But what I was about to ask was different and I knew it. "Yes, I know. But . . ."

He looked at me. "But?"

"I'm afraid of Aiken," I said at last. "He threatens me."

Sawyer frowned. "Threatens you how?"

"He thinks I have plans that involve the women."

"Do you?"

I kept my eyes cast down and didn't answer. Sawyer took my chin in his hands and turned my face to his. "Do you?" he asked again.

My throat was dry, and it was difficult to swallow. At last, I nodded. "Chick is with child," I said.

Sawyer's eyes widened.

"She's afraid when Aiken finds out he'll try to do away with the baby."

I told him about Aiken's methods and the girl who had died because of them. It seemed once I began, I couldn't stop. I told him about Honey and her sad tale and how the night I'd shot Lonnie Smith, Aiken had talked out of both sides of his mouth, telling the men to leave me alone and have me if they would at the same time.

"He's a slave master," I said in conclusion. "An evil one."

Sawyer looked troubled by what I'd told him, but I knew before he spoke that his answer wouldn't be what I hoped for.

"What Aiken does with his women, that's his business. I'm sorry, but that's how it is."

"And what about me?"

"You stay out of his way and he'll stay out of yours."

"That's all you have to say?"

"Ella, I told you once. I'm not their daddy. I'm not here to take care of them."

"And me?"

"You're different."

"How, Sawyer? How am I different? Because I sleep with you? Go ask Honey or Chick or even Athena. Any one of them would take you to their beds."

The words burned in my throat, but they were true. He narrowed his eyes at me as I stood before him, waiting for an answer. Waiting for him to say I was different because he loved me. Because we loved each other. But those words never came.

"They're Aiken's problem, not mine."

"And what does that make me? Your problem?"

"Evidently," he answered.

I knew he meant to tease, but my emotions were raw and I couldn't take it that way. I was hurt and I was scared for my friends, scared for myself.

"I am sorry I've become such a burden," I said stiffly.

He stood, forcing me to step back. His bare chest gleamed in the candlelight, and I knew his skin would feel like warm silk. I knew if I touched him now, if I slipped my hands around his waist and pulled him close, our argument would be over. Sawyer didn't like to fight, and it was I who'd picked this battle. But I also knew that ending it would not include a resolution. I would be in the same state of distress as I'd begun.

Hands on his hips, he made a noise deep in his throat that sounded like a growl. "Become a burden?" he repeated angrily. "Lady, you've been nothing but trouble since the first time I set eyes on you."

I inhaled sharply, willing my tears back. "You don't know how much trouble I can be, Sawyer McCready. I will not see my friends tortured and used anymore. If it means I bring the sheriff here, then I will do that."

Sawyer laughed out loud. "Good plan, but did you forget about Lonnie Smith?"

I hadn't forgotten him, but I hadn't been thinking about him when I'd made my empty threat. I'd only wanted to hurt Sawyer as he was hurting me.

"I can see we have nothing else to say," I said.

"You're wrong there, but I'll let it go. Just stay out of Aiken's business. I mean that."

I lifted my chin. "I will be sure to stay out of yours, as well."

He looked like he might argue, but then he turned his back on me. I bit the inside of my lip as I opened the door and left him alone.

* * *

I'd cried myself to sleep and awoke feeling angry and foolish. What had I expected of Sawyer? That he would don shining armor and rescue us all? My love for him was not conditional, so why had I forced him to make a choice between me and the others? I had vowed to help Chick and I would, but it was not fair that I force Sawyer into such an alliance. He'd invested so much of himself in the Diablo, how could I think he would risk it all?

It was early when I came downstairs. His bedroom door was open, his bed empty. I expected to find him having coffee at the bar or perhaps taking stock of supplies. But though I found an empty cup on a table, I saw no sign of Sawyer. I went to the kitchen where I knew Athena would be and asked if she'd seen him.

"He gone afore sunrise," she told me. Her eyes were angry. Her eyes were always angry.

Had I not been so disappointed, I might have left then. But I wanted to know if he'd told her where he'd gone, and I knew she would keep it from me because she could.

"Why do you hate me, Athena?"

I thought my forthrightness would catch her off guard, but she didn't miss a beat of the eggs in her giant bowl.

"You bring pain to my Chick."

"I do no such thing."

She narrowed her eyes. "You will. I see it."

"You see it?"

"All the time I see trouble come our way and I don't see no face. But you, I see you. I see you bring death."

I was shaking my head, but she glared at me with dark certainty.

"You're wrong. It's not me that brings death. It's Aiken."

"It you."

With that she turned her back and carried her bowl to the stove. There would be no more conversation. Still, I had to ask, "Do you know where Sawyer went?"

"To the bank," she said, not turning.

My surprise couldn't have been greater. I left the kitchen and hurried to the storeroom where he kept the money. The lock was still on the door so I couldn't look inside, not that I would know where exactly he hid it, but I wanted confirmation that this was indeed where he'd gone. A dark feeling had gathered in my belly, and I knew that until I'd seen him and held him and apologized it wouldn't go away.

I poured myself a cup of coffee and sipped it quietly while the girls meandered down the stairs. I braced myself for the moment when Aiken would appear, but he did not follow this morning. The anxiety I felt tightened.

When Meaira plopped down with that distant look about her, I asked, "Where is Aiken?"

"Don't know. He said something about finding Jake Smith, though. Sure, and didn't you make him madder than a priest in a whorehouse." She hummed for a minute, distancing herself from the world with the simple sound. "You made him mad," she repeated in a sort of singsong.

It took a long moment for her words to sink in, but once they did, I jumped to my feet. Did Aiken know where Sawyer had gone? What better opportunity to do away with me than when Sawyer was away. He knew that I was the reason behind Sawyer's change of heart about their "partnership."

"He's bringing Jake here," I said, though I'd heard her clearly enough the first time.

"To hurt you."

I looked at Chick's stricken face and Honey's widened eyes. "I must leave. Chick, we have to go. All of us."

As soon as I spoke, I realized what I'd done. Meaira looked placidly back at me, but I knew she'd betray us at the first opportunity. There was nothing I could do about it now. I wouldn't tell her more, though.

I hurried to the kitchen, gesturing for Chick and Honey to follow. Athena looked up coldly as we entered.

"We have to leave this place," I said. "Aiken is bringing Jake Smith here."

"That ain't our business," she said.

"He'll kill me."

"We leave, Aiken kill us," Athena told me.

"He'll kill Chick either way," I said.

Athena's eyes widened. Honey asked, "Why do you say that?"

I looked into Chick's sweet face, silently apologizing for revealing her secret. But it couldn't be kept any longer. Surely, she must see that?

"I gots a baby in me," Chick said.

The silence that covered the room was chilling. Athena put her hands over her mouth, her eyes widened with pain.

"No," she said.

Chick nodded. "You know what he do to me. Ella right, we gots to go."

Athena shook her head again, refusing to hear the reason in Chick's words.

"I can't," Honey said. "He'll find me or he'll kill everyone I love, but you're right. If you don't leave, he'll kill you both. Take Chick. Go. I'll be fine."

My heart broke for wanting to help her. But I saw the truth of what she said. I wasn't sure any of us would survive this. I would be lucky to help myself and Chick.

"Go get your things," I told her. "You too, Athena. She won't go without you. I have enough money to buy horses for the three of us. We'll go as far as we can, and then we'll figure out what to do next."

Athena slowly sank to a chair, hands still over her face, head shaking in denial. "Not my Chick," she moaned. "Not my baby Chick."

I realized there'd be no reasoning with her until she recovered. All I could do was leave her to Chick while I went to purchase our horses.

On my way out, I saw Meaira still sitting where we'd left her, humming that tuneless melody and staring out at nothing at all. My common sense told me to keep walking, to say nothing more to her. But I'd been raised a Christian, no matter how I lived now, and I couldn't turn my back on someone so obviously lost.

"Meaira," I said. "You heard us, earlier?"

"You'll be going."

"You can come with us."

A soft light entered her eyes, a light that spoke of the woman she'd been before Aiken Tate. "No place left for me, lass."

"Will you tell him?" I asked, when I meant, will you betray us?

The light wavered and became murky, like the woman herself. "I canna promise you I won't."

That was as much as I would get, and I knew it.

* * *

The livery was filled with animals that had been bartered for money to buy mining equipment, and I was fortunate enough to have a pick of three of the heartiest horses. The expense took a toll on my savings, but there was no choice. I had to get away. I would leave a note for Sawyer under the storeroom door where only he could find it. I would explain where I'd gone and why. I would beg for him to understand. I would make amends. But I could do nothing if Jake showed up to kill me and so I had to make haste.

When I returned, Athena and Chick were waiting. I took the horses to the back and we loaded them, knowing that we might not make it through another day. I shuddered when I imagined Aiken's reaction to finding us gone. I wished that Honey would come, too, but I knew for her, death was preferable to being responsible for what he'd do to her family.

"I'll take care of Meaira," Honey told us as she hugged me good-bye.

"And I'll take care of Chick and Athena," I said in an undertone, so Athena wouldn't hear. She'd like as not have my head for such a presumption.

"You're the bravest woman I've ever met," Honey said as she held me tight.

Before she could step away, Aiken rounded the corner . . . and with him was Jake Smith.

It all happened fast, yet each moment imprinted in my mind. Aiken yanked Chick off her horse and pushed her back against the rail. Athena and I had yet to mount and

ERIN QUINN

Athena rushed to Chick's side only to be dealt a leveling blow from Aiken. Jake had his gun pointed at my heart before I saw it clear the leather of his holster. I stared down the barrel of it, knowing my last breath was about to be drawn. "You killed my brother," he said.

"You killed mine first," I said back, nearly laughing at the childish exchange. But there was nothing funny about dying. Nothing funny about having your body riddled with bullets. From the corner of my eye, I saw Athena, sprawled at Aiken's feet. He had one boot pressed against her face and was grinding her cheek into the gravel. He held Chick by the throat, as he had me last night, but there was more restraint than intent in his grip. She was sobbing, begging that he forgive her.

The weight of my failure nearly overwhelmed me. Whatever I'd intended, I'd most certainly sealed our fates with my brash plan. Had I really thought I could outsmart Aiken Tate?

"It your baby, Aiken," Chick sobbed. "It yours cuz ain't no one else wit me then. We was away on the trail. You 'member?"

Aiken looked dumbfounded, and I had a moment to wonder if Chick told the truth. Why hadn't she said so before? Would it make a difference?

Aiken frowned at her. "Baby?" he sneered. "Ain't no baby of mine." He faced Jake again and said, "Are you going to kill her or fuck her?"

Glaring at me, Jake snorted. "Both."

372

He lowered the gun and then whipped my face with it. It felt as if my cheek had exploded and I reeled back, crying out with the pain. I realized as I lay crumpled on the ground, that I was calling Sawyer's name.

Jake leaned over me. "He ain't going to save you, girlie."

Then he yanked my skirts up and tore my undergarments away. My rage became something wild and living.

I had survived too much to give in to this monster. Aiken stood watching with cold enjoyment as Jake fumbled his britches open. I felt the hardness of his belt, the stiff leather of his holster and something else . . . My hands were pinned at my sides, but Jake's knife sheath was just at the tips of my fingers.

He loosened his pants and pulled himself free. I forced myself to relax against the rocky ground and spread my legs so that he slipped between them, bringing my hands within gripping range. My fingers curled around the smooth hilt of his knife, and I slid it free just as he shoved into me. My shout was of humiliation, of violation, but most of all, of rage. I came up hard with the knife, slamming it into his side just beneath his ribs and then yanking it out as he sat straight up, reaching for the wound. Before he could react, I'd buried it to the hilt in his heart. His face contorted with pain and shock. He wavered, still between my legs, his erection not yet aware that the rest of him was dead. I pushed him back and wiggled away as he fell over.

Aiken stared at me like he couldn't believe what he'd seen. I couldn't believe it, either, but I wouldn't cower. I faced him brave and bold and utterly defenseless. I realized too late I'd left Jake's knife embedded in his chest.

Time simply stopped.

His foot still ground Athena's face into the dirt. He still held Chick's throat clenched in his left hand. And I stood before him.

"Let her go," I ordered.

A bemused smile tipped his mouth. "No," he said, but then he pushed Chick away and pulled his gun in one swift movement. All sense of time and place left me as I saw Chick stumble over Athena's inert body at the same moment Aiken cocked his pistol. I heard the sound of the shot crack the air, smelled the smoke, tasted the gunpowder at the back of my throat, and then something slammed into me with a force that knocked me backward. I felt as if I were being smothered. My skirts had somehow tangled around my face as I fell, and I fought to get free, waiting all the while for the paralyzing pain and the blood that would spill with my life.

I heard a sound I didn't understand as, at last, I tore free of the fabrics that caught me like a web. I struggled up and out and only then did I realize what had happened. Chick lay sprawled beside me, the back of her blue dress stained with blood. The sound I heard was Athena, keening like an animal as she clawed her way over to Chick. Her face was bloody where she'd sacrificed the skin of her cheek to get free.

I heard myself screaming, "No, no," over and over as understanding filled me. Chick had pushed me out of the way and taken Aiken's bullet.

I spun to face Aiken, thinking I would rip him apart with my bare hands for what he had done. He didn't hesitate or mourn the sweet girl that lay at our feet. He raised his gun again and pointed at my chest.

"Don't do it, Aiken."

Honey's voice rang out in the same instant the gunshot boomed loud around me. My hands went instinctively to my heart, trying to protect against the hard flash of death. But there was no blood to hold back. No pain to endure. Stunned, I locked eyes with Aiken.

As if rehearsed, the two of us turned our heads to face Honey. She stood on the porch, my daddy's rifle in her hands. A small wisp of smoke drifted from the barrel.

"That's for my baby brother," she said. Her hands shook as she struggled to open the chamber and load it again. I saw Aiken think about how he could get the rifle away from her, but already the feeling must have drained from his fingers as his gun clattered to the ground. Blood spread in a seeping circle from the first bullet she'd put through him, and I knew it was shock more than aggression that kept him standing. She slammed the chamber shut and pointed it again.

"This is for me," she said softly, and pulled the trigger again.

CHAPTER THIRTY-THREE

Reilly had seen violence. He'd been raised on it. But he'd never seen cold-blooded murder. Bill lay bleeding on the floor, and Jonathan, the man Reilly had thought harmless, held the gun pointed at Analise.

His daughter, who he'd only just met.

"I want what's mine. I want the money. I want my *share*."

"Wait," Gracie said, trying to protect Analise. Brendan had moved in closer, looking for an opening. The dogs growled and snapped.

"I'll kill those dogs," Jonathan warned.

Reilly saw Gracie consider the odds of them getting to Jonathan before he could do any harm. Jonathan cocked the gun and kept it trained on Analise's head.

"I'll kill her first, though."

Gracie told the dogs to stay. Then she held her hands out, placating him as she tried to reason with him. "There *was* money. A long time ago. My grandmother gave it to me when she sent me away. Fifty thousand dollars. I never knew where she got it, but she gave it to the woman who took me in. She used it to raise me, to help me and Analise get started in life. It's gone now."

The look on Jonathan's face made Reilly's stomach plunge, and a tightness gathered in his belly. It was a look of desperation. The look of a man who'd banked everything on door number one, only to find nothing behind it.

"It's not gone," he said through gritted teeth. "It's here. He stole it from me." Jonathan waved his free hand at the pulsing light, speaking to it like it was a person. "We was partners, and then you brought *her* here to make a mess of *everything*. You let them gun me down like a *dog*."

He centered his aim at Analise's face, and Reilly took another step, gauging the distance, thinking if he could just move fast enough, he might be able to get between Analise and Gracie and the bullets.

"Get back," Jonathan said. "I will kill both of them without even thinking about it. I *want* to kill them. I've wanted it for a long, long time."

Reilly froze.

"Now," Jonathan said to Gracie. "I want you follow Sawyer and you tell him to give me my *fucking share*."

At their blank looks, he used his chin to point at the glowing orb.

"Sawyer," Chloe breathed. The glowing orb danced and drifted, seemingly with purpose, until it dipped down and touched Gracie.

Jonathan made a sound that crossed anger and excitement. "Is he talking to you? Did he tell you?"

Gracie looked past him to Reilly. Fear gleamed from her eyes, but her voice was steady when she answered. "Yes," Gracie said. "He told me. We need to follow him."

Reilly didn't know if she spoke the truth or if she meant to trick Jonathan, but his ship was bound to hers, no matter where she decided to sail. He'd been a fool and lost her once; he'd die before he let that happen again.

The storm outside slammed into the house, growing in intensity, and rain hit the roof in a never-ending bombardment. The orb passed through the wall and out into the raging tempest. Jonathan shoved Chloe's frail body out front while he took Analise in the same tight, indefensible clutch that he'd held Reilly in when he'd brought him down the stairs. Gracie stayed close to her daughter. Reilly was still looking for a way to intervene without getting them both killed, but hadn't come up with anything yet.

The dogs charged the door as soon as it closed, barking wildly as they watched Gracie and Analise move away.

"Somebody does something I don't like, I pull the trigger. I just need one of you. The other's security. You hear me?"

They heard. They *all* heard.

Gun still aimed at the women, Jonathan shot a fierce look at Reilly. "This is as far as you go."

Reilly didn't move fast enough, but Brendan did. The kid managed to push him just as the gun went off. He felt the bullet part the air where his head had been. Tangled in their momentum, Reilly and Brendan went down in the slippery mud and rolled down a slope, bouncing over rocks and jagged edges until they banked against the side of a boulder. They couldn't see Jonathan anymore, but Reilly hoped that meant Jonathan couldn't see them, either.

He heard the man shout, "You follow me and I will kill her just like I should've done before. I'll kill them both, and I'll like it."

Reilly's mouth was dry. Jonathan moved like a man who'd been born with a pistol in his hand, and Reilly didn't doubt that when he got what he wanted, he would kill the women. He would kill everyone and think nothing of it.

He cast Brendan a look. The kid stared back, eyes hard and determined. He looked like he'd just woken up from a bad dream.

"He means to kill them, no matter what happens," Brendan said. "*Fuck*. That animal's been in my head. I didn't even know he was there."

Understanding finally came—all the little idiosyncrasies in Brendan's personality, the passive-aggressive attitude, the sense that two men had looked out from those blue eyes, but this wasn't the time to dwell on revelations. Reilly needed to think if Gracie and Analise were going to survive this. Nothing else mattered.

Reilly couldn't see Jonathan or the women anymore, but as he clawed his way up the incline he'd just plummeted down, he saw the bobbing light they had been following. It moved toward the springs where other lights

379

waited. Dead Lights, dozens of them, hanging over the rising black waters like stars pinned low in the sky.

"Follow me," he said to Brendan.

He and the kid fought the storm as it tried to sweep them off the slippery planking that led to the springs, keeping the orb in their sights while trying to remain hidden. They needn't have worried. They couldn't see five feet in front them. The flood waters had breached the surface and raced fast over their feet.

They moved swiftly, though, and in minutes, they'd caught up enough that they could hear the conversation.

"Jonathan," Chloe cried, the storm tearing her words out and hurling them into the night. "I know you're still in there. Listen to me. Don't let Aiken use you this way."

Reilly could make out the murky outline of Jonathan's silhouette. He still had the gun pointed at Analise.

"Will killing me bring you peace?" Chloe demanded. "You don't belong in this world. You had your time."

"My time was stolen. My share was taken. *This* is my time."

CHAPTER THIRTY-FOUR

July 1896
Diablo Springs

Aiken's bullet had lodged itself somewhere in Chick's body, but we could not find it to remove it. We were able to staunch the blood and then finally stop it, but her eyes never opened again. Carefully, we took her upstairs and laid her on the bed she'd been so proud to call her own. Athena grew silent and protective and refused to let us help bathe the blood from Chick's frail body. She wrapped Chick in clean cotton strips and took up vigil beside her bed.

As Honey and I left the room, she looked at me. "Death. That all you is. Death. You take all I live for and kill it. I curse you now. No child of yours will walk proud in this world. No child will be blessed with good, only bad. I curse you."

The words came through tears and pain and hurt so raw it scratched as they left her throat. But the words came, and I felt the weight of them settle over my soul.

I wanted to deny the accusation. I wanted to say Chick wasn't dead, that she might recover, but I knew it was a lie.

As if in protest, though, the small babe she carried moved in her womb, and we saw it skim beneath the surface of her skin like a ripple in water. They both managed to cling to life. Maybe there was hope.

I looked back at Athena. Staring into those angry black eyes, I said the only truth I knew for certain. "Aiken is dead. He'll torment you no more."

Honey and I left her alone with Chick and went downstairs to take care of business. It was barely nine in the morning and we had two bodies outside our kitchen door. Had this been another town, someone would have come to investigate. But guns were shot at random all through the day and night in Diablo Springs.

We didn't speak as we heaved Jake Smith up and over his saddle. Nor did we talk as we did the same with Aiken. We led the horses out to the hot springs, taking them around to the far edge where the deepest end of the pool was. In the shelter of the jutting rock to the west, we bound their feet, stuffed stones in their clothing, and threw them in.

Perhaps it was guilt, perhaps it was the hurt of all that had happened. The shock that had been keeping me numb wore off now that the last deed was done. But whatever the reason, as I stood watching Aiken Tate sink, I imagined his eyes opened.

I clapped my hand over my mouth, but even before I could scream, he'd vanished into the murky depths below.

* * *

I waited for Sawyer for a month before I let myself even consider that he might not return. During that time I could do little but berate myself. I'd driven him away. Nothing I could do would ever change that. Still, I waited for him.

The town of Diablo Springs surged up around us, and business continued against all sense and reasoning. I tended bar because I thought it was what Sawyer would want of me. We hired a man to work the tables and throw the dice. We made money hand over fist, but there was no glory in it. No feeling of building something better. By the time I was ready to break into the storage room, I knew what I'd find. Nothing. Sawyer had taken it all . . . and my heart with it.

Upstairs, Chick held on to life with Athena tending to her like a newborn. And almost a month after we killed Aiken and Jake Smith, Chick's baby was born. The delivery was long and hard, but Chick never seemed aware of it. The daughter she gave birth to was tiny and frail, but otherwise perfect in every way . . . except her resemblance to the animal who'd fathered her. Within hours after she was born, Chick quietly passed on to heaven.

Athena named the baby Misery, and as soon as she was able, she packed the squalling newborn up and left us. I gave her all the money I had saved, and she threw it back in my face, spat at my feet, and left on foot. I never saw her again.

We found Meaira dead one morning not long after, her wrists cut open and an empty vial of laudanum on the floor beside her. She'd left no note behind, but she didn't need one. We knew. Instinctively, I understood that I would lose Honey, too, though not by death. She could at last return to her family, and I wished her the best.

It was not long after we buried Meaira that I realized I was with child. I wept for nearly a day afterward, tears of both grief and happiness. There was a part of Sawyer growing inside me, and if I hadn't driven him away, I believed he might have rejoiced with me. Despite Athena's curse, I hoped the baby to be a sign that life went on, and perhaps Sawyer would come back to me. But though I waited until my dying day, he never did.

CHAPTER THIRTY-FIVE

The wind tried to pry Reilly from the boardwalk. The rain and floodwaters tried to wash him away as the Dead Light led them all to a place near the overhang of rock. The thunder boomed at increasing intervals until it felt like the earth was shaking from a quake. The lightning hissed in the sky above, branching into a thousand tributaries as it lit up the night.

Reilly held on to the dilapidated railing with one hand until he reached the bend that looped beneath the rock wall. There, the stone hillside offered a small bit of shelter where he and Brendan could crouch down out of sight. He could see Gracie and Analise huddled together and the Dead Lights hanging over the swirling black pool of the springs. There were no longer ravines and chasms. The water had turned it all into a solid, churning surface. Chloe sat on the ground nearby. Jonathan made sure they knew the gun was still on them.

"What do we do?" Brendan said in a low voice. "Jesus, she's pregnant. And I brought her here."

"Ask him," Jonathan screamed at Chloe. *"Ask him!"*

As if drawn by the violence, the lights began to surge, moving over the water as they raced to the huddle of humanity on the shores. Two orbs that glowed bright as the North Star raced to join the third, creating a luminescent trinity.

Jonathan stared at them suspiciously. "I'm going to count to one," he said. "And then I want answers."

Reilly looked at Brendan. "Here's your chance to make it up to Analise. It's now or never, kid. There's no big plan. You hit from this side. I'll get the gun."

They locked eyes for a second, and Brendan nodded.

Later, Reilly would play the next few seconds over in his head, but even then, he'd still have trouble understanding what had happened. He lunged at Jonathan, grabbing his gun arm and swinging it wide and away from Gracie and Analise while Brendan slammed into Jonathan from behind.

The swirling trio of lights separated and began to solidify. On one side a man took shape, hovering over Reilly's shoulder, glimpsed in choppy seconds as Reilly fought to control the gun. On the other side, a small dark-skinned woman solidified, looking young and lost.

The gun clattered across the rock, and the three men rolled toward the embankment. Brendan caught himself at the very edge and clung to a rock while the churning current tried to suck him away.

Reilly couldn't help, though. He was bigger than Jonathan, but Jonathan seemed superhuman in his rage. He managed to pin Reilly beneath him. The blows came fast about his head and face until stars joined the spider lightning behind his eyes. Reilly struggled to get his arms free, using his legs to try to unseat the other man. It wasn't working.

He saw Brendan gain some traction and pull himself out of the water, but he was too slow, too late. At the same time, Gracie grabbed a big stone and started forward, but Jonathan twisted off Reilly before she could reach him. He dove across the slippery embankment and managed to get the gun again. Reilly was already scrambling to stop him, and Brendan had finally made it to his feet. The kid knocked Analise off her feet just as Jonathan swung the gun wide and fired.

Reilly would never know if Chloe had been his target or Gracie, but in the seconds that moved like lightning, he saw Gracie duck and shove Chloe out of the way just as the bullet reached her.

"No!" Reilly shouted, clambering to catch Gracie as her legs crumpled and blood blossomed across her chest.

Brendan had Analise in his arms as Reilly lowered Gracie to the ground. Jonathan cocked the pistol and aimed again, this time at Reilly. From the corner of his eye, he saw something flare—one of the Dead Lights—and suddenly the shape he'd seen before lurched forward. For one, incredulous moment Reilly saw the face on the man that had formed, felt the sharp bite of recognition as he saw the familiar features of his brother and then the gun flew out of Jonathan's hands again. He didn't have time to dwell on what had happened, though.

"Gracie! Gracie, talk to me," he said, trying to rip her shirt to see the wound. Analise was crying for her mother,

Chloe lay on the ground, and the glowing female who'd materialized hovered around her, seeming to embrace the older woman.

Just then, the third orb darkened and solidified and became man from the picture inside the Diablo—the one who looked like Reilly.

"Where is it, Sawyer?" Jonathan screamed at the apparition.

Reilly knew that if he lived through this, he'd never be able to describe it.

The form leaned forward, looking right at Jonathan. Reilly felt as if the storm itself had begun to throb in time with the glow that surrounded the hovering man. Whatever Jonathan saw in the shape, it compelled him. He took a step forward, reaching out. Reilly saw greed on Jonathan's face. Greed and satisfaction. Was it communicating with the man he saw bathed in light?

Reilly stood transfixed until a movement turned him—Chloe scrabbling across the slick surface, the small female apparition helping her gain her footing. He didn't understand what she was doing until Chloe stood with Jonathan's gun in her hand. The glowing female curved her fingers around Chloe's and helped steady her aim.

"It's time to move on, you bastard," Chloe shouted.

Jonathan was up to his thighs in the dangerous floodwaters, unaware of anything but the apparition and *his share*, whatever that might be.

"You hear me?" she cried.

Jonathan turned and Chloe pulled the trigger.

"That's for my grandma," she said. "Who you treated like an animal."

Her hands shook as she struggled to cock the gun. Once again, the apparition helped her. Jonathan looked down at the spreading blood on his shoulder. Angry, but not fatally injured, he took a step toward Chloe just as she pulled the trigger a second time. "That one's for my mother."

The bullet caught him in the arm and twisted him around for a moment. Furious now, he charged. Chloe was ready, though.

"This is for me," she said, and pulled the trigger one last time.

The bullet hit him dead center, and Jonathan staggered back, looking down with shock at the blood covering his chest. Suddenly, the Dead Lights above them pulled together like a fiery sun. The female who'd helped Chloe, the big man who Reilly would swear had been Matt, and the last one who Aiken had called Sawyer, joined the others until the glow was blinding. The lights pulsed once, twice, and then with a crack of thunder, they vanished into the dark waters just as Jonathan fell back into the freezing embrace of the springs.

Reilly lifted Gracie in his arms, muttering terrified words as he carried her toward the house. Her eyes were closed, her breath ragged, but she was alive.

Brendan followed with Chloe holding on to one arm and Analise on the other. As Reilly made it to the door, he looked back, giving one last look at the dark waters that held so many ghosts.

CHAPTER THIRTY-SIX

B y morning, the storm had blown over, leaving the wreckage of its fury behind. The Diablo had held strong against it, but the rest of the fading town had taken a hit. Reilly doubted anyone would rebuild. In the clear light of day, the springs shivered placidly, but already the water had begun to drain into the underground caverns that had been opened all those years ago by Gracie's grandfather.

The bullet Jonathan had fired at Gracie had passed through the soft flesh of her shoulder and exited the other side without too much damage. He and Chloe had been able to staunch the blood and patch her up until they could get her medical care. Bill was still alive by some miracle, but in much worse condition, and it was touch and go throughout the night. They'd all slept together on the floor of the saloon, horse-dogs snoring in between human bodies. Safe and alive. Bill held on until the ambulance arrived and was now safely at the hospital and expected to recover.

It would be weeks before the water dried up completely and the full extent of the damage could be accounted for, but more than one body had washed up from the caverns during the storm. The Dead Lights had vanished, though, so maybe Diablo Springs had finally taken its last victim.

Later, they talked about the night they'd barely survived, each of them filling in missing pieces.

"I didn't know he was pulling me here," Brendan told them, "but that first time I drove out to the springs, I stayed all night and most of the next day. I missed work. I didn't remember any of it later. Just that I had to come back and bring Analise."

Aiken, ever the manipulator according to Chloe, had brought all the players to the game so that he could get what he wanted—the share of wealth he felt had been stolen from him all those years ago.

"When he—it—whatever was in the light touched me," Gracie said, "I knew it was Sawyer and knew he was there to help. It was like he shared his memory with me. I saw Aiken murder him and toss him into the springs, never realizing that he had all of the saloon's money packed around his body. He sank to the bottom, taking it with him."

"I saw a woman," Analise said. "Out there in the storm. She was young."

"Chick," Chloe said sadly but didn't explain.

Michael, who'd been silent since they'd found him in the basement, finally spoke up. "When I found the ledger, I saw what had happened all those years ago. Chick was Chloe's grandmother. She died when she took a bullet meant for Ella, Gracie's great-grandmother."

"Was she the reason for the curse Ella believe in so passionately?" Gracie asked.

Michael nodded. "And now the curse is broken."

"How?" Gracie asked.

"You stood in front of the bullet meant for me," Chloe answered.

Reilly felt a shiver go through Gracie's body. Then she turned and looked at him. "I thought . . . in the middle of it all, I could've sworn I saw . . ."

"Matt," Reilly finished. "You did. I still can't believe it, but he saved my life."

The words were almost hard to speak but saying them felt cathartic, the first step to healing.

"I think Aiken has been messing with my loved ones for a long time, Gracie," Reilly went on. "It didn't make sense until Brendan said Aiken had been in his head. I think he was in Matt's, too. I took Matt's ashes out to our old house this morning, and I buried them in the backyard, next to the dog." Reilly's mouth tilted at that. "I think he'll like it there. He always loved that dog."

"I still need to decide where Grandma Beck would want to be," Gracie said. "It's just too painful to think about, yet, but she deserves to be somewhere peaceful, at rest."

Reilly pressed a kiss to her temple. "I don't think she'd mind if you wait a bit to make that decision. You'll figure it out. I think the ghosts have finally moved on from Diablo Springs."

"What about Matt?" she asked softly.

"I can only hope my brother moved on with them and has found peace at last," Reilly murmured.

"He has," Chloe said with a knowing smile.

"So is there a lot of money out there waiting to be found?" Brendan asked.

"Not enough to die for," Reilly answered. "You need to stick around. You're going to have your hands full."

* * *

The next morning the roads had cleared, the tow truck pulled Gracie's car out of the ditch, and Chloe left as abruptly as she appeared, stopping only long enough to collect Bill on the way. Gracie felt strangely sad to see her go. Saying good-bye to the woman who'd been haunted for so many years made Gracie think about her own life and where she would go now.

Would Reilly be a part of it? Did he want to be? Life with her wouldn't be a picnic. Aside from her own issues and quirks, there was Analise and yet another baby coming into the world. She wouldn't have wished it for her daughter, any more than it had been wished for herself, but Analise was a blessing that she wouldn't have missed for anything. Perhaps the same would be true for this baby. And Brendan had proved to have more grit than she'd given him credit for. Maybe they would be happy together. Maybe not. But that's what life was, wasn't it? Taking chances and celebrating when they paid off, changing course when they didn't.

As if reading her mind, Reilly moved closer and took Gracie in his arms, holding her like he'd never let her go. He looked deeply into her eyes and asked, "What about us, Gracie?"

In that question, she sensed so many others, questions neither of them could answer. But Gracie knew one thing for certain.

She smiled at him. "I think you and I have enough history between us," she said softly. "I'm ready to start living for today if you are."

His smile started a fire deep within her.

"I like the sound of that. And if I'm lucky, maybe you'll want to think about tomorrow, too."

Gracie wrapped her arms around him and whispered. "I have a feeling you're about to get very lucky, Reilly Alexander. Very, *very* lucky."

Reilly's grin made her fall in love just a little more. She caught her breath as he bent his head and whispered against her lips.

"I'm already the luckiest man alive."

Then, he kissed her, which was exactly what she'd been hoping for.

OTHER BOOKS BY ERIN QUINN

THE BEYOND SERIES

The Five Deaths of Roxanne Love (Book 1)
Available Now

The Forbidden Life of Alex Moore (Novella 1.5)
December 29, 2014

The Three Fates of Ryan Love (Book 2)
January 27, 2015

The Seven Sins of Ruby Love (Book 3)
2015

THE MISTS OF IRELAND SERIES

Haunting Beauty (Book 1)
Haunting Warrior (Book 2)
Haunting Desire (Book 3)
Haunting Embrace (Book 4)

ABOUT THE AUTHOR

Erin Quinn is an NYT bestselling author. Her books have been called "riveting," "brilliantly plotted" and "beautifully written" and have won, placed or showed in the Booksellers Best, WILLA Award for Historical fiction, the Orange Rose, Golden Quill, Best Books, and Award of Excellence.

She lives in Arizona with her husband, two daughters and three dogs (all of whom have made debuts in her stories—the dogs, that is, not the husband and kids.)

Erin Quinn loves to talk to readers. If you have a book club or reading group and would like to discuss one of her books, let her know! Please contact Erin for more information by using the contact form on her website. www.erinquinnbooks.com.

KEEP READING FOR A PREVIEW OF

THE THREE FATES OF RYAN LOVE

BOOK TWO IN THE BEYOND SERIES,
AVAILABLE SOON FROM POCKET BOOKS.

THE THREE FATES OF RYAN LOVE
ERIN QUINN

CHAPTER ONE

Ryan heard the first of the sirens as he turned into the home stretch of his run. He ran most every night after he closed Love's, the bar he owned with his two sisters. The exercise usually cleared his mind, but not tonight. A storm had started brewing as he'd clocked the first mile and the kind of cold that was indigenous to the desert seeped beneath his skin and made old wounds ache. The glowering sky pressed down on him, sinister against the excessive Christmas lights twinkling merrily around every palm tree and the festive banners that snapped in the bitter wind. Instead of clearheaded, Ryan felt chased.

His German shepherd, Brandy, ran at his side, ears up and swiveling. Even she didn't seem to be enjoying the ritual as much as usual.

Glad when Love's came into sight, Ryan slowed his steps and tried to catch his breath. The sirens were closer now and a police car flew past to join more flashing lights about a block down the street. It was after two in the morning, but Mill Avenue near Arizona State University never really slept. Probably drunks out causing trouble.

Maybe even the three he'd thrown out of Love's that night. They'd left him with a bruised face and sore ribs.

Watching through the spitting rain, Ryan cut across an alley and into the parking lot behind Love's. That's when he heard the woman scream.

He spun to face the nook between the south wall of Love's and the cinder-block barrier that hid the side door to the kitchen. He peered into the dark recess, sure that's where the sound had come from, but nothing moved. Brandy's ear swiveled as she barked, trying to sniff and see everything at once. She didn't seem able to pinpoint the scream either.

The next scream echoed around him at the same time pressure filled the space behind his ears and made him feel unbalanced. He stumbled back as lightning flashed and a tremendous bolt snapped down right in front of him. When he looked again, a woman sat inside the small, sheltered alcove with her knees pulled up and her arms wrapped around them. Seconds ago, only darkness had waited there. Long, dark hair gleamed under the muted light, spilling over her shoulders and hiding her face. Her skin had an alabaster sheen. There was a lot of it, too. He frowned. She was naked.

With a hand signal for Brandy to sit, Ryan wiped the rain from his face and approached her cautiously. The walls and awning shielded her from the rain, but not the cold. She shivered violently as he crouched down in front of her.

"Hey," he said in a soft voice. "How'd you get here? Are you okay?"

She looked up with wide, clear eyes as blue as a desert sky. Even in the dark the color was vivid and they shimmered with something he couldn't begin to define. Long lashes the same rich shade as her hair framed them and accented their luminescent glow. They tilted at the corners, catlike. The dark wings of her brows drew focus to the shape of her face, the smooth line of her nose, the dusting of freckles that covered it.

He dropped his gaze and saw a raw scrape on her shin, another up high on her thigh. A third marred her shoulder. He thought of the sirens and police he'd heard. Was she involved in whatever had been happening?

"Ryan?" she whispered, chasing that thought right out of his head.

The sound of his name on her lips raised the hairs at the back of his neck, somehow trumping everything else. Like who she was, what she was doing here stark naked in the middle of the night.

"You know me?"

He peered into her face, sure he'd never seen her before.

"You're Ryan," she said with more certainty.

Her gaze shifted to something behind him. Ryan looked over his shoulder to find Brandy right at his heels with perked ears and a wet, wagging tail, watching the woman. The woman stared back at his dog with what Ryan would swear was wonder.

"Who are you?" he asked.

"Sabelle," she replied, still watching his dog.

Brandy got down on her belly, inching closer in the most unthreatening manner a ninety-five-pound German shepherd could manage.

"Where are your clothes, Sybil?"

She shook her head, pulling her gaze from Brandy to look him in the eye. "S'*belle*," she corrected. "Not Sybil."

"S'belle," he pronounced carefully. "Why are you naked?"

A hot flush turned her skin pink a second before she lied. "I don't remember."

She shifted with agitation and Brandy made a sound low in her throat. Not aggressive. Consoling. The dog had managed to army-crawl close enough to put her big fluffy head on the woman's lap. Sabelle's lips parted as she settled her fingers on Brandy's silky black ear.

She shivered and goose bumps rose on her skin. Ryan quickly reached over his head and pulled off his shirt. It was warm from his body, but damp from the rain. It would cover her, though.

"Here, put this on," he said, handing it over.

She accepted it, fingering the soft fabric before she pressed it to her face, smelling it. The action was so surprising that at first all he could think to do was mumble, "Sorry, it's all I have," while hot embarrassment flooded his face.

"It smells like you," she said.

Like it was a good thing.

His mouth opened but no words came out. He lowered his eyes while she pulled the shirt over her head. When he looked back, she was covered, thank God. His shirt was

4

huge on her. The shoulders drooped to her elbows and the long sleeves hid her hands.

She huddled in it, her gaze roaming his face, lingering on the cut over his nose, the puffy skin on his cheek, and his swollen jaw. He almost felt the quicksilver stare on his bare chest and bruised ribs. He must look like a big ugly thug to her.

She had bruises and scrapes of her own. He could only hope that her wounds had come from something less violent than his.

"What happened to you? Did someone hurt you?" he asked.

"No," she said with a definitive shake of her head.

"You screamed."

"I didn't expect it to be painful."

"You didn't expect *what* to be painful?"

She flinched at his sharp tone. "Coming here."

He didn't know what to say to that. *Here*—in the parking lot in the middle of the night—wasn't anyplace she should be, but she'd obviously been hurt, was probably in shock. She might not even know where she was. He dug his phone out of his pocket and leaned in so the rain running down his back wouldn't get it wet as he dialed 911.

The storm picked up its pace, hitting the asphalt with such force that raindrops bounced and pooled, pounding the awning overhead with fury. Storms moved fast in Arizona, but this was insane.

"Who are you calling?" she asked.

"The police. They'll—"

She snatched the phone out of his hand and hit the screen repeatedly until the ring cut off.

Ryan's mouth was open again. "Okay, now it's getting weird."

"No police," she said. "What time is it?"

When he didn't answer immediately, she repeated the question sharply.

"I don't know. Two? Three in the morning?"

Her eyes rounded and she scrambled to get her feet under her. "We need to go. Now, Ryan."

She stood, long legs protruding from his big shirt. Her hair brushed her shoulders and impatiently she swiped it back. Standing as well, Ryan reached out to steady her as she swayed.

"Easy, girl," he murmured gently. "Slow down. Take a breath. You're safe now. Let's get the police here. They'll get everything worked out."

"No police," she insisted. "They can't help."

"Yeah, well. . . ." *Neither could he.* "Can I have my phone back?"

She turned and started out of the shelter.

"Wait," he said. "Sabelle Whoever-You-Are. Wait."

She seemed more alert, more focused, but she'd obviously hit her head. She tucked her arms tight, hands jammed under her pits and head bent as she gingerly picked her way through the glass, gravel, mud, and puddles covering the parking lot, ignoring him until she stepped on something sharp and gasped.

"Hold up. Would you stop?" he said, exasperated. "Let me help you."

He lifted her in his arms and carried her to the back door before she could protest. She wasn't a big woman, but she was lush with all the right curves in all the right places. She felt solid against his chest and soft in ways that played games with his traitorous thoughts and made him glad for the bracing rain. Brandy escorted them like a devoted admirer, her wet nose brushing Sabelle's feet whenever the dog could reach them. Ryan paused before opening the door, half convinced he was making a big mistake. This was the kind of thing you saw on the news where some dumb putz just trying to help ended up accused of wrongdoing.

He jockeyed her weight as he fumbled his keys from his pocket into the lock. Sabelle tightened her arms around him, pressing all those feminine curves closer as Ryan tried valiantly not to notice.

Darkness clustered just inside and obscured the stairs all the way up. The rain boomed against the roof and the cold made plumes of their breath. His skin felt icy.

Except where he held Sabelle. She was like a furnace heating his bare chest.

The door slammed shut behind them as Ryan hit the lights and set Sabelle on her feet again. She continued to hold onto him, staring into his face as if to memorize his features. For all her crazy talk, her eyes looked clear and focused in the dim glow.

Then she twisted away and started up the stairs to his apartment without asking or waiting for an invitation. With a muttered curse, Ryan started to follow but fingers of disquiet played down his spine, making him pause.

The area under the stairs to his apartment served as storage for cases of beer and other supplies. A door straight ahead made a convenient back entrance to the bar, just as the door behind him was a quick shortcut to the parking lot. Usually the stairwell smelled of cardboard, hops, and old french fries. Familiar, comfortable odors that lingered in most bars. Tonight a whiff of rotten eggs hung over it.

Sabelle was already at his front door, waiting. He'd figured out what smelled after he dealt with her. She tried the knob, found it unlocked, and let herself in before he made it up the stairs. Stunned by her audacity, he picked up his pace. Brandy raced ahead and was beside her as Sabelle padded past the kitchen breakfast bar, trailing fingers over the back of the couch as she took in her surroundings.

His apartment was a loft that stretched over Love's. One room with a wall of windows, it had a spacious, open feel that suited him. Her gaze lingered on the screen sectioning off his bedroom before moving to the clock on the microwave. The digital readout read 2:30. He saw her note it with a deep breath and a nod.

"There's still time." She faced him with determination. "I've come with a warning. Your life is in danger."

He might have smiled if she hadn't looked so distressed. "Okay," he said carefully.

She nodded, apparently satisfied with that response. "Good. I'd hoped you'd understand. We need to leave here." She glanced at the clock again. "Quickly."

"And go where?" he said, not understanding at all.

"Away from here. *Here* is where it happens."

Ryan studied her, suddenly weary to the bone. Ever since his brother's bizarre death—*Murder? Suicide?* Ryan doubted he'd ever know the truth—Love's had been a tourist attraction for lunatics. Fanatics who thought that Ryan's twin brother and sister were blessed by the heavens or cursed by demons had always been on the fringe of their lives. Reece and Roxanne had died (and miraculously been revived) more than once. It went with the territory.

Some of the crazies were dangerous, others merely curious. He didn't know which camp Sabelle fell into, but the sooner he got her out of here, the better.

"You don't believe me," Sabelle said with a hint of disappointment in her voice. "I don't know why I'm surprised. It's in your nature to be suspicious. You have trust issues."

Maybe so. But that was his business. "What's this danger I'm supposedly in?" he asked politely.

"Death," she replied almost eagerly. "Yours, I mean."

He let out a deep breath and shook his head. "Listen, Sabelle. I'd like to help you, get you someplace safe. How about back home?" *Or the psych ward you escaped from?*

"I can never go home," she said vehemently.

He lifted his hands, palms out. "Fair enough. But you can't stay here. I just pulled a twelve-hour shift. I'm tired. All I want is a hot shower and bed."

Her eyes widened and she shot another quick glance at the screen that hid his bed. Something darkly erotic flashed across her features. For a moment, he couldn't look away.

9

"I know you don't believe me," she said, her voice breathy and low, "but this isn't a game or a joke. You can't just take a shower and pretend it will go away. Do you think I would risk so much to warn you if there was nothing to fear?"

"I think you're a confused woman who needs some help."

"I'm not confused. An explosion will decimate this building sometime between now and three a.m. Your apartment will be incinerated. Boom. *Gone.*"

"Between now and three a.m.," he repeated, deadpan.

"Stop it. Stop pretending disbelief you don't feel."

"Oh, I feel it."

Narrowed eyes were the only clue that she'd heard him. She didn't argue, she didn't try to add details to support her claim. Most liars did.

"You'll need the money you have stashed beneath the floorboards in your bedroom," she said with a challenging glance. "Clothes, of course. And Brandy. We'll need her."

"We?"

"I don't know how much time we have, Ryan. I only know that by three, it will all be over. For both of us."

She was all-in when it came to this fantasy quest, and her conviction planted a seed of doubt that startled him.

"You are more important than you know, Ryan."

The laugh he'd tried for earlier finally emerged and his doubt waned. The poor woman was definitely delusional.

"I own a pub. Actually, I own about one-fiftieth of a pub. The bank owns the rest. I spend most of my days and nights behind a bar, serving drinks to people who have less of a life than I do. Unless it's critical that the drunks get their next drink, I'm the opposite of important."

With a superior sounding sniff, she moved behind the Japanese screen and into his bedroom. Dumbfounded, Ryan followed, watching her open his closet. She yanked his backpack off the top shelf and stuffed his favorite jeans, a T-shirt, and a flannel button-down into it.

As she turned, she caught her reflection in the dresser mirror and did a double take. For a moment, she stared at her pale face like she'd expected to see someone else looking back.

He tilted his head to the side, watching her watch herself. She saw the movement and quickly glanced away but her cheeks pinked up and she avoided looking at him. She began opening his drawers like she had every right.

And instead of throwing her out on her pretty little ass, he watched her, still trying to figure out what to do about her. Wrestle his phone away? Humor her back outside and lock the doors behind her?

The storm boomed so loud it shook the walls. He couldn't throw her out in this.

In his top drawer, she found his briefs, added a pair to the pack, and pulled open the next drawer. She rummaged until she retrieved some basketball shorts and held them up to her hips. When she tugged them on, she gave him an eyeful of long legs and bare behind.

She turned and busted him staring. His gaze snared hers and something darkened in the uncertain blue. Neither one of them looked away.

"Do you have shoes I could borrow?" she asked, her voice husky.

He pointed to the other closet door. It took her a moment to turn around and slide the door open. She eyed his size 14 shoes dubiously before she spotted a pair of flip flops on the floor and slipped her feet into them.

"Get the money, Ryan."

Crazy with sprinkles on top. That's what this was.

"You planning on robbing me?" he managed to say.

She faced him. "Is that what you think? Are you afraid I'm going to tackle you and steal all your precious belongings?"

She was swimming in his big shirt. The shorts hung down to her knees and the flip-flops looked like snowshoes on her feet. She had the threat potential of a puppy.

Again, he wished he could muster a laugh. Instead, "No" emerged in a wooden tone.

"Get your stuff and wait it out on the sidewalk with me, then. If nothing happens by three, you can call your police and wash your hands of me."

She handed him his phone like a gesture of good faith. He took it.

"Or I could do that now and save myself the trouble."

"Yes. You could do that. But we'd both pay the price for your stupidity."

"Did you just call me—"

"You are in *danger*," she said, enunciating each syllable sharply. "You're going to die if you don't trust me. How much clearer can I be? I know you're the kind of man who has to see something to believe it. But why not see it from the outside with me?"

With that, she grabbed his backpack and dropped it at his feet.

He still hadn't moved, but Sabelle didn't wait. She crossed to the front door with a stiff back and an air of determination, ridiculous in her borrowed getup and yet somehow . . . convincing.

"How would you know what kind of man I am?" he asked softly.

The question made her pause. She shot a guarded glance over her shoulder, eyes wide and lips parted. Bravado and hunger stared back at him, a combination so mystifying that it shut his mouth.

So what if she was right? It wouldn't be the strangest thing to have happened in the past month. Hell, in the last week. Even as common sense told him that it was more likely she had someone waiting downstairs to relieve him of the money she'd insisted he pack, he felt himself giving in.

She'd said *beneath the floorboards*. If she already knew where he kept the money, why not just break in and steal it while he'd been out for his run? Why the elaborate *naked-and-afraid* act?

"I see you thinking," she said. "You're deciding on all the reasons not to trust me. But that's wasting time you don't have. Look at the clock, Ryan." She paused. "*Please.*"

It was the hitch in her voice that unplugged his common sense and pushed him to the edge.

13

He exhaled a heavy breath. "Let me get a shirt."

The tremulous smile she couldn't hide fast enough called him a fool, but the baby-blues sent another coded message he couldn't be sure he'd read right. He ducked behind the screen that divided the rooms and pried up the floorboard by his bed with a long flathead screwdriver he kept in his nightstand drawer just for that purpose. He stuffed the whole hard-earned 10K into his backpack, shrugged on a shirt, and snagged jackets for both of them on his way out. What could it hurt to sit in his truck and wait it out? If nothing else, maybe he'd get to the bottom of her story.

She waited impatiently by the door, watching the clock switch numbers. Brandy sat at her feet, ready to go. According to Sabelle, they had less than fifteen minutes to get out of there before the whole place was incinerated.

"Hurry," she said and stepped onto the landing without a backward glance.

Shaking his head, Ryan clicked his tongue for Brandy to follow and locked the door behind him.

*To keep reading, buy **The Three Fates of Ryan Love** (Book 2 in the Beyond Series) at your local or online retailer. Available January 2015.*

For a complete book list of Erin Quinn's titles, go to http://www.erinquinnbooks.com/Books.htm